D0642779

PENGUIN CANADA

THE PENGUIN BOOK OF SUMMER STORIES

Internationally acclaimed as an anthologist, translator, essayist, novelist, and editor, ALBERTO MANGUEL is the author of several award-winning books, including *The Dictionary of Imaginary Places, A History of Reading, With Borges, The Penguin Book of Christmas Stories,* and *The Library at Night.* He was born in Buenos Aires, moved to Canada in 1982, and now lives in France, where he was named Officer of the Order of Arts and Letters.

Also by Alberto Manguel

ANTHOLOGIES

The Penguin Book of Christmas Stories

Black Water

Dark Arrows

Other Fires

Evening Games

The Oxford Book of Canadian Ghost Stories

Seasons

Black Water II

Canadian Mystery Stories

The Gates of Paradise

The Second Gates of Paradise

Meanwhile, In Another Part of the Forest *(with Craig Stephenson)*

Lost Words

Why Are You Telling Me This?

Mothers and Daughters

Fathers and Sons

The Ark in the Garden

By the Light of the Glow-Worm's Lamp

God's Spies

NON-FICTION

The Library at Night

A Reading Diary

With Borges

Reading Pictures

Into the Looking-Glass Wood

Bride of Frankenstein

The Dictionary of Imaginary Places
(with Gianni Guadalupi)

A History of Reading

FICTION

Stevenson Under the Palm Trees

News from a Foreign Country Came

The Penguin Book of

SUMMER STORIES

Selected and Introduced by

ALBERTO MANGUEL

PENGUIN
CANADA

PENGUIN CANADA

Published by the Penguin Group

Penguin Group (Canada), 90 Eglinton Avenue East, Suite 700, Toronto, Ontario, Canada M4P 2Y3 (a division of Pearson Canada Inc.)

Penguin Group (USA) Inc., 375 Hudson Street, New York, New York 10014, U.S.A.
Penguin Books Ltd, 80 Strand, London WC2R 0RL, England
Penguin Ireland, 25 St Stephen's Green, Dublin 2, Ireland (a division of Penguin Books Ltd)
Penguin Group (Australia), 250 Camberwell Road, Camberwell, Victoria 3124, Australia (a division of Pearson Australia Group Pty Ltd)
Penguin Books India Pvt Ltd, 11 Community Centre, Panchsheel Park, New Delhi – 110 017, India
Penguin Group (NZ), 67 Apollo Drive, Rosedale, North Shore 0632, Auckland, New Zealand (a division of Pearson New Zealand Ltd)
Penguin Books (South Africa) (Pty) Ltd, 24 Sturdee Avenue, Rosebank, Johannesburg 2196, South Africa

Penguin Books Ltd, Registered Offices: 80 Strand, London WC2R 0RL, England

First published 2007

2 3 4 5 6 7 8 9 10 (WEB)

Manufactured in Canada.

ISBN-13: 978-0-14-305629-4
ISBN-10: 0-14-305629-8

Library and Archives Canada Cataloguing in Publication data available upon request.

Visit Penguin Books' website at **www.penguin.ca**

Special and corporate bulk purchase rates available; please see **www.penguin.ca/corporatesales** or call 1-800-810-3104, ext. 477 or 474

For Edith Sorel,
summer, fall, winter, and spring

Contents

Introduction

by

ALBERTO MANGUEL

Summer afternoon—summer afternoon;
to me those have always been the two
most beautiful words in the English language.

—HENRY JAMES,
IN EDITH WHARTON, *A BACKWARD GLANCE*

SOMETIME IN THE FIRST CENTURY B.C., a Roman poet put into words his memories of summer months spent as a child in the countryside near Mantua. "Fortunate old man!" he wrote. "Here, amid familiar streams and sacred springs, you'll seek the cooling shade. On this side, as in the old days, next to your neighbour's property, the willow hedge will lull you to sleep with the hum of its sipping bees, while over there, under the tall rocks, the peasant's song will fill the air. And the wood-pigeons you loved, and the turtle-doves, will coo in the windblown elms." There was a picnic spread out under the trees, of "ripe apples, tasty chestnuts, and many pressed cheeses," while, "far away, smoke rose from the roofs of distant houses and long shadows fell from the mountain-tops." Virgil was thirty-three years old when he wrote his *Eclogues*. Later he would write about keeping crops and cattle, and about the quest and battles of a hero, but his first book dealt with the sorrows of love and the joys of summer.

There used to be a time in which summer stood for the fulfillment of the year's promise, the moment when, in opposition to the dreaded winter, life became relaxed and mellow, full of warm light that helped us forget the cold and the dark. That, of course, was before we became aware of global warming, of the desert gradually spreading north and south of the equator, of the ice caps melting drastically, and of the increasing warmth no longer felt as a blessing but as a self-inflicted curse. Summer days seem to be over, especially future summers. As Keats said long ago with prophetic candour, "Summer's joys are spoilt by use." Though summer is still the time of birdsong, dog days, short nights and torrid love affairs, to this catalogue of delights we have now added the pleasures of air-conditioning–induced colds, dangerous ultraviolet rays, crowded airports, and high-season prices. And yet …

In spite of climate changes, summer continues to carry its ancient symbolic weight, announcing that the year's cusp has been reached and, though the days now begin their decline toward winter, this is the period for rejoicing with the cuckoo that *"sumer is icumen in,"* as a monk of Reading Abbey joyfully sang out sometime in the mid-thirteenth century. We have always felt that summertime has a different cadence from that of the other seasons.

The history of summer as we know it is not very long. Though the ancient Romans had summer estates and the Chinese emperors summer palaces, the generalized custom of summer holidays is very recent. Up to the nineteenth century, only the aristocracy divided the year between the time spent in town and that spent in the country. Gradually the bourgeoisie began to imitate them, enjoying a *villégiature,* "a season in the provinces," and even though, as late as 1870, the *Larousse du XIXe siècle* considered *villégiature* a neologism, the habit of leaving the city in summer was then shared by all classes (though not of course in the same proportions) and the invention of the summer holidays, a fixture. In 1836, the French workers had won the right to paid summer vacations that lasted up to six weeks; two years later, Stendhal used the word "tourist" in the title of one of his books, to differentiate those who could afford to travel for their holidays from those who could not. The word, meaning "one who travels out of curiosity or idleness," quickly acquired great popularity, together with the scorn of the intelligentsia. "Of all noxious animals," wrote the Reverend Francis Kilvert in his diary on April 5, 1870, "the most noxious is a tourist. And of all the tourists the most vulgar, ill-bred, offensive and loathsome is the British tourist." A sentiment shared by David

Copperfield's aunt, Betsey Trotwood, when she drives off the summer tourists from her lawn in Dover.

Perhaps the best-remembered summers are those of our childhood, days full of momentous discoveries, fulfilled (and unfulfilled) desires, tiny ecstasies, and intimate rejoicing that seemed to fill one endless hot month after another. May Swenson wrote:

> The summer that I was ten—
> Can it be there was only one
> summer when I was ten? It must
> have been a long one then.

More than the other seasons, summer breeds memory: of vanished friendships, strange games, adults who were then inconceivably young, places that were not home, memories of other summer memories. Above all the memory of smells: cut grass, vanilla ice-cream, coconut-scented suntan lotion, salty air, clean sweat on white linen, the smoky pages of cheap detective novels, warm strawberries, chlorine, grilled spicy sausages, lemonade, rubber toys left too long in the sun.

If summer is the season of memory, it is also, for no cogent reason that I can think of, the season of leisurely storytelling. Although books set in winter can no doubt fill a hefty library, writers seem to prefer summer for many of their imaginations. Dostoyevsky's *Crime and Punishment* takes place "on a very hot evening at the beginning of July"; Julien Sorel, in Stendhal's *Le Rouge et le noir,* becomes the lover of Madame de Rênal in the first days of August; in Oscar Wilde's *The Picture of Dorian Gray,* Lord Henry meets the beautiful Dorian when "the light summer wind stirred amidst the trees of the garden"; Gabriel García Márquez begins *One Hundred Years of Solitude* at the end of a torrid South American summer in March; Margaret Atwood's nameless heroine seeks for her father throughout a long Quebec summer in *Surfacing;* in James Joyce's *Ulysses,* Leopold Bloom famously walks the streets of Dublin one long summer's day, June 16, 1904; Lewis Carroll has Alice enter Wonderland on "a golden afternoon" one Oxford summer. While we lie on the beach or on the cabin porch with our books, under the same warm sun Don Quixote wends his way through the dust of La Mancha. Mole and Rat prepare to have their first picnic on the banks of the Thames; Little Nell and her grandfather escape the villainous Quilp through the sunny English countryside; and Elizabeth Bennett agrees to marry the handsome Darcy, thereby bringing pride and prejudice to a happy end. Leisure in the reader is seldom echoed by leisure on the page. As the following stories prove, summer in fiction is a busy time.

The Penguin Book of

SUMMER STORIES

Death by Landscape

by

MARGARET ATWOOD

NOW THAT THE BOYS ARE GROWN UP and Rob is dead, Lois has moved to a condominium apartment in one of the newer waterfront developments. She is relieved not to have to worry about the lawn, or about the ivy pushing its muscular little suckers into the brickwork, or the squirrels gnawing their way into the attic and eating the insulation off the wiring, or about strange noises. This building has a security system, and the only plant life is in pots in the solarium.

Lois is glad she's been able to find an apartment big enough for her pictures. They are more crowded together than they were in the house, but this arrangement gives the walls a European look: blocks of pictures, above and beside one another, rather than one over the chesterfield, one over the fireplace, one in the front hall, in the old acceptable manner of sprinkling art around so it does not get too intrusive. This way has more of an impact. You know it's not supposed to be furniture.

None of the pictures is very large, which doesn't mean they aren't valuable. They are paintings, or sketches and drawings, by artists who were not nearly as well known when Lois began to buy them as they are now. Their work later turned up on stamps, or as silk-screen reproductions hung in the principals' offices of high schools, or as jigsaw puzzles, or on beautifully printed calendars sent out by corporations as Christmas gifts, to their less important clients. These artists painted mostly in the twenties and thirties and forties; they painted landscapes. Lois has two Tom Thomsons, three A.Y. Jacksons, a Lawren Harris. She has an Arthur Lismer, she has a J.E.H. MacDonald. She has a David Milne. They are pictures of convoluted tree trunks on an island of pink wave-smoothed stone, with more islands behind; of a lake with rough, bright, sparsely wooded cliffs; of a vivid river shore with a tangle of bush and two beached canoes, one red, one grey; of a yellow autumn woods with the ice-blue gleam of a pond half-seen through the interlaced branches.

It was Lois who'd chosen them. Rob had no interest in art, although he could see the necessity of having something on the walls. He left all the decorating decisions to her, while providing the money, of course. Because of this collection of hers, Lois's friends—especially the men—have given her the reputation of having a good nose for art investments.

But this is not why she bought the pictures, way back then. She bought them because she wanted them. She wanted something that was in them, although she could not have said at the time what it was. It was not peace: she does not find them peaceful in the least. Looking at them fills her with a wordless unease. Despite the fact that there are no people in them or even animals, it's as if there is something, or someone, looking back out.

WHEN SHE WAS THIRTEEN, Lois went on a canoe trip. She'd only been on overnights before. This was to be a long one, into the trackless wilderness, as Cappie put it. It was Lois's first canoe trip, and her last.

Cappie was the head of the summer camp to which Lois had been sent ever since she was nine. Camp Manitou, it was called; it was one of the better ones, for girls, though not the best. Girls of her age whose parents could afford it were routinely packed off to such camps, which bore a generic resemblance to one another. They favoured Indian names and had hearty, energetic leaders, who were called Cappie or Skip or Scottie. At these camps you learned to swim well and sail, and paddle a canoe, and perhaps ride a horse or play tennis. When you weren't doing these things you could do Arts and Crafts and turn out dingy, lumpish clay ashtrays for your mother—mothers smoked more, then—or bracelets made of coloured braided string.

CHEERFULNESS WAS REQUIRED at all times, even at breakfast. Loud shouting and the banging of spoons on the tables were allowed, and even encouraged, at ritual intervals. Chocolate bars were rationed, to control tooth decay and pimples. At night, after supper, in the dining hall or outside around a mosquito-infested campfire ring for special treats, there were singsongs. Lois can still remember all the words to "My Darling Clementine," and to "My Bonnie Lies Over the Ocean," with acting-out gestures: a rippling of the hands for "the ocean," two hands together under the cheek for "lies." She will never be able to forget them, which is a sad thought.

Lois thinks she can recognize women who went to these camps, and were good at it. They have a hardness to their handshakes, even now; a way of standing, legs planted firmly and farther apart than usual; a way of sizing you up, to see if you'd be any good in a canoe—the front, not the back. They themselves would be in the back. They would call it the stern.

She knows that such camps still exist, although Camp Manitou does not. They are one of the few things that haven't changed much. They now offer copper enamelling, and functionless pieces of stained glass baked in electric ovens, though judging from the productions of her friends' grandchildren the artistic standards have not improved.

To Lois, encountering it in the first year after the war, Camp Manitou seemed ancient. Its log-sided buildings with the white cement in between the half-logs, its flagpole ringed with whitewashed stones, its weathered grey dock jutting out into Lake Prospect, with its woven rope bumpers and its rusty rings for tying up, its prim round flowerbed of petunias near the office door, must surely have been there always. In truth it dated only from the first decade of the century; it had been founded by Cappie's parents, who'd thought of camping as bracing to the character, like cold showers, and had been passed along to her as an inheritance, and an obligation.

Lois realized, later, that it must have been a struggle for Cappie to keep Camp Manitou going, during the Depression and then the war, when money did not flow freely. If it had been a camp for the very rich, instead of the merely well off, there would have been fewer problems. But there must have been enough Old Girls, ones with daughters, to keep the thing in operation, though not entirely shipshape: furniture was battered, painted trim was peeling, roofs leaked. There were dim photographs of these Old Girls dotted around the dining hall, wearing ample woollen bathing suits and showing their fat, dimpled legs, or standing, arms twined, in odd tennis outfits with baggy skirts.

In the dining hall, over the stone fireplace that was never used, there was a huge moulting stuffed moose head, which looked somehow carnivorous. It was a sort of mascot; its name was Monty Manitou. The older campers spread the story that it was haunted, and came to life in the dark, when the feeble and undependable lights had been turned off or, due to yet another generator failure, had gone out. Lois was afraid of it at first, but not after she got used to it.

Cappie was the same: you had to get used to her. Possibly she was forty, or thirty-five, or fifty. She had fawn-coloured hair that looked as if it was cut with a bowl. Her head jutted forward, jigging like a chicken's as she strode around the camp, clutching notebooks and checking things off in them. She was like their minister in church: both of them smiled a lot and were anxious because they wanted things to go well; they both had the same overwashed skins and stringy necks. But all this disappeared when Cappie was leading a singsong, or otherwise leading. Then she was happy, sure of herself, her plain face almost luminous. She wanted to cause joy. At these times she was loved, at others merely trusted.

There were many things Lois didn't like about Camp Manitou, at first. She hated the noisy chaos and spoon-banging of the dining hall, the rowdy singsongs at which you were expected to yell in order to show that you were enjoying yourself. Hers was not a household that encouraged yelling. She hated the necessity of having to write dutiful letters to her parents claiming she was having fun. She could not complain, because camp cost so much money.

She didn't much like having to undress in a roomful of other girls, even in the dim light, although nobody paid any attention, or sleeping in a cabin with seven other girls, some of whom snored because they had adenoids or colds, some of whom had nightmares, or wet their beds and cried about it. Bottom bunks made her feel closed in, and she was afraid of falling out of top ones; she was afraid of heights. She got homesick, and suspected her parents of having a better time when she wasn't there than when she was, although her mother wrote to her every week saying how much they missed her. All this was when she was nine. By the time she was thirteen she liked it. She was an old hand by then.

LUCY WAS HER BEST FRIEND at camp. Lois had other friends in winter, when there was school and itchy woollen clothing and darkness in the afternoons, but Lucy was her summer friend.

She turned up the second year, when Lois was ten, and a Bluejay. (Chickadees, Bluejays, Ravens, and Kingfishers—these were the names Camp Manitou assigned to the different age groups, a sort of totemic clan system. In those days, thinks Lois, it was birds for girls, animals for boys: wolves, and so forth. Though some animals and birds were suitable and some were not. Never vultures, for instance; never skunks, or rats.)

Lois helped Lucy to unpack her tin trunk and place the folded clothes on the wooden shelves, and to make up her bed. She put her in the top bunk right above her, where she could keep an eye on her. Already she knew that Lucy was an exception, to a good many rules; already she felt proprietorial.

Lucy was from the United States, where the comic books came from, and the movies. She wasn't from New York or Hollywood or Buffalo, the only American cities Lois knew the names of, but from Chicago. Her house was on the lakeshore and had gates to it, and grounds. They had a maid, all of the time. Lois's family only had a cleaning lady twice a week.

The only reason Lucy was being sent to *this* camp (she cast a look of minor scorn around the cabin, diminishing it and also offending Lois, while at the same time daunting her) was that her mother had been a camper here. Her mother had been a Canadian once, but had married her father, who had a patch over one eye, like a pirate. She showed Lois the picture of him in her wallet. He got the patch in the war. "Shrapnel," said Lucy. Lois, who was unsure about shrapnel, was so impressed she could only grunt. Her own two-eyed, unwounded father was tame by comparison.

"My father plays golf," she ventured at last.

"*Everyone* plays golf," said Lucy. "My *mother* plays golf."

Lois's mother did not. Lois took Lucy to see the outhouses and the swimming dock and the dining hall with Monty Manitou's baleful head, knowing in advance they would not measure up.

This was a bad beginning; but Lucy was good-natured, and accepted Camp Manitou with the same casual shrug with which she seemed to accept everything. She would make the best of it, without letting Lois forget that this was what she was doing.

However, there were things Lois knew that Lucy did not. Lucy scratched the tops off all her mosquito bites and had to be taken to the infirmary to be daubed with Ozonol. She took her T-shirt off while sailing, and although the counsellor spotted her after a while and made her put it back on, she burned spectacularly, bright red, with the X of her bathing-suit straps standing out in alarming white; she let Lois peel the sheets of whispery-thin burnt skin off her shoulders. When they sang "Alouette" around the campfire, she did not know any of the French words. The difference was that Lucy did not care about the things she didn't know, whereas Lois did.

During the next winter, and subsequent winters, Lucy and Lois wrote to each other. They were both only children, at a time when this was thought to be a disadvantage, so in their letters they pretended to be sisters, or even twins. Lois had to strain a little over this, because Lucy was so blonde, with translucent skin and large blue eyes like a doll's, and Lois was nothing out of the ordinary—just a tallish, thinnish, brownish person with freckles. They signed their letters LL, with the L's entwined together like the monograms on a towel. (Lois and Lucy, thinks Lois. How our names date us. Lois Lane, Superman's girlfriend, enterprising female reporter; *I Love Lucy*. Now we are obsolete, and it's little Jennifers, little Emilys, little Alexandras and Carolines and Tiffanys.)

They were more effusive in their letters than they ever were in person. They bordered their pages with X's and O's, but when they met again in the summers it was always a shock. They had changed so much, or Lucy had. It was like watching someone grow up in jolts. At first it would be hard to think up things to say.

But Lucy always had a surprise or two, something to show, some marvel to reveal. The first year she had a picture of herself in a tutu, her hair in a ballerina's knot on the top of her head; she pirouetted around the swimming dock, to show Lois how it was done, and almost fell off. The next year she had given that up and was taking horseback riding. (Camp Manitou did not have horses.) The next year her mother and father had been divorced, and she had a new stepfather, one with both eyes, and a new house, although the maid was the same. The next year, when they had graduated from Bluejays and entered Ravens, she got her period, right in the first week of camp. The two of them snitched some matches from their counsellor, who smoked illegally, and made a small fire out behind the farthest outhouse, at dusk, using their flashlights. They could set all kinds of fires by now; they had learned how in Campcraft. On this fire they burned one of Lucy's used sanitary napkins. Lois is not sure why they did this, or whose idea it was. But she can remember the feeling of deep satisfaction it gave her as the white fluff singed and the blood sizzled, as if some wordless ritual had been fulfilled.

They did not get caught, but then they rarely got caught at any of their camp transgressions. Lucy had such large eyes, and was such an accomplished liar.

THIS YEAR Lucy is different again: slower, more languorous. She is no longer interested in sneaking around after dark, purloining cigarettes from the counsellor, dealing in blackmarket candy bars. She is pensive, and hard to wake in the mornings. She doesn't like her stepfather, but she doesn't want to live with her real father either, who has a new wife. She thinks her mother may be having a love affair with a doctor; she doesn't know for sure, but she's seen them smooching in his car, out on the driveway, when her stepfather wasn't there. It serves him right. She hates her private school. She has a boyfriend, who is sixteen and works as a gardener's assistant. This is how she met him: in the garden. She describes to Lois what it is like when he kisses her—rubbery at first, but then your knees go limp. She has been forbidden to see him, and threatened with boarding school. She wants to run away from home.

Lois has little to offer in return. Her own life is placid and satisfactory, but there is nothing much that can be said about happiness. "You're so lucky," Lucy tells her, a little smugly. She might as well say *boring* because this is how it makes Lois feel.

LUCY IS APATHETIC about the canoe trip, so Lois has to disguise her own excitement. The evening before they are to leave, she slouches into the campfire ring as if coerced, and sits down with a sigh of endurance, just as Lucy does.

Every canoe trip that went out of camp was given a special send-off by Cappie and the section leader and counsellors, with the whole section in attendance. Cappie painted three streaks of red across each of her cheeks with a lipstick. They looked like three-fingered claw marks. She put a blue circle on her forehead with fountain-pen ink, and tied a twisted bandana around her head and stuck a row of frazzle-ended feathers around it, and wrapped herself in a red-and-black Hudson's Bay blanket. The counsellors, also in blankets but with only two streaks of red, beat on tom-toms made of round wooden cheese boxes with leather stretched over the top and nailed in place. Cappie was Chief Cappeosota. They all had to say "How!" when she walked into the circle and stood there with one hand raised.

Looking back on this, Lois finds it disquieting. She knows too much about Indians: this is why. She knows, for instance, that they should not even be called Indians, and that they have enough worries without other people taking their names and dressing up as them. It has all been a form of stealing.

But she remembers, too, that she was once ignorant of this. Once she loved the campfire, the flickering of light on the ring of faces, the sound of the fake tom-toms, heavy and fast like a scared heartbeat; she loved Cappie in a red blanket and feathers, solemn, as a chief should be, raising her hand and saying, "Greetings, my Ravens." It was not funny, it was not making fun. She wanted to be an Indian. She wanted to be adventurous and pure, and Aboriginal.

"YOU GO ON BIG WATER," says Cappie. This is her idea—all their ideas—of how Indians talk. "You go where no man has ever trod. You go many moons." This is not true. They are only going for a week, not many moons. The canoe route is clearly marked, they have gone over it on a map, and there are prepared campsites with names which are used year after year. But when Cappie says this—and despite the way Lucy rolls up her eyes—Lois can feel the water stretching out, with the shores twisting away on either side, immense and a little frightening.

"You bring back much wampum," says Cappie. "Do good in war, my braves, and capture many scalps." This is another of her pretences: that they are boys, and bloodthirsty. But such a game cannot be played by substituting the word "squaw." It would not work at all.

Each of them has to stand up and step forward and have a red line drawn across her cheeks by Cappie. She tells them they must follow in the paths of their ancestors (who most certainly, thinks Lois, looking out the window of her apartment and remembering the family stash of daguerreotypes and sepia-coloured portraits on her mother's dressing table, the stiff-shirted, black-coated, grim-faced men and the beflounced women with their severe hair and their corseted respectability, would never have considered heading off onto an open lake, in a canoe, just for fun).

At the end of the ceremony they all stood and held hands around the circle, and sang taps. This did not sound very Indian, thinks Lois.

It sounded like a bugle call at a military post, in a movie. But Cappie was never one to be much concerned with consistency, or with archaeology.

AFTER BREAKFAST the next morning they set out from the main dock, in four canoes, three in each. The lipstick stripes have not come off completely, and still show faintly pink, like healing burns. They wear their white denim sailing hats, because of the sun, and thin-striped T-shirts, and pale baggy shorts with the cuffs rolled up. The middle one kneels, propping her rear end against the rolled sleeping bags. The counsellors going with them are Pat and Kip. Kip is no-nonsense; Pat is easier to wheedle, or fool.

There are white puffy clouds and a small breeze. Glints come from the little waves. Lois is in the bow of Kip's canoe. She still can't do a J-stroke very well, and she will have to be in the bow or the middle for the whole trip. Lucy is behind her; her own J-stroke is even worse. She splashes Lois with her paddle, quite a big splash.

"I'll get you back," says Lois.

"There was a stable fly on your shoulder," Lucy says.

Lois turns to look at her, to see if she's grinning. They're in the habit of splashing each other. Back there, the camp has vanished behind the first long point of rock and rough trees. Lois feels as if an invisible rope has broken. They're floating free, on their own, cut loose. Beneath the canoe the lake goes down, deeper and colder than it was a minute before.

"No horsing around in the canoe," says Kip. She's rolled her T-shirt sleeves up to the shoulder; her arms are brown and sinewy, her jaw determined, her stroke perfect. She looks as if she knows exactly what she is doing.

The four canoes keep close together. They sing, raucously and with defiance; they sing "The Quartermaster's Store," and "Clementine," and "Alouette." It is more like bellowing than singing.

After that the wind grows stronger, blowing slantwise against the bows, and they have to put all their energy into shoving themselves through the water.

WAS THERE ANYTHING important, anything that would provide some sort of reason or clue to what happened next? Lois can remember everything, every detail; but it does her no good.

They stopped at noon for a swim and lunch, and went on in the afternoon. At last they reached Little Birch, which was the first campsite for overnight. Lois and Lucy made the fire, while the others pitched the heavy canvas tents. The fireplace was already there, flat stones piled into a U. A burnt tin can and a beer bottle had been left in it. Their fire went out, and they had to restart it. "Hustle your bustle," said Kip. "We're starving."

The sun went down, and in the pink sunset light they brushed their teeth and spat the toothpaste froth into the lake. Kip and Pat put all the food that wasn't in cans into a packsack and slung it into a tree, in case of bears.

Lois and Lucy weren't sleeping in a tent. They'd begged to be allowed to sleep out; that way they could talk without the others hearing. If it rained, they told Kip, they promised not to crawl dripping into the tent over everyone's legs: they would get under the canoes. So they were out on the point.

Lois tried to get comfortable inside her sleeping bag, which smelled of musty storage and of earlier campers, a stale salty sweetness. She curled herself up, with her sweater rolled up under her head for a pillow and her flashlight inside her sleeping bag so it wouldn't roll away. The muscles of her sore arms were making small pings, like rubber bands breaking.

Beside her Lucy was rustling around. Lois could see the glimmering oval of her white face.

"I've got a rock poking into my back," said Lucy.

"So do I," said Lois. "You want to go into the tent?" She herself didn't, but it was right to ask.

"No," said Lucy. She subsided into her sleeping bag. After a moment she said, "It would be nice not to go back."

"To camp?" said Lois.

"To Chicago," said Lucy. "I hate it there."

"What about your boyfriend?" said Lois. Lucy didn't answer. She was either asleep or pretending to be.

There was a moon, and a movement of the trees. In the sky there were stars, layers of stars that went down and down. Kip said that when the stars were bright like that instead of hazy it meant bad weather later on. Out on the lake there were two loons, calling to each other in their insane, mournful voices. At the time it did not sound like grief. It was just background.

THE LAKE IN THE MORNING was flat calm. They skimmed along over the glassy surface, leaving V-shaped trails behind them; it felt like flying. As the sun rose higher it got hot, almost too hot. There were stable flies in the canoes, landing on a bare arm or leg for a quick sting. Lois hoped for wind.

They stopped for lunch at the next of the named campsites, Lookout Point. It was called this because, although the site itself was down near the water on a flat shelf of rock, there was a sheer cliff nearby and a trail that led up to the top. The top was the lookout, although what you were supposed to see from there was not clear. Kip said it was just a view.

Lois and Lucy decided to make the climb anyway. They didn't want to hang around waiting for lunch. It wasn't their turn to cook, though they hadn't avoided much by not doing it, because cooking lunch was no big deal, it was just unwrapping the cheese and getting out the bread and peanut butter, but Pat and Kip always had to do their woodsy act and boil up a billy tin for their own tea.

They told Kip where they were going. You had to tell Kip where you were going, even if it was only a little way into the woods to get dry twigs for kindling. You could never go anywhere without a buddy.

"Sure," said Kip, who was crouching over the fire, feeding driftwood into it. "Fifteen minutes to lunch."

"Where are they off to?" said Pat. She was bringing their billy tin of water from the lake.

"Lookout," said Kip.

"Be careful," said Pat. She said it as an afterthought, because it was what she always said.

"They're old hands," Kip said.

LOIS LOOKS AT HER WATCH: it's ten to twelve. She is the watch-minder; Lucy is careless of time. They walk up the path, which is dry earth and rocks, big rounded pinky-grey boulders or split-open ones with jagged edges. Spindly balsam and spruce trees grow to either side, the lake is blue fragments to the left. The sun is right overhead; there are no shadows anywhere. The heat comes up at them as well as down. The forest is dry and crackly.

It isn't far, but it's a steep climb and they're sweating when they reach the top. They wipe their faces with their bare arms, sit gingerly down on a scorching-hot rock, five feet from the edge but too close for Lois. It's a lookout all right, a sheer drop to the lake and a long view over the water, back the way they've come. It's amazing to Lois that they've travelled so far, over all that water, with nothing to propel them but their own arms. It makes her feel strong. There are all kinds of things she is capable of doing.

"It would be quite a dive off here," says Lucy.

"You'd have to be nuts," says Lois.

"Why?" says Lucy. "It's really deep. It goes straight down." She stands up and takes a step nearer the edge. Lois gets a stab in her midriff, the kind she gets when a car goes too fast over a bump. "Don't," she says.

"Don't what?" says Lucy, glancing around at her mischievously. She knows how Lois feels about heights. But she turns back. "I really have to pee," she says.

"You have toilet paper?" says Lois, who is never without it. She digs in her shorts pocket.

"Thanks," says Lucy.

They are both adept at peeing in the woods: doing it fast so the mosquitoes don't get you, the underwear pulled up between the knees, the squat with the feet apart so you don't wet your legs, facing downhill. The exposed feeling of your bum, as if someone is looking at you from behind. The etiquette when you're with someone else is not to look. Lois stands up and starts to walk back down the path, to be out of sight.

"Wait for me?" says Lucy.

LOIS CLIMBED DOWN, over and around the boulders, until she could not see Lucy; she waited. She could hear the voices of the others, talking and laughing, down near the shore. One voice was yelling, "Ants! Ants!" Someone must have sat on an anthill. Off to the side, in the woods, a raven was croaking, a hoarse single note.

She looked at her watch: it was noon. This is when she heard the shout.

She has gone over and over it in her mind since, so many times that the first, real shout has been obliterated, like a footprint trampled by other footprints. But she is sure (she is almost positive, she is nearly certain) that it was not a shout of fear. Not a scream. More like a cry of surprise, cut off too soon. Short, like a dog's bark.

"Lucy?" Lois said. Then she called "Lucy!" By now she was clambering back up, over the stones of the path. Lucy was not up there. Or she was not in sight.

"Stop fooling around," Lois said. "It's lunchtime." But Lucy did not rise from behind a rock or step out, smiling, from behind a tree. The sunlight was all around; the rocks looked white. "This isn't funny!" Lois said, and it wasn't, panic was rising in her, the panic of a small child who does not know where the bigger ones are hidden. She could hear her own heart. She looked quickly around; she lay down on the ground and looked over the edge of the cliff. It made her feel cold. There was nothing.

She went back down the path, stumbling; she was breathing too quickly; she was too frightened to cry. She felt terrible—guilty and dismayed, as if she had done something very bad, by mistake. Something that could never be repaired. "Lucy's gone," she told Kip.

Kip looked up from her fire, annoyed. The water in the billy can was boiling. "What do you mean, gone?" she said. "Where did she go?"

"I don't know," said Lois. "She's just gone."

No one had heard the shout, but then no one had heard Lois calling, either. They had been talking among themselves, by the water.

Kip and Pat went up to the lookout and searched and called, and blew their whistles. Nothing answered.

Then they came back down, and Lois had to tell exactly what had happened. The other girls all sat in a circle and listened to her. Nobody said anything. They all looked frightened, especially Pat and Kip. They were the leaders. You did not just lose a camper like this, for no reason at all.

"Why did you leave her alone?" said Kip.

"I was just down the path," said Lois. "I told you. She had to go to the bathroom." She did not say *pee* in front of people older than herself.

Kip looked disgusted.

"Maybe she just walked off into the woods and got turned around," said one of the girls.

"Maybe she's doing it on purpose," said another.

Nobody believed either of these theories.

They took the canoes and searched around the base of the cliff, and peered down into the water. But there had been no sound of falling rock; there had been no splash. There was no clue, nothing at all. Lucy had simply vanished.

That was the end of the canoe trip. It took them the same two days to go back that it had taken coming in, even though they were short a paddler. They did not sing.

After that, the police went in a motorboat, with dogs; they were the Mounties and the dogs were German shepherds, trained to follow trails in the woods. But it had rained since, and they could find nothing.

LOIS IS SITTING in Cappie's office. Her face is bloated with crying, she's seen that in the mirror. By now she feels numbed; she feels as if she has drowned. She can't stay here. It has been too much of a shock. Tomorrow her parents are coming to take her away. Several of the other girls who were on the canoe trip are also being collected. The others will have to stay, because their parents are in Europe, or cannot be reached.

Cappie is grim. They've tried to hush it up, but of course everyone in camp knows. Soon the papers will know too. You can't keep it quiet, but what can be said? What can be said that makes any sense? "Girl vanishes in broad daylight, without a trace." It can't be believed. Other things, worse things, will be suspected. Negligence, at the very least. But they have always taken such care. Bad luck will gather around Camp Manitou like a fog; parents will avoid it, in favour of other, luckier places. Lois can see Cappie thinking all this, even through her numbness. It's what anyone would think.

Lois sits on the hard wooden chair in Cappie's office, beside the old wooden desk, over which hangs the thumb-tacked bulletin board of normal camp routine, and gazes at Cappie through her puffy eyelids. Cappie is now smiling what is supposed to be a reassuring smile. Her manner is too casual: she's after something. Lois has seen this look on Cappie's face when she's been sniffing out contraband chocolate bars, hunting down those rumoured to have snuck out of their cabins at night.

"Tell me again," says Cappie, "from the beginning."

Lois has told her story so many times by now, to Pat and Kip, to Cappie, to the police, that she knows it word for word. She knows it, but she no longer believes it. It has become a story. "I told you," she said. "She wanted to go to the bathroom. I gave her my toilet paper. I went down the path, I waited for her. I heard this kind of shout …"

"Yes," says Cappie, smiling confidingly, "but before that. What did you say to one another?"

Lois thinks. Nobody has asked her this before. "She said you could dive off there. She said it went straight down."

"And what did you say?"

"I said you'd have to be nuts."

"Were you mad at Lucy?" says Cappie, in an encouraging voice.

"No," says Lois. "Why would I be mad at Lucy? I wasn't ever mad at Lucy." She feels like crying again. The times when she has in fact been mad at Lucy have been erased already. Lucy was always perfect.

"Sometimes we're angry when we don't know we're angry," says Cappie, as if to herself. "Sometimes we get really mad and we don't even know it. Sometimes we might do a thing without meaning to, or without knowing what will happen. We lose our tempers."

Lois is only thirteen, but it doesn't take her long to figure out that Cappie is not including herself in any of this. By *we* she means Lois. She is accusing Lois of pushing Lucy off the cliff. The unfairness of this hits her like a slap. "I didn't!" she says.

"Didn't what?" says Cappie softly. "Didn't what, Lois?"

Lois does the worst thing, she begins to cry. Cappie gives her a look like a pounce. She's got what she wanted.

LATER, when she was grown up, Lois was able to understand what this interview had been about. She could see Cappie's desperation, her need for a story, a real story with a reason in it; anything but the senseless vacancy Lucy had left for her to deal with. Cappie wanted Lois to supply the reason, to be the reason. It wasn't even for the newspapers or the parents, because she could never make such an accusation without proof. It was for herself: something to explain the loss of Camp Manitou and of all she had worked for, the years of entertaining spoiled children and buttering up parents and making a fool of herself with feathers stuck in her hair. Camp Manitou was in fact lost. It did not survive.

Lois worked all this out, twenty years later. But it was far too late. It was too late even ten minutes afterwards, when she'd left Cappie's office and was walking slowly back to her cabin to pack. Lucy's clothes were still there, folded on the shelves, as if waiting. She felt the other girls in the cabin watching her with speculation in their eyes. *Could she have done it? She must have done it.* For the rest of her life, she has caught people watching her in this way.

Maybe they weren't thinking this. Maybe they were merely sorry for her. But she felt she had been tried and sentenced, and this is what has stayed with her: the knowledge that she had been singled out, condemned for something that was not her fault.

LOIS SITS in the living room of her apartment, drinking a cup of tea. Through the knee-to-ceiling window she has a wide view of Lake Ontario, with its skin of wrinkled blue-grey light, and of the willows of Centre Island shaken by a wind, which is silent at this distance, and on this side of the glass. When there isn't too much pollution she can see the far shore, the foreign shore; though today it is obscured.

Possibly she could go out, go downstairs, do some shopping; there isn't much in the refrigerator. The boys say she doesn't get out enough. But she isn't hungry, and moving, stirring from this space, is increasingly an effort.

She can hardly remember, now, having her two boys in the hospital, nursing them as babies; she can hardly remember getting married, or what Rob looked like. Even at the time she never felt she was paying full attention. She was tired a lot, as if she was living not one life but two: her own, and another, shadowy life that hovered around her and would not let itself be realized—the life of what would have happened if Lucy had not stepped sideways, and disappeared from time.

She would never go up north, to Rob's family cottage or to any place with wild lakes and wild trees and the calls of loons. She would never go anywhere near. Still, it was as if she was always listening for another voice, the voice of a person who should have been there but was not. An echo.

While Rob was alive, while the boys were growing up, she could pretend she didn't hear it, this empty space in sound. But now there is nothing much left to distract her.

She turns away from the window and looks at her pictures. There is the pinkish island, in the lake, with the intertwisted trees. It's the same landscape they paddled through, that distant summer. She's seen travelogues of this country, aerial photographs; it looks different from above, bigger, more hopeless: lake after lake, random blue puddles in dark green bush, the trees like bristles.

How could you ever find anything there, once it was lost? Maybe if they cut it all down, drained it all away, they might find Lucy's bones, sometime, wherever they are hidden. A few bones, some buttons, the buckle from her shorts.

But a dead person is a body; a body occupies space, it exists somewhere. You can see it; you put it in a box and bury it in the ground, and then it's in a box in the ground. But Lucy is not in a box, or in the ground. Because she is nowhere definite, she could be anywhere.

And these paintings are not landscape paintings. Because there aren't any landscapes up there, not in the old, tidy European sense, with a gentle hill, a curving river, a cottage, a mountain in the background, a golden evening sky. Instead there's a tangle, a receding maze, in which you can become lost almost as soon as you step off the path. There are no backgrounds in any of these paintings, no vistas; only a great deal of foreground that goes back and back, endlessly, involving you in its twists and turns of tree and branch and rock. No matter how far back in you go, there will be more. And the trees themselves are hardly trees; they are currents of energy, charged with violent colour.

Who knows how many trees there were on the cliff just before Lucy disappeared? Who counted? Maybe there was one more, afterwards.

Lois sits in her chair and does not move. Her hand with the cup is raised halfway to her mouth. She hears something, almost hears it: a shout of recognition, or of joy.

She looks at the paintings, she looks into them. Every one of them is a picture of Lucy. You can't see her exactly, but she's there, in behind the pink stone island or the one behind that. In the picture of the cliff she is hidden by the clutch of fallen rocks towards the bottom, in the one of the river shore she is crouching beneath the overturned canoe. In the yellow autumn woods she's behind the tree that cannot be seen because of the other trees, over beside the blue sliver of pond; but if you walked into the picture and found the tree, it would be the wrong one, because the right one would be further on.

Everyone has to be somewhere, and this is where Lucy is. She is in Lois's apartment, in the holes that open inwards on the wall, not like windows but like doors. She is here. She is entirely alive.

Dandelion Wine

by

RAY BRADBURY

IT WAS A QUIET MORNING, the town covered over with darkness and at ease in bed. Summer gathered in the weather, the wind had the proper touch, the breathing of the world was long and warm and slow. You had only to rise, lean from your window, and know that this indeed was the first real time of freedom and living, this was the first morning of summer.

Douglas Spaulding, twelve, freshly wakened, let summer idle him on its early-morning stream. Lying in this third-story cupola bedroom, he felt the tall power it gave him, riding high in the June wind, the grandest tower in town. At night, when the trees washed together, he flashed his gaze like a beacon from this lighthouse in all directions over swarming seas of elm and oak and maple. Now …

"Boy," whispered Douglas.

A whole summer ahead to cross off the calendar, day by day. Like the goddess Siva in the travel books, he saw his hands jump everywhere, pluck sour apples, peaches, and midnight plums. He would be clothed in trees and bushes and rivers. He would freeze, gladly, in the hoarfrosted ice-house door. He would bake, happily, with ten thousand chickens, in Grandma's kitchen.

But now—a familiar task awaited him.

One night each week he was allowed to leave his father, his mother, and his younger brother Tom asleep in their small house next door and run here, up the dark spiral stairs to his grandparents' cupola, and in this sorcerer's tower sleep with thunders and visions, to wake before the crystal jingle of milk bottles and perform his ritual magic.

He stood at the open window in the dark, took a deep breath and exhaled.

The street lights, like candles on a black cake, went out. He exhaled again and again and the stars began to vanish.

Douglas smiled. He pointed a finger.

There, and there. Now over here, and here ...

Yellow squares were cut in the dim morning earth as house lights winked slowly on. A sprinkle of windows came suddenly alight miles off in dawn country.

"Everyone yawn. Everyone up."

The great house stirred below.

"Grandpa, get your teeth from the water glass!" He waited a decent interval. "Grandma and Great-grandma, fry hot cakes!"

The warm scent of fried batter rose in the drafty halls to stir the boarders, the aunts, the uncles, the visiting cousins, in their rooms.

"Street where all the Old People live, wake up! Miss Helen Loomis, Colonel Freeleigh, Miss Bentley! Cough, get up, take pills, move around! Mr. Jonas, hitch up your horse, get your junk wagon out and around!"

The bleak mansions across the town ravine opened baleful dragon eyes. Soon, in the morning avenues below, two old women would glide their electric Green Machine, waving at all the dogs. "Mr. Tridden, run to the carbarn!" Soon, scattering hot blue sparks above it, the town trolley would sail the rivering brick streets.

"Ready John Huff, Charlie Woodman?" whispered Douglas to the Street of Children. "Ready!" to baseballs sponged deep in wet lawns, to rope swings hung empty in trees.

"Mom, Dad, Tom, wake up."

Clock alarms tinkled faintly. The courthouse clock boomed. Birds leaped from trees like a net thrown by his hand, singing. Douglas, conducting an orchestra, pointed to the eastern sky.

The sun began to rise.

He folded his arms and smiled a magician's smile. Yes, sir, he thought, everyone jumps, everyone runs when I yell. It'll be a fine season.

He gave the town a last snap of his fingers.

Doors slammed open; people stepped out.

Summer 1928 began.

CROSSING THE LAWN that morning, Douglas Spaulding broke a spider web with his face. A single invisible line on the air touched his brow and snapped without a sound.

So, with the subtlest of incidents, he knew that this day was going to be different. It would be different also, because, as his father explained, driving Douglas and his ten-year-old brother Tom out of town towards the country, there were some days compounded completely of odour, nothing but the world blowing in one nostril and out the other. And some days, he went on, were days of hearing every trump and trill of the universe. Some days were good for tasting and some for touching. And some days were good for all the senses at once. This day now, he nodded, smelled as if a great and nameless orchard had grown up overnight beyond the hills to fill the entire visible land with its warm freshness. The air felt like rain, but there were no clouds. Momentarily, a stranger might laugh off in the woods, but there was silence …

Douglas watched the travelling land. He smelled no orchards and sensed no rain, for without apple trees or clouds he knew neither could exist. And as for that stranger laughing deep in the woods …?

Yet the fact remained—Douglas shivered—this, without reason, was a special day.

The car stopped at the very centre of the quiet forest.

"All right, boys, behave."

They had been jostling elbows.

"Yes, sir."

They climbed out, carrying the blue tin pails away from the lonely dirt road into the smell of fallen rain.

"Look for bees," said Father. "Bees hang around grapes like boys around kitchens. Doug?"

Douglas looked up suddenly.

"You're off a million miles," said Father. "Look alive. Walk with us."

"Yes, sir."

And they walked through the forest, Father very tall, Douglas moving in his shadow, and Tom, very small, trotting in his brother's shade. They came to a little rise and looked ahead. Here, here, did they see? Father pointed. Here was where the big summer-quiet winds lived and passed in the green depths, like ghost whales, unseen.

Douglas looked quickly, saw nothing, and felt put upon by his father who, like Grandpa, lived on riddles. But … but, still … Douglas paused and listened.

Yes, something's going to happen, he thought, I know it!

"Here's maidenhair fern." Dad walked, the tin pail belling in his fist. "Feel this?" He scuffed the earth. "A million years of good rich leaf mould laid down. Think of the autumns that got by to make this."

"Boy, I walk like an Indian," said Tom. "Not a sound."

Douglas felt but did not feel the deep loam, listening, watchful. We're surrounded! he thought. It'll happen! What? He stopped. Come out, wherever you are, whatever you are! he cried silently.

Tom and Dad strolled on the hushed earth ahead.

"Finest lace there is," said Dad quietly.

And he was gesturing up through the trees above to show them how it was woven across the sky or how the sky was woven into the trees, he wasn't sure which. But there it was, he smiled, and the weaving went on, green and blue, if you watched and saw the forest shift its humming loom. Dad stood comfortably saying this and that, the words easy in his mouth. He made it easier by laughing at his own declarations just so often. He liked to listen to the silence, he said, if silence could be listened to, for, he went on, in that silence you could hear wildflower pollen sifting down the bee-fried air, by God, the, bee-fried air! Listen! the waterfall of birdsong beyond those trees!

Now, thought Douglas, here it comes! Running! I don't see it! Running! Almost on me!

"Fox grapes," said Father. "We're in luck, look here!"

Don't! Douglas gasped.

But Tom and Dad bent down to shove their hands deep in rattling bush. The spell was shattered. The terrible prowler, the magnificent runner, the leaper, the shaker of souls, vanished.

Douglas, lost and empty, fell to his knees. He saw his fingers sink through green shadow and come forth stained with such colour that it seemed he had somehow cut the forest and delved his hand in the open wound.

"LUNCHTIME, BOYS!"

With buckets half burdened with fox grapes and wild strawberries, followed by bees which were, no more, no less, said Father, the world humming under its breath, they sat on a green-mossed log, chewing sandwiches and trying to listen to the forest the same way Father did. Douglas felt Dad watching him, quietly amused. Dad started to say something that had crossed his mind, but instead tried another bite of sandwich and mused over it.

"Sandwich outdoors isn't a sandwich any more. Tastes different than indoors, notice? Got more spice. Tastes like mint and pinesap. Does wonders for the appetite."

Douglas's tongue hesitated on the texture of bread and devilled ham. No … no … it was just a sandwich.

Tom chewed and nodded. "Know just what you mean, Dad!"

It almost happened, thought Douglas. Whatever it was it was Big, my gosh, it was Big! Something scared it off. Where is it now? Back of that bush! No, behind me! No, here … almost *here* … He kneaded his stomach secretly.

If I wait, it'll come back. It won't hurt; somehow I know it's not here to hurt me. What then? What? What?

"You know how many baseball games we played this year, last year, year before?" said Tom, apropos of nothing.

Douglas watched Tom's quickly moving lips.

"Wrote it down! One thousand five hundred sixty-eight games! How many times I brushed my teeth in ten years? Six thousand! Washed my hands: fifteen thousand. Slept: four thousand some-odd times, not counting naps. Ate six hundred peaches, eight hundred apples. Pears two hundred. I'm not for pears. Name a thing, I got the statistics. Runs to the billion millions, things I done, add 'em up, in ten years."

Now, thought Douglas, it's coming close again. Why? Tom talking? But why Tom? Tom chatting along, mouth crammed with sandwich, Dad there, alert as a mountain cat on the log, and Tom letting the words rise like quick soda bubbles in his mouth:

"Books I read: four hundred. Matinees I seen: forty Buck Joneses, thirty Jack Hoxies, forty-five Tom Mixes, thirty-nine Hoot Gibsons, one hundred and ninety-two single and separate Felix-the-Cat cartoons, ten Douglas Fairbankses, eight repeats on Lon Chaney in *The Phantom of the Opera,* four Milton Sillses, and one Adolph Menjou thing about love where I spent ninety hours in the theatre toilet waiting for the mush to be over so I could see *The Cat and the Canary* or *The Bat,* where everybody held on to everybody else and screamed for two hours without letting go. During that time I figure four hundred lollipops, three hundred Tootsie Rolls, seven hundred ice cream cones ..."

Tom rolled quietly along his way for another five minutes and then Dad said, "How many berries you picked so far, Tom?"

"Two hundred fifty-six on the nose!" said Tom instantly.

Dad laughed and lunch was over and they moved again into the shadows to find fox grapes and the tiny wild strawberries, bent down, all three of them, hands coming and going, the pails getting heavy, and Douglas holding his breath, thinking, Yes, yes, it's near again! Breathing on my neck, almost! Don't look! Work. Just pick, fill up the pail. If you look you'll scare it off. Don't lose it this time! But how, how do you bring it around here where you can see it, stare it right in the eye? How? How?

"Got a snowflake in a matchbox," said Tom, smiling at the wine-glove on his hand.

Shut up! Douglas wanted to yell. But no, the yell would scare the echoes, and run the Thing away!

And, wait ... the more Tom talked, the closer the great Thing came, it wasn't scared of Tom, Tom drew it with his breath, Tom was part of it!

"Last February," said Tom, and chuckled. "Held a matchbox up in a snowstorm, let one old snowflake fall in, shut it up, ran inside the house, stashed it in the icebox!"

Close, very close. Douglas stared at Tom's flickering lips. He wanted to jump around, for he felt a vast tidal wave lift up behind the forest. In an instant it would smash down, crush them forever ...

"Yes, sir," mused Tom, picking grapes, "I'm the only guy in all Illinois who's got a snowflake in summer. Precious as diamonds, by gosh. Tomorrow I'll open it. Doug, you can look, too ..."

Any other day Douglas might have snorted, struck out, denied it all. But now, with the great Thing rushing near, falling down in the clear air above him, he could only nod, eyes shut.

Tom, puzzled, stopped picking berries and turned to stare over at his brother.

Douglas, hunched over, was an ideal target. Tom leaped, yelling, landed. They fell, thrashed, and rolled.

No! Douglas squeezed his mind shut. No! But suddenly ... Yes, it's all right! Yes! The tangle, the contact of bodies, the falling tumble had not scared off the tidal sea that crashed now, flooding and washing them along the shore of grass deep through the forest. Knuckles struck his mouth. He tasted rusty warm blood, grabbed Tom hard, held him tight, and so in silence they lay, hearts churning, nostrils hissing. And at last, slowly, afraid he would find nothing, Douglas opened one eye.

And everything, absolutely everything, was there.

The world, like a great iris of an even more gigantic eye, which has also just opened and stretched out to encompass everything, stared back at him.

And he knew what it was that had leaped upon him to stay and would not run away now.

I'm alive, he thought.

His fingers trembled, bright with blood, like the bits of a strange flag now found and before unseen, and him wondering what country and what allegiance he owed to it. Holding Tom, but not knowing him there, he touched his free hand to that blood as if it could be peeled away, held up, turned over. Then he let go of Tom and lay on his back with his hand up in the sky and he was a head from which his eyes peered like sentinels through the portcullis of a strange castle out along a bridge, his arm, to those fingers where the bright pennant of blood quivered in the light.

"You all right, Doug?" asked Tom.

His voice was at the bottom of a green moss well somewhere underwater, secret, removed.

The grass whispered under his body. He put his arm down, feeling the sheath of fuzz on it, and, far away, below, his toes creaking in his shoes. The wind sighed over his shelled ears. The world slipped bright over the glassy round of his eyeballs, like images sparked in a crystal sphere. Flowers were sun and fiery spots of sky strewn through the woodland. Birds flickered like skipped stones across the vast inverted pond of heaven. His breath raked over his teeth, going in ice, coming out fire. Insects shocked the air with electric clearness. Ten thousand individual hairs grew a millionth of an inch on his head. He heard the twin hearts beating in each ear, the third heart beating in his throat, the two hearts throbbing his wrists, the real heart pounding his chest. The million pores on his body opened.

I'm *really* alive! he thought. I never knew it before, or if I did I don't remember!

He yelled it loud but silent, a dozen times! Think of it, think of it! Twelve years old and only now! Now discovering this rare timepiece, this clock gold-bright and guaranteed to run threescore and ten, left under a tree and found while wrestling.

"Doug, you okay?"

Douglas yelled, grabbed Tom, and rolled.

"Doug, you're crazy!"

"Crazy!"

They spilled downhill, the sun in their mouths, in their eyes like shattered lemon glass, gasping like trout thrown out on a bank, laughing till they cried.

"Doug, you're not mad?"

"No, no, no, no, no!"

Douglas, eyes shut, saw spotted leopards pad in the dark.

"Tom!" Then quieter. "Tom ... does everyone in the world ... know he's alive?"

"Sure. Heck, yes!"

The leopards trotted soundlessly off through darker lands where eyeballs could not turn to follow.

"I hope they do," whispered Douglas. "Oh, I sure hope they know."

Douglas opened his eyes. Dad was standing high above him there in the green-leaved sky, laughing, hands on hips. Their eyes met. Douglas quickened. Dad knows, he thought. It was all planned! He brought us here on purpose, so this could happen to me! He's in on it, he knows it all. And now he knows that I know.

A hand came down and seized him through the air. Swayed on his feet with Tom and Dad, still bruised and rumpled, puzzled and awed, Douglas held his strange-boned elbows tenderly and licked the fine cut lip with satisfaction. Then he looked at Dad and Tom.

"I'll carry all the pails," he said. "This once, let me haul everything."

They handed over the pails with quizzical smiles.

He stood swaying slightly, the forest collected, full-weighted and heavy with syrup, clenched hard in his down-slung hands. I want to feel all there is to feel, he thought. Let me feel tired, now, let me *feel* tired. I mustn't forget, I'm alive, I know I'm alive, I mustn't forget it tonight or tomorrow or the day after that.

The bees followed and the smell of fox grapes and yellow summer followed as he walked heavy laden and half-drunk, his fingers wondrously calloused, arms numb, feet stumbling so his father caught his shoulder.

"No," mumbled Douglas, "I'm all right. I'm fine ..."

It took half an hour for the sense of the grass, the roots, the stones, the bark of the mossy log, to fade from where they had patterned his arms and legs and back. While he pondered this, let it slip, slide, dissolve away, his brother and his quiet father followed behind, allowing him to pathfind the forest alone out towards that incredible highway which would take them back to the town....

THE TOWN, then, later in the day.

And yet another harvest.

Grandfather stood on the wide front porch like a captain surveying the vast unmotioned calms of a season dead ahead. He questioned the wind and the untouchable sky and the lawn on which stood Douglas and Tom to question only him.

"Grandpa, are they ready? Now?"

Grandfather pinched his chin. "Five hundred, a thousand, two thousand easy. Yes, yes, a good supply. Pick 'em easy, pick 'em all. A dime for every sack delivered to the press!"

"Hey!"

The boys bent, smiling. They picked the golden flowers. The flowers that flooded the world, dripped off lawns on to brick streets, tapped softly at crystal cellar windows and agitated themselves so that on all sides lay the dazzle and glitter of molten sun.

"Every year," said Grandfather. "They run amuck; I let them. Pride of lions in the yard. Stare, and they burn a hole in your retina. A common flower, a weed that no one sees, yes. But for us, a noble thing, the dandelion."

So, plucked carefully, in sacks, the dandelions were carried below. The cellar dark glowed with their arrival. The wine press stood open, cold. A rush of flowers warmed it. The press, replaced, its screw rotated, twirled by Grandfather, squeezed gently on the crop.

"There ... so ..."

The golden tide, the essence of this fine fair month ran, then gushed from the spout below, to be crocked, skimmed of ferment, and bottled in clean ketchup shakers, then ranked in sparkling rows in cellar gloom.

Dandelion wine.

The words were summer on the tongue. The wine was summer caught and stoppered. And now that Douglas knew, he really knew he was alive, and moved turning through the world to touch and see it all, it was only right and proper that some of his new knowledge, some of this special vintage day would be sealed away for opening on a January day with snow falling fast and the sun unseen for weeks or months and perhaps some of the miracle by then forgotten and in need of renewal. Since this was going to be a summer of unguessed wonders, he wanted it all salvaged and labelled so that any time he wished he might tiptoe down in this dank twilight and reach up his fingertips.

And there, row upon row, with the soft gleam of flowers opened at morning, with the light of this June sun glowing through a faint skin of dust, would stand the dandelion wine. Peer through it at the wintry day—the snow melted to grass, the trees were reinhabited with bird, leaf, and blossoms like a continent of butterflies breathing on the wind. And peering through, colour sky from iron to blue.

Hold summer in your hand, pour summer in a glass, a tiny glass of course, the smallest tingling sip for children; change the season in your veins by raising glass to lip and tilting summer in.

"Ready, now, the rain barrel!"

Nothing else in the world would do but the pure waters which had been summoned from the lakes far away and the sweet fields of grassy dew on early morning, lifted to the open sky, carried in laundered clusters nine hundred miles, brushed with wind, electrified with high voltage, and condensed upon cool air. This water, falling, raining, gathered yet more of the heavens in its crystals. Taking something of the east wind and the west wind and the north wind and the south, the water made rain and the rain, within this hour of rituals, would be well on its way to wine.

Douglas ran with the dipper. He plunged it deep in the rain barrel. "Here we go!"

The water was silk in the cup; clear, faintly blue silk. It softened the lip and the throat and the heart, if drunk. This water must be carried in dipper and bucket to the cellar, there to be leavened in freshets, in mountain streams, upon the dandelion harvest.

Even Grandma, when snow was whirling fast, dizzying the world, blinding windows, stealing breath from gasping mouths, even Grandma, one day in February, would vanish to the cellar.

Above, in the vast house, there would be coughings, sneezings, wheezings, and groans, childish fevers, throats raw as butchers' meat, noses like bottled cherries, the stealthy microbe everywhere.

Then, rising from the cellar like a June goddess, Grandma would come, something hidden but obvious under her knitted shawl. This, carried to every miserable room upstairs-and-down, would be dispensed with aroma and clarity into neat glasses, to be swigged neatly. The medicines of another time, the balm of sun and idle August afternoons, the faintly heard sounds of ice wagons passing on brick avenues, the rush of silver sky-rockets and the fountaining of lawn mowers moving through ant countries, all these, all these in a glass.

Yes, even Grandma, drawn to the cellar of winter for a June adventure, might stand alone and quietly, in secret conclave with her own soul and spirit, as did Grandfather and Father and Uncle Bert, or some of the boarders, communing with a last touch of a calendar long departed, with the picnics and the warm rains and the smell of wheat and new popcorn and bending hay. Even Grandma, repeating and repeating the fine and golden words, even as they were said now in this moment when the flowers were dropping into the press, as they would be repeated every winter for all the white winters in time. Saying them over and over on the lips, like a smile, like a sudden patch of sunlight in the dark.

Dandelion wine. Dandelion wine. Dandelion wine.

Under the Jaguar Sun

by

ITALO CALVINO

"OAXACA" IS PRONOUNCED "Wa*ha*ka." Originally, the hotel where we were staying had been the Convent of Santa Catalina. The first thing we noticed was a painting in a little room leading to the bar. The bar was called Las Novicias. The painting was a large, dark canvas that portrayed a young nun and an old priest standing side by side; their hands, slightly apart from their sides, almost touched. The figures were rather stiff for an eighteenth-century picture; the painting had the somewhat crude grace characteristic of colonial art, but it conveyed a distressing sensation, like an ache of contained suffering.

The lower part of the painting was filled by a long caption, written in cramped lines in an angular, italic hand, white on black. The words devoutly celebrated the life and death of the two characters, who had been chaplain and abbess of the convent (she, of noble birth, had entered it as a novice at the age of eighteen). The reason for their being painted together was the extraordinary love (this word, in the pious Spanish prose, appeared charged with ultra-terrestrial yearning) that had bound the abbess and her confessor for thirty years, a love so great (the word in its spiritual sense sublimated but did not erase the physical emotion) that when the priest came to die, the abbess, twenty years younger, in the space of a single day fell ill and literally expired of love (the word blazed with a truth in which all meanings converge), to join him in Heaven.

Olivia, whose Spanish is better than mine, helped me decipher the story, suggesting to me the translation of some obscure expressions, and these words proved to be the only ones we exchanged during and after the reading, as if we had found ourselves in the presence of a drama, or of a happiness, that made any comment out of place. Something intimidated us—or, rather, frightened us, or, more precisely, filled us with a kind of uneasiness. So I will try to describe what I felt: the sense of a lack, a consuming void. What Olivia was thinking, since she remained silent, I cannot guess.

Then Olivia spoke. She said, "I would like to eat *chiles en nogada.*" And, walking like somnambulists, not quite sure we were touching the ground, we headed for the dining room.

In the best moments of a couple's life, it happens: I immediately reconstructed the train of Olivia's thought, with no need of further speech, because the same sequence of associations had unrolled in my mind, though in a more foggy, murky way. Without her, I would never have gained awareness of it.

Our trip through Mexico had already lasted over a week. A few days earlier, in Tepotzotlán, in a restaurant whose tables were set among the orange trees of another convent's cloister, we had savoured dishes prepared (at least, so we were told) according to the traditional recipes of the nuns. We had eaten a *tamal de elote*—a fine semolina of sweet corn, that is, with ground pork and very hot pepper, all steamed in a bit of corn-husk—and then *chiles en nogada,* which were reddish brown, somewhat wrinkled little peppers, swimming in a walnut sauce whose harshness and bitter aftertaste were drowned in a creamy, sweetish surrender.

After that, for us, the thought of nuns called up the flavours of an elaborate and bold cuisine, bent on making the flavours' highest notes vibrate, juxtaposing them in modulations, in chords, and especially in dissonances that would assert themselves as an incomparable experience—a point of no return, an absolute possession exercised on the receptivity of all the senses.

The Mexican friend who had accompanied us on that excursion, Salustiano Velazco by name, in answering Olivia's inquiries about these recipes of conventual gastronomy, lowered his voice as if confiding indelicate secrets to us. It was his way of speaking—or, rather, one of his ways; the copious information Salustiano supplied (about the history and customs and nature of his country his erudition was inexhaustible) was either stated emphatically like a war proclamation or slyly insinuated as if it were charged with all sorts of implied meanings.

Olivia remarked that such dishes involved hours and hours of work and, even before that, a long series of experiments and adjustments. "Did these nuns spend their whole day in the kitchen?" she asked, imagining entire lives devoted to the search for new blends of ingredients, new variations in the measurements, to alert and patient mixing, to the handing down of an intricate, precise lore.

"Tenían sus criadas," Salustiano answered. ("They had their servants.") And he explained to us that when the daughters of noble families entered the convent, they brought their maids with them; thus, to satisfy the venial whims of gluttony, the only cravings allowed them, the nuns could rely on a swarm of eager, tireless helpers. And as far as they themselves were concerned, they had only to conceive and compare and correct the recipes that expressed

their fantasies confined within those walls: the fantasies, after all, of sophisticated women, bright and introverted and complex women who needed absolutes, whose reading told of ecstasies and transfigurations, martyrs and tortures, women with conflicting calls in their blood, genealogies in which the descendants of the conquistadores mingled with those of Indian princesses or slaves, women with childhood recollections of the fruits and fragrances of a succulent vegetation, thick with ferments, though growing from those sun-baked plateaus.

Nor should sacred architecture be overlooked, the background to the lives of those religious; it, too, was impelled by the same drive toward the extreme that led to the exacerbation of flavours amplified by the blaze of the most spicy *chiles*. Just as colonial baroque set no limits on the profusion of ornament and display, in which God's presence was identified in a closely calculated delirium of brimming, excessive sensations, so the curing of the hundred or more native varieties of hot peppers carefully selected for each dish opened vistas of a flaming ecstasy.

At Tepotzotlán, we visited the church the Jesuits had built in the eighteenth century for their seminary (and no sooner was it consecrated than they had to abandon it, as they were expelled from Mexico forever): a theatre-church, all gold and bright colours, in a dancing and acrobatic baroque, crammed with swirling angels, garlands, panoplies of flowers, shells. Surely the Jesuits meant to compete with the splendour of the Aztecs, whose ruined temples and palaces—the royal palace of Quetzalcóatl!—still stood, to recall a rule imposed through the impressive effects of a grandiose, transfiguring art. There was a challenge in the air, in this dry and thin air at an altitude of two thousand metres: the ancient rivalry between the civilizations of America and Spain in the art of bewitching the senses with dazzling seductions. And from architecture this rivalry extended to cuisine, where the two civilizations had merged, or perhaps where the conquered had triumphed, strong in the condiments born from their very soil. Through the white hands of novices and the brown hands of lay sisters, the cuisine of the new Indo-Hispanic civilization had become also the field of battle between the aggressive ferocity of the ancient gods of the mesa and the sinuous excess of the baroque religion.

On the supper menu we didn't find *chiles en nogada*. From one locality to the next the gastronomic lexicon varied, always offering new terms to be recorded and new sensations to be defined. Instead, we found *guacamole,* to be scooped up with crisp tortillas that snap into many shards and dip like spoons into the thick cream (the fat softness of the *aguacate*—the Mexican national fruit, known to the rest of the world under the distorted name of "avocado"—is accompanied and underlined by the angular dryness of the tortilla, which, for its part, can have many flavours, pretending to have none); then *guajolote con mole poblano*—that is, turkey with Puebla-style *mole* sauce, one of the noblest among the many *moles,* and most laborious (the preparation never takes less than two days), and most complicated, because it requires several different varieties of *chile,* as well as garlic, onion, cinnamon, cloves, pepper, cumin, coriander, and sesame, almonds, raisins, and peanuts, with a touch of chocolate; and finally *quesadillas* (another kind of tortilla, really, for which cheese is incorporated in the dough, garnished with ground meat and refried beans).

Right in the midst of chewing, Olivia's lips paused, almost stopped, though without completely interrupting their continuity of movement, which slowed down, as if reluctant to allow an inner echo to fade, while her gaze became fixed, intent on no specific object, in apparent alarm. Her face had a special concentration that I had observed during meals ever since we began our trip to Mexico. I followed the tension as it moved from her lips to her nostrils, flaring one moment, contracting the next (the plasticity of the nose is quite limited—especially for a delicate, harmonious nose like Olivia's—and each barely perceptible attempt to expand the capacity of the nostrils in the longitudinal direction actually makes them thinner, while the corresponding reflex movement, accentuating their breadth, then seems a kind of withdrawal of the whole nose into the surface of the face).

What I have just said might suggest that, in eating, Olivia became closed into herself, absorbed with the inner course of her sensations; in reality, on the contrary, the desire her whole person expressed was that of communicating to me what she was tasting: communicating with me through flavours, or communicating with flavours through a double set of taste buds, hers and mine. "Did you taste that? Are you tasting it?" she was asking me, with a kind of anxiety, as if at that same moment our incisors had pierced an identically composed morsel and the same drop of savour had been caught by the membranes of my tongue and of hers. "Is it *cilantro*? Can't you taste *cilantro*?" she insisted, referring to an herb whose local name hadn't allowed us to identify it with certainty (was it coriander, perhaps?) and of which a little thread in the morsel we were chewing sufficed to transmit to the nostrils a sweetly pungent emotion, like an impalpable intoxication.

Olivia's need to involve me in her emotions pleased me greatly, because it showed that I was indispensable to her and that, for her, the pleasures of existence could be appreciated only if we shared them. Our subjective, individual selves, I was thinking, find their amplification and completion only in the unity of the couple. I needed confirmation of this conviction all the more since, from the beginning of our Mexican journey, the physical bond between Olivia and me was going through a phase of rarefaction, if not eclipse: a momentary phenomenon, surely, and not in itself disturbing—part of the normal ups and downs to which, over a long period, the life of every couple is subject. And I couldn't help remarking how certain manifestations of Olivia's vital energy, certain prompt reactions or delays on her part, yearnings or throbs, continued to take place before my eyes, losing none of their intensity, with only one significant difference: their stage was no longer the bed of our embraces but a dinner table.

During the first few days I expected the gradual kindling of the palate to spread quickly to all our senses. I was mistaken: aphrodisiac this cuisine surely was, but in itself and for itself (this is what I thought to understand, and what I am saying applies only to us at that moment; I cannot speak for others or for us if we had been in a different humour). It stimulated desires, in other words, that sought their satisfaction only within the very sphere of sensation that had aroused them—in eating new dishes, therefore, that would generate and extend those same desires. We were thus in the ideal situation for imagining what the love between the abbess and the chaplain might have been like: a love that, in the eyes of the world and in their own eyes, could have been perfectly chaste and at the same time infinitely carnal in that experience of flavours gained through secret and subtle complicity.

"Complicity": the word, the moment it came into my mind—referring not only to the nun and the priest but also to Olivia and me—heartened me. Because if what Olivia sought was complicity in the almost obsessive passion that had seized her, then this suggested we were not losing—as I had feared—a parity between us. In fact, it had seemed to me during the last few days that Olivia, in her gustatory exploration, had wanted to keep me in a subordinate position: a presence necessary, indeed, but subaltern, obliging me to observe the relationship between her and food as a confidant or as a compliant pander. I dispelled this irksome notion that had somehow or other occurred to me. In reality, our complicity could not be more total, precisely because we experienced the same passion in different ways, in accord with our temperaments: Olivia more sensitive to perceptive nuances and endowed with a more analytical memory, where every recollection remained distinct and unmistakable, I tending more to define experiences verbally and conceptually, to mark the ideal line of journey within ourselves contemporaneously with our geographical journey. In fact, this was a conclusion of mine that Olivia had instantly adopted (or perhaps Olivia had been the one to prompt the idea and I had simply proposed it to her again in words of my own): the true journey, as the introjection of an "outside" different from our normal one, implies a complete change of nutrition, a digesting of the visited country—its fauna and flora and its culture (not only the different culinary practices and condiments but the different implements used to grind the flour or stir the pot)—making it pass between the lips and down the esophagus. This is the only kind of travel that has a meaning nowadays, when everything visible you can see on television without rising from your easy chair. (And you mustn't rebut that the same result can be achieved by visiting the exotic restaurants of our big cities; they so counterfeit the reality of the cuisine they claim to follow that, as far as our deriving real knowledge is concerned, they are the equivalent not of an actual locality but of a scene reconstructed and shot in a studio.)

ALL THE SAME, in the course of our trip Olivia and I saw everything there was to see (no small exploit, in quantity or quality). For the following morning we had planned a visit to the excavations at Monte Albán, and the guide came for us at the hotel promptly with a little bus. In the sunny, arid countryside grow the agaves used for mescal and tequila, and *nopales* (which we call prickly pears) and cereus—all thorns—and jacaranda, with its blue flowers. The road climbs up into the mountains. Monte Albán, among the heights surrounding a valley, is a complex of ruins: temples, reliefs, grand stairways, platforms for human sacrifice. Horror, sacredness, and mystery are consolidated by tourism, which dictates preordained forms of behaviour, the modest surrogates of those rites. Contemplating these stairs, we try to imagine the hot blood spurting from the breast split by the stone axe of the priest.

Three civilizations succeeded one another at Monte Albán, each shifting the same blocks: the Zapotecs building over the works of the Olmecs, and the Mixtecs doing the same to those of the Zapotecs. The calendars of the ancient Mexican civilizations, carved on the reliefs, represent a cyclic, tragic concept of time: every fifty-two years the universe ended, the gods died, the temples were destroyed, every celestial and terrestrial thing changed its name. Perhaps the peoples that history defines as the successive occupants of these territories were merely a single people, whose continuity was never broken even through a series of massacres like those the reliefs depict. Here are the conquered villages, their names written in hieroglyphics, and the god of the village, his head hung upside down; here are the chained prisoners of war, the severed heads of the victims.

The guide to whom the travel agency entrusted us, a burly man named Alonso, with flattened features like an Olmec head (or Mixtec? Zapotec?), points out to us, with exuberant mime, the famous bas-reliefs called "Los Danzantes." Only some of the carved figures, he says, are portraits of dancers, with their legs in movement (Alonso performs a few steps); others might be astronomers, raising one hand to shield their eyes and study the stars (Alonso strikes an astronomer's pose). But for the most part, he says, they represent women giving birth (Alonso acts this out). We learn that this temple was meant to ward off difficult childbirths; the reliefs were perhaps votive images. Even the dance, for that matter, served to make births easier, through magic mimesis—especially when the baby came out feet first (Alonso performs the magic mimesis). One relief depicts a Cesarean operation, complete with uterus and Fallopian tubes (Alonso, more brutal than ever, mimes the entire female anatomy, to demonstrate that a sole surgical torment linked births and deaths).

Everything in our guide's gesticulation takes on a truculent significance, as if the temples of the sacrifices cast their shadow on every act and every thought. When the most propitious date had been set, in accordance with the stars, the sacrifices were accompanied by the revelry of dances, and even births seemed to have no purpose beyond supplying new soldiers for the wars to capture victims. Though some figures are shown running or wrestling or playing football, according to Alonso these are not peaceful athletic competitions but, rather, the games of prisoners forced to compete in order to determine which of them would be the first to ascend the altar.

"And the loser in the games was chosen for the sacrifice?" I ask.

"No! The winner!" Alonso's face becomes radiant. "To have your chest split open by the obsidian knife was an honour!" And in a crescendo of ancestral patriotism, just as he had boasted of the excellence of the scientific knowledge of the ancient peoples, so now this worthy descendant of the Olmecs feels called upon to exalt the offering of a throbbing human heart to the sun to assure that the dawn would return each morning and illuminate the world.

That was when Olivia asked, "But what did they do with the victims' bodies afterward?"

Alonso stopped.

"Those limbs—I mean, those entrails," Olivia insisted. "They were offered to the gods, I realize that. But, practically speaking, what happened to them? Were they burned?"

No, they weren't burned.

"Well, what then? Surely a gift to the gods couldn't be buried, left to rot in the ground."

"Los zopilotes," Alonso said. "The vultures. They were the ones who cleared the altars and carried the offerings to Heaven."

The vultures. "Always?" Olivia asked further, with an insistence I could not explain to myself.

Alonso was evasive, tried to change the subject; he was in a hurry to show us the passages that connected the priests' houses with the temples, where they made their appearance, their faces covered by terrifying masks. Our guide's pedagogical enthusiasm had something irritating about it, because it gave the impression he was imparting to us a lesson that was simplified so that it would enter our poor profane heads, though he actually knew far more, things he kept to himself and took care not to tell us. Perhaps this was what Olivia had sensed and what, after a certain point, made her maintain a closed, vexed silence through the rest of our visit to the excavations and on the jolting bus that brought us back to Oaxaca.

Along the road, all curves, I tried to catch Olivia's eye as she sat facing me, but thanks to the bouncing of the bus or the difference in the level of our seats, I realized my gaze was resting not on her eyes but on her teeth (she kept her lips parted in a pensive expression), which I happened to be seeing for the first time not as the radiant glow of a smile but as the instruments most suited to their purpose: to be dug into flesh, to sever it, tear it. And as you try to read a person's thoughts in the expression of his eyes, so now I looked at those strong, sharp teeth and sensed there a restrained desire, an expectation.

AS WE REENTERED the hotel and headed for the large lobby (the former chapel of the convent), which we had to cross to reach the wing where our room was, we were struck by a sound like a cascade of water flowing and splashing and gurgling in a thousand rivulets and eddies and jets. The closer we got, the more this homogeneous noise was broken down into a complex of chirps, trills, caws, clucks, as of a flock of birds flapping their wings in an aviary. From the doorway (the room was a few steps lower than the corridor), we saw an expanse of little spring hats on the heads of ladies seated around tea tables. Throughout the country a campaign was in progress for the election of a new president of the republic, and the wife of the favoured candidate was giving a tea party of impressive proportions for the wives of the prominent men of Oaxaca. Under the broad, empty vaulted ceiling, three hundred Mexican ladies were conversing all at once; the spectacular acoustical event that had immediately subdued us was produced by their voices mingled with the tinkling of cups and spoons and of knives cutting slices of cake. Looming over the assembly was a gigantic full-colour picture of a round-faced lady with her black, smooth hair drawn straight back, wearing a blue dress of which only the buttoned collar could be seen; it was not unlike the official portraits of Chairman Mao Tse-tung, in other words.

To reach the patio and, from it, our stairs, we had to pick our way among the little tables of the reception. We were already close to the far exit when, from a table at the back of the hall, one of the few male guests rose and came toward us, arms extended. It was our friend Salustiano Velazco, a member of the would-be president's staff and, in that capacity, a participant in the more delicate stages of the electoral campaign. We hadn't seen him since leaving the capital, and to show us, with all his ebullience, his joy on seeing us again and to inquire about the latest stages of our journey (and perhaps to escape momentarily that atmosphere in which the triumphal female predominance compromised his chivalrous certitude of male supremacy) he left his place of honour at the symposium and accompanied us into the patio.

Instead of asking us about what we had seen, he began by pointing out the things we had surely failed to see in the places we had visited and could have seen only if he had been with us—a conversational formula that impassioned connoisseurs of a country feel obliged to adopt with visiting friends, always with the best intentions, though it successfully spoils the pleasure of those who have returned from a trip and are quite proud of their experiences, great or small. The convivial din of the distinguished gynoecium followed us even into the patio and drowned at least half the words he and we spoke, so I was never sure he wasn't reproaching us for not having seen the very things we had just finished telling him we had seen.

"And today we went to Monte Albán," I quickly informed him, raising my voice. "The stairways, the reliefs, the sacrificial altars ..."

Salustiano put his hand to his mouth, then waved it in midair—a gesture that, for him, meant an emotion too great to be expressed in words. He began by furnishing us archaeological and ethnographical details I would have very much liked to hear sentence by sentence, but they were lost in the reverberations of the feast. From his gestures and the scattered words I managed to catch (*"Sangre ... obsidiana ... divinidad solar"*), I realized he was talking about the human sacrifices and was speaking with a mixture of awed participation and sacred horror—an attitude distinguished from that of our crude guide by a greater awareness of the cultural implications.

Quicker than I, Olivia managed to follow Salustiano's speech better, and now she spoke up, to ask him something. I realized she was repeating the question she had asked Alonso that afternoon: "What the vultures didn't carry off—what happened to that, afterward?"

Salustiano's eyes flashed knowing sparks at Olivia, and I also grasped then the purpose behind her question, especially as Salustiano assumed his confidential, abettor's tone. It seemed that, precisely because they were softer, his words now overcame more easily the barrier of sound that separated us.

"Who knows? The priests ... This was also a part of the rite—I mean among the Aztecs, the people we know better. But even about them, not much is known. These were secret ceremonies. Yes, the ritual meal ... The priest assumed the functions of the god, and so the victim, divine food ..."

Was this Olivia's aim? To make him admit this? She insisted further, "But how did it take place? The meal ..."

"As I say, there are only sonic suppositions. It seems that the princes, the warriors also joined in. The victim was already part of the god, transmitting divine strength." At this point, Salustiano changed his tone and became proud, dramatic, carried away. "Only the warrior who had captured the sacrificed prisoner could not touch his flesh. He remained apart, weeping."

Olivia still didn't seem satisfied. "But this flesh—in order to eat it ... The way it was cooked, the sacred cuisine, the seasoning—is anything known about that?"

Salustiano became thoughtful. The banqueting ladies had redoubled their noise, and now Salustiano seemed to become hypersensitive to their sounds; he tapped his ear with one finger, signalling that he couldn't go on in all that racket. "Yes, there must have been some rules. Of course, that food couldn't be consumed without a special ceremony ... the due honour ... the respect for the sacrificed, who were brave youths ... respect for the gods ... flesh that couldn't be eaten just for the sake of eating, like any ordinary food. And the flavour ..."

"They say it isn't good to eat?"

"A strange flavour, they say."

"It must have required seasoning—strong stuff."

"Perhaps that flavour had to be hidden. All other flavours had to be brought together, to hide that flavour."

And Olivia asked, "But the priests ... About the cooking of it—they didn't leave any instructions? Didn't hand down anything?"

Salustiano shook his head. "A mystery. Their life was shrouded in mystery."

And Olivia—Olivia now seemed to be prompting him. "Perhaps that flavour emerged, all the same—even through the other flavours."

Salustiano put his fingers to his lips, as if to filter what he was saying. "It was a sacred cuisine. It had to celebrate the harmony of the elements achieved through sacrifice—a terrible harmony, flaming, incandescent ..." He fell suddenly silent, as if sensing he had gone too far, and as if the thought of the repast had called him to his duty, he hastily apologized for not being able to stay longer with us. He had to go back to his place at the table.

WAITING FOR EVENING TO FALL, we sat in one of the cafés under the arcades of the *zócalo,* the regular little square that is the heart of every old city of the colony—green, with short, carefully pruned trees called *almendros,* though they bear no resemblance to almond trees. The tiny paper flags and the banners that greeted the official candidate did their best to convey a festive air to the *zócalo*. The proper Oaxaca families strolled under the arcades. American hippies waited for the old woman who supplied them with *mescalina*. Ragged vendors unfurled coloured fabrics on the ground. From another square nearby came the echo of the loudspeakers of a sparsely attended rally of the opposition. Crouched on the ground, heavy women were frying tortillas and greens.

In the kiosk in the middle of the square, an orchestra was playing, bringing back to me reassuring memories of evenings in a familiar, provincial Europe I was old enough to have known and forgotten. But the memory was like a trompe-l'oeil, and when I examined it a little, it gave me a sense of multiplied distance, in space and in time. Wearing black suits and neckties, the musicians, with their dark, impassive Indian faces, played for the varicoloured, shirt-sleeved tourists—inhabitants, it seemed, of a perpetual summer—for parties of old men and women, meretriciously young in all the gleam of their dentures, and for groups of the really young, hunched over and meditative, as if waiting for age to come and whiten their blond beards and flowing hair; bundled in rough clothes, weighed down by their knapsacks, they looked like the allegorical figures of winter in old calendars.

"Perhaps time has come to an end, the sun has grown weary of rising, Chronos dies of starvation for want of victims to devour, the ages and the seasons are turned upside down," I said.

"Perhaps the death of time concerns only us," Olivia answered. "We who tear one another apart, pretending not to know it, pretending not to taste flavours any more."

"You mean that here—that they need stronger flavours here because they know, because here they ate ..."

"The same as at home, even now. Only we no longer know it, no longer dare look, the way they did. For them there was no mystification: the horror was right there, in front of their eyes. They ate as long as there was a bone left to pick clean, and that's why the flavours ..."

"To hide that flavour?" I said, again picking up Salustiano's chain of hypotheses.

"Perhaps it couldn't be hidden. *Shouldn't* be. Otherwise, it was like not eating what they were really eating. Perhaps the other flavours served to enhance that flavour, to give it a worthy background, to honour it."

At these words I felt again the need to look her in the teeth, as I had done earlier, when we were coming down in the bus. But at that very moment her tongue, moist with saliva, emerged from between her teeth, then immediately drew back, as if she were mentally savouring something. I realized Olivia was already imagining the supper menu.

It began, this menu, offered us by a restaurant we found among low houses with curving grilles, with a rose-coloured liquid in a hand-blown glass: *sopa de camarones*—shrimp soup, that is, immeasurably hot, thanks to some variety of *chiles* we had never come upon previously, perhaps the famous *chiles jalapeños*. Then *cabrito*—roast kid—every morsel of which provoked surprise, because the teeth would encounter first a crisp bit, then one that melted in the mouth.

"You're not eating?" Olivia asked me. She seemed to concentrate only on savouring her dish, though she was very alert, as usual, while I had remained lost in thought, looking at her. It was the sensation of her teeth in my flesh that I was imagining, and I could feel her tongue lift me against the roof of her mouth, enfold me in saliva, then thrust me under the tips of the canines. I sat there facing her, but at the same time it was as if a part of me, or all of me, were contained in her mouth, crunched, torn shred by shred. The situation was not entirely passive, since while I was being chewed by her I felt also that I was acting on her, transmitting sensations that spread from the taste buds through her whole body. I was the one who aroused her every vibration—it was a reciprocal and complete relationship, which involved us and overwhelmed us.

I regained my composure; so did she. We looked carefully at the salad of tender prickly-pear leaves (*ensalada de nopalitos*)—boiled, seasoned with garlic, coriander, red pepper, and oil and vinegar—then the pink and creamy pudding of *maguey* (a variety of agave), all accompanied by a carafe of *sangrita* and followed by coffee with cinnamon.

But this relationship between us, established exclusively through food, so much so that it could be identified in no image other than that of a meal—this relationship which in my imaginings I thought corresponded to Olivia's deepest desires—didn't please her in the slightest, and her irritation was to find its release during that same supper.

"How boring you are! How monotonous!" she began by saying, repeating an old complaint about my uncommunicative nature and my habit of giving her full responsibility for keeping the conversation alive—an argument that flared up whenever we were alone together at a restaurant table, including a list of charges whose basis in truth I couldn't help admitting but in which I also discerned the fundamental reasons for our unity as a couple; namely, that Olivia saw and knew how to catch and isolate and rapidly define many more things than I, and therefore my relationship with the world was essentially via her. "You're always sunk into yourself, unable to participate in what's going on around you, unable to put yourself out for another, never a flash of enthusiasm on your own, always ready to cast a pall on anybody else's, depressing, indifferent—" And to the inventory of my faults she added this time a new adjective, or one that to my ears now took on a new meaning: "Insipid!"

There: I was insipid, I thought, without flavour. And the Mexican cuisine, with all its boldness and imagination, was needed if Olivia was to feed on me with satisfaction. The spiciest flavours were the complement—indeed, the avenue of communication, indispensable as a loudspeaker that amplifies sounds—for Olivia to be nourished by my substance.

"I may seem insipid to you," I protested, "but there are ranges of flavour more discreet and restrained than that of red peppers. There are subtle tastes that one must know how to perceive!"

THE NEXT MORNING we left Oaxaca in Salustiano's car. Our friend had to visit other provinces on the candidate's tour, and offered to accompany us for part of our itinerary. At one point on the trip he showed us some recent excavations not yet overrun by tourists. A stone statue rose barely above the level of the ground, with the unmistakable form that we had learned to recognize on the very first days of our Mexican archaeological wanderings: the *chacmool,* or half-reclining human figure, in an almost Etruscan pose, with a tray resting on his belly. He looks like a rough, good-natured puppet, but it was on that tray that the victims' hearts were offered to the gods.

"Messenger of the gods—what does that mean?" I asked. I had read that definition in a guidebook. "Is he a demon sent to earth by the gods to collect the dish with the offering? Or an emissary from human beings who must go to the gods and offer them the food?"

"Who knows?" Salustiano answered, with the suspended attitude he took in the face of unanswerable questions, as if listening to the inner voices he had at his disposal, like reference books. "It could be the victim himself, supine on the altar, offering his own entrails on the dish. Or the sacrificer, who assumes the pose of the victim because he is aware that tomorrow it will be his turn. Without this reciprocity, human sacrifice would be unthinkable. All were potentially both sacrificer and victim—the victim accepted his role as victim because he had fought to capture the others as victims."

"They could be eaten because they themselves were eaters of men?"

I added, but Salustiano was talking now about the serpent as symbol of the continuity of life and the cosmos.

Meanwhile I understood: my mistake with Olivia was to consider myself eaten by her, whereas I should be myself (I always had been) the one who ate her. The most appetizingly flavoured human flesh belongs to the eater of human flesh. It was only by feeding ravenously on Olivia that I would cease being tasteless to her palate.

This was in my mind that evening when I sat down with her to supper. "What's wrong with you? You're odd this evening," Olivia said, since nothing ever escaped her. The dish they had served us was called *gorditas pellizcadas con manteca*—literally, "plump girls pinched with butter." I concentrated on devouring, with every meatball, the whole fragrance of Olivia—through voluptuous mastication, a vampire extraction of vital juices. But I realized that in a relationship that should have been among three terms—me, meatball, Olivia—a fourth term had intruded, assuming a dominant role: the name of the meatballs. It was the name *"gorditas pellizcadas con manteca"* that I was especially savouring and assimilating and possessing. And, in fact, the magic of that name continued affecting me even after the meal, when we retired together to our hotel room in the night. And for the first time during our Mexican journey the spell whose victims we had been was broken, and the inspiration that had blessed the finest moments of our joint life came to visit us again.

The next morning we found ourselves sitting up in our bed in the *chacmool* pose, with the dulled expression of stone statues on our faces and, on our laps, the tray with the anonymous hotel breakfast, to which we tried to add local flavours, ordering with it mangoes, papayas, cherimoyas, guayabas—fruits that conceal in the sweetness of their pulp subtle messages of asperity and sourness.

OUR JOURNEY MOVED into the Maya territories. The temples of Palenque emerged from the tropical forest, dominated by thick, wooded mountains: enormous ficus trees with multiple trunks like roots, lilac-coloured *macuilis, aguacates*—every tree wrapped in a cloak of lianas and climbing vines and hanging plants. As I was going down the steep stairway of the Temple of the Inscriptions, I had a dizzy spell. Olivia, who disliked stairs, had chosen not to follow me and had remained with the crowd of noisy groups, loud in sound and colour, that the buses were disgorging and ingesting constantly in the open space among the temples. By myself, I had climbed to the Temple of the Sun, to the relief of the jaguar sun, to the Temple of the Foliated Cross, to the relief of the *quetzal* in profile, then to the Temple of the Inscriptions, which involves not only climbing up (and then down) a monumental stairway but also climbing down (and then up) the smaller, interior staircase that leads down to the underground crypt. In the crypt there is the tomb of the king-priest (which I had already been able to study far more comfortably a few days previously in a perfect facsimile at the Anthropological Museum in Mexico City), with the highly complicated carved stone slab on which you see the king operating a science-fiction apparatus that to our eyes resembles the sort of thing used to launch space rockets, though it represents, on the contrary, the descent of the body to the subterranean gods and its rebirth as vegetation.

I went down, I climbed back up into the light of the jaguar sun—into the sea of the green sap of the leaves. The world spun, I plunged down, my throat cut by the knife of the king-priest, down the high steps onto the forest of tourists with super-8s and usurped, broad-brimmed sombreros. The solar energy coursed along dense networks of blood and chlorophyll; I was living and dying in all the fibres of what is chewed and digested and in all the fibres that absorb the sun, consuming and digesting.

Under the thatched arbour of a restaurant on a riverbank, where Olivia had waited for me, our teeth began to move slowly, with equal rhythm, and our eyes stared into each other's with the intensity of serpents'—serpents concentrated in the ecstasy of swallowing each other in turn, as we were aware, in our turn, of being swallowed by the serpent that digests us all, assimilated ceaselessly in the process of ingestion and digestion, in the universal cannibalism that leaves its imprint on every amorous relationship and erases the lines between our bodies and *sopa de frijoles, huachinango a la vera cruzana,* and *enchiladas.*

The Adulterous Woman

by

ALBERT CAMUS

A HOUSEFLY had been circling for the last few minutes in the bus, though the windows were closed. An odd sight here, it had been silently flying back and forth on tired wings. Janine lost track of it, then saw it light on her husband's motionless hand. The weather was cold. The fly shuddered with each gust of sandy wind that scratched against the windows. In the meagre light of the winter morning, with a great fracas of sheet metal and axles, the vehicle was rolling, pitching, and making hardly any progress. Janine looked at her husband. With wisps of greying hair growing low on a narrow forehead, a broad nose, a flabby mouth, Marcel looked like a pouting faun. At each hollow in the pavement she felt him jostle against her. Then his heavy torso would slump back on his widespread legs and he would become inert again and absent, with vacant stare. Nothing about him seemed active but his thick hairless hands, made even shorter by the flannel underwear extending below his cuffs and covering his wrists. His hands were holding so tight to a little canvas suitcase set between his knees that they appeared not to feel the fly's halting progress.

Suddenly the wind was distinctly heard to howl and the gritty fog surrounding the bus became even thicker. The sand now struck the windows in packets as if hurled by invisible hands. The fly shook a chilled wing, flexed its legs, and took flight. The bus slowed and seemed on the point of stopping. But the wind apparently died down, the fog lifted slightly, and the vehicle resumed speed. Gaps of light opened up in the dust-drowned landscape. Two or three frail, whitened palm trees which seemed cut out of metal flashed into sight in the window only to disappear the next moment.

"What a country!" Marcel said.

The bus was full of Arabs pretending to sleep, shrouded in their burnooses. Some had folded their legs on the seat and swayed more than the others in the car's motion. Their silence and impassivity began to weigh upon Janine; it seemed to her as if she had been travelling for days with that mute escort. Yet the bus had left only at dawn from the end of the rail line and for two hours in the cold morning it had been advancing on a stony, desolate plateau which, in the beginning at least, extended its straight lines all the way to reddish horizons. But the wind had risen and gradually swallowed up the vast expanse. From that moment on, the passengers had seen nothing more; one after another, they had ceased talking and were silently progressing in a sort of sleepless night, occasionally wiping their lips and eyes irritated by the sand that filtered into the car.

"Janine!" She gave a start at her husband's call. Once again she thought how ridiculous that name was for someone tall and sturdy like her. Marcel wanted to know where his sample case was. With her foot she explored the empty space under the seat and encountered an object which she decided must be it. She could not stoop over without gasping somewhat. Yet in school she had won the first prize in gymnastics and hadn't known what it was to be winded. Was that so long ago? Twenty-five years. Twenty-five years were nothing, for it seemed to her only yesterday when she was hesitating between an independent life and marriage, just yesterday when she was thinking anxiously of the time she might be growing old alone. She was not alone and that law-student who always wanted to be with her was now at her side. She had eventually accepted him although he was a little shorter than she and she didn't much like his eager, sharp laugh or his black protruding eyes. But she liked his courage in facing up to life, which he shared with all the French of this country. She also liked his crestfallen look when events or men failed to live up to his expectations. Above all, she liked being loved, and he had showered her with attentions. By so often making her aware that she existed for him he made her exist in reality. No, she was not alone....

The bus, with many loud honks, was plowing its way through invisible obstacles. Inside the car, however, no one stirred. Janine suddenly felt someone staring at her and turned toward the seat across the aisle. He was not an Arab, and she was surprised not to have noticed him from the beginning. He was wearing the uniform of the French regiments of the Sahara and an unbleached linen cap above his tanned face, long and pointed like a jackal's. His grey eyes were examining her with a sort of glum disapproval, in a fixed stare. She suddenly blushed and turned back to her husband, who was still looking straight ahead in the fog and wind. She snuggled down in her coat. But she could still see the French soldier, long and thin, so thin in his fitted tunic that he seemed constructed of a dry, friable material, a mixture of sand and bone. Then it was that she saw the thin hands and burnt faces of the Arabs in front of her and noticed that they seemed to have plenty of room, despite their ample garments, on the seat where she and her husband felt wedged in. She pulled her coat around her knees. Yet she wasn't so fat—tall and well rounded rather, plump and still desirable, as she was well aware when men looked at her, with her rather childish face, her bright, naïve eyes contrasting with this big body she knew to be warm and inviting.

No, nothing had happened as she had expected. When Marcel had wanted to take her along on his trip she had protested. For some time he had been thinking of this trip—since the end of the war, to be precise, when business had returned to normal. Before the war the small dry-goods business he had taken over from his parents on giving up his study of law had provided a fairly good living. On the coast the years of youth can be happy ones. But he didn't much like physical effort and very soon had given up taking her to the beaches. The little car took them out of town solely for the Sunday afternoon ride. The rest of the time he preferred his shop full of multicoloured piece-goods shaded by the arcades of this half-native, half-European quarter. Above the shop they lived in three rooms furnished with Arab hangings and furniture from the Galerie Barbès. They had not had children. The years had passed in the semi-darkness behind the half-closed shutters. Summer, the beaches, excursions, the mere sight of the sky were things of the past. Nothing seemed to interest Marcel but business. She felt she had discovered his true passion to be money, and, without really knowing why, she didn't like that. After all, it was to her advantage. Far from being miserly, he was generous, especially where she was concerned. "If something happened to me," he used to say, "you'd be provided for." And, in fact, it is essential to provide for one's needs. But for all the rest, for what is not the most elementary need, how to provide? This is what she felt vaguely, at infrequent intervals. Meanwhile she helped Marcel keep his books and occasionally substituted for him in the shop. Summer was always the hardest, when the heat stifled even the sweet sensation of boredom.

Suddenly, in summer as it happened, the war, Marcel called up then rejected on grounds of health, the scarcity of piece-goods, business at a standstill, the streets empty and hot. If something happened now, she would no longer be provided for. This is why, as soon as piece-goods came back on the market, Marcel had thought of covering the villages of the Upper Plateaus and of the South himself in order to do without a middleman and sell directly to the Arab merchants. He had wanted to take her along. She knew that travel was difficult, she had trouble breathing, and she would have preferred staying at home. But he was obstinate and she had accepted because it would have taken too much energy to refuse. Here they were and, truly, nothing was like what she had imagined. She had feared the heat, the swarms of flies, the filthy hotels reeking of aniseed. She had not thought of the cold, of the biting wind, of these semi-polar plateaus cluttered with moraines. She had dreamt too of palm trees and soft sand. Now she saw that the desert was not that at all, but merely stone, stone everywhere, in the sky full of nothing but stone-dust, rasping and cold, as on the ground, where nothing grew among the stones except dry grasses.

The bus stopped abruptly. The driver shouted a few words in that language she had heard all her life without ever understanding it. "What's the matter?" Marcel asked. The driver, in French this time, said that the sand must have clogged the carburetor, and again Marcel cursed this country. The driver laughed hilariously and asserted that it was nothing, that he would clean the carburetor and they'd be off again. He opened the door and the cold wind blew into the bus, lashing their faces with a myriad grains of sand. All the Arabs silently plunged their noses into their burnooses and huddled up. "Shut the door," Marcel shouted. The driver laughed as he came back to the door. Without hurrying, he took some tools from under the dash-board, then, tiny in the fog, again disappeared ahead without closing the door. Marcel sighed. "You may be sure he's never seen a motor in his life." "Oh, be quiet!" said Janine. Suddenly she gave a start. On the shoulder of the road close to the bus, draped forms were standing still. Under the burnoose's hood and behind a rampart of veils, only their eyes were visible. Mute, come from nowhere, they were staring at the travellers. "Shepherds," Marcel said.

Inside the car there was total silence. All the passengers, heads lowered, seemed to be listening to the voice of the wind loosed across these endless plateaus. Janine was all of a sudden struck by the almost complete absence of luggage. At the end of the railroad line the driver had hoisted their trunk and a few bundles onto the roof. In the racks inside the bus could be seen nothing but gnarled sticks and shopping-baskets. All these people of the South apparently were travelling empty-handed.

But the driver was coming back, still brisk. His eyes alone were laughing above the veils with which he too had masked his face. He announced that they would soon be under way. He closed the door, the wind became silent, and the rain of sand on the windows could be heard better. The motor coughed and died. After having been urged at great length by the starter, it finally sparked and the driver raced it by pressing on the gas. With a big hiccup the bus started off. From the ragged clump of shepherds, still motionless, a hand rose and then faded into the fog behind them. Almost at once the vehicle began to bounce on the road, which had become worse. Shaken up, the Arabs constantly swayed. Nonetheless, Janine was feeling overcome with sleep when there suddenly appeared in front of her a little yellow box filled with lozenges. The jackal-soldier was smiling at her. She hesitated, took one, and thanked him. The jackal pocketed the box and simultaneously swallowed his smile. Now he was staring at the road, straight in front of him. Janine turned toward Marcel and saw only the solid back of his neck. Through the window he was watching the denser fog rising from the crumbly embankment.

They had been travelling for hours and fatigue had extinguished all life in the car when shouts burst forth outside. Children wearing burnooses, whirling like tops, leaping, clapping their hands, were running around the bus. It was now going down a long street lined with low houses; they were entering the oasis. The wind was still blowing, but the walls intercepted the grains of sand which had previously cut off the light. Yet the sky was still cloudy. Amidst shouts, in a great screeching of brakes, the bus stopped in front of the adobe arcades of a hotel with dirty windows. Janine got out and, once on the pavement, staggered. Above the houses she could see a slim yellow minaret. On her left rose the first palm trees of the oasis, and she would have liked to go toward them. But although it was close to noon, the cold was bitter; the wind made her shiver. She turned toward Marcel and saw the soldier coming toward her. She was expecting him to smile or salute. He passed without looking at her and disappeared. Marcel was busy getting down the trunk of piece-goods, a black foot-locker perched on the bus's roof. It would not be easy. The driver was the only one to take care of the luggage and he had already stopped, standing on the roof, to hold forth to the circle of burnooses gathered around the bus. Janine, surrounded with faces that seemed cut out of bone and leather, besieged by guttural shouts, suddenly became aware of her fatigue. "I'm going in," she said to Marcel, who was shouting impatiently at the driver.

She entered the hotel. The manager, a thin, laconic Frenchman, came to meet her. He led her to a second-floor balcony overlooking the street and into a room which seemed to have but an iron bed, a white-enamelled chair, an uncurtained wardrobe, and, behind a rush screen, a washbasin covered with fine sand-dust. When the manager had closed the door, Janine felt the cold coming from the bare, white-washed walls. She didn't know where to put her bag, where to put herself. She had either to lie down or to remain standing, and to shiver in either case. She remained standing, holding her bag and staring at a sort of window-slit that opened onto the sky near the ceiling. She was waiting, but she didn't know for what. She was aware only of her solitude, and of the penetrating cold, and of a greater weight in the region of her heart. She was in fact dreaming, almost deaf to the sounds rising from the street along with Marcel's vocal outbursts, more aware on the other hand of that sound of a river coming from the window-slit and caused by the wind in the palm trees, so close now, it seemed to her. Then the wind seemed to increase and the gentle ripple of waters became a hissing of waves. She imagined, beyond the walls, a sea of erect, flexible palm trees unfurling in the storm. Nothing was like what she had expected, but those invisible waves refreshed her tired eyes. She was standing, heavy, with dangling arms, slightly stooped, as the cold climbed her thick legs. She was dreaming of the erect and flexible palm trees and of the girl she had once been.

AFTER HAVING WASHED, they went down to the dining room. On the bare walls had been painted camels and palm trees drowned in a sticky background of pink and lavender. The arcaded windows let in a meagre light. Marcel questioned the hotel manager about the merchants. Then an elderly Arab wearing a military decoration on his tunic served them. Marcel, preoccupied, tore his bread into little pieces. He kept his wife from drinking water. "It hasn't been boiled. Take wine." She didn't like that, for wine made her sleepy. Besides, there was pork on the menu. "They don't eat it because of the Koran. But the Koran didn't know that well-done pork doesn't cause illness. We French know how to cook. What are you thinking about?" Janine was not thinking of anything, or perhaps of that victory of the cooks over the prophets. But she had to hurry. They were to leave the next morning for still farther south; that afternoon they had to see all the important merchants. Marcel urged the elderly Arab to hurry the coffee. He nodded without smiling and pattered out. "Slowly in the morning, not too fast in the afternoon," Marcel said, laughing. Yet eventually the coffee came. They barely took time to swallow it and went out into the dusty, cold street. Marcel called a young Arab to help him carry the trunk, but as a matter of principle quibbled about the payment. His opinion, which he once more expressed to Janine, was in fact based on the vague principle that they always asked for twice as much in the hope of settling for a quarter of the amount. Janine, ill at ease, followed the two trunk-bearers. She had put on a wool dress under her heavy coat and would have liked to take up less space. The pork, although well done, and the small quantity of wine she had drunk also bothered her somewhat.

They walked along a diminutive public garden planted with dusty trees. They encountered Arabs who stepped out of their way without seeming to see them, wrapping themselves in their burnooses. Even when they were wearing rags, she felt they had a look of dignity unknown to the Arabs of her town. Janine followed the trunk, which made a way for her through the crowd. They went through the gate in an earthen rampart and emerged on a little square planted with the same mineral trees and bordered on the far side, where it was widest, with arcades and shops. But they stopped on the square itself in front of a small construction shaped like an artillery shell and painted chalky blue. Inside, in the single room lighted solely by the entrance, an old Arab with white moustaches stood behind a shiny plank. He was serving tea, raising and lowering the teapot over three tiny multicoloured glasses. Before they could make out anything else in the darkness, the cool scent of mint tea greeted Marcel and Janine at the door. Marcel had barely crossed the threshold and dodged the garlands of pewter teapots, cups and trays, and the postcard displays when he was up against the counter. Janine stayed at the door. She stepped a little aside so as not to cut off the light. At that moment she perceived in the darkness behind the old merchant two Arabs smiling at them, seated on the bulging sacks that filled the back of the shop. Red-and-black rugs and embroidered scarves hung on the walls; the floor was cluttered with sacks and little boxes filled with aromatic seeds. On the counter, beside a sparkling pair of brass scales and an old yardstick with figures effaced, stood a row of loaves of sugar. One of them had been unwrapped from its coarse blue paper and cut into on top. The smell of wool and spices in the room became apparent behind the scent of tea when the old merchant set down the teapot and said good day.

Marcel talked rapidly in the low voice he assumed when talking business. Then he opened the trunk, exhibited the wools and silks, pushed back the scale and yardstick to spread out his merchandise in front of the old merchant. He got excited, raised his voice, laughed nervously, like a woman who wants to make an impression and is not sure of herself. Now, with hands spread wide, he was going through the gestures of selling and buying. The old man shook his head, passed the tea tray to the two Arabs behind him, and said just a few words that seemed to discourage Marcel. He picked up his goods, piled them back into the trunk, then wiped an imaginary sweat from his forehead. He called the little porter and they started off toward the arcades. In the first shop, although the merchant began by exhibiting the same Olympian manner, they were a little luckier. "They think they're God almighty," Marcel said, "but they're in business too! Life is hard for everyone."

Janine followed without answering. The wind had almost ceased. The sky was clearing in spots. A cold, harsh light came from the deep holes that opened up in the thickness of the clouds. They had now left the square. They were walking in narrow streets along earthen walls over which hung rotted December roses or, from time to time, a pomegranate, dried and wormy. An odour of dust and coffee, the smoke of a wood fire, the smell of stone and of sheep permeated this quarter. The shops, hollowed out of the walls, were far from one another; Janine felt her feet getting heavier. But her husband was gradually becoming more cheerful. He was beginning to sell and was feeling more kindly; he called Janine "Baby"; the trip would not be wasted. "Of course," Janine said mechanically, "it's better to deal directly with them."

They came back by another street, toward the centre. It was late in the afternoon; the sky was now almost completely clear. They stopped in the square. Marcel rubbed his hands and looked affectionately at the trunk in front of them. "Look," said Janine. From the other end of the square was coming a tall Arab, thin, vigorous, wearing a sky-blue burnoose, soft brown boots and gloves, and bearing his bronzed aquiline face loftily. Nothing but the *chèche* that he was wearing swathed as a turban distinguished him from those French officers in charge of native affairs whom Janine had occasionally admired. He was advancing steadily toward them, but seemed to be looking beyond their group as he slowly removed the glove from one hand. "Well," said Marcel as he shrugged his shoulders, "there's one who thinks he's a general." Yes, all of them here had that look of pride; but this one, really, was going too far. Although they were surrounded by the empty space of the square, he was walking straight toward the trunk without seeing it, without seeing them. Then the distance separating them decreased rapidly and the Arab was upon them when Marcel suddenly seized the handle of the foot-locker and pulled it out of the way. The Arab passed without seeming to notice anything and headed with the same regular step toward the ramparts. Janine looked at her husband; he had his crestfallen look. "They think they can get away with anything now," he said. Janine did not reply. She loathed that Arab's stupid arrogance and suddenly felt unhappy. She wanted to leave and thought of her little apartment. The idea of going back to the hotel, to that icy room, discouraged her. It suddenly occurred to her that the manager had advised her to climb up to the terrace around the fort to see the desert. She said this to Marcel and that he could leave the trunk at the hotel. But he was tired and wanted to sleep a little before dinner. "Please," said Janine. He looked at her, suddenly attentive. "Of course, my dear," he said.

She waited for him in the street in front of the hotel. The white-robed crowd was becoming larger and larger. Not a single woman could be seen, and it seemed to Janine that she had never seen so many men. Yet none of them looked at her. Some of them, without appearing to see her, slowly turned toward her that thin, tanned face that made them all look alike to her, the face of the French soldier in the bus and that of the gloved Arab, a face both shrewd and proud. They turned that face toward the foreign woman, they didn't see her, and then, light and silent, they walked around her as she stood there with swelling ankles. And her discomfort, her need of getting away increased. "Why did I come?" But already Marcel was coming back.

When they climbed the stairs to the fort, it was five o'clock. The wind had died down altogether. The sky, completely clear, was now periwinkle blue. The cold, now drier, made their cheeks smart. Halfway up the stairs an old Arab, stretched out against the wall, asked them if they wanted a guide, but didn't budge, as if he had been sure of their refusal in advance. The stairs were long and steep despite several landings of packed earth. As they climbed, the space widened and they rose into an ever broader light, cold and dry, in which every sound from the oasis reached them pure and distinct. The bright air seemed to vibrate around them with a vibration increasing in length as they advanced, as if their progress struck from the crystal of light a sound wave that kept spreading out. And as soon as they reached the terrace and their gaze was lost in the vast horizon beyond the palm grove, it seemed to Janine that the whole sky rang with a single short and piercing note, whose echoes gradually filled the space above her, then suddenly died and left her silently facing the limitless expanse.

From east to west, in fact, her gaze swept slowly, without encountering a single obstacle, along a perfect curve. Beneath her, the blue-and-white terraces of the Arab town overlapped one another, splattered with the dark-red spots of peppers drying in the sun. Not a soul could be seen, but from the inner courts, together with the aroma of roasting coffee, there rose laughing voices or incomprehensible stamping of feet. Farther off, the palm grove, divided into uneven squares by clay walls, rustled its upper foliage in a wind that could not be felt up on the terrace. Still farther off and all the way to the horizon extended the ochre-and-grey realm of stones, in which no life was visible. At some distance from the oasis, however, near the wadi that bordered the palm grove on the west could be seen broad black tents. All around them a flock of motionless dromedaries, tiny at that distance, formed against the grey ground the black signs of a strange handwriting, the meaning of which had to be deciphered. Above the desert, the silence was as vast as the space.

Janine, leaning her whole body against the parapet, was speechless, unable to tear herself away from the void opening before her. Beside her, Marcel was getting restless. He was cold; he wanted to go back down. What was there to see here, after all? But she could not take her gaze from the horizon. Over yonder, still farther south, at that point where sky and earth met in a pure line—over yonder it suddenly seemed there was awaiting her something of which, though it had always been lacking, she had never been aware until now. In the advancing afternoon the light relaxed and softened; it was passing from the crystalline to the liquid. Simultaneously, in the heart of a woman brought there by pure chance a knot tightened by the years, habit, and boredom was slowly loosening. She was looking at the nomads' encampment. She had not even seen the men living in it; nothing was stirring among the black tents, and yet she could think only of them whose existence she had barely known until this day. Homeless, cut off from the world, they were a handful wandering over the vast territory she could see, which however was but a paltry part of an even greater expanse whose dizzying course stopped only thousands of miles farther south, where the first river finally waters the forest. Since the beginning of time, on the dry earth of this limitless land scraped to the bone, a few men had been ceaselessly trudging, possessing nothing but serving no one, poverty-stricken but free lords of a strange kingdom. Janine did not know why this thought filled her with such a sweet, vast melancholy that it closed her eyes. She knew that this kingdom had been eternally promised her and yet that it would never be hers, never again, except in this fleeting moment perhaps when she opened her eyes again on the suddenly motionless sky and on its waves of steady light, while the voices rising from the Arab town suddenly fell silent. It seemed to her that the world's course had just stopped and that, from that moment on, no one would ever age any more or die. Everywhere, henceforth, life was suspended—except in her heart, where, at the same moment, someone was weeping with affliction and wonder.

But the light began to move; the sun, clear and devoid of warmth, went down toward the west, which became slightly pink, while a grey wave took shape in the east ready to roll slowly over the vast expanse. A first dog barked and its distant bark rose in the now even colder air. Janine noticed that her teeth were chattering. "We are catching our death of cold," Marcel said. "You're a fool. Let's go back." But he took her hand awkwardly. Docile now, she turned away from the parapet and followed him. Without moving, the old Arab on the stairs watched them go down toward the town. She walked along without seeing anyone, bent under a tremendous and sudden fatigue, dragging her body, whose weight now seemed to her unbearable. Her exaltation had left her. Now she felt too tall, too thick, too white too for this world she had just entered. A child, the girl, the dry man, the furtive jackal were the only creatures who could silently walk that earth. What would she do there henceforth except to drag herself toward sleep, toward death?

She dragged herself, in fact, toward the restaurant with a husband suddenly taciturn unless he was telling how tired he was, while she was struggling weakly against a cold, aware of a fever rising within her. Then she dragged herself toward her bed, where Marcel came to join her and put the light out at once without asking anything of her. The room was frigid. Janine felt the cold creeping up while the fever was increasing. She breathed with difficulty, her blood pumped without warming her; a sort of fear grew within her. She turned over and the old iron bedstead groaned under her weight. No, she didn't want to fall ill. Her husband was already asleep; she too had to sleep; it was essential. The muffled sounds of the town reached her through the window-slit. With a nasal twang old phonographs in the Moorish cafés ground out tunes she recognized vaguely; they reached her borne on the sound of a slow-moving crowd. She must sleep. But she was counting black tents; behind her eyelids motionless camels were grazing; immense solitudes were whirling within her. Yes, why had she come? She fell asleep on that question.

She awoke a little later. The silence around her was absolute. But, on the edges of town, hoarse dogs were howling in the soundless night. Janine shivered. She turned over, felt her husband's hard shoulder against hers, and suddenly, half asleep, huddled against him. She was drifting on the surface of sleep without sinking in and she clung to that shoulder with unconscious eagerness as her safest haven. She was talking, but no sound issued from her mouth. She was talking, but she herself hardly heard what she was saying. She could feel only Marcel's warmth. For more than twenty years every night thus, in his warmth, just the two of them, even when ill, even when travelling, as at present ... Besides, what would she have done alone at home? No child! Wasn't that what she lacked? She didn't know. She simply followed Marcel, pleased to know that someone needed her. The only joy he gave her was the knowledge that she was necessary. Probably he didn't love her. Love, even when filled with hate, doesn't have that sullen face. But what is his face like? They made love in the dark by feel, without seeing each other. Is there another love than that of darkness, a love that would cry aloud in daylight? She didn't know, but she did know that Marcel needed her and that she needed that need, that she lived on it night and day, at night especially—every night, when he didn't want to be alone, or to age or die, with that set expression he assumed which she occasionally recognized on other men's faces, the only common expression of those madmen hiding under an appearance of wisdom until the madness seizes them and hurls them desperately toward a woman's body to bury in it, without desire, everything terrifying that solitude and night reveals to them.

Marcel stirred as if to move away from her. No, he didn't love her; he was merely afraid of what was not she, and she and he should long ago have separated and slept alone until the end. But who can always sleep alone? Some men do, cut off from others by a vocation or misfortune, who go to bed every night in the same bed as death. Marcel never could do so—he above all, a weak and disarmed child always frightened by suffering, her own child indeed who needed her and who, just at that moment, let out a sort of whimper. She cuddled a little closer and put her hand on his chest. And to herself she called him with the little love-name she had once given him, which they still used from time to time without even thinking of what they were saying.

She called him with all her heart. After all, she too needed him, his strength, his little eccentricities, and she too was afraid of death. "If I could overcome that fear, I'd be happy...." Immediately, a nameless anguish seized her. She drew back from Marcel. No, she was overcoming nothing, she was not happy, she was going to die, in truth, without having been liberated. Her heart pained her; she was stifling under a huge weight that she suddenly discovered she had been dragging around for twenty years. Now she was struggling under it with all her strength. She wanted to be liberated even if Marcel, even if the others, never were! Fully awake, she sat up in bed and listened to a call that seemed very close. But from the edges of night the exhausted and yet indefatigable voices of the dogs of the oasis were all that reached her ears. A slight wind had risen and she heard its light waters flow in the palm grove. It came from the south, where desert and night mingled now under the again unchanging sky, where life stopped, where no one would ever age or die any more. Then the waters of the wind dried up and she was not even sure of having heard anything except a mute call that she could, after all, silence or notice. But never again would she know its meaning unless she responded to it at once. At once—yes, that much was certain at least!

She got up gently and stood motionless beside the bed, listening to her husband's breathing. Marcel was asleep. The next moment, the bed's warmth left her and the cold gripped her. She dressed slowly, feeling for her clothes in the faint light coming through the blinds from the street lamps. Her shoes in her hand, she reached the door. She waited a moment more in the darkness, then gently opened the door. The knob squeaked and she stood still. Her heart was beating madly. She listened with her body tense and, reassured by the silence, turned her hand a little more. The knob's turning seemed to her interminable. At last she opened the door, slipped outside, and closed the door with the same stealth. Then, with her cheek against the wood, she waited. After a moment she made out, in the distance, Marcel's breathing. She faced about, felt the icy night air against her cheek, and ran the length of the balcony. The outer door was closed. While she was slipping the bolt, the night watchman appeared at the top of the stairs, his face blurred with sleep, and spoke to her in Arabic. "I'll be back," said Janine as she stepped out into the night.

Garlands of stars hung down from the black sky over the palm trees and houses. She ran along the short avenue, now empty, that led to the fort. The cold, no longer having to struggle against the sun, had invaded the night; the icy air burned her lungs. But she ran, half blind, in the darkness. At the top of the avenue, however, lights appeared, then descended toward her zigzagging. She stopped, caught the whir of turning sprockets and, behind the enlarging lights, soon saw vast burnooses surmounting fragile bicycle wheels. The burnooses flapped against her; then three red lights sprang out of the black behind her and disappeared at once. She continued running toward the fort. Halfway up the stairs, the air burned her lungs with such cutting effect that she wanted to stop. A final burst of energy hurled her despite herself onto the terrace, against the parapet, which was now pressing her belly. She was panting and everything was hazy before her eyes. Her running had not warmed her and she was still trembling all over. But the cold air she was gulping down soon flowed evenly inside her and a spark of warmth began to glow amidst her shivers. Her eyes opened at last on the expanse of night.

Not a breath, not a sound—except at intervals the muffled crackling of stones that the cold was reducing to sand—disturbed the solitude and silence surrounding Janine. After a moment, however, it seemed to her that the sky above her was moving in a sort of slow gyration. In the vast reaches of the dry, cold night, thousands of stars were constantly appearing, and their sparkling icicles, loosened at once, began to slip gradually toward the horizon. Janine could not tear herself away from contemplating those drifting flares. She was turning with them, and the apparently stationary progress little by little identified her with the core of her being, where cold and desire were now vying with each other. Before her the stars were falling one by one and being snuffed out among the stones of the desert, and each time Janine opened a little more to the night. Breathing deeply, she forgot the cold, the dead weight of others, the craziness or stuffiness of life, the long anguish of living and dying. After so many years of mad, aimless fleeing from fear, she had come to a stop at last. At the same time, she seemed to recover her roots and the sap again rose in her body, which had ceased trembling. Her whole belly pressed against the parapet as she strained toward the moving sky; she was merely waiting for her fluttering heart to calm down and establish silence within her. The last stars of the constellations dropped their clusters a little lower on the desert horizon and became still. Then, with unbearable gentleness, the water of night began to fill Janine, drowned the cold, rose gradually from the hidden core of her being and overflowed in wave after wave, rising up even to her mouth full of moans. The next moment, the whole sky stretched out over her, fallen on her back on the cold earth.

When Janine returned to the room, with the same precautions, Marcel was not awake. But he whimpered as she got back in bed and a few seconds later sat up suddenly. He spoke and she didn't understand what he was saying. He got up, turned on the light, which blinded her. He staggered toward the washbasin and drank a long draft from the bottle of mineral water. He was about to slip between the sheets when, one knee on the bed, he looked at her without understanding. She was weeping copiously, unable to restrain herself. "It's nothing, dear," she said, "it's nothing."

Le Chevalier

by

MOHAMED CHOUKRI

I WAS HATING THE SUMMER. The heat was stifling and there wasn't a lot about it that was enjoyable. Even when I had the occasional good idea, the weather was so hot that it made me dizzy and the ideas evaporated like the morning dew. When I was a kid I used to enjoy the summer. I'm the kind who prefers the moist sand of the sea to the dry sand of the desert—I don't like wind and sand hitting you full in the face so that you can't see a thing. I'm not the sort to hang onto dreams, except when desires get the better of me, and I only tend to remember my anxieties when I sit down to write.

I found Le Chevalier sitting and looking depressed out in front of the Café Central. He called me over:

"I want to ask you a favour. I need you to give me a hand with something."

This was the first time I'd ever heard him ask anyone round there for help. Evening was drawing on. He got up slowly and said:

"You know. When people like me get old, we find ourselves wishing we could start life all over again."

As I sit here writing these notes I'm listening to the Ode to Joy from Beethoven's Ninth Symphony, and Chopin's First Nocturne. I'll leave it to the reader to imagine how they sound.

The heat in Le Chevalier's room was like an oven. There was a bottle of rosé on the table. He only ever drank water when he had no wine. He used to say jokingly that water was only for frogs and camels. He poured me a glass of the wine: it was warm and sour-tasting, and you could smell the cork in it. He pointed to a shabby suitcase near the bed.

"I didn't really want to trouble you ... would you mind carrying this to the beach for me?"

"To the beach?" I said.

I wondered whether he was going ga-ga.

"I know it sounds strange, but just do what I ask. I won't tell you what's in it—you can see for yourself when we get there."

As we walked, he asked me to slow down and wait for him. I'd never seen him as tired and pathetic as this. He was the sort of person who wouldn't complain even if there really was something wrong with him, but as we went along he stumbled and almost fell. His suitcase wasn't heavy. I found myself wondering what it could possibly contain. Several people were already on their way home, abandoning the beautiful Tangier evening; others were still enjoying the pleasures of its moist sands. We reached a spot on the beach and I opened the magical suitcase. It had various things in it. Some short stories, some of which he'd read to me previously. They'd never been published. A stack of faded photographs. Medals awarded in two world wars. He asked me to burn the lot without taking anything out of the case. The thought of this upset me. Needless to say, I would do what he asked, but I did ask if I could have one of the photos of him to keep. He was adamant:

"No. Please just do as I ask. Don't argue. We can take plenty of pictures of you and me together whenever you like."

As the blackened pages flew about, he gazed across at an evening horizon that was suffused with the colour of almond flowers. Here were memories going back more than sixty years, wiped out without pity or remorse. He seemed on the verge of tears. The redness of his face reflected the turmoil inside him. All of a sudden I began to see him in a new light. All the stories he'd read to me previously had been devoid of any literary imagination. They were simply unadorned accounts of things that had happened in his life. Everything in them was pre-cooked and ready-made. Obviously his isolation didn't help, as far as developing his literary talents was concerned. He was the kind of person who, when they read or hear something, always want to know whether it's true.

He had a particular aversion to going to church on Sundays and saints' days. By this time the only pleasure he had from life was from the past: for him, the good old days had ended in the late 1940s, despite the disasters of wars large and small. This was his unhappiness. After his retirement from the army he'd decided to take up autosuggestive therapy. He'd been interested in it when he was younger. As far as I was concerned, it was all hocus-pocus, but I changed my mind when I saw him treat Sarah in my presence. He began by saying things and getting her to repeat them. Then he passed the palm of his hand over her belly, which seemed to take away her pain, to such an extent that she was able to get up from her sick bed.

Le Chevalier had been our doctor in pain and in sorrow, and now he was the one who was in pain. Once, when I was suffering from anemia, he had prescribed meatballs of raw horsemeat mixed with the yolk of a raw egg, garlic, spices and wine. I understood, through things he said to me, that it's not possible for people to live with memories that are of failure and betrayal. He had no memories that were worth living for. He'd become alienated from everyone close to him, and they'd effectively killed him off while he was still alive.

His allowance cheque was more than usually late in arriving. He was getting depressed. He wouldn't look you in the eye. This was unusual for him. I heard him mumble:

"In the land of promises the poor man died of hunger."

I didn't ask what he meant. As I left I wondered what it would be like to be 75. If it was ordained for me to live that long, I wondered what pleasures or miseries life would have in store for me. That earlier phrase of his kept coming back to me, obsessively: "When we get old, we find ourselves wishing we could start life all over again." So as to dispel the gathering gloom I told myself that I would never get old like that. I never met anyone of his age who didn't complain about time robbing him of the things he loved doing, or complaining about life itself. But Le Chevalier wasn't the kind of person to complain about his lot. I began to dread the end of my life as I saw it foreshadowed in his life. There's nothing worse than comparing your life with other people's lives.

As it turned out, there was a three-week delay in his allowance cheque arriving. The silent drop is the drop which breaks the silence. He had to cut back on food until he was eating only butter, tomatoes, onions and lemons. On most days I got a bottle of wine to share with him, out of sympathy for the poor man having to drink the water that he found so repellent. The French Cultural Centre invited him to give a lecture on auto-suggestive therapy, but his enthusiasm evaporated when he saw only about ten people in the hall, so he shortened his presentation to twenty minutes. This earned him 500 dirhams, which was enough to ward off poverty while he waited for his cheque to arrive. That evening he treated me in the restaurant of the hotel where we lived: food and drink, conversation and jokes, to while away the tedium of the night.

Last year he was disappointed in one of his ambitions. He was at the Café Zagourah, and he had asked the lady pianist and her violinist husband to accompany him in an old song from the 1930s. As soon as his voice began to ring out, all the passers-by began stopping outside the café. The waiter politely asked him to stop because singing was not allowed. I suppose reality had deserted Le Chevalier because he lived in a world that was foreign to him. He was like a man hanging from a branch over an abyss, weighed down by his burden of sadness.

He found me at the Café Central enjoying a morning of idleness. His depression had left him. He invited me to go with him to visit his friend Georges, in Dahiyat 'Awama. It was a scorching day and I had nothing better to do with my time, so I went along. He bought a rabbit and some wine, a tin of mushrooms and some barley bread. We took the bus. From the last stop we still had about a kilometre to walk to reach Georges' little smallholding. The road was scorching hot under our feet. A small snake, about half a metre long, was crossing in front of us. Le Chevalier stopped and struck up a conversation with it:

He said: "Go ahead, you cross first ... You were here before us," and he told me not to move.

The sweat was dripping from us. Georges earned his living from keeping bees. Hardly anyone ever visited him except for Le Chevalier, and myself when I went with him. Sometimes I bought honey from him. He was clearly delighted as he welcomed us. It was a tin hut, fairly roomy, that he'd built himself. It was stiflingly hot in summer and freezing cold in winter. His entire wealth consisted of livestock in the shape of cows and chickens. He led an abstemious life. The only furniture he owned was a bed, a table, some chairs and a small radio.

I felt like strolling in the shade of his orange and pear trees. Some of the pears were over-ripe and several had been eaten into by insects.

I ate two that had fallen from the tree. Georges and Le Chevalier cooked the rabbit. I thought it best to leave them alone. Given that they were both of French origin, they had a lot in common. Le Chevalier was an unbeliever and Georges a believer, but they had an understanding. I never once heard them argue about religion. Georges had planted two wooden crosses, one in the field and the other near the well, and over the door of the hut he had another cross, made of dark wood, which looked more like a scarecrow. There was no room for Satan there! I wondered how he could possibly be happy in this almost total isolation. He had no books except for a few faded grey volumes. No sign of any newspapers or magazines. He probably nourished himself with meditation, like saints and hermits. Small birds were flitting between the trees. A black bird sat on a branch. It began to quiver and sing. It was probably a starling. I thought of Aïn Khabbès, and Busatin Kaytan, and the Sirimin fields in Oran. A person is how he ends his life, not how he begins it. That was another of Le Chevalier's sayings. If I lived that long, I wondered what kind of old age would await me. For sure I wouldn't end up burning a caseful of my memories on the beach.

Up until that point, I'd never allowed any emotion to betray me. I'd always lived in a kind of state of emergency. I only loved what was fleeting. Love, in fact, didn't interest me unless it was big and fantastic, like in a book. I spoke about it without touching it or embracing it. And most of the young women who attracted me were hermaphrodites. Deep down I probably had a hidden tendency to homosexuality. For me a woman's greatest attraction was probably her youth. I also found that the negativity of some women inspired nothing but an impulse of rape.

I'd been looking for life's games and symbols, not its reality; looking for the obscure and the riddle, not the clear and the simple; the unknown and not the known, the mirage and not the water. A very ripe pear fell to the ground next to me. It rolled towards me, so

I picked it up. I ate it, thinking of Isaac Newton, and Henry Thoreau, and Robert Frost. I also thought of the Jew who threw himself out of a sixth-floor window in Tetuan. He landed on top of a Moroccan labourer and drove his head and neck into his chest. I prefer the cow mooing to the sound of a nightingale singing. The shadow of that tree carried me back to the shadowy greenery of my childhood: Aïn el Qetiout, Aïn el Hayani, Aïn Khabbès—all springs where I had drunk the water of cold and muddy misery.

This was the first time, as an adult, that I'd lain down to relax and think in a tree-filled, sunny spot like this. Previously I'd always walked straight past trees and only ever stopped to pick their fruit. Now I was enjoying a tree's shelter and feeding on its maturity. Time was no longer my prison. I was beginning to be able to hold it at bay whenever I wanted. I was grateful to my friend Le Chevalier. If it hadn't been for him, I wouldn't have experienced this intoxicating surge of memories which flooded me with their gentleness, their softness and their depth. My tiredness melted from me in a sensation of total, delightful relaxation, which then gave way to a delicious sleep.

Georges brought me an earthenware tumbler filled with wine. He was a real old-timer in everything he did, this amiable Georges—so gentle in his voice and his movements. As I sat and smoked, I began to see things more clearly with every sip of the wine. The various stages of my life seemed to parade before my eyes: the old and the new, the bad and the good, the pleasant and the painful—an intricate interweaving of light and shade, like the branches of this pear tree. A breeze began to blow, bringing a pleasant coolness with it. Le Chevalier called me over to eat. He always enjoyed his cooking. Rabbit cooked with wine and mushrooms was his special favourite. He really was rooted in this nomad-like life of his.

Summer

by

JULIO CORTÁZAR

IN THE LATE AFTERNOON Florencio went down to the cabin with his little girl, taking the back road full of holes and loose stones that only Mariano and Zulma were up to following in their Jeep. Zulma opened the door for them, and Florencio thought that her eyes looked as if she had been peeling onions. Mariano appeared from the other room; he told them to come in, but Florencio only wanted to ask them to take care of the little girl until the next morning because he had to go to the coast on an urgent matter and there was nobody in the village he could ask to do him this favour. Of course, said Zulma, leave her, don't worry, we'll set up a bed for her here downstairs. Come on in and have a drink, Mariano insisted, it'll only take five minutes, but Florencio had left his car in the village square, he had to take off right away; he thanked them and kissed his little girl, who had already spotted the stack of magazines on the bench. When the door closed, Zulma and Mariano looked at each other almost questioningly, as if everything had happened too fast. Mariano shrugged his shoulders and returned to his workshop, where he was gluing an old chair; Zulma asked the little girl if she was hungry, she suggested she play with the magazines, in the closet there was a ball and a net for catching butterflies; the little girl said thank you and began to look at the magazines; Zulma watched her a moment while she prepared the artichokes for dinner that evening and thought she could let her play by herself.

Dusk fell early in the south now; they barely had a month left before returning to the capital and getting into that other life during the winter which, in any case, was only a continuation of this one, distantly together, amicably friends, respecting and performing the many trivial, delicate, conventional ceremonies of a couple, as now, when Mariano needed one of the burners to heat the glue jar and Zulma took the pot of potatoes off saying she'd finish cooking them later, and Mariano said thanks because the chair was almost ready and it would be better to do all the gluing in one application, but he had to heat the jar first, of course. The little girl was leafing through the magazines at the end of the large room that was used both as a kitchen and as a living room. Mariano looked in the pantry for some candy to give her; it was time to go out into the garden to have a drink as they watched night fall upon the hills. There was never anybody on the road; the first house in the village could barely be seen at the highest point; in front of them the slope kept on descending to the bottom of the valley, which was already in the shadows. Go ahead and pour, I'll be right there, said Zulma. Everything was done in cyclical fashion, each thing in its time and a time for each thing, except for the little girl, who had suddenly disturbed the pattern just a bit; a stool and a glass of milk for her, a stroke of her hair, and praise for how well she was behaving. The cigarettes, the swallows clustering above the cabin; everything went along repeating itself, fitting into the right slot, the chair must be almost dry by now, stuck together like that new day which had nothing new about it. The insignificant difference was the little girl that afternoon, as sometimes the mailman would draw them out of their solitude for a moment at midday with a letter for Mariano or Zulma that the addressee would receive and put away without saying a word. One more month of foreseeable repetitions, like rehearsals, and the Jeep loaded to the top would take them back to the apartment in the capital, to the life that was only different in form, Zulma's group or Mariano's artist friends, afternoons in the stores for her and evenings in the cafés for Mariano, a coming-and-going separately although they always got together to perform the linking ceremonies, the morning kiss, the neutral programs in common, as now when Mariano offered her another drink and Zulma accepted with her eyes lost in the most distant hills, which were tinted already in deep violet.

What would you like to have for supper, little one? Me? Anything you say, ma'am. She probably doesn't like artichokes, said Mariano. Yes, I like them, said the little girl, with oil and vinegar, but only a little salt because it burns. They laughed; they would make a special vinaigrette dressing for her. And boiled eggs, how do you like them? With a teaspoon, said the little girl. And only a little salt, because it burns, teased Mariano. Salt burns a lot, said the little girl, I give my doll her mashed potatoes without salt, today I didn't bring her because my daddy was in a hurry and wouldn't let me. It's going to be a lovely night, thought Zulma out loud, see how clear the air is toward the north. Yes, it won't be too hot, said Mariano, bringing the chairs into the downstairs room and turning on the lamps next to the picture window that faced the valley. Automatically he also turned on the radio. Nixon is going to Peking, how about that, said Mariano. There's nothing sacred, said Zulma, and they both laughed at the same time. The little girl was into the magazines and marking the comic strip pages as though she planned to reread them.

Night arrived in between the insecticide Mariano was spraying in the bedroom upstairs and the fragrance of an onion Zulma cut while humming along with a pop tune on the radio. Midway through supper the little girl began to doze over the boiled egg; they joked with her, they prodded her to finish; Mariano had already prepared the cot for her with an inflatable mattress in the farthest corner of the kitchen so they wouldn't bother her if they stayed a while in the room downstairs listening to records or reading. The little girl ate her peach and admitted she was sleepy. Go to bed, sweetie, said Zulma, don't forget if you have to tinkle, you only have to go upstairs, we'll leave the stairway light on. The little girl, half-asleep, gave them each a kiss on the cheek, but before she lay down she selected a magazine and placed it under the pillow. They're unbelievable, said Mariano, such an unattainable world and to think it once was ours, everybody's. Perhaps it's not so different, said Zulma, clearing the table, you too have your compulsions, the bottle of cologne on the left and the razor on the right, and as for me, forget it. But they weren't compulsions, thought Mariano, rather a response to death and nothingness, fixing things and times, establishing rituals and passages in opposition to chaos, which was full of holes and smudges. Only now he no longer said it aloud, more and more there seemed to be less of a need to talk to Zulma, and Zulma didn't say anything either that might prompt an exchange of ideas. Take the coffee pot, I've already set the cups on the stool by the chimney. Check to see if there's any sugar left in the bowl, there's a new package in the pantry. I can't find the corkscrew, this bottle of rum has a good colour, don't you think? Yes, a lovely colour. Since you're going up, bring the cigarettes I left on the dresser. This rum is really good stuff. It's hot, don't you think so? Yes, it's stifling, we'd better not open the windows, the place will fill with moths and mosquitoes.

WHEN ZULMA HEARD the first sound, Mariano was looking among the stack of records for a Beethoven sonata which he hadn't listened to that summer. He stood still with his hand in the air, he looked at Zulma. A noise as if on the stone steps of the garden, but nobody came to the cabin at that hour, nobody ever came at night. From the kitchen he switched on the light that illuminated the nearest part of the garden, saw no one and turned it off. Probably a dog looking around for something to eat, said Zulma. It sounded strange, almost like a snort, said Mariano. An enormous white blur lashed against the window. Zulma muffled a scream, Mariano, with his back toward her, turned around too late, the pane reflected only the pictures and furniture in the room. He had no time to ask anything, the snort resounded near the north wall; a whinny that was smothered just like Zulma's scream, her hands up to her mouth and pressing against the back wall, staring at the window. It's a horse, said Mariano, I hear his hooves, he's galloping through the garden. His mane, his lips, almost as if they were bleeding, an enormous white head was grazing the window; the horse barely looked at them, the white blotch was erased on the right, they heard his hooves again, an abrupt silence coming from the side of the stone steps, the neighing, the flight. But there are no horses in these parts, said Mariano, who had grabbed the bottle of rum by the neck before realizing it and now put it back on the stool. He wants to come in, said Zulma, glued to the rear wall, Of course not, what a foolish idea, he probably escaped from some herd in the valley and headed for the light. I tell you, he wants to come in, he's rabid and wants to get inside. Horses don't get rabies, as far as I know, said Mariano, I think he's gone, I'll take a look from the upstairs window. No, please, stay here, I can still hear him, he's on the terrace steps, he's stomping on the plants, he'll be back, and what if he breaks the window and gets in? Don't be silly, what do you mean he'll break the window, said Mariano weakly, maybe if we turn off the lights he'll go away. I don't know, I don't know, said Zulma, sliding down until she was sitting on the stool, I heard how he whinnied, he's there upstairs. They heard the hooves coming down the steps, the irritated heavy snort against the door, Mariano thought he felt something like pressure on the door, a repeated rubbing, and Zulma ran to him screaming hysterically. He cast her off, not violently, extended his hand toward the light switch; in the dark (the only light still on was in the kitchen, where the little girl was sleeping), the neighing and the hooves became louder, but the horse was no longer in front of the door; he could be heard going back and forth in the garden. Mariano ran to turn out the kitchen light without even looking toward the corner where they had put the little girl to bed; he returned to put his arms around Zulma, who was sobbing. He caressed her hair and face, asking her to be quiet so he could listen better. In the window the horse rubbed his head against the large pane, not too forcefully, the white blotch appeared transparent in the darkness; they sensed the horse looking inside, as though searching for something, but he could not see them any longer, and yet there he still was, whinnying and puffing, bolting abruptly from side to side. Zulma's body slipped through Mariano's arms and he helped her sit on the stool again, propping her up against the wall. Don't move, don't say anything, he's leaving now, you'll see. He wants to come in, Zulma said feebly, I know he wants to come in, and what if he breaks the window, what's going to happen if he kicks it in? Shh, said Mariano, please shut up. He's going to come in, muttered Zulma. And I don't even have a shotgun, said Mariano, I'd blast five shots into his head, the son of a bitch. He's not there any more, said Zulma, rising suddenly, I hear him up there, if he sees the terrace door he might come in. It's shut tight, don't be afraid, remember in the dark he's not about to enter a house where he couldn't even move around, he's not that dumb. Oh yes, said Zulma, he wants to come in, he'll crush us against the walls, I know he wants to come in. Shh, repeated Mariano, who also was thinking about it, and could do nothing but wait with his back soaked in cold perspiration. Once again the hooves echoed upon the flagstone steps, and suddenly silence, the distant crickets, a bird high in a walnut tree.

Without turning on the light, now that the window let the night's vague clarity enter, Mariano filled a glass with rum and held it against Zulma's lips, forcing her to drink even though her teeth hit the glass and the liquor spilled on her blouse; then holding the bottle by the neck he took a long swig and went to the kitchen to check on the little girl. With her hand under the pillow as if clutching the precious magazine, incredibly she was asleep and had heard nothing, she hardly seemed to be there, while in the big room Zulma's sobbing broke every so often into a smothered hiccup, almost a shout. It's all over, it's over, said Mariano, sitting up against her and shaking her gently, it was nothing but a scare. He'll be back, said Zulma, her eyes nailed to the window. No, he's probably far off by now, no doubt he escaped from some herd down below. No horse does that, said Zulma, no horse tries to enter a house like that. It's strange, I'll grant you that, said Mariano, maybe we'd better take a look outside, I have the lantern right here. But Zulma had pressed herself against the wall, the idea of opening the door, of going out toward the white shadow that might be near, waiting under the trees, ready to charge. Look, if we don't check to see if he's gone, nobody will sleep tonight, said Mariano. Let's give him a little more time; meanwhile you go to bed, and I'll give you a tranquilizer; an extra dose, poor kid, you've certainly earned it.

ZULMA ENDED UP by accepting passively; without turning on the lights, they went toward the stairs and with his hand Mariano motioned toward the little girl asleep, but Zulma scarcely looked at her, she was climbing the stairs reeling, Mariana had to hold her as they entered the bedroom because she was about to bump into the doorframe. From the window that faced the eaves they looked at the stone steps, the highest terrace of the garden. You see, he's gone, said

Mariano, fixing Zulma's pillow, watching her undress mechanically, staring at the window. He made her drink the drops, dabbed cologne on her neck and hands, gently lifted the sheet up to Zulma's shoulders as she closed her eyes and trembled. He wiped her cheeks, waited a moment, and went downstairs to look for the lantern; carrying it unlit in one hand and an axe in the other, little by little he opened the door of the large room and went out to the lower terrace, where he could get full view of the entire side of the house facing eastward; the night was identical to so many other summer nights, the crickets chirped in the distance, a frog let fall two alternating drops of sound. Not needing the lantern, Mariano saw the trampled lilac bush, the huge prints in the pansy bed, the flowerpot overturned at the bottom of the steps; so it wasn't a hallucination, and, of course, it was better that it not be; in the morning he would go with Florencio to check on the herds in the valley, they weren't going to get the upper hand so easily. Before going in he set the flowerpot straight, went up to the front trees and listened for a long while to the crickets and the frog; when he looked toward the house, Zulma was standing at the bedroom window, naked, motionless.

THE LITTLE GIRL had not moved. Mariano went upstairs without making any noise and began to smoke a cigarette next to Zulma. You see, he's gone, now we can sleep in peace, tomorrow we'll see. Little by little he led her toward the bed, undressed, stretched out on his back still smoking. Go to sleep, everything is all right, it was only an absurd fright. He stroked her hair, his fingers slid down to her shoulder, grazing her breasts lightly. Zulma turned on her side, her back toward him, not speaking; this too was like so many other summer nights.

GETTING TO SLEEP should have been difficult, but no sooner had Mariano put out his cigarette than he dropped off suddenly; the window was still open and no doubt mosquitoes would enter, but sleep came first, with no dreams, total nothingness from which he emerged at some moment driven by an indescribable panic, the pressure of Zulma's fingers on one shoulder, the panting. Almost without realizing it, he was now listening to the night, the perfect silence punctuated by the crickets. Go to sleep, Zulma, it's nothing, you must have been dreaming. Insisting she agree with him, that she lie down again, her back turned to him now that she had suddenly withdrawn her hand and was sitting up rigid, looking toward the closed door. He got up at the same time as Zulma, helpless to stop her from opening the door and going to the top of the stairs, clinging to her and asking himself vaguely if it wouldn't be better to slap her, to bring her back to bed by force, to break such petrified remoteness. In the middle of the staircase Zulma stopped, taking hold of the banister. You know why the little girl is there? With a voice that must have still belonged to the nightmare. The little girl? Two more steps, now almost in the bend that led to the kitchen. Zulma, please. And her voice cracking, almost in falsetto: she's there to let him in, I tell you she's going to let him in. Zulma, don't make me do something I'll regret. And her voice, almost triumphant, still rising in tone, look, just look if you don't believe me; the bed's empty, the magazine on the floor. With a start Mariano headed for Zulma, he sprang toward the light switch. The little girl looked at them, her pink pyjamas against the door that faced the large room, her face drowsy. What are you doing up at this hour, said Mariano wrapping a dish towel around his waist. The little girl looked at Zulma naked, somewhere between being asleep and embarrassed she looked at her as if wanting to go back to bed, on the brink of tears. I got up to tinkle, she said. And you went out to the garden when we had told you to go upstairs to the bathroom.

The little girl began to pout, her hands comically lost in the pockets of her pyjamas. It's okay, go to bed, said Mariano, stroking her hair. He covered her, and placed the magazine under the pillow for her; the little girl turned toward the wall, a finger in her mouth as if to console herself. Go ahead up, said Mariano, you see there's nothing wrong, don't stand there like a sleepwalker. He saw Zulma take a couple of steps toward the door of the large room, he blocked her path; everything was fine now, damn it. But don't you realize she's opened the door for him, said Zulma with that voice which wasn't hers. Stop the nonsense, Zulma. Go see if it's not so, or let me go. Mariano's hand closed around her trembling forearm. Get upstairs right now, pushing her till he had led her to the foot of the steps, looking as he went by at the little girl, who hadn't moved, she must be asleep by now. On the first step Zulma screamed and tried to escape, but the stairway was narrow and Mariano kept shoving her with his whole body; the towel unfastened and fell to the bottom of the stairs. Holding on to her by the shoulders, he hurled her upward to the landing and flung her into the bedroom, shutting the door behind him. She's going to let him in, Zulma repeated, the door is open and he'll get in. Lie down, said Mariano. I'm telling you the door is open. It doesn't matter if he comes in or not, let him come in if he wants to, I don't give a damn now whether he comes in or not. He caught Zulma's hands as they tried to repel him, from behind he pushed against the bed, they fell together, Zulma sobbing and begging, powerless to move under the weight of a body that pressed her nearer and nearer, that bent her to a will murmured mouth to mouth, wildly amidst tears and obscenities. I don't want to, I don't want to, I don't want to ever again, I don't want to, but it was too late now, her strength and pride yielding to that levering weight, returning her to an impossible past, to the summers without letters and without horses. Later in the night—it was beginning to get light—Mariano dressed in silence and went down to the kitchen; the little girl was sleeping with her finger in her mouth, the door of the big room was open. Zulma had been right, the little girl had opened the door but the horse hadn't entered the house, Unless, he thought, lighting his first cigarette and looking at the blue ridge of the hills, unless Zulma had been right about that too and the horse had entered the house, but how could they prove it if they had not heard him, if everything was in order, if the clock would continue to measure the morning and later Florencio would come to get the little girl, probably around twelve the mailman would arrive whistling from afar, leaving for them on the garden table the letters that he or Zulma would pick up without saying anything, shortly before deciding by mutual consent what was best to prepare for lunch.

Games at Twilight

by

ANITA DESAI

IT WAS STILL TOO HOT to play outdoors. They had had their tea, they had been washed and had their hair brushed, and after the long day of confinement in the house that was not cool but at least a protection from the sun, the children strained to get out. Their faces were red and bloated with the effort, but their mother would not open the door, everything was still curtained and shuttered in a way that stifled the children, made them feel that their lungs were stuffed with cotton wool and their noses with dust and if they didn't burst out into the light and see the sun and feel the air, they would choke.

"Please, ma, please," they begged. "We'll play in the veranda and porch—we won't go a step out of the porch."

"You will, I know you will, and then—"

"No—we won't, we won't," they wailed so horrendously that she actually let down the bolt of the front door so that they burst out like seeds from a crackling, overripe pod into the veranda, with such wild, maniacal yells that she retreated to her bath and the shower of talcum powder and the fresh sari that were to help her face the summer evening.

THEY FACED THE AFTERNOON. It was too hot. Too bright. The white walls of the veranda glared stridently in the sun. The bougainvillea hung about it, purple and magenta, in livid balloons. The garden outside was like a tray made of beaten brass, flattened out on the red gravel and the stony soil in all shades of metal—aluminium, tin, copper and brass. No life stirred at this arid time of day—the birds still drooped, like dead fruit, in the papery tents of the trees; some squirrels lay limp on the wet earth under the garden tap. The outdoor dog lay stretched as if dead on the veranda mat, his paws and ears and tail all reaching out like dying travellers in search of water. He rolled his eyes at the children—two white marbles rolling in the purple sockets, begging for sympathy—and attempted to lift his tail in a wag but could not. It only twitched and lay still.

Then, perhaps roused by the shrieks of the children, a band of parrots suddenly fell out of the eucalyptus tree, tumbled frantically in the still, sizzling air, then sorted themselves out into battle formation and streaked away across the white sky.

The children, too, felt released. They too began tumbling, shoving, pushing against each other, frantic to start. Start what? Start their business. The business of the children's day which is—play.

"Let's play hide-and-seek."

"Who'll be It?"

"You be It."

"Why should I? You be—"

"You're the eldest—"

"That doesn't mean—"

The shoves became harder. Some kicked out. The motherly Mira intervened. She pulled the boys roughly apart. There was a tearing sound of cloth but it was lost in the heavy panting and angry grumbling and no one paid attention to the small sleeve hanging loosely off a shoulder.

"Make a circle, make a circle!" she shouted, firmly pulling and pushing till a kind of vague circle was formed. "Now clap!" she roared and, clapping, they all chanted in melancholy unison: "Dip, dip, dip—my blue ship—" and every now and then one or the other saw he was safe by the way his hands fell at the crucial moment—palm on palm, or back of hand on palm—and dropped out of the circle with a yell and a jump of relief and jubilation.

Raghu was It. He started to protest, to cry "You cheated—Mira cheated—Anu cheated—" but it was too late, the others had all already streaked away. There was no one to hear when he called out, "Only in the veranda—the porch—Ma said—Ma *said* to stay in the porch!" No one had stopped to listen, all he saw were their brown legs flashing through the dusty shrubs, scrambling up brick walls, leaping over compost heaps and hedges, and then the porch stood empty in the purple shade of the bougainvillea and the garden was as empty as before; even the limp squirrels had whisked away, leaving everything gleaming, brassy and bare.

Only small Manu suddenly reappeared, as if he had dropped out of an invisible cloud or from a bird's claws, and stood for a moment in the centre of the yellow lawn, chewing his finger and near to tears as he heard Raghu shouting, with his head pressed against the veranda wall, "Eighty-three, eighty-five, eighty-nine, ninety ..." and then made off in a panic, half of him wanting to fly north, the other half counselling south. Raghu turned just in time to see the flash of his white shorts and the uncertain skittering of his red sandals, and charged after him with such a bloodcurdling yell that Manu stumbled over the hosepipe, fell into its rubber coils and lay there weeping, "I won't be It—you have to find them all—all—All!"

"I know I have to, idiot," Raghu said, superciliously kicking him with his toe. "You're dead," he said with satisfaction, licking the beads of perspiration off his upper lip, and then stalked off in search of worthier prey, whistling spiritedly so that the hiders should hear and tremble.

RAVI HEARD the whistling and picked his nose in a panic, trying to find comfort by burrowing the finger deep-deep into that soft tunnel. He felt himself too exposed, sitting on an upturned flower-pot behind the garage. Where could he burrow? He could run around the garage if he heard Raghu come—around and around and around—but he hadn't much faith in his short legs when matched against Raghu's long, hefty, hairy footballer legs. Ravi had a frightening glimpse of them as Raghu combed the hedge of crotons and hibiscus, trampling delicate ferns underfoot as he did so. Ravi looked about him desperately, swallowing a small ball of snot in his fear.

The garage was locked with a great heavy lock to which the driver had the key in his room, hanging from a nail on the wall under his work-shirt. Ravi had peeped in and seen him still sprawling on his string-cot in his vest and striped underpants, the hair on his chest and the hair in his nose shaking with the vibrations of his phlegm-obstructed snores. Ravi had wished he were tall enough, big enough to reach the key on the nail, but it was impossible, beyond his reach for years to come. He had sidled away and sat dejectedly on the flowerpot. That at least was cut to his own size.

But next to the garage was another shed with a big green door. Also locked. No one even knew who had the key to the lock. That shed wasn't opened more than once a year when Ma turned out all the old broken bits of furniture and rolls of matting and leaking buckets, and the white anthills were broken and swept away and Flit sprayed into the spider webs and rat holes so that the whole operation was like the looting of a poor, ruined and conquered city. The green leaves of the door sagged. They were nearly off their rusty hinges. The hinges were large and made a small gap between the door and the walls—only just large enough for rats, dogs and, possibly, Ravi to slip through.

Ravi had never cared to enter such a dark and depressing mortuary of defunct household goods seething with such unspeakable and alarming animal life but, as Raghu's whistling grew angrier and sharper and his crashing and storming in the hedge wilder, Ravi suddenly slipped off the flowerpot and through the crack and was gone. He chuckled aloud with astonishment at his own temerity so that Raghu came out of the hedge, stood silent with his hands on his hips, listening, and finally shouted "I heard you! I'm coming! *Got you*—" and came charging round the garage only to find the upturned flowerpot, the yellow dust, the crawling of white ants in a mud-hill against the closed shed door—nothing. Snarling, he bent to pick up a stick and went off, whacking it against the garage and shed walls as if to beat out his prey.

RAVI SHOOK, then shivered with delight, with self-congratulation. Also with fear. It was dark, spooky in the shed. It had a muffled smell, as of graves. Ravi had once got locked into the linen cupboard and sat there weeping for half an hour before he was rescued. But at least that had been a familiar place, and even smelled pleasantly of starch, laundry and, reassuringly, of his mother. But the shed smelled of rats, anthills, dust and spider webs. Also of less definable, less recognizable horrors. And it was dark. Except for the white-hot cracks along the door, there was no light. The roof was very low. Although Ravi was small, he felt as if he could reach up and touch it with his fingertips. But he didn't stretch. He hunched himself into a ball so as not to bump into anything, touch or feel anything. What might there not be to touch him and feel him as he stood there, trying to see in the dark? Something cold, or slimy—like a snake. Snakes! He leaped up as Raghu whacked the wall with his stick—then, quickly realizing what it was, felt almost relieved to hear Raghu, hear his stick. It made him feel protected.

But Raghu soon moved away. There wasn't a sound once his footsteps had gone around the garage and disappeared. Ravi stood frozen inside the shed. Then he shivered all over. Something had tickled the back of his neck. It took him a while to pick up the courage to lift his hand and explore. It was an insect—perhaps a spider—exploring *him*. He squashed it and wondered how many more creatures were watching him, waiting to reach out and touch him, the stranger.

There was nothing now. After standing in that position—his hand still on his neck, feeling the wet splodge of the squashed spider gradually dry—for minutes, hours, his legs began to tremble with the effort, the inaction. By now he could see enough in the dark to make out the large solid shapes of old wardrobes, broken buckets and bedsteads piled on top of each other around him. He recognized an old bathtub—patches of enamel glimmered at him and at last he lowered himself onto its edge.

He contemplated slipping out of the shed and into the fray. He wondered if it would not be better to be captured by Raghu and be returned to the milling crowd as long as he could be in the sun, the light, the free spaces of the garden and the familiarity of his brothers, sisters and cousins. It would be evening soon. Their games would become legitimate. The parents would sit out on the lawn on cane basket chairs and watch them as they tore around the garden or gathered in knots to share a loot of mulberries or black, teeth-splitting *jamun* from the garden trees. The gardener would fix the hosepipe to the water tap and water would fall lavishly through the air to the ground, soaking the dry yellow grass and the red gravel and arousing the sweet, the intoxicating scent of water on dry earth—that loveliest scent in the world. Ravi sniffed for a whiff of it. He half-rose from the bathtub, then heard the despairing scream of one of the girls as Raghu bore down upon her. There was the sound of a crash, and of rolling about in the bushes, the shrubs, then screams and accusing sobs of, "I touched the den—" "You did not—" "I did—" "You liar, you did *not*" and then a fading away and silence again.

Ravi sat back on the harsh edge of the tub, deciding to hold out a bit longer. What fun if they were all found and caught—he alone left unconquered! He had never known that sensation. Nothing more wonderful had ever happened to him than being taken out by an uncle and bought a whole slab of chocolate all to himself, or being flung into the soda-man's pony cart and driven up to the gate by the friendly driver with the red beard and pointed ears. To defeat Raghu—that hirsute, hoarse-voiced football champion—and to be the winner in a circle of older, bigger, luckier children—that would be thrilling beyond imagination. He hugged his knees together and smiled to himself almost shyly at the thought of so much victory, such laurels.

THERE HE SAT SMILING, knocking his heels against the bathtub, now and then getting up and going to the door to put his ear to the broad crack and listening for sounds of the game, the pursuer and the pursued, and then returning to his seat with the dogged determination of the true winner, a breaker of records, a champion.

It grew darker in the shed as the light at the door grew softer, fuzzier, turned to a kind of crumbling yellow pollen that turned to yellow fur, blue fur, grey fur. Evening. Twilight. The sound of water gushing, falling. The scent of earth receiving water, slaking its thirst in great gulps and releasing that green scent of freshness, coolness. Through the crack Ravi saw the long purple shadows of the shed and the garage lying still across the yard. Beyond that, the white walls of the house. The bougainvillea had lost its lividity, hung in dark bundles that quaked and twittered and seethed with masses of homing sparrows. The lawn was shut off from his view. Could he hear the children's voices? It seemed to him that he could. It seemed to him that he could hear them chanting, singing, laughing. But what about the game? What had happened? Could it be over? How could it when he was still not found?

It then occurred to him that he could have slipped out long ago, dashed across the yard to the veranda and touched the "den." It was necessary to do that to win. He had forgotten. He had only remembered the part of hiding and trying to elude the seeker. He had done that so successfully, his success had occupied him so wholly that he had quite forgotten that success had to be clinched by that final dash to victory and the ringing cry of "Den!"

With a whimper he burst through the crack, fell on his knees, got up and stumbled on stiff, benumbed legs across the shadowy yard, crying heartily by the time he reached the veranda so that when he flung himself at the white pillar and bawled, "Den! Den! Den!" his voice broke with rage and pity at the disgrace of it all and he felt himself flooded with tears and misery.

Out on the lawn, the children stopped chanting. They all turned to stare at him in amazement. Their faces were pale and triangular in the dusk. The trees and bushes around them stood inky and sepulchral, spilling long shadows across them. They stared, wondering at his reappearance, his passion, his wild animal howling. Their mother rose from her basket chair and came towards him, worried, annoyed, saying, "Stop it, stop it, Ravi. Don't be a baby. Have you hurt yourself?" Seeing him attended to, the children went back to clasping their hands and chanting "The grass is green, the rose is red...."

But Ravi would not let them. He tore himself out of his mother's grasp and pounded across the lawn into their midst, charging at them with his head lowered so that they scattered in surprise. "I won, I won, I won," he bawled, shaking his head so that the big tears flew. "Raghu didn't find me. I won, I won—"

It took them a minute to grasp what he was saying, even who he was. They had quite forgotten him. Raghu had found all the others long ago. There had been a fight about who was to be It next. It had been so fierce that their mother had emerged from her bath and made them change to another game. Then they had played another and another. Broken mulberries from the tree and eaten them. Helped the driver wash the car when their father returned from work. Helped the gardener water the beds till he roared at them and swore he would complain to their parents. The parents had come out, taken up their positions on the cane chairs. They had begun to play again, sing and chant. All this time no one had remembered Ravi. Having disappeared from the scene, he had disappeared from their minds. Clean.

"Don't be a fool," Raghu said roughly, pushing him aside, and even Mira said, "Stop howling, Ravi. If you want to play, you can stand at the end of the line," and she put him there very firmly.

The game proceeded. Two pairs of arms reached up and met in an arc. The children trooped under it again and again in a lugubrious circle, ducking their heads and intoning

"The grass is green,
The rose is red;
Remember me
When I am dead, dead, dead, dead ..."

And the arc of thin arms trembled in the twilight, and the heads were bowed so sadly, and their feet tramped to that melancholy refrain so mournfully, so helplessly, that Ravi could not bear it. He would not follow them, he would not be included in this funereal game. He had wanted victory and triumph—not a funeral. But he had been forgotten, left out and he would not join them now. The ignominy of being forgotten—how could he face it? He felt his heart go heavy and ache inside him unbearably. He lay down full length on the damp grass, crushing his face into it, no longer crying, silenced by a terrible sense of his insignificance.

Postcards from Surfers

by

HELEN GARNER

"One night I dreamed that I did not love, and that night, released from all bonds, I lay as though in a kind of soothing death."

—COLETTE

WE ARE DRIVING north from Coolangatta airport. Beside the road the ocean heaves and heaves into waves which do not break. The swells are dotted with boardriders in black wet-suits, grim as sharks.

"Look at those idiots," says my father.

"They must be freezing," says my mother.

"But what about the principle of the wet-suit?" I say. "Isn't there a thin layer of water between your skin and the suit, and your body heat …"

"Could be," says my father.

The road takes a sudden swing round a rocky outcrop. Miles ahead of us, blurred in the milky air, I see a dream city: its cream, its silver, its turquoise towers thrust in a cluster from a distant spit.

"What—is that Brisbane?" I say.

"No," says my mother. "That's Surfers."

My father's car has a built-in computer. If he exceeds the speed limit, the dashboard emits a discreet but insistent pinging. Lights flash, and the pressure of his right foot lessens. He controls the windows from a panel between the two front seats. We cruise past a Valiant parked by the highway with a FOR SALE sign propped in its back window.

"Look at that," says my mother. "A WA number-plate. Probably thrashed it across the Nullarbor and now they reckon they'll flog it."

"Pro'ly stolen," says my father. "See the sticker? ALL YOU VIRGINS, THANKS FOR NOTHING. You can just see what sort of a pin'ead he'd be. Brain the size of a pea."

Close up, many of the turquoise towers are not yet sold.

"Every conceivable feature," the signs say. They have names like Capricornia, Biarritz, The Breakers, Acapulco, Rio.

I had a Brazilian friend when I lived in Paris. He showed me a postcard, once, of Rio where he was born and brought up. The card bore an aerial shot of a splendid, curved tropical beach, fringed with palms, its sand pure as snow.

"Why don't you live in Brazil," I said, "if it's as beautiful as this?"

"Because," said my friend, "right behind that beach there is a huge military base."

In my turn I showed him a postcard of my country. It was a reproduction of that Streeton painting called *The Land of the Golden Fleece* which in my homesickness I kept standing on the heater in my bedroom. He studied it carefully. At last he turned his currant-coloured eyes to me and said,

"Les arbres sont rouges?" Are the trees red?

Several years later, six months ago, I was rummaging through a box of old postcards in a junk shop in Rathdowne Street. Among the photos of damp cottages in Galway, of Raj hotels crumbling in bicycle-thronged Colombo, of glassy Canadian lakes flawed by the wake of a single canoe, I found two cards that I bought for a dollar each. One was a picture of downtown Rio, in black-and-white. The other, crudely tinted, showed Geelong, the town where I was born. The photographer must have stood on the high grassy bank that overlooks the Eastern Beach. He lined up his shot through the never-flowing fountain with its quartet of concrete wading birds (storks? cranes? I never asked my father: they have long orange beaks and each bird holds one leg bent, as if about to take a step); through the fountain and out over the curving wooden promenade, from which we dived all summer, unsupervised, into the flat water; and across the bay to the You Yangs, the double-humped, low, volcanic cones, the only disturbance in the great basalt plains that lie between Geelong and Melbourne. These two cards in the same box! And I find them! Imagine! *"Cher Rubens,"* I wrote. *"Je t'envoie ces deux cartes postales, de nos deux villes natales ..."*

Auntie Lorna has gone for a walk on the beach. My mother unlocks the door and slides open the flywire screen. She goes out into the bright air to tell her friend of my arrival. The ocean is right in front of the unit, only a hundred and fifty yards away. How can people be so sure of the boundary between land and sea that they have the confidence to build houses on it? The white doorsteps of the ocean travel and travel.

"Twelve o'clock," says my father.

"Getting on for lunchtime," I say.

"Getting towards it. Specially with that nice cold corned beef sitting there, and fresh brown bread. Think I'll have to try some of that choko relish. Ever eaten a choko?"

"I wouldn't know a choko if I fell over it," I say.

"Nor would I."

He selects a serrated knife from the magnetized holder on the kitchen wall and quickly and skilfully, at the bench, makes himself a thick sandwich. He works with powerful concentration: when the meat flaps off the slice of bread, he rounds it up with a large, dramatic scooping movement and a sympathetic grimace of the lower lip. He picks up the sandwich in two hands, raises it to his mouth and takes a large bite. While he chews he breathes heavily through his nose.

"Want to make yourself something?" he says with his mouth full.

I stand up. He pushes the loaf of bread towards me with the back of his hand. He puts the other half of his sandwich on a green bread and butter plate and carries it to the table. He sits with his elbows on the pine wood, his knees wide apart, his belly relaxing on to his thighs, his high-arched, long-boned feet planted on the tiled floor. He eats, and gazes out to sea. The noise of his eating fills the room.

My mother and Auntie Lorna come up from the beach. I stand inside the wall of glass and watch them stop at the tap to hose the sand off their feet before they cross the grass to the door. They are two old women: they have to keep one hand on the tap in order to balance on the left foot and wash the right. I see that they are two old women, and yet they are neither young nor old. They are my mother and Auntie Lorna, two institutions. They slide back the wire door, smiling.

"Don't tramp sand everywhere," says my father from the table.

They take no notice. Auntie Lorna kisses me, and holds me at arms' length with her head on one side. My mother prepares food and we eat, looking out at the water.

"You've missed the coronary brigade," says my father. "They get out on the beach about nine in the morning. You can pick 'em. They swing their arms up really high when they walk." He laughs, looking down.

"Do you go for a walk every day too?" I ask.

"Six point six kilometres," says my father.

"Got a pedometer, have you?"

"I just nutted it out," says my father. "We walk as far as a big white building, down that way, then we turn round and come back. Six point six altogether, there and back."

"I might come with you."

"You can if you like," he says. He picks up his plate and carries it to the sink. "We go after breakfast. You've missed today's."

He goes to the couch and opens the newspaper on the low coffee table. He reads with his glasses down his nose and his hands loosely linked between his spread knees. The women wash up.

"Is there a shop nearby?" I ask my mother. "I have to get some tampons."

"Caught short, are you?" she says. "I think they sell them at the shopping centre, along Sunbrite Avenue there near the bowling club. Want me to come with you?"

"I can find it."

"I never could use those things," says my mother, lowering her voice and glancing across the room at my father. "Hazel told me about a terrible thing that happened to her. For days she kept noticing this revolting smell that was … emanating from her. She washed and washed, and couldn't get rid of it. Finally she was about to go to the doctor, but first she got down and had a look with the mirror. She saw this bit of thread and pulled it. The thing was *green*. She must've forgotten to take it out—it'd been there for days and days and *days*."

We laugh with the teatowels up to our mouths. My father, on the other side of the room, looks up from the paper with the bent smile of someone not sure what the others are laughing at. I am always surprised when my mother comes out with a word like "emanating." At home I have a book called *An Outline of English Verse* which my mother used in her matriculation year. In the margins of *The Rape of the Lock* she has made notations: "bathos; reminiscent of Virgil; parody of Homer." Her handwriting in these pencilled jottings, made forty-five years ago, is exactly as it is today: this makes me suspect, when I am not with her, that she is a closet intellectual.

Once or twice, on my way from the unit to the shopping centre, I think to see roses along a fence and run to look, but I find them to be some scentless, fleshy flower. I fall back. Beside a patch of yellow grass, pretty trees in a row are bearing and dropping white blossom-like flowers, but they look wrong to me, I do not recognize them: the blossoms too large, the branches too flat. I am dizzy from the flight. In Melbourne it is still winter, everything is bare.

I buy the tampons and look for the postcards. There they are, displayed in a tall revolving rack. There is a great deal of blue. Closer, I find colour photos of white beaches, duneless, palmless, on which half-naked people lie on their backs with their knees raised. The frequency of this posture, at random through the crowd, makes me feel like laughing. Most of the cards have GREETINGS FROM THE GOLD COAST or BROADBEACH or SURFERS PARADISE embossed in gold in one corner: I search for pictures without words. Another card, in several slightly differing versions, shows a graceful, big-breasted young girl lying in a seductive pose against some rocks: she is wearing a bikini and her whole head is covered by one of those latex masks that are sold in trick shops, the ones you pull on as a bandit pulls on a stocking. The mask represents the hideous, raddled, grinning face of an old woman, a witch. I stare at this photo for a long time. Is it simple, or does it hide some more mysterious signs and symbols?

I buy twelve GREETINGS FROM cards with views, some aerial, some from the ground. They cost twenty-five cents each.

"Want the envelopes?" says the girl. She is dressed in a flowered garment which is drawn up between her thighs like a nappy.

"Yes please." The envelopes are so covered with coloured maps, logos and drawings of Australian fauna that there is barely room to write an address, but something about them attracts me. I buy a packet of Licorice Chews and eat them all on the way home: I stuff them in two at a time: my mouth floods with saliva. There are no rubbish bins so I put the papers in my pocket. Now that I have spent money here, now that I have rubbish to dispose of, I am no longer a stranger. In Paris there used to be signs in the streets that said, *"Le commerce, c'est la vie de la ville."* Any traveller knows this to be the truth.

The women are knitting. They murmur and murmur. What they say never requires an answer. My father sharpens a pencil stub with his pocket knife, and folds the paper into a pad one-eighth the size of a broadsheet page.

"Five down, spicy meat jelly. ASPIC. Three across, counterfeit. BOGUS! Howzat."

"You're in good nick," I say. "I would've had to rack my brains for BOGUS. Why don't you do harder ones?"

"Oh, I can't do those other ones, the cryptic."

"You have to know Shakespeare and the Bible off by heart to do those," I say.

"Yairs. Course, if you got hold of the answer and filled it out looking at that, with a lot of practice you could come round to their way of thinking. They used to have good ones in the *Weekly Times*. But I s'pose they had so many complaints from cockies who couldn't do 'em that they had to ease off."

I do not feel comfortable yet about writing the postcards. It would seem graceless. I flip through my mother's pattern book.

"There's some nice ones there," she says. "What about the one with the floppy collar?"

"Want to buy some wool?" says my father. He tosses the finished crossword on to the coffee table and stands up with a vast yawn. "Oh—

ee—oh—ooh. Come on, Miss. I'll drive you over to Pacific Fair."

I choose the wool and count out the number of balls specified by the pattern. My father rears back to look at it: this movement struck terror into me when I was a teenager but I now recognize it as short-sightedness.

"Pure wool, is it?" he says. As soon as he touches it he will know. He fingers it, and looks at me.

"No," I say. "Got a bit of synthetic in it. It's what the pattern says to use."

"Why don't you—" He stops. Once he would have tried to prevent me from buying it. His big blunt hands used to fling out the fleeces, still warm, on to the greasy table. His hands looked as if they had no feeling in them but they teased out the wool, judged it, classed it, assigned it a fineness and a destination: Italy, Switzerland, Japan. He came home with thorns embedded deep in the flesh of his palms. He stood patiently while my mother gouged away at them with a needle. He drove away at shearing time in a yellow car with running boards, up to the big sheds in the country; we rode on the running boards as far as the corner of our street, then skipped home. He went to the Melbourne Show for work, not pleasure, and once he brought me home a plastic trumpet. "Fordie," he called me, and took me to the wharves and said, "See that rope? It's not a rope. It's a hawser." "Hawser," I repeated, wanting him to think I was a serious person. We walked along Strachan Avenue, Manifold Heights, hand in hand. "Listen," he said. "Listen to the wind in the wires." I must have been very little then, for the wires were so high I can't remember seeing them.

He turns away from the fluffy pink balls and waits with his hands in his pockets for me to pay.

"What do you do all day, up here?" I say on the way home.

"Oh ... play bowls. Follow the real estate. I ring up the firms that advertise these flash units and I ask 'em questions. I let 'em lower and lower their price. See how low they'll go. How many more discounts they can dream up." He drives like a farmer in a ute, leaning forward with his arms curved round the wheel, always about to squint up through the windscreen at the sky, checking the weather.

"Don't they ask your name?"

"Yep."

"What do you call yourself?"

"Oh, Jackson or anything." He flicks a glance at me. We begin to laugh, looking away from each other.

"It's bloody crook up here," he says. "Jerry-built. Sad. 'Every conceivable luxury!' They can't get rid of it. They're desperate. Come on. We'll go up and you can have a look."

The lift in Biarritz is lined with mushroom-coloured carpet. We brace our backs against its wall and it rushes us upwards. The salesman in the display unit has a moustache, several gold bracelets, a beige suit, and a clipboard against his chest. He is engaged with an elderly couple and we are able to slip past him into the living room.

"Did you see that peanut?" hisses my father.

"A gilded youth," I say. "'Their eyes are dull, their heads are flat, they have no brains at all.'"

He looks impressed, as if he thinks I have made it up on the spot. *"The Man from Ironbark,"* I add.

"I only remember *The Geebung Polo Club,*" he says. He mimes leaning off a horse and swinging a heavy implement. We snort with laughter. Just inside the living room door stand five Ionic pillars in a half-moon curve. Beyond them, through the glass, are views of a river and some mountains. The river winds in a plain, the mountains are sudden, lumpy and crooked.

"From the other side you can see the sea," says my father.

"Would you live up here?"

"Not on your life. Not with those flaming pillars."

From the bedroom window he points out another high-rise building closer to the sea. Its name is Chelsea. It is battle-ship grey with a red trim. Its windows face away from the ocean. It is tall and narrow, of mean proportions, almost prison-like. "I wouldn't mind living in that one," he says. I look at it in silence. He has unerringly chosen the ugliest one. It is so ugly that I can find nothing to say.

It is Saturday afternoon. My father is waiting for the Victorian football to start on TV. He rereads the paper.

"Look at this," he says. "Mum, remember that seminar we went to about investment in diamonds?"

"Up here?" I say. "A *seminar*?"

"S'posed to be an investment that would double its value in six days. We went along one afternoon. They were obviously con-men. Ooh, setting up a big con, you could tell. They had sherry and sandwiches."

"That's all we went for, actually," says my mother.

"What sort of people went?" I ask.

"Oh … people like ourselves," says my father.

"Do you think anybody bought any?"

"Sure. Some idiots. Anyway, look at this in today's *Age*. 'The Diamond Dreamtime. World diamond market plummets.' Haw haw haw."

He turns on the TV in time for the bounce. I cast on stitches as instructed by the pattern and begin to knit. My mother and Auntie Lorna, well advanced in complicated garments for my sister's teenage children, conduct their monologues which cross, coincide and run parallel. My father mumbles advice to the footballers and emits bursts of contemptuous laughter. "Bloody idiot," he says.

I go to the room I am to share with Auntie Lorna and come back with the packet of postcards. When I get out my pen and the stamps and set myself up at the table my father looks up and shouts to me over the roar of the crowd,

"Given up on the knitting?"

"No. Just knocking off a few postcards. People expect a postcard when you go to Queensland."

"Have to keep up your correspondence, Father," says my mother.

"I'll knit later," I say.

"How much have you done?" asks my father.

"This much." I separate thumb and forefinger.

"Dear Philip," I write. I make my writing as thin and small as I can: the back of the postcard, not the front, is the art form. "Look where I am. A big red setter wet from the surf shambles up the side way of the unit, looking lost and anxious as setters always do. My parents send it packing with curses in an inarticulate tongue. Go orn, get orf, gorn!"

"Dear Philip. THE IDENTIFICATION OF THE BIRDS AND FISHES. *My father:* 'Look at those albatross. They must have eyes that can see for a hundred miles. As soon as one dives, they come from everywhere. Look at 'em dive! Bang! Down they go.' *Me:* 'What sort of fish would they be diving for?' *My father:* 'Whiting. They only eat whiting.' *Me:* 'They do not!' *My father:* 'How the hell would *I* know what sort of fish they are.'"

"Dear Philip. My father says they are albatross, but my mother (in the bathroom, later) remarks to me that albatross have shorter, more hunched necks."

"Dear Philip. I share a room with Auntie Lorna. She also is writing postcards and has just asked me how to spell TOO. I like her very much and *she likes me*. 'I'll keep the stickybeaks in the Woomelang post office guessing,' she says. 'I won't put my name on the back of the envelope.'"

"Dear Philip. OUTSIDE THE POST OFFICE. My father, Auntie Lorna and I wait in the car for my mother to go in and pick up the mail from the locked box. *My father:* 'Gawd, amazing, isn't it, what people do. See that sign there, ENTER, with the arrow pointing upwards? What sort of a thing is that? Is it a joke, or just some no-hoper foolin' around? That woman's been in the phone box for half an hour, I bet. How'd you be, outside the public phone waiting for some silly coot to finish yackin' on about everything under the sun, while you had something important to say. That happened to us, once, up at—' My mother opens the door and gets in. 'Three letters,' she says. 'All for me.'"

Sometimes my little story overflows the available space and I have to run over on to a second postcard. This means I must find a smaller, secondary tale, or some disconnected remark, to fill up card number two.

"*Me:* (opening cupboard) 'Hey! Scrabble! We can have a game of Scrabble after tea!' *My father:* (with a scornful laugh) 'I can't wait.'"

"Dear Philip. I know you won't write back. I don't even know whether you are still at this address."

"Dear Philip. One Saturday morning I went to Coles and bought a scarf. It cost four and sixpence and I was happy with my purchase. He whisked it out of my hand and looked at the label. 'Made in China. Is it real silk? Let's test it.' He flicked on his cigarette lighter. We all screamed and my mother said, 'Don't *bite*! He's only teasing you.'"

"Dear Philip. Once, when I was fourteen, I gave cheek to him at the dinner table. He hit me across the head with his open hand. There was silence. My little brother gave a high, hysterical giggle and I laughed too, in shock. He hit me again. After the washing up I was sent for. He was sitting in an armchair, looking down. 'The reason why we don't get on any more,' he said, 'is because we're so much alike.' This idea filled me with such revulsion that I turned my swollen face away. It was swollen from crying, not from the blows, whose force had been more symbolic than physical."

"Dear Philip. Years later he read my mail. He found the contraceptive pills. He drove up to Melbourne and found me and made me come home. He told me I was letting men use my body. He told me I ought to see a psychiatrist. I was in the front seat and my mother was in the back. I thought, 'If I open the door and jump out, I won't have to listen to this any more.' My mother tried to stick up for me. He shouted at her. 'It's your fault,' he said. 'You were too soft on her.'"

"Dear Philip. I know you've heard all this before. I also know it's no worse than anyone else's story."

"Dear Philip. And again years later he asked me a personal question. He was driving, I was in the suicide seat. 'What went wrong,' he said, 'between you and Philip?' Again I turned my face away. 'I don't want to talk about it,' I said. There was silence. He never asked again. And years after *that,* in a café in Paris on my way to work, far enough away from him to be able to, I thought of that question and began to cry. Dear Philip. I forgive you for everything."

Late in the afternoon my mother and Auntie Lorna and I walk along the beach to Surfers. The tide is out: our bare feet scarcely *mark* the firm sand. Their two voices run on, one high, one low. If I speak they pretend to listen, just as I feign attention to their endless, looping discourses: these are our courtesies: this is love. Everything is spoken, nothing is said. On the way back I point out to them the smoky orange clouds that are massing far out to sea, low over the horizon. Obedient, they stop and face the water. We stand in a row, Auntie Lorna in a pretty frock with sandals dangling from her finger, my mother and I with our trousers rolled up. Once I asked my Brazilian friend a stupid question. He was listening to a conversation between me and a Frenchman about our countries' electoral systems. He was not speaking and, thinking to include him, I said, "And how do people vote *chez toi,* Rubens?" He looked at me with a small smile. "We don't have elections," he said. Where's Rio from here? "Look at those clouds!" I say. "You'd think there was another city out there, wouldn't you, burning."

Just at dark the air takes on the colour and dampness of the subtropics. I walk out the screen door and stand my gin on a fence post. I lean on the fence and look at the ocean. Soon the moon will thrust itself over the line. If I did a painting of a horizon, I think, I would make it look like a row of rocking, inverted Vs, because that's what I see when I look at it. The flatness of a horizon is intellectual. A cork pops on the first floor balcony behind me. I glance up. In the half dark two men with moustaches are smiling down at me.

"Drinking champagne tonight?" I say.

"Wonderful sound, isn't it," says the one holding the bottle.

I turn back to the moonless horizon. Last year I went camping on the Murray River. I bought the cards at Tocumwal. I had to write fast for the light was dropping and spooky noises were coming from the trees. "Dear Dad," I wrote. "I am up on the Murray, sitting by the campfire. It's nearly dark now but earlier it was beautiful, when the sun was going down and the dew was rising." Two weeks later, at home, I received a letter from him written in his hard, rapid, slanting hand, each word ending in a sharp upward flick. The letter itself concerned a small financial matter, and consisted of two sentences on half a sheet of quarto, but on the back of the envelope he had dashed off a personal message: "P.S. Dew does not rise. It *forms*."

The moon does rise, as fat as an orange, out of the sea straight in front of the unit. A child upstairs sees it too and utters long werewolf howls. My mother makes a meal and we eat it. "Going to help Mum with the dishes, are you, Miss?" says my father from his armchair. My shoulders stiffen. I am, I do. I lie on the couch and read an old *Woman's Day*. Princess Caroline of Monaco wears a black dress and a wide white hat. The knitting needles make their mild clicking. Auntie Lorna and my father come from the same town, Hopetoun in the Mallee, and when the news is over they begin again.

"I always remember the cars of people," says my father. "There was an old four-cylinder Dodge, belonging to Whatsisname. It had—"

"Would that have been one of the O'Lachlans?" says Auntie Lorna.

"Jim O'Lachlan. It had a great big exhaust pipe coming out the back. And I remember stuffing a potato up it."

"A *potato*?" I say.

"The bloke was a councillor," says my father. "He came out of the Council chambers and got into the Dodge and started her up. He only got fifty yards up the street when BA—BANG! This damn thing shot out the back—I reckon it's still going!" He closes his lips and drops his head back against the couch to hold in his laughter.

I walk past Biarritz, where globes of light float among shrubbery, and the odd balcony on the half-empty tower holds rich people out into the creamy air. A barefoot man steps out of the take-away food shop with a hamburger in his hand. He leans against the wall to unwrap it, and sees me hesitating at the slot of the letterbox, holding up the postcards and reading them over and over in the weak light from the public phone. "Too late to change it now," he calls. I look up. He grins and nods and takes his first bite of the hamburger. Beside the letterbox stands a deep rubbish bin with a swing lid. I punch open the bin and drop the postcards in.

All night I sleep safely in my bed. The waves roar and hiss, and slam like doors. Auntie Lorna snores, but when I tug at the corner of her blanket she sighs and turns over and breathes more quietly. In the morning the rising sun hits the front windows and floods the place with a light so intense that the white curtains can hardly net it. Everything is pink and golden. In the sink a cockroach lurks. I try to swill it down the drain with a cup of water but it resists strongly. The air is bright, is milky with spray. My father is already up: while the kettle boils he stands out on the edge of the grass, the edge of his property, looking at the sea.

On Fire

by

ISABEL HUGGAN

THEY OPEN THE FIRST BOTTLES of beer in the early afternoon, sitting by the water where two small children are paddling. The children (as well as a baby asleep in the cottage behind the cedar hedge) belong to Alex and Casey, who have invited David and Lily up to the lake to spend the last weekend of summer. Casey sits under a large navy-blue umbrella, while Lily lies near her on a towel, turning to brown her body with a mixture of tanning oils and lotions. But the late August sun hasn't much power and although she's been on the beach since morning her skin appears unchanged. Lily likes to go into the winter with a little additional colour, she says, or else she looks washed out by the new year (she and David have not yet begun their annual Christmas trips to Cozumel).

Casey, on the other hand, guards her paleness like a virtue and is the same shade of ivory all year round. A decade before skin cancer becomes a fashionable concern, Casey is making pronouncements about the sun being her enemy, about dangerous rays and who-knows-what-all; Lily is really getting fed up with these exaggerated claims and phobias.

Casey never used to be like this when they lived together—there was a casual ease to her then, a daring. But now she is so careful, measuring out time and food and experience in precise bits, everything weighed and measured. Lily thinks having three babies in less than six years has affected Casey's brain as well as her body for she has changed in some terrible and irrevocable way. She'd expected Casey to be a wonderful mother, possibly a little frazzled and disorganized but happy, definitely happy; instead, she has become tight-lipped and tidy. Even with all her attention to diet she has gained weight and she sits now in the blue shade of the big umbrella like an early Picasso, thickened and humourless. Worrying.

Lily finds herself annoyed by her old friend much of the time they are together (which is not often any more, maybe twice a year). She suspects that her irritation isn't only because of Casey's fretful ways, but probably has to do with her own deep frustration at being childless. She cannot prevent herself from believing that she'd be much better at motherhood than Casey is, that she'd be more relaxed, more joyfully maternal. Yes, and grateful. Casey seems not to have a shred of gratitude for these wonderful babies.

Lily turns over on her stomach and lets the sun do its business on her spine, the backs of her long legs, the soles of her feet. But what can you do, she thinks, trying to bend her thoughts in a more philosophical direction. This is just the way things are. Maybe it doesn't seem fair but who ever said life was fair?

David is further down the beach with Roger, the eldest child, who has come out of the water blue-lipped, rubbing at himself with a beach towel in a sad, little-old-man way. David is kneeling, trying to distract the small boy from his shivering by building something in the sand. Hearing his voice, Lily raises her head and watches—it is only David who is making the fort, piling up pails of sand, laughing and talking as he works. He uses a small red shovel to smooth the sides, to fashion the turrets and towers with crenellated edges. He has sent three-year-old Vicki in search of sticks and feathers—fevvers, he calls them—to decorate the top when they are done.

Roger is sitting to one side, idly arranging piles of stones. He has clearly lost interest but David is happily humming to himself and starting to dig a small trench down to the water's edge. His idea of being a father, thinks Lily as she closes her eyes against the scene, is to become a child again himself. Perhaps it is not such a bad thing that they do not yet have children. Perhaps they will never have children and that will be for the best, the laws of nature working to prevent them from becoming the awful parents they'd no doubt be. She probably wouldn't be a better mother than Casey is, not really. She'd just end up being David's mother too.

With that, she feels the prickle of self-pitying tears and blinks rapidly, burying her head in the sandy towel. She has ended up crying about one thing or another the last few visits with Alex and Casey and she can't let it happen again.

The four of them have been friends for a long time, she and Casey since their first week at university when they met in a line signing up for Journalism. "How come *you're* taking this bird course?" Casey had asked her, and Lily had been astounded and offended. She wasn't going to study journalism because it was meant to be an *easy* option: she'd already decided it would be her major. She wanted to write for a newspaper, she loved writing more than anything in the world: she'd been cultivating a fantasy of herself as a hotshot reporter since she was fourteen. But this wasn't the answer she gave to the short rude girl next to her in line.

"Because I'm a bird," she'd said, drawing herself up to full height, one foot curled around her other leg, her thin arms wrenched up and out like spindly wings, and her large, rather beakish nose thrust out in what she hoped was the supercilious demeanour of a stork or flamingo.

"Oh, thank you," Casey had sighed, her grey eyes round with delight. "I've been really worried there wasn't going to be anybody to *like* around this place. What's your name?"

They had become inseparable after that, sharing rooms and flats for the next four years until, the summer of their graduation, Casey had married Alex and had gone off with him to Pasadena where he'd been given a large and prestigious fellowship. Alex was a graduate student in astronomy when they met him; he'd turned up auditing the same music appreciation course they were taking, given by a dotty old professor who'd known Stravinsky's daughter and who played all his music at top volume in a small basement room in the chemistry building.

Those Thursday evening music classes had had such an unlikely air about them it had heightened the romantic sense of destiny surrounding Casey's falling in love. Alex didn't much appeal to Lily—she found him too moody and remote. She much preferred the sociable, gregarious boys with whom she worked on the student paper, with whom she could talk easily and crack jokes and be herself. Alex always made her feel awkward and apprehensive. But she found herself spellbound by the dazzling intensity of Casey's passion, felt herself drawn into their ardour. It had happened so swiftly; one night, after the old man had played *Rites of Spring,* Alex had declared himself and instantly Casey was his. Their love was radiant, magical, as mysterious and overwhelming as Stravinsky's strange music. Even after Lily met and married David, she still felt a lingering nostalgia for that time, that place—the stuffy little room, the eccentric professor, that richly complex, dissonant music. A lingering envy.

With David, love had taken more time. There had been a lengthy engagement while she worked for a small newspaper in the town where he was establishing his law practice, since they both wanted to make sure they were compatible before committing themselves. For Lily, it had been a period of disillusionment, discovering that the career she'd dreamt of did not satisfy her at all; she knew she ought not be bored and restless, but she was.

She thought it might have been different if she'd started on a big city daily—there'd be excitement there, a core of energy—but as it was she found daily reporting a monotonous chore and began to think more and more about raising a family. She threw out her pills and waited for the signs which would mean she could ask for maternity leave, knowing in her heart she would never return to the paper.

They've stayed in that town, David and Lily, renovating a large, turn-of-the-century house, room by room. Nearly two years ago Lily quit her job hoping, as her mother had suggested, that staying home and leading a less stressful life would allow her to get pregnant. But although she and David have followed all the suggested procedures, nothing has happened. They are considering putting their name in at the Children's Aid Society, since everyone says adoption is a surefire way to suddenly find yourself expecting, and Lily thinks she wouldn't mind having two babies at once. But the only babies available seem to be ones with problems or mixed parentage, and neither she nor David are entirely sure about shouldering that kind of burden. Still, sometimes it seems to her that anything, anything would be better than this waiting for something to happen.

She has a standard answer now whenever friends inquire how she's getting along. "I'm just a lady in waiting," she says, and gives a small self-mocking and apologetic chuckle. One night at a party David overhears her saying this and adds, "Brooding about breeding is more like it!" She laughs as loudly as everyone else at the time, but when he repeats the same thing later she looks at him sharply to see whether he is trying to wound her with his wordplay. But no, his big handsome face is flushed with good humour, he is simply enjoying the sound of language, the taste of it in his mouth. It is what makes him such a fine litigation lawyer and is why his practice is flourishing, why they can afford to have Lily stay home. She has been thinking of doing some freelance writing for magazines, maybe trying her hand at some fiction, but the house seems to take so much of her time. She is stripping the varnish off all the woodwork, doing the jobs that might be difficult or dangerous once a baby comes.

Alex has left the beach. He has gone up to the cottage to check on the sleeping baby and to bring down more beer. Casey has said she won't have any more, one is enough, but Lily is already looking forward to the bitter liquid sliding ice-cold down her throat. She hopes Alex won't take too long, and with that passing thought suddenly realizes she misses Alex when he is absent. She is at a loss to know why, for in all the years they've known each other she and he have seldom talked alone: she has known him through Casey and with David, but never directly.

To some extent she still sees him as he was a decade ago, slouching in his chair at the back of the music class, thin and sullen and burning with desire for Casey. He wasn't talkative then and seems to speak even less as time passes. He only teaches one course now at the university and the rest of his time is spent doing calculations. His work is solitary, enormous, bright with portent and infinite possibility.

But he never speaks of it, maybe because none of them will understand what he's talking about. He barely talks at all, is even more self-absorbed than he was as a student. And yet as she thinks of him now, Lily sees him as the silent centre of their circle, the still pivot around whom the other three turn, talking, talking. Perhaps, she thinks, spending so much time on her own has brought her to a new appreciation of Alex, a feeling of unspoken affinity and connection—for she has found, working on the house day after day, a pocket of quiet within herself, a need for solitude she'd never known was there.

Sometimes when David comes home in the evening, spilling over with the news of his day in court, wanting to share everything word by word, she wishes he would stop. He is too overwhelming, too verbose. She will often pick up a book, or busy herself with something to avoid these conversations. "Could we chat later, Davey? I'm just in the middle of this right now." Always nice about it, or at least she means to be.

David is singing something silly and hearty from Gilbert and Sullivan as he cheerfully digs the moat deeper on Roger's instruction. The little boy is charmed by the way the sides cave in as the water rises and he urges David to go faster, faster. Soon the walls of the fort give way to the water and David is laughing along with Roger at the ruins, not minding that all his work has been for naught. He seems to have a child's easy understanding of pleasure as an end in itself.

Watching him place a small feather in Vicki's hair, Lily is moved by the exquisite gentleness of the gesture. Maybe he would be an excellent father after all, she thinks.

Alex reappears carrying three bottles of beer held against his chest and the baby slung on one shoulder. He calls out as he comes through the hedge, "Travis was awake, Case." Lily looks up from her towel to see a grimace pass across the other woman's face, but she can't tell whether it is from resignation or resentment.

"Oh Alex, you bugger, I'll bet you woke him. He should have been good for another hour."

Alex plumps the baby down on Casey's legs in a jolly way, as if his movements might forestall the anger he sees flashing from her eyes. In her pale face the round grey eyes have always been startling, but now they are quite haunting—she has a way of opening her lids very wide, as if to see through the endless dark tunnel of baby-bound fatigue, which makes them seem even rounder and more expressive.

There is a grim set to Casey's jaw as she turns her attention to Travis, a yellow-haired and pink-skinned baby rolling in fat. "Little pig," she says, but she says it fondly, tenderly, almost as if she were speaking to a lover. "Little pig," again, as she pulls up her shirt on one side to reveal a large, brownish-purple nipple which has begun to leak milk even before the baby attaches himself.

Lily is both attracted and slightly nauseated by the sight of the blue-veined and bruised-looking breast. She tries to imagine herself with that slurping infant pulling at her body, but she cannot. "God, Casey, you must feel so useful doing that," she says affectionately.

"That's what you always say, Lil," says Casey, tossing her head back and looking at her old friend as from a long distance. "You think I'm feeling utterly fulfilled, don't you? Well I'm here to tell you what I feel is *drained*. Don't sit there and create a fantasy about motherhood, I'm telling you."

Lily feels a surge of indignation at Casey's tone of maternal condescension—it seems to her this is increasingly Casey's manner—but all she says is: "Here then, drink some of my beer and replace your bodily fluids. I'm going to swim."

She walks to the water's edge where Vicki sits with her short chubby legs stretched out in front of her, whooping with glee every time a wave washes over her feet. Lying beside her is Alex, eyes closed, balancing a bottle of beer on his flat stomach. His dry skin is freckled and almost entirely hairless (unlike David's, whose entire body is covered in crisp, wiry dark hair). On his chest the nipples are small and bright pink, like two sugar rosebuds on a cake; looking down at him, Lily thinks what foolish and futile things men's nipples are, only for decoration. As she stands there, she is filled with a rushing desire to crouch down and taste their sweetness. Alex opens his eyes and looks up at her, one eyebrow arched quizzically. "Would you care to dance?" he says.

Lily has the unnerving idea that her forehead has opened up and Alex has seen the picture in her mind. She feels her face redden and so she scuffs the sand with her toe and does a comic turn.

"Can't dance. It's against my religion," she says, and runs into the lake. She is stricken by the intimacy that has passed between them—nothing remotely like this has ever happened before. Even little Vicki seems to be caught in the crackling web of electricity and has thrown herself upon her father's body, smothering him with kisses and upsetting his beer. Alex is smiling.

Lily runs out through the shallow water to where it is deep enough to swim. This late in the summer the bottom never really gets warm during the daylight hours and the coldness Lily feels around her ankles and knees is somehow thrilling. Her bones ache as she plunges down into the dark water, her racing pulse slowed by the murky silence around her. Swimming, she feels her long hair streaming out behind her, feels it falling like scarves around her shoulders as she rises to the surface. She has swum directly out into the lake and is unable to touch bottom; she does this every time she comes here. Being frightened and not succumbing to the fear always makes her feel powerful, in control of her life. Something left over from her childhood, she guesses, this moment of decision, this moment of knowing she *will not* drown. She never allows the welling panic in her chest to rise up and close her throat.

As she swims back to shore Lily squints to see more clearly but from this far away the people on the sand are only blurs and smudges. Like a Seurat painting, she thinks, small dots of colour, my universe broken into fragments of light. Casey, the children, Alex, even David no longer solid ... just dots of colour, unconnected. Dots. (Her mother, sitting very close to her on the couch, both of them perspiring in the summer heat, that summer she had turned nine. Her mother, explaining the facts of life. "And the little egg from which you came is no bigger than the dot a pencil makes, like the period at the end of this page.") Dots. Tiny little dots within her body which somehow are not making themselves available to David's eager and dizzyheaded sperm. Her fault, her dots.

With a smooth crawl she slices through the water until her knees drag on the sand and then she rises and runs toward David, shaking her hair so that the spray flings out wildly and glistens all over his body and face.

"You should have come in," she says. "It was wonderful."

David wipes away the droplets of water from his eyes and looks up at her mildly. "But you were having such a nice time out there by yourself, Lil, I could see that. I didn't want to intrude."

She feels absurdly angry at his observing her so closely and knowing her so well. He's right, she would have felt encroached upon had he joined her—but this knowing of her is invasive, too. Is this how Casey feels about her baby sucking at her, she wonders. Is this part of marriage and motherhood inevitable, this sense of being known, being owned, being completely overtaken?

"Another beer," says Lily. "I need another beer. You want one?" He shakes his head and she walks up the beach without asking Alex and Casey who are sitting together, talking intently over Travis's head. There are four stone steps up through the hedge to the cottage which belongs to Alex's parents; they allow Alex and Casey to use it every August. It is at least sixty years old, a white clapboard structure with dark green trim around the windows and eaves and a wide screened-in porch which once looked out over the lake but now has its view blocked by the cedar windbreak. There is a sparse, dry lawn, and on either side of a flagstone path leading to the porch there is a round bed of straggly petunias made even more forlorn-looking by a rim of white-painted rocks. The yard is rich in aromas—cedar, and the honeysuckle and trumpetvine growing up over the porch, and the sweet grass which thrives in this sandy soil.

Inside the cottage there are strong, specific smells of mothballs and damp wood and years of spilt coffee on the old woodstove. The cottage has electricity (there is an ancient Kelvinator out of which Lily takes the beer) but this family of Alex's clings to old ways as much as possible when they are at the lake. As if going back in time can provide some kind of balance to their present lives, as if not flicking on a light switch can somehow transform them into people with "real" values.

Lily leans against the refrigerator to drink the first half of her beer, enjoying the coolness of the kitchen and the way its vine-covered windows convert sharp sunlight to dappled green shadows. There is something secretive and hidden about this little cottage she likes a lot; she feels as if she were still down in the cold dark water of the lake. Maybe Casey's right, she thinks. Maybe the sun *is* our enemy.

Later, in the early evening, the kitchen has become bright and warm. The four adults jostle each other within its confines, sharing the tasks of making supper and feeding the children. David is inventing a new spaghetti sauce concocted from various tins found in the cupboard; Casey is making salad and Alex is setting the table and supervising Roger and Vicki, who are eating hot dogs with ketchup. There is a steamy closeness which is not unpleasant, a grittiness which comes from sand underfoot and the sensation of still-damp bathing suits on the skin.

They will change into comfortable clothing once the children are down ("putting the children down" is Casey's phrase and strikes Lily as peculiarly sinister, suggestive of doing away with them). Lily has asked if she might give Travis his nightly bath in the sink and Casey has agreed, adding, "Just don't get moony, Lil."

It seems to Lily that with each visit the last year or so Casey has taken on more responsibility for her emotional well-being, monitoring her every shift and swell of feeling, constantly on the alert for any display of sentimentality or self-pity. As if she can't bear to see the reality of Lily's unrequited longing for babies. Lily keeps reminding herself that intervention is a kind of love, but she wishes Casey would simply let her be sad.

At this moment, she has pretended not to hear her, and has gone instead to open herself another beer—her fifth—while the tap is running for the baby's bath. She feels languid and happy, as if she were still in the lake. Travis is a remarkably placid baby, nearly nine months old and very bright-eyed. As she lathers his fat body with soap he squirms with pleasure and as she washes the folds along his thigh he squeals and splashes her. She is conscious of his small penis floating in the bubbles like a wrinkled little rosebud, and she is shy of touching it, afraid he will emit such a scream of delight the others will turn and say, "Lily, what are you up to with that child?"

Lily wonders if there is any difference between her enjoyment of Travis as she washes him and what a mother would feel. Are there levels of feeling which can be identified, labelled, and categorized? She lifts Travis out of the sink, amazed at the weight and heft of his shining body. "He's not a little pig, he's a Buddha," she says to the room at large. "A little pink Buddha."

Beside her, David is chopping onions for the sauce, and he slides his hip along the counter so that he is touching Lily as she is drying Travis. She feels surrounded by sensation—the baby's flesh, David's hip, the smell of onion, smoke, soap, beer—enveloped and enclosed. She looks at David, whose cheeks are streaming with tears, and at first she thinks that he is overcome by the sight of her holding the baby and then realizes it's the onions making him cry. Still, she feels interfered with, as if he is attempting to join her in whatever she is experiencing with small Travis. Why should she be so antagonistic, she wonders; it doesn't make sense. Yet both Casey and David set her teeth on edge with their caring.

The meal, when it is finally served after many lullabies to the children, is exactly like scores of others they have shared. The pasta is overcooked, David's sauce is highly original and almost inedible, and the salad is too sharp, tingling with lemon juice and garlic. There is a lot of bread and a lot of wine—two bottles of Hungarian red—and the local mild cheddar they always buy on the way up to the lake. Two oil lamps are burning on a shelf above the table and from outside night sounds drift in: a few final whippoorwills, crickets, frogs, and the occasional lap of a wave. Alex says that every seventh wave is larger than the previous six. He always says this and no one ever challenges him or asks if it is really true. Because he knows about the heavens, somehow they all assume he must know about the natural world as well. Even David, who loves to argue and ordinarily will not accept statements without question, gives Alex a kind of elevated station and never disputes the business of the waves.

Alex goes at the close of the meal to a cupboard and brings out a bottle of German dessert wine. "It should be cold, honey," says Casey, in a tight, careful way they all understand means that she wishes him not to open the bottle. Instead, he goes to the Kelvinator and takes out a metal tray of ice cubes, and as he drops a cube in each glass of white wine, he smiles at Casey. It is much the same way he plopped the baby on her lap earlier in the afternoon, deliberately merry, making a movement which in itself swerves around disaster.

Lily knows this oversweet wine will give her a headache but she is past caring. She wants to drink more, she feels reckless. Casey used to drink as much as the others, but the last few years she has been breast-feeding or pregnant much of the time and so there's always been a reason to avoid excess. Lily wonders if Alex drinks this much when he and Casey are alone together or if it is only when she and David are around.

For now they are sitting around a table as they have so often, the wine slowing them down and bringing them into tight focus: they belong in the same frame. Alex is smoking Camel cigarettes steadily and David is lighting and relighting his pipe with his usual earnest, jaunty dignity.

Casey, who once went through a pack a day, has become an ardent non-smoker, but even her show of being affected by the smoke—clearing her throat, wiping her eyes—does not deter the men. Alex shoves a pack across the table toward Lily and although she has never felt at ease with Casey's disapproval, she takes a cigarette out and smokes it. The gesture feels strangely defiant and adolescent.

Casey has become the centre of attention. She is animated, her grey eyes luminous, her round face glowing like a pearl in the light from the lamps. She is heated, having had just enough wine to fuel the rage she is now loosing upon them. "I'd damn well rather do it myself than have to have my husband's signature," she says.

She is telling about her latest conversation with her doctor, the obstetrician-gynecologist who has brought her three babies into the world, who knows her, she says, inside-out. She speaks of him with the fierceness women reserve for their fathers and doctors, those men with too much power. This man—she calls him Mac, they've been friends for years—is denying her the right to have a tubal ligation without Alex's consent.

"Consent!" she says, her voice harsh, and higher than usual in its force. "Consent! It's *my* bloody body and it's mine to do with as I bloody please!"

Lily looks at her friend and thinks how beautiful she is; with the extra layer of milky fat covering her bones, her even features are still perfectly defined but riper, more sensual. The bright colour now in her cheeks and the way she holds her head high are somehow thrilling, make her seem nearly glamorous in her fury at Mac. Someone else entirely from that frowning blue woman on the beach. Lily has the wildly unsettling notion, all of a sudden, that neither of these Caseys bears any resemblance to the one she thinks of as her old friend. She doesn't really know who this woman is. Nor does Casey know Lily, neither of them are the same any more. They've changed beyond recall.

"Be fair," Alex says softly. "It isn't just Mac, you know, it's the hospital's policy. And he has to work there, he has to do the operation within their regulations."

"Oh Christ, Alex, don't stick up for him." Casey's voice cuts in like a scalpel before Alex is finished, scornful and dismissive. "Mac is part of the system, he's no better than that old fart whatsisname who runs the place. He goes along with it all, he's a pig at heart the same as the rest of them."

David sucks noisily on his pipe, leans back in his chair the way he likes to do before making some sort of legal pronouncement. Lily watches him and wonders what on earth he does in court without his pipe as a prop. He is very calm and his large body stretches out from the chair, his face ruddy from the wine and the earlier laughter. But she can tell from his tone that he is upset by Casey's agitation and is responding in the only way he knows—by dampening her vehemence with reason and composure.

"Now you see, Case," he is saying, "these fellas are in a real bind. They can get themselves in trouble if they go ahead with one of these sterilizations and then later the husband says he didn't know, or he only wants her if she's fertile, et cetera, et cetera. Believe me, this is fresh ground for the courts, and everyone's being careful, not just your Mac. There are lawsuits and nasty precedents in the offing if anybody makes a wrong move. They aren't asking for consent so much as your husband's acknowledgment."

"Bullshit, David," says Casey. "If Alex signs, then that's consent. Look, you only see it from your point of view, the law. See it from mine. I don't want any more babies. Me, the baby machine."

Alex, who has been hunching over his last glass of wine and smoking heavily, speaks directly to David now as if somehow he, in his legal role, has become the arbiter of this dispute. "Look, Dave, I told her I'd go and have it done, I don't care, it means nothing to me, I only want Case to be happy. It's easier for us anyway, snip-snip in the doctor's office and done. I've told her."

His face beneath his freckles is livid with emotion. When he drinks he never gets sweaty and red-faced the way David does, he seems to become even drier. How does he drink so much and stay so lean, Lily wonders. For that matter, how do I?

"Oh, Alex, can't you hear what I'm *saying*?" Casey speaks now in a tone of sorrowful exasperation, as if to a child. "I'm fighting this on the very issue you're talking about. You don't need my permission for your snip-snip, but I need *yours*. Can't you understand? It's about my subordinate role, it's about male domination, but it's not theoretical stuff, Alex, it's real. Goddammit, listen to me!"

Lily realizes she may be a little drunk because she feels as if she is in a play but she has forgotten her lines. She knows she is meant to be on Casey's side and yet her sympathies are shifting somewhere else. "Surely having babies is not subordinate," she says. "It's because it's the most important thing in the world that these men get so uptight about it. Face it, Casey, you're only thirty years old. Couldn't Mac be concerned that in a few years you might want to have a baby again?"

Casey turns on Lily with quick, icy disdain. "You're such a romantic, Lil."

Lily is hurt but self-righteous—it makes perfect sense to her that a husband should know what's going on, after all, it takes two, doesn't it? She takes the rebuff with a thin smile, and gets up, goes to the bedroom and takes from David's overnight bag the bottle of French brandy he had stuck in at the last minute. He'd bought it last week after winning a particularly long and difficult case. "Didn't we bring this to celebrate with?" she says to David as she comes back to the table.

"What in heaven's name are we celebrating?" Casey asks, raising her eyebrows and making her eyes very round.

"The complexities of our existence," says David, in his pompous lawyer's voice, taking on a comic role to divert attention from the hostility in the air, anger so intense it is almost tangible. He loosens the heavy cork stopper and pours a little of the caramel-coloured liquid into four plastic tumblers. "You have some too, Casey," he says. "It'll do young Travis good to get some Courvoisier with his milk tonight. Here." He passes round the glasses and lifts his high above them. "To our complexities."

Lily drinks hers at one swallow while the others are still sipping. She feels an urgent need to act, to prevent the conversation from slipping back to that perilous place they've just been. She leans forward and takes the bottle by the neck, pouring herself another two fingers.

"I feel like a swim again," she says, inspired.

"You talkin' suit or you talkin' skinny?" David asks, in a mock accent he often affects to make people laugh. He has a good-ol'-boy aspect himself that makes the accent seem appropriate, even engaging.

"Skinny, honey," Lily says, flirting back in a way she never does if they are alone. "Have I evah been anythin' but skinny?"

They all laugh, for it is one of David's longstanding jokes that her knees, elbows, and hipbones are lethal weapons in bed, all of them sharp enough to draw blood. Lily *does* seem a ludicrous name for someone so angular and so unlike a flower, she thinks.

(She has had, over the past few months, a battery of fertility tests, one of which was meant to discover whether her hormonal development was retarded, but the results are inconclusive; her boyish body is no indication. There have been other tests of her inner workings as well, which have so assaulted her sense of privacy she is still, weeks later, injured in her spirit. She had lain, strapped down on a metal table under the eye of a camera, and watched on a small monitor her uterus, a white pear-shaped object glowing and fluttering on the dark screen; and then, not the neat bull's horns of medical diagram but two winding bits of thread, two tendrils of a climbing vine. Casey wants these same slender, slivery tubes of life cut, or cauterized, or plugged with plastic. Getting your tubes tied. A simple operation, nothing to it.)

"Listen, Lil, honestly, we can't go out on the beach naked. You know, we're not in the middle of nowhere." Casey is sober and sensible, and although she is laughing she is taking it upon herself to keep Lily and David in line.

"Goodness, chile," David says, "it's after midnight. There ain't gonna be no pryin' eyes down there this hour. Why don' you jest whip off them rags and come dippin' with me and my fren'?" He turns the full force of his charm upon her, a man who can disarm with his caution-to-the-wind lopsided smile—and Casey is suddenly and inexplicably taken with this jovial mood he offers. She abandons her stance and rises from the table, agreeing to swim skinny.

"But we'll take the oil lamps down with us," she says. "I don't want to leave them alight in the cottage with the kids asleep. And we have to be quiet, I mean it, David. No chortling!" She is going along with him but she is making rules—as always, Lily thinks. She always has to be the mother now.

Lily looks across the table at Alex, who is stubbing out a cigarette. His clear green eyes make her think of water, which is odd because his skin is so dry and patchy, his tangled blond hair like a small forest fire springing from his forehead. "You're coming too, aren't you?" she says, knowing his preference would be to stay quietly at the table alone. He responds by taking the lamps in his hands and holding them out as if he were leading a parade. Casey gathers the towels and they all enter the night, David and Lily giggling and shushing each other.

Out on the sand there are transparent layers of mist lying between them and the water, shreds and strands of gauze floating in the dark. Only the occasional star glitters, only a handful of distant cottage lights glimmer along the shore. The sole sounds are of crickets in the hedge, the small lapping of waves, and from down the lake someone's stereo playing music which is too urban for this setting—the sad, sophisticated undulations of a tenor sax. Alex places the lamps on the sand and Casey piles the towels beside them, glancing anxiously back at the dark cottage and her sleeping children.

Lily knows that by convention she must not look at the others while they undress but she is caught by the sight of her husband as he slips off his shorts and underwear, by the clownlike appearance of his penis hanging from its fur collar of black hair—like a false nose, like a fleshy handle. (David had done his tests first, since after all his was the easiest, involving only one hilarious morning in which he had to jump immediately in the car and drive to the medical labs with the precious vial of semen. He and his equipment had passed with flying colours.)

She cannot help it, she looks over to see what Casey looks like naked now, and is startled by the despondent heaviness of her hips and belly, the hanging breasts grotesque rather than voluptuous. Even in the resigned and ungainly way she removes her clothes Casey seems deliberately unsexy, as if she wants to be old and done with that business forever. Lily's own thin body by contrast seems a blessing, and she moves her hands along the ridges of her ribs and along her flat stomach with pride. Well, everything has its price, she thinks. Nothing new about that. She looks now to see Alex, who is pulling off his sweatshirt, standing behind Casey. He is even more of an ectomorph than she is, sinew and bone. She waits for him to take off his underpants, feeling ashamed of her prurience yet unable to turn away.

But he doesn't. He keeps his white briefs on and taking Casey's hand walks quickly into the lake, edgy and furtive. Lily wishes they were like the people she's read about in California, at Esalen and places like that, who would hold hands and chant mantras together as they entered the water, four bodies in one mind. She feels the need of ceremony and ritual to cleanse them of that conversation about

Casey tying her tubes. A conversation that is already hooking itself into their lives.

The cool night air makes the lake seem warmer than it was earlier in the day as she slides beneath the surface, enjoying the silky texture of the water on her skin. She flips over on her back and with a gentle flutter kick steers herself out past the shoreline mist, looking up at the cloud-studded sky, the drifting stars. The life Alex has chosen for himself, the security of unobtainable galaxies.

She hears David's voice calling her softly. "Don't go out too far, Lil, there's an undertow" And she turns, with a firm and graceful breast stroke making her way back to where he stands, chest-deep. He is only a little taller than she is, a wall of a man against whom she now leans, letting her wet hair drape over his shoulder. She feels the jutting of his erect penis against her thigh and brings herself closer to him, excited.

"Help," she says. "There's an enemy submarine down there." She wraps her legs around his waist and burrows her face into his throat, playfully kissing and biting the flesh of his shoulder, and then biting again so sharply that he pushes her away.

"Hey, that hurts, Lil. Cut it out!"

"Sorry," she says, unrepentant, and swims off in a dreamy way back out to deep water. She can hear Alex and Casey murmuring—they are sitting in the shallows, splashing each other softly from time to time—but she cannot hear what they are saying. It seems to Lily specifically matrimonial, this splashing of each other. The saxophone's lonely melody slips over the water and winds itself around them. But what is the tune? She almost catches it once but lets it go, and is left with an image of neon-speckled puddles on city pavement, footsteps of a departing lover down the dark street.

The haze on the lake is lifting and the night is moonless but clear when David announces he is going back to the cottage. Lily knows she has hurt him in some irredeemable way by swimming off when he wanted her; she swims back now to where he is and tries to smooth things over. "I'm coming too, Davey," she says and stands up, the nipples on her flat breasts like small thimbles in the chilly air. They dry each other and then wrap the towels around themselves, carrying their clothes and shoes. Lily takes one of the lamps and leaves the other for Casey and Alex who have begun to swim a little, still talking.

It is only Casey's voice which is audible, and there is something brittle about it, something accusatory and plaintive. Alex's voice comes and goes in monosyllabic scraps, whetting Lily's curiosity as she walks slowly back to the cottage. It reminds her of how she used to listen to them talking in the kitchen of the flat she and Casey had shared their last year at school. Alex would bring Casey back from his place late at night and she'd make him coffee and they'd sit together at the chrome and red Formica table, talking and smoking cigarettes until dawn. Lily would hear their blurred voices through her bedroom door, not yet in love herself but on the outer shell of it, knowing the sound of it from the outside in. In the morning she'd see their coffee cups and ashtrays, proof of a complicity in which she had no part.

She sets the lamp down inside the porch and gets dressed: she pulls on one of Alex's father's old cardigans which hangs on a nail by the door and holds it around herself to stop the sudden trembling that has overtaken her. Seeing her shudder, David pours her a full tumbler of brandy, which smells strangely like rotting fruit to Lily now, vile and evil. But she drinks it anyway, needing its warmth to give her strength, and curls up in a wicker chair to wait for the other two.

First to appear is Casey, clad in a towel with her clothes around her neck, not covering her large swinging breasts. They are full—she has gone past Travis's usual feeding time—and they seem bursting with self-importance. She clutches her clothes and towels to her body and runs to the cottage, her ankles splaying out from side to side as if she has a tight skirt on. She rushes past David who is sitting with his pipe on the wooden steps, past Lily and into the bedroom where they hear her getting the baby from his bed. When she re-emerges, in a blue bathrobe with Travis at her breast, her face has a lovely serenity and she is perfectly beautiful again. She settles into a chair next to Lily and smiles, stroking the fine blond hair on her son's small head.

The music from down the beach has stopped and the night is completely silent. There is only the uneven flutter of one oil lamp and then coming through the hedge the other one, held high by Alex. In his other hand he carries his clothing and towel; he is shining wet and bare to the night except for his white underpants. The light from the lamp reveals him, Eros and Psyche in one body.

Alex sets the lamp down in the centre of a petunia bed and piles his clothes beside it. He bows toward the porch and speaks in the manner of a ringmaster, a showman. "Ta-daa!" he says, and then again louder. "Ta-daa!"

This is so unlike anything Alex has ever done the other three sit open-mouthed, waiting to hear what he will say next. He is announcing that he will now dance a farewell to summer and will they all please hold their applause until he is through. David looks back over his shoulder at Lily and grins, shaking his head; Casey mutters to Travis, "Your daddy is drunk again, sweetheart." Lily is mesmerized, taut with expectation, wondering what he is going to do.

What he does is to leap over the lamp, making the flame waver and nearly go out, and then leap again, higher in the air, his arms straight out at his sides, his head held aloft and haughty. Clearly this is meant to be a spoof, a late-night amusement to send them to bed with a laugh. But there is also something very serious about his dancing, serious in the way he is demanding their attention. It reminds Lily of the way small boys play games as if their lives depend on it. Now he is jumping and pirouetting in a furious parody of ballet, now crouching and stamping in crazy imitation of African tribal dancing, but noiselessly. He snaps his fingers sharply every so often as if to keep in his mind some marking of the rhythms he must be hearing. The music of the spheres, Lily thinks and plans to offer that up next morning at breakfast. A good astronomer's joke.

As Alex dances the three others settle into themselves and begin to feel comfortable with the strangeness of his performance. His body is making shadows on the hedge, deformed and lacy shapes which stretch and shrink out of all proportion as he circles the lamp. His eyes are ablaze with excitement—he is obviously having the time of his life—and it occurs to Lily watching him that as long as there is a hedge between Alex and the outside world he feels safe and capable of liberating himself in their midst. With this dance he is taking them all with him into the most profound and private part of his soul, she thinks, and wonders if Casey knows this. She looks over at her old friend, awash in fondness for her after all the years they've shared, and sees that Casey has closed her eyes, has nestled herself closer to the sucking baby.

It seems to Lily watching Alex that his long bony fingers stream fire, that his yellow hair has caught fire too, and that there are tongues of flame licking the air around his face. Even his bare feet have a brightness, seem to be strung on wires of gold, threads of fire itself. He is an unexpected comet searing crazily through the August night, he is a puppet sprung free of its master. He is dancing faster and faster, he is becoming a firebird, he is burning up and disappearing into the ether.

But it is really only Alex, a thirty-five-year-old astronomer given to one moment of frenzy; thin, freckled Alex in his wet underwear dashing and prancing over the grass.

It is a dance of goodbye to more than summer but none of them know that at the time. Years later, after one of the marriages has ended in divorce and the two women have let their friendship dwindle into oblivion, Lily will find a postcard Casey sent to her after that last

August weekend together. It has an old black-and-white photograph of Nijinsky dancing on the front and, on the back, only this: *Booze is bad for the heart.* Lily will be shaken when she realizes the truth of what she reads, and how much Casey had understood, even with her eyes closed.

Glowing with sweat, Alex twists himself into one last glorious leap and for a grand finale lands at David's feet, arms outstretched. "The end," he says, panting, out of breath. David claps his hands softly. "Bravo," he says. "You're a real star." His voice is warm and appreciative.

Alex goes up the steps and through the door, and stands looking at Casey holding Travis, who has fallen asleep against the blue bathrobe. Lily gets up from her chair and reaches out her hand, her fingers pointing toward his chest. She touches one of his nipples, recoiling immediately as if she's received a shock.

"You're on fire," she says, herself as breathless as if she had been dancing. She will say this again later to Alex, much later when they have finally become lovers, but this is the first time she says it.

The Wasps

by

SHIMAKI KENSAKU

SOME LIVELY VISITORS to my sickroom in early summer were the wasps. Certainly the stately, dashing appearance of the wasps befitted the forerunners of an active, prosperous season. Even the melancholy sickroom seemed suddenly to acquire an air of gaiety. The wasps were never still. Of course not when they were flying around but even when they alighted, a brimful energy kept their bodies pulsing as they moved about in short, mincing steps. A waist narrow as a thread connected their chests and abdomens. At first sight their bodies seemed all an elegant slenderness, but in fact they possessed a flexible toughness and durability. Judging from their exiguous midriffs, you might think they could be easily pulled apart or snapped in two like a twig, but I doubt if they could. They had a steely lustre about them, which partook not of iron blackness but of a beautiful, gleaming blue.

Their wings, too, as they took the light, were a lovely glistening purple. There was a persimmon tree that reached down its branches an arm's length away from my sickroom window. Its small white flowers were falling now. The honeybees hummed about it busily, as if time were short. Compared with the wasps, they seemed like hardworking, honest citizens. Those mountain bandits, the hornets, were more like good-natured peasants. The wasps were like mettlesome samurai, out for glory. Once a wasp that I had just seen zoom up to the ceiling, with a resonant buzz that I couldn't believe was his, dive-bombed my pillow. No time to think that it was the wasp of just now—it was like a black pebble flung hard at me. It seemed to fly straight at my face. I threw up my right hand. I knew it was the wasp when it levelled off with a droning noise. It landed with a corpulent horsefly that lay on its side with its legs loosely bunched. As I watched, the fly gave a few spastic twitches. After a while it could not move at all. Embracing the big horsefly with its whole body—head, legs, and stinger—the wasp gave it the *coup de grâce*. They rolled over together like a burr.

Another time I saw a wasp caught in a spider's web under the eaves. It was a freshly made web, as yet unbroken. "Now you're caught," I thought. Just then the wasp, with a violent shuddering and buzzing, adroitly made its escape from the web. As if nothing had happened, it flew up toward the high summer sky. The spider, who had instantly glided down from its hiding place in the upper part of the web, seemed as surprised as myself to find its likely prey gone. That sort of resolute quickness was just like the wasps.

But there were so many of them! Busily spelling each other in their labours—not even the flies, whose numbers abruptly increased at this time, could compare with them. "So many wasps!" my human visitors would say, their eyes widening as they suddenly noticed them all. Was there a reason why the wasps liked my room?

In the lintel and window-posts of the paper door, there were a lot of little round holes. Up to now, I had not cared at all what they were, or when and why they'd been made. This was an old, remodelled farmhouse and they were just naturally there. Why they were naturally there had never occurred to me. It was only as I lay in bed day after day that I saw there was a special relationship between those holes and the wasps. When they flew in the room and alighted on the lintel or the sides of the window, the wasps walked around as if looking for something. When they found one of those holes, they always went inside it. Not once but four or five times, they came out and went back in. They seemed to conduct a minute inspection tour around each and every hole. Then they went inside. Then they came out again. The wasps were clearing some kind of trash out of the holes. In it was mixed what looked like fragments of insect wings. The holes were evidently deep enough to conceal four-fifths of the wasps' bodies. The wasps took fairly long with their housecleaning. Afterward they would fly out of the room. When one wasp came back, I saw that it was carrying something between its legs, perhaps a small, winged insect. Its legs stilled locked around its prey, the wasp entered the hole. When it had stored its booty in there, it flew away. But it was back again soon, with a new victim. This time it was something as big as the wasp itself. When I looked closely, it seemed to be a small grasshopper. Unhurriedly, the wasp pushed it inside the hole. The third time, it brought back a green caterpillar or grub. If it could hold so much, the hole must be larger than I'd thought. Most likely it wound its way back to a hollowed chamber. The wasp flew away again. By now, however, the summer's day was at an end. The wasp did not come back again.

The next day, the wasp was back by the time I'd finished breakfast. I had wondered if it would repeat the previous day's routine. As I watched, it circled and recircled the hole as if on the lookout for something. Slowly drawing the circle tighter, it circumspectly approached the hole. This time it entered not head first but by backing itself in. Once its hindquarters were inside, it stopped so that its front half protruded from the hole.

For a while it continued quietly in that pose. Quietly but not idly, as I saw when I looked closer. It was in the midst of some work that was very important to it. Now and then it would move just slightly. Then it would be still again. While straining its whole body to accomplish one thing, the wasp constantly looked about it as if for enemies that might do it harm. There was a stillness about the wasp that I could not have imagined as other than of death. I thought that its strange little face expressed an unusual seriousness. Clearly this work had to do with life … at last even I understood. The wasp was laying its eggs.

It was a long hard job. Finally the wasp came all the way out of the hole. Eased of its burden, it showed its relief at having discharged an important duty by wagging its abdomen up and down. Again it patrolled the area around the hole. Then it flew away. When it came back again, it had something else. Thrusting its head in along with whatever it was, the wasp laboured intently in the hole. When it backed out again, I was surprised. The mouth of the hole had been beautifully sealed with something like mud. A white, beautiful mud wall. I realized that what the wasp had brought before was a crumb of dirt, that it had mixed this with its own secretion and plastered up the hole. And yet, how had it achieved such whiteness? Had it kneaded its own honey into the earth?

Just as if well pleased with itself, the wasp waved its feelers around. Then, with a sonorous buzzing, it flew away.

The next day, it came by again. When it had made sure that everything was all right, it buzzed away again.

I now looked at the other holes. I saw that all of them had been plastered over in the same way.

We were midway through a torrid August. The heat that summer was the worst in many years. Already ill, I was laid low by the heat. It had worn me out to watch the wasp go about its little business for two days. The same vitality that had cheered me up in early summer now got on my nerves. Even what had been self-evident from the start, that these lively activities were on behalf of reproduction, was now repulsive to me. What if I poked a twig or straw through those white walls? I had such thoughts. No doubt if I'd been well enough to get up I would have acted on my bad impulse. It oppressed me to think that next year those eggs would hatch out. If I thought ahead even so far as a month, the future seemed vague and hazardous. But then, I also steeped myself in grandiose dreams of my life ten or twenty years from now. It seemed to me that this sort of inconsistency was a sign that my illness was getting worse. I thought of the theory that hopelessly ill persons are apt to indulge themselves in grand dreams of the future. And yet I found a pleasure, an ease of heart, in developing such dreams and dwelling on their details.

The summer passed, and autumn became winter. My lively insect-companions also went away. A few, however, were left. Flies in winter were not unusual. But what was I to make of soldier bugs in winter, and praying mantises? Until early December, you could see praying mantises by the roadside, dragging themselves along as if on stilts. But I would find them clinging to my paper door until the end of January. As for the soldier bugs, they lasted into February. They had lost all their summer greenness—perhaps it was a different species—and were now the colour of shrivelled turnip leaves. There was no trace of that smelly froth that soldier bugs exude. In the afternoon, I would place a rattan chaise longue by the south-facing window and lie on it in the sun. Then I would notice that the soldier bugs had moved along with me. Maybe a foot away from my face, they lined up companionably. We stayed there until the sun went down.

One day, I slid open the window in front of my writing table. Something like small beans fell pit-a-pat onto the table. They were ladybugs. A bevy of them had chosen to spend the winter in the warmth of my room. Soon they were everywhere: on the paper door, on the desk, and even on my books. Bearing on their black shards the rising sun of Japan, they continued their lively promenade. Some even crawled up on my bedding.

With such friendly insects, I spent the winter indoors. During that time my illness hung in the balance.

The warm time of the year came around again. One day, I heard a familiar spirited buzzing noise. It startled me. My heart beat faster. I'd forgotten all about the wasps. At the sudden memory, I looked across the room at last year's holes. Slowly sitting up, I dragged myself toward them. I examined the white, sealed entrance of one of the holes. At tiny aperture had been punched through its mud-paper wall. I looked at the other holes. Each had been broken out of, and was empty again.

Meanwhile the sound of buzzing, of one, two, and more winged insects, grew steadily louder and stronger. Soon it was everywhere in the room. For the first time, my weakened body and mind were filled by the joy of being alive.

A Pornographer Woos

by

BERNARD MACLAVERTY

I AM SITTING on the warm sand with my back to a rock watching you, my love. You have just come from a swim and the water is still in beads all over you, immiscible with the suntan oil. There are specks of sand on the thickening folds of your waist. The fine hairs on your legs below the knee are black and slicked all the one way with the sea. Now your body is open to the sun, willing itself to a deeper brown. You tan well by the sea. Your head is turned away from the sun into the shade of your shoulder and occasionally you open one eye to check on the children. You are wearing a black bikini. Your mother says nothing but it is obvious that she doesn't approve. Stretch marks, pale lightning flashes, descend into your groin.

Your mother sits rustic between us in a print dress. She wears heavy brogue shoes and those thick lisle stockings. When she crosses her legs I can see she is wearing pink bloomers. She has never had a holiday before and finds it difficult to know how to act. She is trying to read the paper but what little breeze there is keeps blowing and turning the pages. Eventually she folds the paper into a small square and reads it like that. She holds the square with one hand and shades her glasses with the other.

Two of the children come running up the beach with that curious quickness they have when they run barefoot over ribbed sand. They are very brown and stark naked, something we know again is disapproved of, by reading their grandmother's silence. They have come for their bucket and spade because they have found a brown ogee thing and they want to bring it and show it to me. The eldest girl, Maeve, runs away becoming incredibly small until she reaches the water's edge. Anne, a year younger, stands beside me with her Kwashiorkor tummy. She has forgotten the brown ogee and is examining something on the rock behind my head. She says "bloodsuckers" and I turn round. I see one, then look to the side and see another and another. They are all over the rock, minute, pin-point, scarlet spiders.

Maeve comes back with the brown ogee covered with seawater in the bucket. It is a sea-mat and I tell her its name. She contorts and says it is horrible. It is about the size of a child's hand, an elliptical mound covered with spiky hairs. I carry it over to you and you open one eye. I say, "Look." Your mother becomes curious and says, "What is it?" I show it to you, winking with the eye farthest from her but you don't get the allusion because you too ask, "What is it?" I tell you it is a sea-mat. Maeve goes off waving her spade in the air.

I have disturbed you because you sit up on your towel, gathering your knees up to your chest. I catch your eye and it holds for infinitesimally longer than as if you were just looking. You rise and come over to me and stoop to look in the bucket. I see the whiteness deep between your breasts. Leaning over, your hands on your knees, you raise just your eyes and look at me from between the hanging of your hair. I pretend to talk, watching your mother, who turns away. You squat by the bucket opening your thighs towards me and purse your mouth. You say, "It is hot," and smile, then go maddeningly back to lie on your towel.

I reach over into your basket. There is an assortment of children's clothes, your underwear bundled secretly, a squash-bottle, suntan lotion and at last—my jotter and Biro. It is a small jotter, the pages held by a wire spiral across the top. I watch you lying in front of me shining with oil. When you lie your breasts almost disappear. There are some hairs peeping at your crotch. Others, lower, have been coyly shaved. On the inside of your right foot is the dark varicose patch which came up after the third baby.

I begin to write what we should, at that minute, be doing. I have never written pornography before and I feel a conspicuous bump appearing in my bathing trunks. I laugh and cross my legs and continue writing. As I come to the end of the second page I have got the couple (with our own names) as far as the hotel room. They begin to strip and caress. I look up and your mother is looking straight at me. She smiles and I smile back at her. She knows I write for a living. I am working. I have just peeled your pants beneath your knees. I proceed to make us do the most fantastical things. My mind is pages ahead of my pen. I can hardly write quickly enough.

At five pages the deed is done and I tear the pages off from the spiral and hand them to you. You turn over and begin to read.

This flurry of movement must have stirred your mother because she comes across to the basket and scrabbles at the bottom for a packet of mints. She sits beside me on the rock, offers me one which I refuse, then pops one into her mouth. For the first time on the holiday she has overcome her shyness to talk to me on her own. She talks of how much she is enjoying herself. The holiday, she says, is taking her out of herself. Her hair is steel-grey darkening at the roots. After your father's death left her on her own we knew that she should get away. I have found her a woman who hides her emotion as much as she can. The most she would allow herself was to tell us how, several times, when she got up in the morning she had put two eggs in the pot. It's the length of the day, she says, that gets her. I knew she was terrified at first in the dining room but now she is getting used to it and even criticizes the slowness of the service. She has struck up an acquaintance with an old priest whom she met in the sitting-room. He walks the beach at low tide, always wearing his hat and carries a rolled pac-a-mac in one hand.

I look at you and you are still reading the pages. You lean on your elbows, your shoulders high and, I see, shaking with laughter. When you are finished you fold the pages smaller and smaller, then turn on your back and close your eyes without so much as a look in our direction.

Your mother decides to go to the water's edge to see the children. She walks with arms folded, unused to having nothing to carry. I go over to you. Without opening your eyes you tell me I am filthy, whispered even though your mother is fifty yards away. You tell me to burn it, tearing it up would not be safe enough. I feel annoyed that you haven't taken it in the spirit in which it was given. I unfold the pages and begin to read it again. The bump reinstates itself. I laugh at some of my artistic attempts—"the chittering noise of the venetian blinds," "luminous pulsing tide"—I put the pages in my trousers pocket on the rock.

Suddenly Anne comes running. Her mouth is open and screaming. Someone has thrown sand in her face. You sit upright, your voice incredulous that such a thing should happen to your child. Anne, standing, comes to your shoulder. You wrap your arms round her nakedness and call her "Lamb" and "Angel" but the child still cries. You take a tissue from your bag and lick one corner of it and begin to wipe the sticking sand from round her eyes. I watch your face as you do this. Intent, skilful, a beautiful face focused on other-than-me. This, the mother of my children. Your tongue licks out again wetting the tissue. The crying goes on and you begin to scold lightly giving the child enough confidence to stop. "A big girl like you?" You take the child's cleaned face into the softness of your neck and the tears subside. From the basket miraculously you produce a mint and then you are both away walking, you stooping at the waist to laugh on a level with your child's face.

You stand talking to your mother where the glare of the sand and the sea meet. You are much taller than she. You come back to me covering half the distance in a stiff-legged run. When you reach the rock you point your feet and begin pulling on your jeans. I ask where you are going. You smile at me out of the head hole of your T-shirt, your midriff bare and say that we are going back to the hotel.

"Mummy will be along with the children in an hour or so."

"What did you tell her?"

"I told her you were dying for a drink before tea."

We walked quickly back to the hotel. At first we have an arm around each other's waist but it is awkward, like a three-legged race, so we break and just hold hands. In the hotel room there are no venetian blinds but the white net curtains belly and fold in the breeze of the open window. It is hot enough to lie on the coverlet.

It has that special smell by the seaside and afterwards in the bar as we sit, slaked from the waist down, I tell you so. You smile and we await the return of your mother and our children.

The Pool

by

DAPHNE DU MAURIER

THE CHILDREN RAN OUT on to the lawn. There was space all around them, and light, and air, with the trees indeterminate beyond. The gardener had cut the grass. The lawn was crisp and firm now, because of the hot sun through the day; but near the summer-house where the tall grass stood there were dew-drops like frost clinging to the narrow stems.

The children said nothing. The first moment always took them by surprise. The fact that it waited, thought Deborah, all the time they were away; that day after day while they were at school, or in the Easter holidays with the aunts at Hunstanton being blown to bits, or in the Christmas holidays with their father in London riding on buses and going to theatres—the fact that the garden waited for them was a miracle known only to herself. A year was so long. How did the garden endure the snows clamping down upon it, or the chilly rain that fell in November? Surely sometimes it must mock the slow steps of Grandpapa pacing up and down the terrace in front of the windows, or Grandmama calling to Patch? The garden had to endure month after month of silence, while the children were gone. Even the spring and the days of May and June were wasted, all those mornings of butterflies and darting birds, with no one to watch but Patch gasping for breath on a cool stone slab. So wasted was the garden, so lost.

"You must never think we forget," said Deborah in the silent voice she used to her own possessions. "I remember, even at school, in the middle of French"—but the ache then was unbearable, that it should be the hard grain of a desk under her hands, and not the grass she bent to touch now. The children had had an argument once about whether there was more grass in the world or more sand, and Roger said that of course there must be more sand, because of under the sea; in every ocean all over the world there would be sand, if you looked deep down. But there could be grass too, argued Deborah, a waving grass, a grass that nobody had ever seen, and the colour of that ocean grass would be darker than any grass on the surface of the world, in fields or prairies or people's gardens in America. It would be taller than trees and it would move like corn in a wind.

They had run in to ask somebody adult, "What is there most of in the world, grass or sand?", both children hot and passionate from the argument. But Grandpapa stood there in his old panama hat looking for clippers to trim the hedge—he was rummaging in the drawer full of screws—and he said, "What? What?" impatiently.

The boy turned red—perhaps it was a stupid question—but the girl thought, he doesn't know, they never know, and she made a face at her brother to show that she was on his side. Later they asked their grandmother, and she, being practical, said briskly, "I should think sand. Think of all the grains," and Roger turned in triumph, "I told you so!" The grains. Deborah had not considered the grains. The magic of millions and millions of grains clinging together in the world and under the oceans made her sick. Let Roger win, it did not matter. It was better to be in the minority of the waving grass.

Now, on this first evening of summer holiday, she knelt and then lay full-length on the lawn, and stretched her hands out on either side like Jesus on the Cross, only face downwards, and murmured over and over again the words she had memorized from Confirmation preparation. "A full, perfect and sufficient sacrifice … a full, perfect and sufficient sacrifice … satisfaction, and oblation, for the sins of the whole world." To offer herself to the earth, to the garden, the garden that had waited patiently all these months since last summer, surely this must be her first gesture.

"Come on," said Roger, rousing himself from his appreciation of how Willis the gardener had mowed the lawn to just the right closeness for cricket, and without waiting for his sister's answer he ran to the summer house and made a dive at the long box in the corner where the stumps were kept. He smiled as he lifted the lid. The familiarity of the smell was satisfying. Old varnish and chipped paint, and surely that must be the same spider and the same cobweb? He drew out the stumps one by one, and the bails, and there was the ball—it had not been lost after all, as he had feared. It was worn, though, a greyish red—he smelled it and bit it, to taste the shabby leather. Then he gathered the things in his arms and went out to set up the stumps.

"Come and help me measure the pitch," he called to his sister, and looking at her, squatting in the grass with her face hidden, his heart sank, because it meant that she was in one of her absent moods and would not concentrate on the cricket.

"Deb?" he called anxiously. "You are going to play?"

Deborah heard his voice through the multitude of earth sounds, the heartbeat and the pulse. If she listened with her ear to the ground there was a humming much deeper than anything that bees did, or the sea at Hunstanton. The nearest to it was the wind, but the wind was reckless. The humming of the earth was patient. Deborah sat up, and her heart sank just as her brother's had done, for the same reason in reverse. The monotony of the game ahead would be like a great chunk torn out of privacy.

"How long shall we have to be?" she called.

The lack of enthusiasm damped the boy. It was not going to be any fun at all if she made a favour of it. He must be firm, though. Any concession on his part she snatched and turned to her advantage.

"Half-an-hour," he said, and then, for encouragement's sake, "You can bat first."

Deborah smelled her knees. They had not yet got the country smell, but if she rubbed them in the grass, and in the earth too, the white London look would go.

"All right," she said, "but no longer than half-an-hour."

He nodded quickly, and so as not to lose time measured out the pitch and then began ramming the stumps in the ground. Deborah went into the summer house to get the bats. The familiarity of the little wooden hut pleased her as it had her brother. It was a long time now, many years, since they had played in the summer house, making yet another house inside this one with the help of broken deck-chairs; but, just as the garden waited for them a whole year, so did the summer house, the windows on either side, cobweb-wrapped and stained, gazing out like eyes. Deborah did her ritual of bowing twice. If she should forget this, on her first entrance, it spelled ill-luck.

She picked out the two bats from the corner, where they were stacked with old croquet-hoops, and she knew at once that Roger would choose the one with the rubber handle, even though they could not bat at the same time, and for the whole of the holidays she must make do with the smaller one, that had half the whipping off. There was a croquet clip lying on the floor. She picked it up and put it on her nose and stood a moment, wondering how it would be if forever more she had to live thus, nostrils pinched, making her voice like Punch. Would people pity her?

"Hurry," shouted Roger, and she threw the clip into the corner, then quickly returned when she was halfway to the pitch, because she knew the clip was lying apart from its fellows, and she might wake in the night and remember it. The clip would turn malevolent, and haunt her. She replaced him on the floor with two others, and now she was absolved and the summer house at peace.

"Don't get out too soon," warned Roger as she stood in the crease he had marked for her, and with a tremendous effort of concentration Deborah forced her eyes to his retreating figure and watched him roll up his sleeves and pace the required length for his run-up. Down came the ball and she lunged out, smacking it in the air in an easy catch. The impact of ball on bat stung her hands. Roger missed the catch on purpose. Neither of them said anything.

"Who shall I be?" called Deborah.

The game could only be endured, and concentration kept, if Roger gave her a part to play. Not an individual, but a country.

"You're India," he said, and Deborah felt herself grow dark and lean. Part of her was tiger, part of her was sacred cow, the long grass fringing the lawn was jungle, the roof of the summer house a minaret.

Even so, the half-hour dragged, and, when her turn came to bowl, the ball she threw fell wider every time, so that Roger, flushed and self-conscious because their grandfather had come out on to the terrace and was watching them, called angrily, "Do try."

Once again the effort of concentration, the figure of their grandfather—a source of apprehension to the boy, for he might criticize them—acting as a spur to his sister. Grandpapa was an Indian God, and tribute must be paid to him, a golden apple. The apple must be flung to slay his enemies. Deborah muttered a prayer, and the ball she bowled came fast and true and hit Roger's off-stump. In the moment of delivery their grandfather had turned away and pottered back again through the French windows of the drawing-room.

Roger looked round swiftly. His disgrace had not been seen. "Jolly good ball," he said. "It's your turn to bat again."

But his time was up. The stable clock chimed six. Solemnly Roger drew stumps.

"What shall we do now?" he asked.

Deborah wanted to be alone, but if she said so, on this first evening of the holiday, he would be offended.

"Go to the orchard and see how the apples are coming on," she suggested, "and then round by the kitchen-garden in case the raspberries haven't all been picked. But you have to do it all without meeting anyone. If you see Willis or anyone, even the cat, you lose a mark."

It was these sudden inventions that saved her. She knew her brother would be stimulated at the thought of outwitting the gardener. The aimless wander round the orchard would turn into a stalking exercise.

"Will you come too?" he asked.

"No," she said, "you have to test your skill."

He seemed satisfied with this and ran off towards the orchard, stopping on the way to cut himself a switch from the bamboo.

As soon as he had disappeared Deborah made for the trees fringing the lawn, and once in the shrouded wood felt herself safe. She walked softly along the alleyway to the pool. The late sun sent shafts of light between the trees and on to the alleyway, and a myriad insects webbed their way in the beams, ascending and descending like angels on Jacob's ladder. But were they insects, wondered Deborah, or particles of dust, or even split fragments of light itself, beaten out and scattered by the sun?

It was very quiet. The woods were made for secrecy. They did not recognize her as the garden did. They did not care that for a whole year she could be at school, or at Hunstanton, or in London. The woods would never miss her: they had their own dark, passionate life.

Deborah came to the opening where the pool lay, with the five alleyways branching from it, and she stood a moment before advancing to the brink, because this was holy ground and required atonement. She crossed her hands on her breast and shut her eyes. Then she kicked off her shoes. "Mother of all things wild, do with me what you will," she said aloud. The sound of her own voice gave her a slight shock. Then she went down on her knees and touched the ground three times with her forehead.

The first part of her atonement was accomplished, but the pool demanded sacrifice, and Deborah had come prepared. There was a stub of pencil she had carried in her pocket throughout the school term which she called her luck. It had teeth marks on it, and a chewed piece of rubber at one end. This treasure must be given to the pool just as other treasures had been given in the past, a miniature jug, a crested button, a china pig. Deborah felt for the stub of pencil and kissed it. She had carried and caressed it for so many lonely months, and now the moment of parting had come. The pool must not be denied. She flung out her right hand, her eyes still shut, and heard the faint plop as the stub of pencil struck the water. Then she opened her eyes, and saw in mid-pool a ripple. The pencil had gone, but the ripple moved, gently shaking the water lilies. The movement symbolized acceptance.

Deborah, still on her knees and crossing her hands once more, edged her way to the brink of the pool and then, crouching there beside it, looked down into the water. Her reflection wavered up at her, and it was not the face she knew, not even the looking-glass face which anyway was false, but a disturbed image, dark-skinned and ghostly. The crossed hands were like the petals of the water lilies themselves, and the colour was not waxen white but phantom green. The hair too was not the live clump she brushed every day and tied back with ribbon, but a canopy, a shroud. When the image smiled it became more distorted still. Uncrossing her hands, Deborah leaned forward, took a twig, and drew a circle three times on the smooth surface. The water shook in ever-widening ripples, and her reflection, broken into fragments, heaved and danced, a sort of monster, and the eyes were there no longer, nor the mouth.

Presently the water became still. Insects, long-legged flies and beetles with spread wings hummed upon it. A dragon-fly had all the magnificence of a lily leaf to himself. He hovered there, rejoicing. But when Deborah took her eyes off him for a moment he was gone. At the far end of the pool, beyond the clustering lilies, green scum had formed, and beneath the scum were rooted, tangled weeds. They were so thick, and had lain in the pool so long, that if a man walked into them from the bank he would be held and choked. A fly, though, or a beetle, could sit upon the surface, and to him the pale green scum would not be treacherous at all, but a resting-place, a haven. And if someone threw a stone, so that the ripples formed, eventually they came to the scum, and rocked it, and the whole of the mossy surface moved in rhythm, a dancing-floor for those who played upon it.

There was a dead tree standing by the far end of the pool. He could have been fir or pine, or even larch, for time had stripped him of identity. He had no distinguishing mark upon his person, but with grotesque limbs straddled the sky. A cap of ivy crowned his raked head. Last winter a dangling branch had broken loose, and this now lay in the pool half-submerged, the green scum dripping from the withered twigs. The soggy branch made a vantage-point for birds, and as Deborah watched a nestling suddenly flew from the undergrowth enveloping the dead tree, and perched for an instant on the mossy filigree. He was lost in terror. The parent bird cried warningly from some dark safety, and the nestling, pricking to the cry, took off from the branch that had offered him temporary salvation. He swerved across the pool, his flight mistimed, yet reached security. The chitter from the undergrowth told of his scolding. When he had gone silence returned to the pool.

It was, so Deborah thought, the time for prayer. The water lilies were folding upon themselves. The ripples ceased. And that dark hollow in the centre of the pool, that black stillness where the water was deepest, was surely a funnel to the kingdom that lay below. Down that funnel had travelled the discarded treasures. The stub of pencil had lately plunged the depths. He had now been received as an equal among his fellows. This was the single law of the pool, for there were no other commandments. Once it was over, that first cold headlong flight, Deborah knew that the softness of the welcoming water took away all fear. It lapped the face and cleansed the eyes, and the plunge was not into darkness at all but into light. It did not become blacker as the pool was penetrated, but paler, more golden-green, and the mud that people told themselves was there was only a defence against strangers. Those who belonged, who knew, went to the source at once, and there were caverns and fountains and rainbow-coloured seas. There were shores of the whitest sand. There was soundless music.

Once again Deborah closed her eyes and bent lower to the pool. Her lips nearly touched the water. This was the great silence, when she had no thoughts, and was accepted by the pool. Waves of quiet ringed themselves about her, and slowly she lost all feeling, and had no knowledge of her legs, or of her kneeling body, or of her cold, clasped hands. There was nothing but the intensity of peace. It was a deeper acceptance than listening to the earth, because the earth was of the world, the earth was a throbbing pulse, but the acceptance of the pool meant another kind of hearing, a closing in of the waters, and just as the lilies folded so did the soul submerge.

"Deborah ... ? Deborah ... ?" Oh, no! Not now, don't let them call me back now! It was as though someone had hit her on the back, or jumped out at her from behind a corner, the sharp and sudden clamour of another life destroying the silence, the secrecy. And then came the tinkle of the cowbells. It was the signal from their grandmother that the time had come to go in. Not imperious and ugly with authority, like the clanging bell at school summoning those at play to lessons or chapel, but a reminder, nevertheless, that Time was all-important, that life was ruled to order, that even here, in the holiday home the children loved, the adult reigned supreme.

"All right, all right," muttered Deborah, standing up and thrusting her numbed feet into her shoes. This time the rather raised tone of "Deborah?", and the more hurried clanging of the cowbells, brought long ago from Switzerland, suggested a more imperious Grandmama than the tolerant one who seldom questioned. It must mean their supper was already laid, soup perhaps getting cold, and the farce of washing hands, of tidying, of combing hair, must first be gone through.

"Come on, Deb," and now the shout was close, was right at hand, privacy lost forever, for her brother came running down the alleyway swishing his bamboo stick in the air.

"What *have* you been doing?" The question was an intrusion and a threat. She would never have asked him what he had been doing, had he wandered away wanting to be alone, but Roger, alas, did not claim privacy. He liked companionship, and his question now, asked half in irritation, half in resentment, came really from the fear that he might lose her.

"Nothing," said Deborah,

Roger eyed her suspiciously. She was in that morning mood. And it meant, when they went to bed, that she would not talk. One of the best things, in the holidays, was having the two adjoining rooms and calling through to Deb, making her talk.

"Come on," he said, "they've rung," and the making of their grandmother into "they," turning a loved individual into something impersonal, showed Deborah that even if he did not understand he was on her side. He had been called from play, just as she had.

They ran from the woods to the lawn, and on to the terrace. Their grandmother had gone inside, but the cowbells hanging by the French window were still jangling

The custom was for the children to have their supper first, at seven, and it was laid for them in the dining room on a hot plate. They served themselves. At a quarter-to-eight their grandparents had dinner. It was called dinner, but this was a concession to their status. They ate the same as the children, though Grandpapa had a savoury which was not served to the children. If the children were late for supper then it put out Time, as well as Agnes, who cooked for both generations, and it might mean five minutes' delay before Grandpapa had his soup. This shook routine.

The children ran up to the bathroom to wash, then downstairs to the dining room. Their grandfather was standing in the hall. Deborah sometimes thought that he would have enjoyed sitting with them while they ate their supper, but he never suggested it. Grandmama had warned them, too, never to be a nuisance, or indeed to shout, if Grandpapa was near. This was not because he was nervous, but because he liked to shout himself.

"There's going to be a heat wave," he said. He had been listening to the news.

"That will mean lunch outside tomorrow," said Roger swiftly. Lunch was the meal they took in common with the grandparents, and it was the moment of the day he disliked. He was nervous that his grandfather would ask him how he was getting on at school.

"Not for me, thank you," said Grandpapa. "Too many wasps."

Roger was at once relieved. This meant that he and Deborah would have the little round garden-table to themselves. But Deborah felt sorry for her grandfather as he went back into the drawing-room. Lunch on the terrace could be gay, and would liven him up. When people grew old they had so few treats.

"What do you look forward to most in the day?" she once asked her grandmother.

"Going to bed," was the reply, "and filling my two hot water bottles." Why work through being young, thought Deborah, to this?

Back in the dining room the children discussed what they should do during the heat wave. It would be too hot, Deborah said, for cricket. But they might make a house, suggested Roger, in the trees by the paddock. If he got a few old boards from Willis, and nailed them together like a platform, and borrowed the orchard ladder, then they could take fruit and bottles of orange squash and keep them up there, and it would be a camp from which they could spy on Willis afterwards.

Deborah's first instinct was to say she did not want to play, but she checked herself in time. Finding the boards and fixing them would take Roger a whole morning. It would keep him employed. "Yes, it's a good idea," she said, and to foster his spirit of adventure she looked at his notebook, as they were drinking their soup, and approved of items necessary for the camp while he jotted them down. It was all part of the daylong deceit she practised to express understanding of his way of life.

When they had finished supper they took their trays to the kitchen and watched Agnes, for a moment, as she prepared the second meal for the grandparents. The soup was the same, but garnished. Little croutons of toasted bread were added to it. And the butter was made into pats, not cut in a slab. The savoury tonight was to be cheese straws. The children finished the ones that Agnes had burned. Then they went through to the drawing-room to say good night. The older people had both changed. Grandpapa was in a smoking-jacket, and wore soft slippers. Grandmama had a dress that she had worn several years ago in London. She had a cardigan round her shoulders like a cape.

"Go carefully with the bathwater," she said. "We'll be short if there's no rain."

They kissed her smooth, soft skin. It smelled of rose leaves. Grandpapa's chin was sharp and bony. He did not kiss Roger.

"Be quiet overhead," whispered their grandmother. The children nodded. The dining room was underneath their rooms, and any jumping about or laughter would make a disturbance.

Deborah felt a wave of affection for the two old people. Their lives must be empty and sad. "We *are* glad to be here," she said. Grandmama smiled. This was how she lived, thought Deborah, on little crumbs of comfort.

Once out of the room their spirits soared, and to show relief Roger chased Deborah upstairs, both laughing for no reason. Undressing, they forgot the instructions about the bath, and when they went into the bathroom—Deborah was to have first go—the water was gurgling into the overflow. They tore out the plug in a panic, and listened to the waste roaring down the pipe to the drain below. If Agnes did not have the wireless on she would hear it.

The children were too old now for boats or play, but the bathroom was a place for confidences, for a sharing of those few tastes they agreed upon, or, after quarrelling, for moody silence. The one who broke silence first would then lose face.

"Willis has a new bicycle," said Roger. "I saw it propped against the shed. I couldn't try it because he was there. But I shall tomorrow. It's a Raleigh."

He liked all practical things, and the trying of the gardener's bicycle would give an added interest to the morning of next day. Willis had a bag of tools in a leather pouch behind the saddle. These could all be felt and the spanners, smelling of oil, tested for shape and usefulness.

"If Willis died," said Deborah, "I wonder what age he would be."

It was the kind of remark that Roger resented always. What had death to do with bicycles? "He's sixty-five," he said, "so he'd be sixty-five."

"No," said Deborah, "what age when he got *there*."

Roger did not want to discuss it. "I bet I can ride it round the stables if I lower the seat," he said. "I bet I don't fall off."

But if Roger would not rise to death, Deborah would not rise to the wager. "Who cares?" she said.

The sudden streak of cruelty stung the brother. Who cared indeed ... The horror of an empty world encompassed him, and to give himself confidence he seized the wet sponge and flung it out of the window. They heard it splosh on the terrace below.

"Grandpapa will step on it, and slip," said Deborah, aghast.

The image seized them, and choking back laughter they covered their faces. Hysteria doubled them up. Roger rolled over and over on the bathroom floor. Deborah, the first to recover, wondered why laughter was so near to pain, why Roger's face, twisted now in merriment, was yet the same crumpled thing when his heart was breaking.

"Hurry up," she said briefly, "let's dry the floor," and as they wiped the linoleum with their towels the action sobered them both.

Back in their bedrooms, the door open between them, they watched the light slowly fading. But the air was warm like day. Their grandfather and the people who said what the weather was going to be were right. The heat wave was on its way. Deborah, leaning out of the open window, fancied she could see it in the sky, a dull haze where the sun had been before; and the trees beyond the lawn, day-coloured when they were having their supper in the dining room, had turned into night-birds with outstretched wings. The garden knew about the promised heat wave, and rejoiced: the lack of rain was of no consequence yet, for the warm air was a trap, lulling it into a drowsy contentment.

The dull murmur of their grandparents' voices came from the dining room below. What did they discuss, wondered Deborah. Did they make those sounds to reassure the children, or were their voices part of their unreal world? Presently the voices ceased, and then there was a scraping of chairs, and voices from a different quarter, the drawing-room now, and a faint smell of their grandfather's cigarette.

Deborah called softly to her brother but he did not answer. She went through to his room, and he was asleep. He must have fallen asleep suddenly, in the midst of talking. She was relieved. Now she could be alone again, and not have to keep up the pretence of sharing conversation. Dusk was everywhere, the sky a deepening black. "When they've gone up to bed," thought Deborah, "then I'll be truly alone." She knew what she was going to do. She waited there, by the open window, and the deepening sky lost the veil that covered it, the haze disintegrated, and the stars broke through. Where there had been nothing was life, dusty and bright, and the waiting earth gave off a scent of knowledge. Dew rose from the pores. The lawn was white.

Patch, the old dog, who slept at the end of Grandpapa's bed on a plaid rug, came out on to the terrace and barked hoarsely. Deborah leaned out and threw a piece of creeper on to him. He shook his back. Then he waddled slowly to the flower-tub above the steps and cocked his leg. It was his nightly routine. He barked once more, staring blindly at the hostile trees, and went back into the drawing-room. Soon afterwards, someone came to close the windows—Grandmama, thought Deborah, for the touch was light. "They are shutting out the best," said the child to herself, "all the meaning, and all the point." Patch, being an animal, should know better. He ought to be in a kennel where he could watch, but instead, grown fat and soft, he preferred the bumpiness of her grandfather's bed. He had forgotten the secrets. So had they, the old people.

Deborah heard her grandparents come upstairs. First her grandmother, the quicker of the two, and then her grandfather, more laboured, saying a word or two to Patch as the little dog wheezed his way up. There was a general clicking of lights and shutting of doors. Then silence. How remote, the world of the grandparents, undressing with curtains closed. A pattern of life unchanged for so many years. What went on without would never be known. "He that has ears to hear, let him hear," said Deborah, and she thought of the callousness of Jesus which no priest could explain. Let the dead bury their dead. All the people in the world, undressing now, or sleeping, not just in the village but in cities and capitals, they were shutting out the truth, they were burying their dead. They wasted silence.

The stable clock struck eleven. Deborah pulled on her clothes. Not the cotton frock of the day, but her old jeans that Grandmama disliked, rolled up above her knees. And a jersey. Sandshoes with a hole that did not matter. She was cunning enough to go down by the back stairs. Patch would bark if she tried the front stairs, close to the grandparents' rooms. The backstairs led past Agnes' room, which smelled of apples though she never ate fruit. Deborah could hear her snoring. She would not even wake on Judgment Day. And this led her to wonder on the truth of that fable too, for there might be so many millions by then who liked their graves—Grandpapa, for instance, fond of his routine, and irritated at the sudden riot of trumpets.

Deborah crept past the pantry and the servants' hall—it was only a tiny sitting-room for Agnes, but long usage had given it the dignity of the name—and unlatched and unbolted the heavy back door. Then she stepped outside, on to the gravel, and took the long way round by the front of the house so as not to tread on the terrace, fronting the lawns and the garden.

The warm night claimed her. In a moment it was part of her. She walked on the grass, and her shoes were instantly soaked. She flung up her arms to the sky. Power ran to her fingertips. Excitement was communicated from the waiting trees, and the orchard, and the paddock; the intensity of their secret life caught at her and made her run. It was nothing like the excitement of ordinary looking forward, of birthday presents, of Christmas stockings, but the pull of a magnet—her grandfather had shown her once how it worked, little needles springing to the jaws—and now night and the sky above were a vast magnet, and the things that waited below were needles, caught up in the great demand.

Deborah went to the summer house, and it was not sleeping like the house fronting the terrace but open to understanding, sharing complicity. Even the dusty windows caught the light, and the cobwebs shone. She rummaged for the old lilo and the moth-eaten car rug that Grandmama had thrown out two summers ago, and bearing them over her shoulder she made her way to the pool. The alleyway was ghostly, and Deborah knew, for all her mounting tension, that the test was hard. Part of her was still body-bound, and afraid of shadows. If anything stirred she would jump and know true terror. She must show defiance, though. The woods expected it. Like old wise lamas they expected courage.

She sensed approval as she ran the gauntlet, the tall trees watching. Any sign of turning back, of panic, and they would crowd upon her in a choking mass, smothering protest. Branches would become arms, gnarled and knotty, ready to strangle, and the leaves of the higher trees fold in and close like the sudden furling of giant umbrellas. The smaller undergrowth, obedient to the will, would become a briary of a million thorns where animals of no known world crouched snarling, their eyes on fire. To show fear was to show misunderstanding. The woods were merciless.

Deborah walked the alleyway to the pool, her left hand holding the lilo and the rug on her shoulder, her right hand raised in salutation. This was a gesture of respect. Then she paused before the pool and laid down her burden beside it. The lilo was to be her bed, the rug her cover. She took off her shoes, also in respect, and lay down upon the lilo. Then, drawing the rug to her chin, she lay flat, her eyes upon the sky. The gauntlet of the alleyway over, she had no more fear. The woods had accepted her, and the pool was the final resting-place, the doorway, the key.

"I shan't sleep," thought Deborah. "I shall just lie awake here all the night and wait for morning, but it will be a kind of introduction to life, like being confirmed."

The stars were thicker now than they had been before. No space in the sky without a prick of light, each star a sun. Some, she thought, were newly born, white-hot, and others wise and colder, nearing completion. The law encompassed them, fixing the riotous path, but how they fell and tumbled depended upon themselves. Such peace, such stillness, such sudden quietude, excitement gone. The trees were no longer menacing but guardians and the pool was primeval water, the first, the last.

Then Deborah stood at the wicket-gate, the boundary, and there was a woman with outstretched hand, demanding tickets, "Pass through," she said when Deborah reached her. "We saw you coming." The wicket-gate became a turnstile. Deborah pushed against it and there was no resistance, she was through.

"What is it?" she asked. "Am I really here at last? Is this the bottom of the pool?"

"It could be," smiled the woman. "There are so many ways. You just happened to choose this one."

Other people were pressing to come through. They had no faces, they were only shadows. Deborah stood aside to let them by, and in a moment they had gone, all phantoms.

"Why only now, tonight?" asked Deborah. "Why not in the afternoon, when I came to the pool?"

"It's a trick," said the woman. "You seize on the moment in time. We were here this afternoon. We're always here. Our life goes on around you, but nobody knows it. The trick's easier by night, that's all."

"Am I dreaming, then?" asked Deborah.

"No," said the woman, "this isn't a dream. And it isn't death, either. It's the secret world."

The secret world.... It was something Deborah had always known, and now the pattern was complete. The memory of it, and the relief, were so tremendous that something seemed to burst inside her heart.

"Of course ..." she said, "of course ..." and everything that had ever been fell into place. There was no disharmony. The joy was indescribable, and the surge of feeling, like wings about her in the air, lifted her away from the turnstile and the woman, and she had all knowledge. That was it—the invasion of knowledge.

"I'm not myself, then, after all," she thought. "I knew I wasn't. It was only the task given," and, looking down, she saw a little child who was blind trying to find her way. Pity seized her. She bent down and put her hands on the child's eyes, and they opened, and the child was herself at two years old. The incident came back. It was when her mother died and Roger was born.

"It doesn't matter after all," she told the child. "You are not lost. You don't have to go on crying." Then the child that had been herself melted, and became absorbed in the water and the sky, and the joy of the invading flood intensified so that there was no body at all but only being. No words, only movements. And the beating of wings. This above all, the beating of wings.

"Don't let me go!" It was a pulse in her ear, and a cry, and she saw the woman at the turnstile put up her hands to hold her. Then there was such darkness, such dragging, terrible darkness, and the beginning of pain all over again, the leaden heart, the tears, the misunderstanding. The voice saying "No!" was her own harsh, worldly voice, and she was staring at the restless trees, black and ominous against the sky. One hand trailed in the water of the pool.

Deborah sat up, sobbing. The hand that had been in the pool was wet and cold. She dried it on the rug. And suddenly she was seized with such fear that her body took possession, and throwing aside the rug she began to run along the alleyway, the dark trees mocking and the welcome of the woman at the turnstile turned to treachery. Safety lay in the house behind the closed curtains, security was with the grandparents sleeping in their beds, and like a leaf driven before a whirlwind Deborah was out of the woods and across the silver soaking lawn, up the steps beyond the terrace and through the garden-gate to the back door.

The slumbering solid house received her. It was like an old staid person who, surviving many trials, had learned experience. "Don't take any notice of them," it seemed to say, jerking its head—did a house have a head?—towards the woods beyond. "They've made no contribution to civilization. I'm man-made and different. This is where you belong, dear child. Now settle down."

Deborah went back again upstairs and into her bedroom. Nothing had changed. It was still the same. Going to the open window she saw that the woods and the lawn seemed unaltered from the moment, how long back she did not know, when she had stood there, deciding upon the visit to the pool. The only difference now was in herself. The excitement had gone, the tension too. Even the terror of those last moments, when her flying feet had brought her to the house, seemed unreal.

She drew the curtains, just as her grandmother might have done, and climbed into bed. Her mind was now preoccupied with practical difficulties, like explaining the presence of the lilo and the rug beside the pool. Willis might find them, and tell her grandfather. The feel of her own pillow, and of her own blankets, reassured her. Both were familiar. And being tired was familiar too, it was a solid bodily ache, like the tiredness after too much jumping or cricket. The thing was, though—and the last remaining conscious thread of thought decided to postpone conclusion until the morning—which was real? This safety of the house, or the secret world?

2

When Deborah woke next morning she knew at once that her mood was bad. It would last her for the day. Her eyes ached, and her neck was stiff, and there was a taste in her mouth like magnesia. Immediately Roger came running into her room, his face refreshed and smiling from some dreamless sleep, and jumped on her bed.

"It's come," he said, "the heat wave's come. It's going to be ninety in the shade."

Deborah considered how best she could damp his day. "It can go to a hundred for all I care," she said. "I'm going to read all morning."

His face fell. A look of bewilderment came into his eyes. "But the house?" he said. "We'd decided to have a house in the trees, don't you remember? I was going to get some planks from Willis."

Deborah turned over in bed and humped her knees. "You can, if you like," she said. "I think it's a silly game."

She shut her eyes, feigning sleep, and presently she heard his feet patter slowly back to his own room, and then the thud of a ball against the wall. If he goes on doing that, she thought maliciously, Grandpapa will ring his bell, and Agnes will come panting up the stairs. She hoped for destruction, for grumbling and snapping, and everyone falling out, not speaking. That was the way of the world.

The kitchen, where the children breakfasted, faced west, so it did not get the morning sun. Agnes had hung up fly-papers to catch wasps. The cereal, puffed wheat, was soggy. Deborah complained, mashing the mess with her spoon.

"It's a new packet," said Agnes. "You're mighty particular all of a sudden."

"Deb's got out of bed the wrong side," said Roger.

The two remarks fused to make a challenge. Deborah seized the nearest weapon, a knife, and threw it at her brother. It narrowly missed his eye, but cut his cheek. Surprised, he put his hand to his face and felt the blood. Hurt, not by the knife but by his sister's action, his face turned red and his lower lip quivered. Deborah ran out of the kitchen and slammed the door. Her own violence distressed her, but the power of the mood was too strong. Going on to the terrace, she saw that the worst had happened. Willis had found the lilo and the rug, and had put them to dry in the sun. He was talking to her grandmother. Deborah tried to slip back into the house, but it was too late.

"Deborah, how very thoughtless of you," said Grandmama. "I tell you children every summer that I don't mind your taking the things from the hut into the garden if only you'll put them back."

Deborah knew she should apologize, but the mood forbade it. "That old rug is full of moth," she said contemptuously, "and the lilo has a rainproof back. It doesn't hurt them."

They both stared at her, and her grandmother flushed, just as Roger had done when she had thrown the knife at him. Then her grandmother turned her back and continued giving some instructions to the gardener.

Deborah stalked along the terrace, pretending that nothing had happened, and skirting the lawn she made her way towards the orchard and so to the fields beyond. She picked up a windfall, but as soon as her teeth bit into it the taste was green. She threw it away. She went and sat on a gate and stared in front of her, looking at nothing. Such deception everywhere. Such sour sadness. It was like Adam and Eve being locked out of paradise. The Garden of Eden was no more. Somewhere, very close, the woman at the turnstile waited to let her in, the secret world was all about her, but the key was gone. Why had she ever come back? What had brought her?

People were going about their business. The old man who came three days a week to help Willis was sharpening his scythe behind the toolshed. Beyond the field where the lane ran towards the main road she could see the top of the postman's head. He was pedalling his bicycle towards the village. She heard Roger calling, "Deb? Deb … ?", which meant that he had forgiven her, but still the mood held sway and she did not answer. Her own dullness made her own punishment. Presently a knocking sound told her that he had got the planks from Willis and had embarked on the building of his house. He was like his grandfather; he kept to the routine set for himself.

Deborah was consumed with pity. Not for the sullen self humped upon the gate, but for all of them going about their business in the world who did not hold the key. The key was hers, and she had lost it. Perhaps if she worked her way through the long day the magic would return with evening and she would find it once again. Or even now, by the pool, there might be a clue, a vision.

Deborah slid off the gate and went the long way round. By skirting the fields, parched under the sun, she could reach the other side of the wood and meet no one. The husky wheat was stiff. She had to keep close to the hedge to avoid brushing it, and the hedge was tangled. Foxgloves had grown too tall and were bending with empty sockets, their flowers gone. There were nettles everywhere. There was no gate into the wood, and she had to climb the pricking hedge with the barbed wire tearing her knickers. Once in the wood some measure of peace returned, but the alleyways this side had not been scythed, and the grass was long. She had to wade through it like a sea, brushing it aside with her hands.

She came upon the pool from behind the monster tree, the hybrid whose naked arms were like a dead man's stumps, projecting at all angles. This side, on the lip of the pool, the scum was carpet-thick, and all the lilies, coaxed by the risen sun, had opened wide. They basked as lizards bask on hot stone walls. But here, with stems in water, they swung in grace, cluster upon cluster, pink and waxen white. "They're asleep," thought Deborah. "So is the wood. The morning is not their time," and it seemed to her beyond possibility that the turnstile was at hand and the woman waiting, smiling. "She said they were always there, even in the day, but the truth is that being a child I'm blinded in the day. I don't know how to see."

She dipped her hands in the pool, and the water was tepid brown. She tasted her fingers, and the taste was rank. Brackish water, stagnant from long stillness. Yet beneath ... beneath, she knew, by night the woman waited, and not only the woman but the whole secret world. Deborah began to pray. "Let it happen again," she whispered. "Let it happen again. Tonight. I won't be afraid."

The sluggish pool made no acknowledgment, but the very silence seemed a testimony of faith, of acceptance. Beside the pool, where the imprint of the lilo had marked the moss, Deborah found a kirby-grip, fallen from her hair during the night. It was proof of visitation. She threw it into the pool as part of the treasury. Then she walked back into the ordinary day and the heat wave, and her black mood was softened. She went to find Roger in the orchard. He was busy with the platform. Three of the boards were fixed, and the noisy hammering was something that had to be borne. He saw her coming, and as always, after trouble, sensed that her mood had changed and mention must never be made of it. Had he called, "Feeling better?", it would have revived the antagonism, and she might not play with him all the day. Instead, he took no notice. She must be the first to speak.

Deborah waited at the foot of the tree, then bent, and handed him up an apple. It was green, but the offering meant peace. He ate it manfully. "Thanks," he said. She climbed into the tree beside him and reached for the box of nails. Contact had been renewed. All was well between them.

3

The hot day spun itself out like a web. The heat haze stretched across the sky, dun-coloured and opaque. Crouching on the burning boards of the apple tree, the children drank ginger beer and fanned themselves with dock-leaves. They grew hotter still. When the cowbells summoned them for lunch they found that their grandmother had drawn the curtains of all the rooms downstairs, and the drawing-room was a vault and strangely cool. They flung themselves into chairs. No one was hungry. Patch lay under the piano, his soft mouth dripping saliva. Grandmama had changed into a sleeveless linen dress never before seen, and Grandpapa, in a dented panama, carried a fly-whisk used years ago in Egypt.

"Ninety-one," he said grimly, "on the Air Ministry roof. It was on the one o'clock news."

Deborah thought of the men who must measure heat, toiling up and down on this Ministry roof with rods and tapes and odd-shaped instruments. Did anyone care but Grandpapa?

"Can we take our lunch outside?" asked Roger.

His grandmother nodded. Speech was too much effort, and she sank languidly into her chair at the foot of the dining-room table. The roses she had picked last night had wilted.

The children carried chicken drumsticks to the summer house. It was too hot to sit inside, but they sprawled in the shadow it cast, their heads on faded cushions shedding kapok. Somewhere, far above their heads, an aeroplane climbed like a small silver fish, and was lost in space.

"A Meteor," said Roger. "Grandpapa says they're obsolete."

Deborah thought of Icarus, soaring towards the sun. Did he know when his wings began to melt? How did he feel? She stretched out her arms and thought of them as wings. The fingertips would be the first to curl, and then turn cloggy soft, and useless. What terror in the sudden loss of height, the drooping power …

Roger, watching her, hoped it was some game. He threw his picked drumstick into a flower-bed and jumped to his feet.

"Look," he said, "I'm a Javelin," and he too stretched his arms and ran in circles, banking. Jet noises came from his clenched teeth. Deborah dropped her arms and looked at the drumstick. What had been clean and white from Roger's teeth was now earth-brown. Was it offended to be chucked away? Years later, when everyone was dead, it would be found, moulded like a fossil. Nobody would care.

"Come on," said Roger.

"Where to?" she asked.

"To fetch the raspberries," he said.

"You go," she told him.

Roger did not like going into the dining room alone. He was self-conscious. Deborah made a shield from the adult eyes. In the end he consented to fetch the raspberries without her on condition that she played cricket after tea. After tea was a long way off.

She watched him return, walking very slowly, bearing the plates of raspberries and clotted cream. She was seized with sudden pity, that same pity which, earlier, she had felt for all people other than herself. How absorbed he was, how intent on the moment that held him. But tomorrow he would be some old man far away, the garden forgotten, and this day long past.

"Grandmama says it can't go on," he announced. "There'll have to be a storm."

But why? Why not forever? Why not breathe a spell so that all of them could stay locked and dreaming like the courtiers in the *Sleeping Beauty,* never knowing, never waking, cobwebs in their hair and on their hands, tendrils imprisoning the house itself?

"Race me," said Roger, and to please him she plunged her spoon into the mush of raspberries but finished last, to his delight.

No one moved during the long afternoon. Grandmama went upstairs to her room. The children saw her at her window in her petticoat drawing the curtains close. Grandpapa put his feet up in the drawing-room, a handkerchief over his face. Patch did not stir from his place under the piano. Roger, undefeated, found employment still. He first helped Agnes to shell peas for supper, squatting on the back-door step while she relaxed on a lop-sided basket chair dragged from the servants' hall. This task finished, he discovered a tin-bath, put away in the cellar, in which Patch had been washed in younger days. He carried it to the lawn and filled it with water. Then he stripped to bathing-trunks and sat in it solemnly, an umbrella over his head to keep off the sun.

Deborah lay on her back behind the summer house, wondering what would happen if Jesus and Buddha met. Would there be discussion, courtesy, an exchange of views like politicians at summit talks? Or were they after all the same person, born at separate times? The queer thing was that this topic, interesting now, meant nothing in the secret world. Last night, through the turnstile, all problems disappeared. They were non-existent. There was only the knowledge and the joy.

She must have slept, because when she opened her eyes she saw to her dismay that Roger was no longer in the bath but was hammering the cricket-stumps into the lawn. It was a quarter-to-five.

"Hurry up," he called, when he saw her move. "I've had tea."

She got up and dragged herself into the house, sleepy still, and giddy. The grandparents were in the drawing-room, refreshed from the long repose of the afternoon. Grandpapa smelled of eau-de-cologne. Even Patch had come to and was lapping his saucer of cold tea.

"You look tired," said Grandmama critically. "Are you feeling all right?"

Deborah was not sure. Her head was heavy. It must have been sleeping in the afternoon, a thing she never did.

"I think so," she answered, "but if anyone gave me roast pork I know I'd be sick."

"No one suggested you should eat roast pork," said her grandmother, surprised. "Have a cucumber sandwich, they're cool enough."

Grandpapa was lying in wait for a wasp. He watched it hover over his tea, grim, expectant. Suddenly he slammed at the air with his whisk. "Got the brute," he said in triumph. He ground it into the carpet with his heel. It made Deborah think of Jehovah.

"Don't rush around in the heat," said Grandmama. "It isn't wise. Can't you and Roger play some nice, quiet game?"

"What sort of game?" asked Deborah.

But her grandmother was without invention. The croquet mallets were all broken. "We might pretend to be dwarfs and use the heads," said Deborah, and she toyed for a moment with the idea of squatting to croquet. Their knees would stiffen, though, it would be too difficult.

"I'll read aloud to you, if you like," said Grandmama.

Deborah seized upon the suggestion. It delayed cricket. She ran out on to the lawn and padded the idea to make it acceptable to Roger.

"I'll play afterwards," she said, "and that ice-cream that Agnes has in the fridge, you can eat all of it. I'll talk tonight in bed."

Roger hesitated. Everything must be weighed. Three goods to balance evil.

"You know that stick of sealing-wax Daddy gave you?" he said.

"Yes."

"Can I have it?"

The balance for Deborah too. The quiet of the moment in opposition to the loss of the long thick stick so brightly red.

"All right," she grudged.

Roger left the cricket stumps and they went into the drawing-room. Grandpapa, at the first suggestion of reading aloud, had disappeared, taking Patch with him. Grandmama had cleared away the tea. She found her spectacles and the book. It was *Black Beauty*. Grandmama kept no modern children's books, and this made common ground for the three of them. She read the terrible chapter where the stable lad lets Beauty get overheated and gives him a cold drink and does not put on his blanket. The story was suited to the day. Even Roger listened entranced. And Deborah, watching her grandmother's calm face and hearing her careful voice reading the sentences, thought how strange it was that Grandmama could turn herself into Beauty with such ease, She *was* a horse, suffering there with pneumonia in the stable, being saved by the wise coachman.

After the reading, cricket was anti-climax, but Deborah must keep her bargain. She kept thinking of Black Beauty writing the book. It showed how good the story was, Grandmama said, because no child had ever yet questioned the practical side of it, or posed the picture of a horse with a pen in its hoof.

"A modern horse would have a typewriter," thought Deborah, and she began to bowl to Roger, smiling to herself as she did so because of the twentieth-century Beauty clacking with both hoofs at a machine.

This evening, because of the heat wave, the routine was changed. They had their baths first, before their supper, for they were hot and exhausted from the cricket. Then, putting on pyjamas and cardigans, they ate their supper on the terrace. For once Grandmama was indulgent. It was still so hot that they could not take chill, and the dew had not yet risen. It made a small excitement, being in pyjamas on the terrace. Like people abroad, said Roger. Or natives in the South Seas, said Deborah. Or beachcombers who had lost caste. Grandpapa, changed into a white tropical jacket, had not lost caste.

"He's a white trader," whispered Deborah. "He's made a fortune out of pearls."

Roger choked. Any joke about his grandfather, whom he feared, had all the sweet agony of danger.

"What's the thermometer say?" asked Deborah.

Her grandfather, pleased at her interest, went to inspect it.

"Still above eighty," he said with relish.

Deborah, when she cleaned her teeth later, thought how pale her face looked in the mirror above the wash-basin. It was not brown, like Roger's, from the day in the sun, but wan and yellow. She tied back her hair with a ribbon, and the nose and chin were peaky sharp. She yawned largely, as Agnes did in the kitchen on Sunday afternoons.

"Don't forget you promised to talk," said Roger quickly.

Talk.... That was the burden. She was so tired she longed for the white smoothness of her pillow, all blankets thrown aside, bearing only a single sheet. But Roger, wakeful on his bed, the door between them wide, would not relent. Laughter was the one solution, and to make him hysterical, and so exhaust him sooner, she fabricated a day in the life of Willis, from his first morning kipper to his final glass of beer at the village inn. The adventures in between would have tried Gulliver. Roger's delight drew protests from the adult world below. There was the sound of a bell, and then Agnes came up the stairs and put her head round the corner of Deborah's door.

"Your Granny says you're not to make so much noise," she said.

Deborah, spent with invention, lay back and closed her eyes. She could go no further. The children called good night to each other, both speaking at the same time, from age-long custom, beginning with their names and addresses and ending with the world, the universe, and space. Then the final main "Good night," after which neither must ever speak, on pain of unknown calamity.

"I must try and keep awake," thought Deborah, but the power was not in her. Sleep was too compelling, and it was hours later that she opened her eyes and saw her curtains blowing and the forked flash light the ceiling, and heard the trees tossing and sobbing against the sky. She was out of bed in an instant. Chaos had come. There were no stars, and the night was sulphurous. A great crack split the heavens and tore them in two. The garden groaned. If the rain would only fall there might be mercy, and the trees, imploring, bowed themselves this way and that, while the vivid lawn, bright in expectation, lay like a sheet of metal exposed to flame. Let the waters break. Bring down the rain.

Suddenly the lightning forked again, and standing there, alive yet immobile, was the woman by the turnstile. She stared up at the windows of the house, and Deborah recognized her. The turnstile was there, inviting entry, and already the phantom figures, passing through it, crowded towards the trees beyond the lawn. The secret world was waiting. Through the long day, while the storm was brewing, it had hovered there unseen beyond her reach, but now that night had come, and the thunder with it, the barriers were down. Another crack, mighty in its summons, the turnstile yawned, and the woman with her hand upon it smiled and beckoned.

Deborah ran out of the room and down the stairs. Somewhere somebody called—Roger, perhaps, it did not matter—and Patch was barking; but caring nothing for concealment she went through the dark drawing-room and opened the French window on to the terrace. The lightning searched the terrace and lit the paving, and Deborah ran down the steps on to the lawn where the turnstile gleamed.

Haste was imperative. If she did not run the turnstile might be closed, the woman vanish, and all the wonder of the sacred world be taken from her. She was in time. The woman was still waiting. She held out her hand for tickets, but Deborah shook her head. "I have none." The woman, laughing, brushed her through into the secret world where there were no laws, no rules, and all the faceless phantoms ran before her to the woods, blown by the rising wind. Then the rain came. The sky, deep brown as the lightning pierced it, opened, and the water hissed to the ground, rebounding from the earth in bubbles. There was no order now in the alleyway. The ferns had turned to trees, the trees to Titans. All moved in ecstasy, with sweeping limbs, but the rhythm was broken up, tumultuous, so that some of them were bent backwards, torn by the sky, and others dashed their heads to the undergrowth where they were caught and beaten.

In the world behind, laughed Deborah as she ran, this would be punishment, but here in the secret world it was a tribute. The phantoms who ran beside her were like waves. They were linked one with another, and they were, each one of them, and Deborah too, part of the night force that made the sobbing and the laughter. The lightning forked where they willed it, and the thunder cracked as they looked upwards to the sky.

The pool had come alive. The water lilies had turned to hands, with palms upraised, and in the far corner, usually so still under the green scum, bubbles sucked at the surface, steaming and multiplying as the torrents tell. Everyone crowded to the pool. The phantoms bowed and crouched by the water's edge, and now the woman had set up her turnstile in the middle of the pool, beckoning them once more. Some remnant of a sense of social order rose in Deborah and protested.

"But we've already paid," she shouted, and remembered a second later that she had passed through free. Must there be duplication? Was the secret world a rainbow, always repeating itself, alighting on another hill when you believed yourself beneath it? No time to think. The phantoms had gone through. The lightning, streaky white, lit the old dead monster tree with his crown of ivy, and because he had no spring now in his joints he could not sway in tribute with the trees and ferns, but had to remain there, rigid, like a crucifix.

"And now … and now … and now …" called Deborah.

The triumph was that she was not afraid, was filled with such wild acceptance.… She ran into the pool. Her living feet felt the mud and the broken sticks and all the tangle of old weeds, and the water was up to her armpits and her chin. The lilies held her. The rain blinded her. The woman and the turnstile were no more.

"Take me too," cried the child. "Don't leave me behind!" In her heart was a savage disenchantment. They had broken their promise, they had left her in the world. The pool that claimed her now was not the pool of secrecy, but dank, dark, brackish water choked with scum.

4

"Grandpapa says he's going to have it fenced round," said Roger. 'It should have been done years ago. A proper fence, then nothing can ever happen. But barrow-loads of shingle tipped in it first. Then it won't be a pool, but just a dewpond. Dewponds aren't dangerous."

He was looking at her over the edge of her bed. He had risen in status, being the only one of them downstairs, the bearer of tidings good or ill, the go-between. Deborah had been ordered two days in bed.

"I should think by Wednesday," he went on, "you'd be able to play cricket. It's not as if you're hurt. People who walk in their sleep are just a bit potty."

"I did not walk in my sleep," said Deborah.

"Grandpapa said you must have done," said Roger. "It was a good thing that Patch woke him up and he saw you going across the lawn ..." Then, to show his release from tension, he stood on his hands.

Deborah could see the sky from her bed. It was flat and dull. The day was a summer day that had worked through storm. Agnes came into the room with junket on a tray. She looked important.

"Now run off," she said to Roger. "Deborah doesn't want to talk to you. She's supposed to rest."

Surprisingly, Roger obeyed, and Agnes placed the junket on the table beside the bed. "You don't feel hungry, I expect," she said. "Never mind, you can eat this later, when you fancy it. Have you got a pain? It's usual, the first time."

"No," said Deborah.

What had happened to her was personal. They had prepared her for it at school, but nevertheless it was a shock, not to be discussed with Agnes. The woman hovered a moment, in case the child asked questions; but, seeing that none came, she turned and left the room.

Deborah, her cheek on her hand, stared at the empty sky The heaviness of knowledge lay upon her, a strange, deep sorrow.

"I won't come back," she thought. "I've lost the key."

The hidden world, like ripples on the pool so soon to be filled in and fenced, was out of her reach forever.

Miss Forbes's Summer of Happiness

by

GABRIEL GARCÍA MÁRQUEZ

WHEN WE CAME BACK to the house in the afternoon, we found an enormous sea serpent nailed by the neck to the door frame. Black and phosphorescent, it looked like a Gypsy curse with its still-flashing eyes and its saw-like teeth in gaping jaws. I was about nine years old at the time, and at the sight of that vision out of a delirium I felt a terror so intense that I lost my voice. But my brother, who was two years younger, dropped the oxygen tanks, the masks, the fins, and fled, screaming in panic. Miss Forbes heard him from the tortuous stone steps that wound along the reefs from the dock to the house, and she ran to us, panting and livid, yet she had only to see the beast crucified on the door to understand the cause of our horror. She always said that when two children were together they were both guilty of what each did alone, and so she scolded the two of us for my brother's screams and continued to reprimand us for our lack of self-control. She spoke in German, not in the English stipulated in her tutor's contract, perhaps because she too was frightened and refused to admit it. But as soon as she caught her breath she returned to her stony English and her pedagogical obsession.

"It is a *Muraena helena,*" she told us, "so called because it was an animal sacred to the ancient Greeks."

All at once Oreste, the local boy who taught us how to swim in deep waters, appeared behind the agave plants. He was wearing his diving mask on his forehead, a minuscule bathing suit, and a leather belt that held six knives of different shapes and sizes, for he could conceive of no other way to hunt underwater than by engaging in hand-to-hand combat with his prey. He was about twenty years old and spent more time at the bottom of the sea than on solid ground, and with motor oil always smeared over his body he even looked like a sea animal. When she saw him for the first time, Miss Forbes told my parents that it was impossible to imagine a more beautiful human being. But his beauty could not save him from her severity: He too had to endure a reprimand, in Italian, for having hung the moray eel on the door, with no other possible reason than his desire to frighten the children. Then Miss Forbes ordered him to take it down with the respect due a mythical creature, and told us to dress for supper.

We did so without delay, trying not to commit a single error, because after two weeks under the regime of Miss Forbes we had learned that nothing was more difficult than living. As we showered in the dim light of the bathroom, I knew that my brother was still thinking about the moray. "It had people's eyes," he said. I agreed, but made him think otherwise and managed to change the subject until I finished washing. Yet when I stepped out of the shower he asked me to stay and keep him company.

"It's still daytime," I said.

I opened the curtains. It was the middle of August, and through the window you could see the burning lunar plain all the way to the other side of the island, and the sun that had stopped in the sky.

"That's not why," my brother said. "I'm just scared of being scared."

But when we came down to the table he seemed calm, and he had done everything with so much care that he earned special praise from Miss Forbes and two more points in the week's good-conduct report. I, on the other hand, lost two of the five points I had already earned, because at the last minute I permitted myself to hurry and came into the dining room out of breath. Every fifty points entitled us to a double portion of dessert, but neither of us had earned more than fifteen. It was a shame, really, because we never again tasted any desserts as delicious as those made by Miss Forbes.

Before beginning supper we would stand and pray behind our empty plates. Miss Forbes was not Catholic, but her contract stipulated that she would have us pray six times a day, and she had learned our prayers in order to fulfill those terms. Then the three of us would sit down, and we held our breath while she scrutinized our deportment down to the slightest detail, and only when everything seemed perfect would she ring the bell. Then the cook, Fulvia Flaminea, came in, carrying the eternal vermicelli soup of that abominable summer.

At first, when we were alone with our parents, meals were a fiesta. Fulvia Flaminea giggled all around the table as she served us, with a vocation for disorder that brought joy to our lives, and then sat down with us and ate a little bit from everyone's plate. But ever since Miss Forbes had taken charge of our destiny, she served in such dark silence that we could hear the bubbling of the soup as it boiled in the tureen. We ate with our spines against the back of our chairs, chewing ten times on one side and ten times on the other, never taking our eyes off the iron, languid, autumnal woman who recited etiquette lessons by heart. It was just like Sunday Mass, but without the consolation of people singing.

On the day we found the moray eel hanging from the door, Miss Forbes spoke to us of our patriotic obligations. After the soup, Fulvia Flaminea, almost floating on the air rarefied by our tutor's voice, served a broiled fillet of snowy flesh with an exquisite aroma. I have always preferred fish to any other food on land or in the sky, and that memory of our house in Guacamayal eased my heart. But my brother refused the dish without tasting it.

"I don't like it," he said.

Miss Forbes interrupted her lesson.

"You cannot know that," she told him. "You have not even tasted it."

She shot a warning glance at the cook, but it was too late.

"Moray is the finest fish in the world, *figlio mio,*" Fulvia Flaminea told him. "Try it and see."

Miss Forbes remained calm. She told us, with her unmerciful methodology, that moray had been a delicacy of kings in antiquity and that warriors fought over its bile because it gave them supernatural courage. Then she repeated, as she had so often in so short a time, that good taste was not an innate faculty, nor was it taught at any particular age; rather, it was imposed from infancy. Therefore we had no valid reason not to eat. I had tasted the moray before I knew what it was, and remembered the contradiction forever after: It had a smooth, rather melancholy taste, yet the image of the serpent nailed to the door frame was more compelling than my appetite. My brother made a supreme effort with his first bite, but he could not bear it: He vomited.

"You will go to the bathroom," Miss Forbes told him without losing her calm, "you will wash yourself with care, and you will come back to eat."

I felt great anguish for him, because I knew how difficult he found it to cross the entire house in the early darkness and stay alone in the bathroom for the time he needed to wash. But he returned very soon in a clean shirt, pale and quivering with a hidden tremor, and he bore up very well under the rigorous inspection of his cleanliness. Then Miss Forbes sliced a piece of moray and ordered us to continue. I just managed a second bite. But my brother did not even pick up his knife and fork.

"I'm not going to eat it," he said.

His determination was so obvious that Miss Forbes withdrew.

"All right," she said, "but you will have no dessert."

My brother's relief filled me with his courage. I crossed my knife and fork on my plate, just as Miss Forbes had taught us to do when we were finished, and said:

"I won't have dessert either."

"And you will not watch television," she replied.

"And we will not watch television," I said.

Miss Forbes placed her napkin on the table, and the three of us stood to pray. Then she sent us to our bedroom, with the warning that we had to be asleep by the time she finished eating. All our good-conduct points were cancelled, and only after we had earned twenty more would we again enjoy her cream cakes, her vanilla tarts, her exquisite plum pastries, the likes of which we would not taste again for the rest of our lives.

The break was bound to come sooner or later. For an entire year we had looked forward to a summer of freedom on the island of Pantelleria, at the far southern end of Sicily, and that is what it really had been for the first month, when our parents were with us. I still remember as if it were a dream the solar plain of volcanic rock, the eternal sea, the house painted with quicklime up to the brickwork; on windless nights you could see from its windows the luminous beams of lighthouses in Africa. Exploring the sleeping ocean floor around the island with our father, we had discovered a row of yellow torpedoes, half buried since the last war; we had brought up a Greek amphora almost a metre high, with petrified garlands and the dregs of an immemorial and poisonous wine in its depths; we had bathed in a steaming pool of waters so dense you almost could walk on them. But the most dazzling revelation for us had been Fulvia Flaminea. She looked like a cheerful bishop and was always accompanied by a troop of sleepy cats who got in her way when she walked. But she said she put up with them not out of love but to keep from being devoured by rats. At night, while our parents watched programs for adults on television, Fulvia Flaminea took us to her house, less than a hundred metres from ours, and taught us to distinguish the remote babbling, the songs, the outbursts of weeping on the winds from Tunis. Her husband was a man too young for her, who worked in the summer at the tourist hotels on the far end of the island and came home only to sleep. Oreste lived a little farther away with his parents, and always appeared at night with strings of fish and baskets of fresh-caught lobster, which he hung in the kitchen so that Fulvia Flaminea's husband could sell them the next day at the hotels. Then he would put his diving lantern back on his forehead and take us to catch the field rats as big as rabbits that lay in wait for kitchen scraps. Sometimes we came home after our parents had gone to bed, and it was hard for us to sleep with the racket the rats made as they fought over the garbage in the courtyards. But even that annoyance was a magical ingredient in our happy summer.

The decision to hire a German governess could have occurred only to my father, a writer from the Caribbean with more presumption than talent. Dazzled by the ashes of the glories of Europe, he always seemed too eager to excuse his origins, in his books as well as in real life, and he had succumbed to the fantasy that no vestige of his own past would remain in his children. My mother was still as unassuming as she had been when she was an itinerant teacher in Alta Guajira, and she never imagined her husband could have an idea that was less than providential. And therefore they could not have asked themselves in their hearts what our lives would be like with a sergeant from Dortmund intent on inculcating in us by force the most ancient, stale habits of European society, while they and forty other fashionable writers participated in a five-week cultural encounter on the islands of the Aegean Sea.

Miss Forbes arrived on the last Saturday in July on the regular boat from Palermo, and from the moment we first saw her we knew the party was over. She arrived in that southern heat wearing combat boots, a dress with overlapping lapels, and hair cut like a man's under her felt hat. She smelled of monkey urine. "That's how every European smells, above all in summer," our father told us. "It's the smell of civilization." But despite her military appearance, Miss Forbes was a poor creature who might have awakened a certain compassion in us if we had been older or if she had possessed any trace of tenderness. The world changed. Our six hours in the ocean, which from the beginning of the summer had been a continual exercise of our imagination, were turned into one identical hour repeated over and over again. When we were with our parents we had all the time we wanted to swim with Oreste and be astonished at the art and daring with which he confronted octopuses in their own environment murky with ink and blood, using no other weapons than his combat knives. He still arrived as always at eleven o'clock in his little outboard motorboat, but Miss Forbes did not allow him to stay with us a minute longer than required for our lesson in deep-sea diving. She forbade us to go to Fulvia Flaminea's house at night because she considered it excessive familiarity with servants, and we had to devote the hours we had once spent in the pleasurable hunting of rats to analytical readings of Shakespeare. Accustomed to stealing mangoes from courtyards and stoning dogs to death on the burning streets of Guacamayal, we could not imagine a crueller torture than that princely life.

But we soon realized that Miss Forbes was not as strict with herself as she was with us, and this was the first chink in her authority. In the beginning she stayed on the beach under the multicoloured umbrella, dressed for war and reading ballads by Schiller, while Oreste taught us to dive, and then, for hours and hours, she gave us theoretical lectures on proper behaviour in society, until it was time for lunch.

One day she asked Oreste to take her in his boat to the hotel tourist shops, and she came back with a one-piece bathing suit as black and iridescent as a sealskin, yet she never went in the water. She sunbathed on the beach while we swam, and wiped away the perspiration with a towel but did not take a shower, so that after three days she looked like a boiled lobster and the smell of her civilization had become unbreathable.

At night she gave vent to her emotions. From the very start of her reign we heard someone walking through the house, feeling his way in the darkness, and my brother was tormented by the idea that it was one of the wandering drowning victims that Fulvia Flaminea had told us so much about. We soon discovered, however, that it was Miss Forbes, who spent the night living her real life as a lonely woman, which she herself would have censured during the day. One morning at dawn we surprised her in the kitchen in her schoolgirl's nightdress, preparing her splendid desserts. Her entire body, including her face, was covered with flour, and she was drinking a glass of port with a mental abandon that would have scandalized the other Miss Forbes. By then we knew that after we were in bed she did not go to her bedroom but went down to swim in secret, or stayed in the living room until very late, watching movies forbidden to minors on television, with the sound turned off, eating entire cakes and even drinking from the bottle of special wine that my father saved with so much devotion for memorable occasions. In defiance of her own sermons on austerity and composure, she wolfed everything down, choking on it with a kind of uncontrolled passion. Later we heard her talking to herself in her room, we heard her reciting complete excerpts from *Die Jungfrau von Orleans* in melodious German, we heard her singing, we heard her sobbing in her bed until dawn, and then she would appear at breakfast, her eyes swollen with tears, more gloomy and authoritarian than ever. My brother and I were never again as unhappy as we were then, but I was prepared to endure her to the end, for I knew that in any case her word would prevail over ours. My brother, however, confronted her with all the force of his character, and the summer of happiness became hellish for us. The episode of the moray eel was the final straw. That same night, as we lay in our beds listening to the incessant coming and going of Miss Forbes in the sleeping house, my brother released all the hatred rotting in his soul.

"I'm going to kill her," he said.

I was surprised, not so much by his decision as by the fact that I had been thinking the same thing since supper. I tried, however, to dissuade him.

"They'll cut off your head," I told him.

"They don't have guillotines in Sicily," he said. "Besides, nobody will know who did it."

I thought about the amphora salvaged from the water, where the dregs of fatal wine still lay. My father had kept it because he wanted a more thorough analysis to determine the nature of the poison, which could not be the product of the simple passage of time. Using the wine on Miss Forbes would be so easy that nobody would think it was not an accident or suicide. And so at dawn, when we heard her collapse, exhausted by the rigours of her vigil, we poured wine from the amphora into my father's bottle of special wine. From what we had heard, that dose was enough to kill a horse.

We ate breakfast in the kitchen at nine o'clock sharp, Miss Forbes herself serving us the sweet rolls that Fulvia Flaminea left on the top of the stove very early in the morning. Two days after we had substituted the wine, while we were having breakfast, my brother let me know with a disillusioned glance that the poisoned bottle stood untouched on the sideboard. That was a Friday, and the bottle remained untouched over the weekend. Then on Tuesday night, Miss Forbes drank half the wine while she watched dissolute movies on television.

Yet on Wednesday she came to breakfast with her customary punctuality. As usual, her face looked as if she had spent a bad night; as always, her eyes were uneasy behind the heavy glasses, and they became even more uneasy when she found a letter with German stamps in the basket of rolls. She read it while she drank her coffee, which she had told us so many times one must not do, and while she read, flashes of light radiating from the written words passed over her face. Then she removed the stamps from the envelope and put them in the basket with the remaining rolls so that Fulvia Flaminea's husband could have them for his collection. Despite her initial bad experience, she accompanied us that day in our exploration of the ocean depths, and we wandered through a sea of delicate water until the air in our tanks began to run out, and we went home without our lesson in good manners. Not only was Miss Forbes in a floral mood all day, but at supper she seemed even more animated. My brother, however, could not tolerate his disappointment. As soon as we received the order to begin, he pushed away the plate of vermicelli soup with a provocative gesture.

"This worm water gives me a pain in the ass," he said.

It was as if he had tossed a grenade on the table. Miss Forbes turned pale, her lips hardened until the smoke of the explosion began to clear away, and the lenses of her glasses blurred with tears. Then she took them off, dried them with her napkin, placed the napkin on the table with the bitterness of an inglorious defeat, and stood up.

"Do whatever you wish," she said. "I do not exist."

She was locked in her room from seven o'clock on. But before midnight, when she supposed we were asleep, we saw her pass by in her schoolgirl's nightdress, carrying half a chocolate cake and the bottle with more than four fingers of poisoned wine back to her bedroom. I felt a tremor of pity.

"Poor Miss Forbes," I said.

My brother did not breathe easy.

"Poor us if she doesn't die tonight," he said.

That night she talked to herself again for a long time, declaimed Schiller in a loud voice inspired by a frenetic madness, and ended with a final shout that filled the entire house. Then she sighed many times from the depths of her soul and succumbed with a sad, continuous whistle like a boat adrift. When we awoke, still exhausted by the tension of the night, the sun was cutting through the blinds but the house seemed submerged in a pond. Then we realized it was almost ten and we had not been awakened by Miss Forbes's morning routine. We did not hear the toilet flush at eight, or the faucet turn in the sink, or the noise of the blinds, or the metallic sound of her boots, or the three mortal blows on the door with the flat of her slave driver's hand. My brother put his ear to the wall, held his breath in order to detect the slightest sign of life from the next room, and at last breathed a sigh of liberation.

"That's it!" he said. "All you can hear is the ocean."

We prepared our breakfast a little before eleven, and then, before Fulvia Flaminea arrived with her troop of cats to clean the house, we went down to the beach with two air tanks each and another two as spares. Oreste was already on the dock, gutting a six-pound gilthead he had just caught. We told him we had waited for Miss Forbes until eleven, and since she was still sleeping we decided to come down to the ocean by ourselves. We told him too that she had suffered an attack of weeping at the table the night before, and perhaps she had not slept well and wanted to stay in bed. Just as we expected, Oreste was not very interested in our explanation, and he accompanied us on our pillaging of the ocean floor for a little more than an hour. Then he told us we should go up for lunch, and left in his boat to sell the gilthead at the tourist hotels. We waved goodbye from the stone steps, making him think we were about to climb up to the house, until he disappeared around the cliff. Then we put on our air tanks and continued to swim without anyone's permission.

The day was cloudy and there was a rumble of dark thunder on the horizon, but the sea was smooth and clear and its own light was enough. We swam on the surface to the line of the Pantelleria lighthouse, then turned a hundred metres to the right and dove at the spot where we calculated we had seen the torpedoes at the beginning of the summer. There they were: six of them, painted sun-yellow with their serial numbers intact, and lying on the volcanic bottom in an order too perfect to be accidental. We kept circling the lighthouse, looking for the submerged city that Fulvia Flaminea had told us about so often, and with so much awe, but we could not find it. After two hours, convinced there were no new mysteries to discover, we surfaced with our last gulp of oxygen.

A summer storm had broken while we were swimming, the sea was rough, and a flock of bloodthirsty birds flew with fierce screams over the trail of dying fish on the beach. Yet without Miss Forbes the afternoon light seemed brand-new and life was good. But when we finished struggling up the steps cut into the cliff, we saw a crowd of people at the house and two police cars by the door, and for the first time we were conscious of what we had done. My brother began to tremble and tried to turn back.

"I'm not going in," he said.

I, on the other hand, had the confused notion that if we just looked at the body we would be safe from all suspicion.

"Take it easy," I told him. "Take a deep breath, and think about just one thing: We don't know anything."

No one paid attention to us. We left our tanks, masks, and flippers at the gate and went to the side veranda, where two men sat on the floor next to a stretcher and smoked. Then we realized there was an ambulance at the back door, and several soldiers armed with rifles. In the living room women from the area were sitting on chairs that had been pushed against the wall and praying in dialect, while their men crowded into the courtyard talking about anything that did not have to do with death. I squeezed my brother's hard, icy hand even tighter, and we walked into the house through the back door. Our bedroom door was open, and the room was just as we had left it that morning. In Miss Forbes's room, which was next to ours, an armed *carabinieriere* stood guarding the entrance, but the door was open. We walked toward it with heavy hearts, and before we had a chance to look in, Fulvia Flaminea came out of the kitchen like a bolt of lightning and shut the door with a scream of horror:

"For God's sake, *figlioli,* don't look at her!"

It was too late. Never, for the rest of our lives, would we forget what we saw in that fleeting instant. Two plainclothesmen were measuring the distance from the bed to the wall with a tape, while another was taking pictures with a black-sleeve camera like the ones park photographers used. Miss Forbes was not on the unmade bed. She was stretched on her side, naked in a pool of dried blood that had stained the entire floor, and her body was riddled by stab wounds. There were twenty-seven fatal cuts, and by their number and brutality one could see that the attack had been made with the fury of a love that found no peace, and that Miss Forbes had received it with the same passion, without even screaming or crying, reciting Schiller in her beautiful soldier's voice, conscious of the fact that this was the inexorable price of her summer of happiness.

Hired Girl

by

ALICE MUNRO

MRS. MONTJOY WAS SHOWING me how to put the pots and pans away. I had put some of them in the wrong places.

Above all things, she said, she hated a higgledy-piggledy cupboard.

"You waste more time," she said. "You waste more time looking for something because it wasn't where it was last time."

"That's the way it was with our hired girls at home," I said. "The first few days they were there they were always putting things away where we couldn't find them.

"We called our maids hired girls," I added. "That was what we called them, at home."

"Did you?" she said. A moment of silence passed. "And the colander on that hook there."

Why did I have to say what I had said? Why was it necessary to mention that we had hired girls at home?

Anybody could see why. To put myself somewhere near her level. As if that was possible. As if anything I had to say about myself or the house I came from could interest or impress her.

IT WAS TRUE, though, about the hired girls. In my early life there was a procession of them. There was Olive, a soft drowsy girl who didn't like me because I called her Olive Oyl. Even after I was made to apologize she didn't like me. Maybe she didn't like any of us much because she was a Bible Christian, which made her mistrustful and reserved. She used to sing as she washed the dishes and I dried. *There is a Balm in Gilead* ... If I tried to sing with her she stopped.

Then came Jeanie, whom I liked, because she was pretty and she did my hair up in pin curls at night when she did her own. She kept a list of the boys she went out with and made peculiar signs after their names: x x x o o * *. She did not last long.

Neither did Dorothy, who hung the clothes on the line in an eccentric way—pinned up by the collar, or by one sleeve or one leg—and swept the dirt into a corner and propped the broom up to hide it.

And when I was around ten years old hired girls became a thing of the past. I don't know if it was because we became poorer or because I was considered old enough to be a steady help. Both things were true.

Now I was seventeen and able to be hired out myself, though only as summer help because I had one more year to go at high school. My sister was twelve, so she could take over at home.

MRS. MONTJOY had picked me up at the railway station in Pointe au Baril, and transported me in an outboard-motor boat to the island. It was the woman in the Pointe au Baril store who had recommended me for the job. She was an old friend of my mother's—they had taught school together. Mrs. Montjoy had asked her if she knew of a country girl, used to doing housework, who would be available for the summer, and the woman had thought that it would be the very thing for me. I thought so too—I was eager to see more of the world.

Mrs. Montjoy wore khaki shorts and a tucked-in shirt. Her short, sun-bleached hair was pushed behind her ears. She leapt aboard the boat like a boy and gave a fierce tug to the motor, and we were flung out on the choppy evening waters of Georgian Bay. For thirty or forty minutes we dodged around rocky and wooded islands with their lone cottages and boats bobbing beside the docks. Pine trees jutted out at odd angles, just as they do in the paintings.

I held on to the sides of the boat and shivered in my flimsy dress.

"Feeling a tad sick?" said Mrs. Montjoy, with the briefest possible smile. It was like the signal for a smile, when the occasion did not warrant the real thing. She had large white teeth in a long tanned face, and her natural expression seemed to be one of impatience barely held in check. She probably knew that what I was feeling was fear, not sickness, and she threw out this question so that I—and she—need not be embarrassed.

Here was a difference, already, from the world I was used to. In that world, fear was commonplace, at least for females. You could be afraid of snakes, thunderstorms, deep water, heights, the dark, the bull, and the lonely road through the swamp, and nobody thought any the worse of you. In Mrs. Montjoy's world, however, fear was shameful and always something to be conquered.

The island that was our destination had a name—Nausicaa. The name was written on a board at the end of the dock. I said it aloud, trying to show that I was at ease and quietly appreciative, and Mrs. Montjoy said with slight surprise, "Oh, yes. That was the name it already had when Daddy bought it. It's for some character in Shakespeare."

I opened up my mouth to say no, no, not Shakespeare, and to tell her that Nausicaa was the girl on the beach, playing ball with her friends, surprised by Ulysses when he woke up from his nap. I had learned by this time that most of the people I lived amongst did not welcome this kind of information, and I would probably have kept quiet even if the teacher had asked us in school, but I believed that people out in the world—the real world—would be different. Just in time I recognized the briskness of Mrs. Montjoy's tone when she said "some character in Shakespeare"—the suggestion that Nausicaa, and Shakespeare, as well as any observations of mine, were things she could reasonably do without.

The dress I was wearing for my arrival was one I had made myself, out of pink and white striped cotton. The material had been cheap, the reason being that it was not really meant for a dress but for a blouse or a nightgown, and the style I had chosen—the full-skirted, tight-waisted style of those days—was a mistake. When I walked, the cloth bunched up between my legs, and I kept having to yank it loose. Today was the first day the dress had been worn, and I still thought that the trouble might be temporary—with a firm enough yank the material might be made to hang properly. But I found when I took off my belt that the day's heat and my hot ride on the train had created a worse problem. The belt was wide and elasticized, and of a burgundy colour, which had run. The waistline of the dress was circled with strawberry dye.

I made this discovery when I was getting undressed in the loft of the boathouse, which I was to share with Mrs. Montjoy's ten-year-old daughter, Mary Anne.

"What happened to your dress?" Mary Anne said. "Do you sweat a lot? That's too bad."

I said that it was an old dress anyway and that I hadn't wanted to wear anything good on the train.

Mary Anne was fair-haired and freckled, with a long face like her mother's. But she didn't have her mother's look of quick judgments marshalled at the surface, ready to leap out at you. Her expression was benign and serious, and she wore heavy glasses even when sitting up in bed. She was to tell me soon that she had had an operation to get her eyes straightened, but even so her eyesight was poor.

"I've got Daddy's eyes," she said. "I'm intelligent like him too, so it's too bad I'm not a boy."

Another difference. Where I came from, it was generally held to be more suspect for boys to be smart than for girls to be, though not particularly advantageous for one or the other. Girls could go on to be teachers, and that was all right—though quite often they became old maids—but for boys to continue with school usually meant they were sissies.

All night long you could hear the water slapping against the boards of the boathouse. Morning came early. I wondered whether I was far enough north of home for the sun to actually be rising sooner. I got up and looked out. Through the front window, I saw the silky water, dark underneath but flashing back from its surface the light of the sky. The rocky shores of this little cove, the moored sailboats, the open channel beyond, the mound of another island or two, shores and channels beyond that. I thought that I would never, on my own, be able to find my way back to the mainland.

I did not yet understand that maids didn't have to find their way anywhere. They stayed put, where the work was. It was the people who made the work who could come and go.

The back window looked out on a grey rock that was like a slanting wall, with shelves and crevices on it where little pine and cedar trees and blueberry bushes had got a foothold. Down at the foot of this wall was a path—which I would take later on—through the woods, to Mrs. Montjoy's house. Here everything was still damp and almost dark, though if you craned you could see bits of the sky whitening through the trees on top of the rock. Nearly all of the trees were strict-looking, fragrant evergreens, with heavy boughs that didn't allow much growth underneath—no riot of grapevine and brambles and saplings such as I was used to in the hardwood forest. I had noticed that when I looked out from the train on the day before—how what we called the bush turned into the more authentic-looking *forest,* which had eliminated all lavishness and confusion and seasonal change. It seemed to me that this real forest belonged to rich people—it was their proper though sombre playground—and to Indians, who served the rich people as guides and exotic dependents, living out of sight and out of mind, somewhere that the train didn't go.

Nevertheless, on this morning I was really looking out, eagerly, as if this was a place where I would live and everything would become familiar to me. And everything did become familiar, at least in the places where my work was and where I was supposed to go. But a barrier was up. Perhaps *barrier* is too strong a word—there was not a warning so much as something like a shimmer in the air, an indolent reminder. *Not for you.* It wasn't a thing that had to be said. Or put on a sign.

Not for you. And though I felt it, I would not quite admit to myself that such a barrier was there. I would not admit that I ever felt humbled or lonely, or that I was a real servant. But I stopped thinking about leaving the path, exploring among the trees. If anybody saw me I would have to explain what I was doing and *they*—Mrs. Montjoy—would not like it.

And to tell the truth, this wasn't so different from the way things were at home, where taking any impractical notice of the out-of-doors, or mooning around about Nature—even using that word, *Nature*—could get you laughed at.

MARY ANNE LIKED TO TALK when we were lying on our cots at night. She told me that her favourite book was *Kon-Tiki* and that she did not believe in God or Heaven.

"My sister is dead," she said. "And I don't believe she is floating around somewhere in a white nightie. She is just dead, she is just nothing.

"My sister was pretty," she said. "Compared to me she was, anyway. Mother wasn't ever pretty and Daddy is really ugly. Aunt Margaret used to be pretty but now she's fat, and Nana used to be pretty but now she's old. My friend Helen is pretty but my friend Susan isn't. You're pretty, but it doesn't count because you're the maid. Does it hurt your feelings for me to say that?"

I said no.

"I'm only the maid when I'm here."

It wasn't that I was the only servant on the island. The other servants were a married couple, Henry and Corrie. They did not feel diminished by their jobs—they were grateful for them. They had come to Canada from Holland a few years before and had been hired by Mr. and Mrs. Foley, who were Mrs. Montjoy's parents. It was Mr. and Mrs. Foley who owned the island, and lived in the large white bungalow, with its awnings and verandas, that crowned the highest point of land. Henry cut the grass and looked after the tennis court and repainted the lawn chairs and helped Mr. Foley with the boats and the clearing of paths and the repairs to the dock. Corrie did the housework and cooked the meals and looked after Mrs. Foley.

Mrs. Foley spent every sunny morning sitting outside on a deck chair, with her feet stretched out to get the sun and an awning attached to the chair protecting her head. Corrie came out and shifted her around as the sun moved, and took her to the bathroom, and brought her cups of tea and glasses of iced coffee. I was witness to this when I went up to the Foleys' house from the Montjoys' house on some errand, or to put something into or remove something from the freezer. Home freezers were still rather a novelty and a luxury at this time, and there wasn't one in the Montjoys' cottage.

"You are not going to suck the ice cubes," I heard Corrie say to Mrs. Foley. Apparently Mrs. Foley paid no attention and proceeded to suck an ice cube, and Corrie said, "Bad. No. Spit out. Spit right out in Corrie's hand. Bad. You didn't do what Corrie say."

Catching up to me on the way into the house, she said, "I tell them she could choke to death. But Mr. Foley always say, give her the ice cubes, she wants a drink like everybody else. So I tell her and tell her. Do not suck ice cubes. But she won't do what I say."

Sometimes I was sent up to help Corrie polish the furniture or buff the floors. She was very exacting. She never just wiped the kitchen counters—she scoured them. Every move she made had the energy and concentration of somebody rowing a boat against the current and every word she said was flung out as if into a high wind of opposition. When she wrung out a cleaning rag she might have been wringing the neck of a chicken. I thought it might be interesting if I could get her to talk about the war, but all she would say was that everybody was very hungry and they saved the potato skins to make soup.

"No good," she said. "No good to talk about that."

She preferred the future. She and Henry were saving their money to go into business. They meant to start up a nursing home. "Lots of people like her," said Corrie, throwing her head back as she worked to indicate Mrs. Foley out on the lawn. "Soon more and more. Because they give them the medicine, that makes them not die so soon. Who will be taking care?"

One day Mrs. Foley called out to me as I crossed the lawn.

"Now, where are you off to in such a hurry?" she said. "Come and sit down by me and have a little rest."

Her white hair was tucked up under a floppy straw hat, and when she leaned forward the sun came through the holes in the straw, sprinkling the pink and pale-brown patches of her face with pimples of light. Her eyes were a colour so nearly extinct I couldn't make it out and her shape was curious—a narrow flat chest and a swollen stomach under layers of loose, pale clothing. The skin of the legs she stuck out into the sunlight was shiny and discoloured and covered with faint cracks.

"Pardon my not having put my stockings on," she said. "I'm afraid I'm feeling rather lazy today. But aren't you the remarkable girl. Coming all that way by yourself. Did Henry help you carry the groceries up from the dock?"

Mrs. Montjoy waved to us. She was on her way to the tennis court, to give Mary Anne her lesson. Every morning she gave Mary Anne a lesson, and at lunch they discussed what Mary Anne had done wrong.

"There's that woman who comes to play tennis," Mrs. Foley said of her daughter. "She comes every day, so I suppose it's all right. She may as well use it if she hasn't a court of her own."

Mrs. Montjoy said to me later, "Did Mrs. Foley ask you to come over and sit on the grass?"

I said yes. "She thought I was somebody who'd brought the groceries."

"I believe there was a grocery girl who used to run a boat. There hasn't been any grocery delivery in years. Mrs. Foley does get her wires crossed now and then."

"She said you were a woman who came to play tennis."

"Did she really?" Mrs. Montjoy said.

THE WORK that I had to do here was not hard for me. I knew how to bake, and iron, and clean an oven. Nobody tracked barnyard mud into this kitchen and there were no heavy men's work clothes to wrestle through the wringer. There was just the business of putting everything perfectly in place and doing quite a bit of polishing. Polish the rims of the burners of the stove after every use, polish the taps, polish the glass door to the deck till the glass disappears and people are in danger of smashing their faces against it.

The Montjoys' house was modern, with a flat roof and a deck extending over the water and a great many windows, which Mrs. Montjoy would have liked to see become as invisible as the glass door.

"But I have to be realistic," she said. "I know if you did that you'd hardly have time for anything else." She was not by any means a slave driver. Her tone with me was firm and slightly irritable, but that was the way it was with everybody. She was always on the lookout for inattention or incompetence, which she detested. *Sloppy* was a favourite word of condemnation. Others were *wishy-washy* and *unnecessary.* A lot of things that people did were unnecessary, and some of these were also wishy-washy. Other people might have used the words *arty* or *intellectual* or *permissive.* Mrs. Montjoy swept all those distinctions out of the way.

I ate my meals alone, between serving whoever was eating on the deck or in the dining room. I had almost made a horrible mistake about that. When Mrs. Montjoy caught me heading out to the deck with three plates—held in a show-off waitress-style—for the first lunch, she said, "Three plates there? Oh, yes, two out on the deck and yours in here. Right?"

I read as I ate. I had found a stack of old magazines—*Life and Look* and *Time* and *Collier's*—at the back of the broom closet. I could tell that Mrs. Montjoy did not like the idea of my sitting reading these magazines as I ate my lunch, but I did not quite know why. Was it because it was bad manners to eat as you read, or because I had not asked permission? More likely she saw my interest in things that had nothing to do with my work as a subtle kind of impudence. Unnecessary.

All she said was, "Those old magazines must be dreadfully dusty."

I said that I always wiped them off.

Sometimes there was a guest for lunch, a woman friend who had come over from one of the nearby islands. I heard Mrs. Montjoy say "... have to keep your girls happy or they'll be off to the hotel, off to the port. They can get jobs there so easily. It's not the way it used to be."

The other woman said, "That's so true."

"So you just make allowances," said Mrs. Montjoy. "You do the best with them you can." It took me a moment to realize who they were talking about. Me. "Girls" meant girls like me. I wondered, then, how I was being kept happy. By being taken along on the occasional alarming boat ride when Mrs. Montjoy went to get supplies? By being allowed to wear shorts and a blouse, or even a halter, instead of a uniform with a white collar and cuffs?

And what hotel was this? What port?

"WHAT ARE YOU BEST AT?" Mary Anne said. "What sports?"

After a moment's consideration, I said, "Volleyball." We had to play volleyball at school. I wasn't very good at it, but it was my best sport because it was the only one.

"Oh, I don't mean team sports," said Mary Anne. "I mean, what are you *best* at. Such as tennis. Or swimming or riding or what? My really best thing is riding, because that doesn't depend so much on your eyesight. Aunt Margaret's best used to be tennis and Nana's used to be tennis too, and Grandad's was always sailing, and Daddy's is swimming I guess and Uncle Stewart's is golf and sailing and Mother's is golf and swimming and sailing and tennis and everything, but maybe tennis a little bit the best of all. If my sister Jane hadn't died I don't know what hers would have been, but it might have been swimming because she could swim already and she was only three."

I had never been on a tennis court and the idea of going out in a sailboat or getting up on a horse terrified me. I could swim, but not very well. Golf to me was something that silly-looking men did in cartoons. The adults I knew never played any games that involved physical action. They sat down and rested when they were not working, which wasn't often. Though on winter evenings they might play cards. Euchre. Lost Heir. Not the kind of cards Mrs. Montjoy ever played.

"Everybody I know works too hard to do any sports," I said. "We don't even have a tennis court in our town and there isn't any golf course either." (Actually we had once had both these things, but there hadn't been the money to keep them up during the Depression and they had not been restored since.) "Nobody I know has a sailboat."

I did not mention that my town did have a hockey rink and a baseball park.

"Really?" said Mary Anne thoughtfully. "What do they do then?"

"*Work*. And they never have any money, all of their lives."

Then I told her that most people I knew had never seen a flush toilet unless it was in a public building and that sometimes old people (that is, people too old to work) had to stay in bed all winter in order to keep warm. Children walked barefoot until the frost came in order to save on shoe leather, and died of stomach aches that were really appendicitis because their parents had no money for a doctor. Sometimes people had eaten dandelion leaves, nothing else, for supper.

Not one of these statements—even the one about dandelion leaves—was completely a lie. I had heard of such things. The one about flush toilets perhaps came closest to the truth, but it applied to country people, not town people, and most of those it applied to would be of a generation before mine. But as I talked to Mary Anne all the isolated incidents and bizarre stories I had heard spread out in my mind, so that I could almost believe that I myself had walked with bare blue feet on cold mud—I who had benefited from cod liver oil and inoculations and been bundled up for school within an inch of my life, and had gone to bed hungry only because I refused to eat such things as junket or bread pudding or fried liver. And this false impression I was giving seemed justified, as if my exaggerations or near lies were substitutes for something I could not make clear.

How to make clear, for instance, the difference between the Montjoys' kitchen and our kitchen at home. You could not do that simply by mentioning the perfectly fresh and shining floor surfaces of one and the worn-out linoleum of the other, or the fact of soft water being pumped from a cistern into the sink contrasted with hot and cold water coming out of taps. You would have to say that you had in one case a kitchen that followed with absolute correctness a current notion of what a kitchen ought to be, and in the other a kitchen that changed occasionally with use and improvisation, but in many ways never changed at all, and belonged entirely to one family and to the years and decades of that family's life. And when I thought of that kitchen, with the combination wood and electric stove that I polished with waxed-paper bread wrappers, the dark old spice tins with their rusty rims kept from year to year in the cupboards, the barn clothes hanging by the door, it seemed as if I had to protect it from contempt—as if I had to protect a whole precious and intimate though hardly pleasant way of life from contempt. Contempt was what I imagined to be always waiting, swinging along on live wires, just under the skin and just behind the perceptions of people like the Montjoys.

"That isn't fair," said Mary Anne. "That's awful. I didn't know people could eat dandelion leaves." But then she brightened. "Why don't they go and catch some fish?"

"People who don't need the fish have come and caught them all already. Rich people. For fun."

Of course some of the people at home did catch fish when they had time, though others, including me, found the fish from our river too bony. But I thought that would keep Mary Anne quiet, especially since I knew that Mr. Montjoy went on fishing trips with his friends.

She could not stop mulling over the problem. "Couldn't they go to the Salvation Army?"

"They're too proud."

"Well I feel sorry for them," she said. "I feel really sorry for them, but I think that's stupid. What about the little babies and the children? They ought to think about them. Are the children too proud too?"

"Everybody's proud."

WHEN MR. MONTJOY CAME to the island on weekends, there was always a great deal of noise and activity. Some of that was because there were visitors who came by boat to swim and have drinks and watch sailing races. But a lot of it was generated by Mr. Montjoy himself. He had a loud blustery voice and a thick body with a skin that would never take a tan. Every weekend he turned red from the sun, and during the week the burned skin peeled away and left him pink and muddy with freckles, ready to be burned again. When he took off his glasses you could see that one eye was quick and squinty and the other boldly blue but helpless-looking, as if caught in a trap.

His blustering was often about things that he had misplaced, or dropped, or bumped into. "Where the hell is the—?" he would say, or "You didn't happen to see the—?" So it seemed that he had also misplaced, or failed to grasp in the first place, even the name of the thing he was looking for. To console himself he might grab up a handful of peanuts or pretzels or whatever was nearby, and eat handful after handful until they were all gone. Then he would stare at the empty bowl as if that too astounded him.

One morning I heard him say, "Now where in hell is that—?" He was crashing around out on the deck.

"Your book?" said Mrs. Montjoy, in a tone of bright control. She was having her midmorning coffee.

"I thought I had it out here," he said. "I was reading it."

"The Book-of-the-Month one?" she said. "I think you left it in the living room."

She was right. I was vacuuming the living room, and a few moments before I had picked up a book pushed partway under the sofa. Its title was *Seven Gothic Tales*. The title made me want to open it, and even as I overheard the Montjoys' conversation I was reading, holding the book open in one hand and guiding the vacuum cleaner with the other. They couldn't see me from the deck.

"Nay, I speak from the heart," said Mira. "I have been trying for a long time to understand God. Now I have made friends with him. To love him truly you must love change, and you must love a joke, these being the true inclinations of his own heart."

"There it is," said Mr. Montjoy, who for a wonder had come into the room without his usual bumping and banging—or none at least that I had heard. "Good girl, you found my book. Now I remember. Last night I was reading it on the sofa."

"It was on the floor," I said. "I just picked it up."

He must have seen me reading it. He said, "It's a queer kind of book, but sometimes you want to read a book that isn't like all the others."

"I couldn't make heads or tails of it," said Mrs. Montjoy, coming in with the coffee tray. "We'll have to get out of the way here and let her get on with the vacuuming."

Mr. Montjoy went back to the mainland, and to the city, that evening. He was a bank director. That did not mean, apparently, that he worked in a bank. The day after he had gone I looked everywhere. I looked under the chairs and behind the curtains, in case he might have left that book behind. But I could not find it.

"I ALWAYS THOUGHT it would be nice to live up here all the year round, the way you people do," said Mrs. Foley. She must have cast me again as the girl who brought the groceries. Some days she said, "I know who you are now. You're the new girl helping the Dutch woman in the kitchen. But I'm sorry, I just can't recall your name." And other days she let me walk by without giving any greeting or showing the least interest.

"We used to come up here in the winter," she said. "The bay would be frozen over and there would be a road across the ice. We used to go snowshoeing. Now that's something people don't do anymore. Do they? Snowshoeing?"

She didn't wait for me to answer. She leaned towards me. "Can you tell me something?" she said with embarrassment, speaking almost in a whisper. "Can you tell me where Jane is? I haven't seen her running around here for the longest time."

I said that I didn't know. She smiled as if I was teasing her, and reached out a hand to touch my face. I had been stooping down to listen to her, but now I straightened up, and her hand grazed my chest instead. It was a hot day and I was wearing my halter, so it happened that she touched my skin. Her hand was light and dry as a wood shaving, but the nail scraped me.

"I'm sure it's all right," she said.

After that I simply waved if she spoke to me and hurried on my way.

ON A SATURDAY AFTERNOON towards the end of August, the Montjoys gave a cocktail party. The party was given in honour of the friends they had staying with them that weekend—Mr. and Mrs. Hammond. A good many small silver forks and spoons had to be polished in preparation for this event, so Mrs. Montjoy decided that all the silver might as well be done at the same time. I did the polishing and she stood beside me, inspecting it.

On the day of the party, people arrived in motorboats and sailboats. Some of them went swimming, then sat around on the rocks in their bathing suits, or lay on the dock in the sun. Others came up to the house immediately and started drinking and talking in the living room or out on the deck. Some children had come with their parents, and older children by themselves, in their own boats. They were not children of Mary Anne's age—Mary Anne had been taken to stay with her friend Susan, on another island. There were a few very young ones, who came supplied with folding cribs and playpens, but most were around the same age as I was. Girls and boys fifteen or sixteen years old.

They spent most of the afternoon in the water, shouting and diving and having races to the raft.

Mrs. Montjoy and I had been busy all morning, making all the different things to eat, which we now arranged on platters and offered to people. Making them had been fiddly and exasperating work. Stuffing various mixtures into mushroom caps and sticking one tiny slice of something on top of a tiny slice of something else on top of a precise fragment of toast or bread. All the shapes had to be perfect—perfect triangles, perfect rounds and squares, perfect diamonds.

Mrs. Hammond came into the kitchen several times and admired what we were doing.

"How marvellous everything looks," she said. "You notice I'm not offering to help. I'm a perfect mutt at this kind of thing."

I liked the way she said that. *I'm a perfect mutt.* I admired her husky voice, its weary good-humoured tone, and the way she seemed to suggest that tiny geometrical bits of food were not so necessary, might even be a trifle silly. I wished I could be her, in a sleek black bathing suit with a tan like dark toast, shoulder-length smooth dark hair, orchid-coloured lipstick.

Not that she looked happy. But her air of sullenness and complaint seemed glamorous to me, her hints of cloudy drama enviable. She and her husband were an altogether different type of rich people from Mr. and Mrs. Montjoy. They were more like the people I had read about in magazine stories and in books like *The Hucksters*—people who drank a lot and had love affairs and went to psychiatrists.

Her name was Carol and her husband's name was Ivan. I thought of them already by their first names—something I had never been tempted to do with the Montjoys.

Mrs. Montjoy had asked me to put on a dress, so I wore the pink and white striped cotton, with the smudged material at its waist tucked under the elasticized belt. Nearly everybody else was in shorts and bathing suits. I passed among them, offering food. I was not sure how to do this. Sometimes people were laughing or talking with such vigour that they didn't notice me, and I was afraid that their gestures would send the food bits flying. So I said, "Excuse me—would you like one of these?" in a raised voice that sounded very determined or even reproving. Then they looked at me with startled amusement, and I had the feeling that my interruption had become another joke.

"Enough passing for now," said Mrs. Montjoy. She gathered up some glasses and told me to wash them. "People never keep track of their own," she said. "It's easier just to wash them and bring in clean ones. And it's time to get the meatballs out of the fridge and heat them up. Could you do that? Watch the oven—it won't take long."

While I was busy in the kitchen I heard Mrs. Hammond calling, "Ivan! Ivan!" She was roaming through the back rooms of the house. But Mr. Hammond had come in through the kitchen door that led to the woods. He stood there and did not answer her. He came over to the counter and poured gin into his glass.

"Oh, Ivan, there you are," said Mrs. Hammond, coming in from the living room.

"Here I am," said Mr. Hammond.

"Me, too," she said. She shoved her glass along the counter.

He didn't pick it up. He pushed the gin towards her and spoke to me. "Are you having fun, Minnie?"

Mrs. Hammond gave a yelp of laughter. "Minnie? Where did you get the idea her name was Minnie?"

"Minnie," said Mr. Hammond. Ivan. He spoke in an artificial, dreamy voice. "Are you having fun, Minnie?"

"Oh yes," I said, in a voice that I meant to make as artificial as his. I was busy lifting the tiny Swedish meatballs from the oven and I wanted the Hammonds out of my way in case I dropped some. They would think that a big joke and probably report on me to Mrs. Montjoy, who would make me throw the dropped meatballs out and be annoyed at the waste. If I was alone when it happened I could just scoop them up off the floor.

Mr. Hammond said, "Good."

"I swam around the point," Mrs. Hammond said. "I'm working up to swimming around the entire island."

"Congratulations," Mr. Hammond said, in the same way that he had said "Good."

I wished that I hadn't sounded so chirpy and silly. I wished that I had matched his deeply skeptical and sophisticated tone.

"Well then," said Mrs. Hammond. Carol. "I'll leave you to it."

I had begun to spear the meatballs with toothpicks and arrange them on a platter. Ivan said, "Care for some help?" and tried to do the same, but his toothpicks missed and sent meatballs skittering onto the counter.

"Well," he said, but he seemed to lose track of his thoughts, so he turned away and took another drink. "Well, Minnie."

I knew something about him. I knew that the Hammonds were here for a special holiday because Mr. Hammond had lost his job. Mary Anne had told me this. "He's very depressed about it," she had said. "They won't be poor, though. Aunt Carol is rich."

He did not seem depressed to me. He seemed impatient–chiefly with Mrs. Hammond—but on the whole rather pleased with himself. He was tall and thin, he had dark hair combed straight back from his forehead, and his mustache was an ironic line above his upper lip. When he talked to me he leaned forward, as I had seen him doing earlier, when he talked to women in the living room. I had thought then that the word for him was *courtly*.

"Where do you go swimming, Minnie? Do you go swimming?"

"Yes," I said. "Down by the boathouse." I decided that his calling me Minnie was a special joke between us.

"Is that a good place?"

"Yes." It was, for me, because I liked being close to the dock. I had never, till this summer, swum in water that was over my head.

"Do you ever go in without your bathing suit on?"

I said, "No."

"You should try it."

Mrs. Montjoy came through the living-room doorway, asking if the meatballs were ready.

"This is certainly a hungry crowd," she said. "It's the swimming does it. How are you getting on, Ivan? Carol was just looking for you."

"She was here," said Mr. Hammond.

Mrs. Montjoy dropped parsley here and there among the meatballs. "Now," she said to me. "I think you've done about all you need to here. I think I can manage now. Why don't you just make yourself a sandwich and run along down to the boathouse?"

I said I wasn't hungry. Mr. Hammond had helped himself to more gin and ice cubes and had gone into the living room.

"Well. You'd better take something," Mrs. Montjoy said. "You'll be hungry later."

She meant that I was not to come back.

On my way to the boathouse I met a couple of the guests—girls of my own age, barefoot and in their wet bathing suits, breathlessly laughing. They had probably swum partway round the island and climbed out of the water at the boathouse. Now they were sneaking back to surprise somebody. They stepped aside politely, not to drip water on me, but did not stop laughing. Making way for my body without a glance at my face.

They were the sort of girls who would have squealed and made a fuss over me, if I had been a dog or a cat.

THE NOISE OF THE PARTY continued to rise. I lay down on my cot without taking off my dress. I had been on the go since early morning and I was tired. But I could not relax. After a while I got up and changed into my bathing suit and went down to swim. I climbed down the ladder into the water cautiously as I always did—I thought that I would go straight to the bottom and never come up if I jumped—and swam around in the shadows. The water washing my limbs made me think of what Mr. Hammond had said and I worked the straps of my bathing suit down, finally pulling out one arm after the other so that my breasts could float free. I swam that way, with the water sweetly dividing at my nipples ...

I thought it was not impossible that Mr. Hammond might come looking for me. I thought of him touching me. (I could not figure out exactly how he would get into the water—I did not care to think of him stripping off his clothes. Perhaps he would squat down on the dock and I would swim over to him.) His fingers stroking my bare skin like ribbons of light. The thought of being touched and desired by a man that old—forty, forty-five?—-was in some way repulsive, but I knew I would get pleasure from it, rather as you might get pleasure from being caressed by an amorous tame crocodile. Mr. Hammond's—Ivan's—skin might be smooth, but age and knowledge and corruptness would be on him like invisible warts and scales.

I dared to lift myself partly out of the water, holding with one hand to the dock. I bobbed up and down and rose into the air like a mermaid. Gleaming, with nobody to see.

Now I heard steps. I heard somebody coming. I sank down into the water and held still.

For a moment I believed that it was Mr. Hammond, and that I had actually entered the world of secret signals, abrupt and wordless forays of desire. I did not cover myself but shrank against the dock, in a paralyzed moment of horror and submission.

The boathouse light was switched on, and I turned around noiselessly in the water and saw that it was old Mr. Foley, still in his party outfit of white trousers and yachting cap and blazer. He had stayed for a couple of drinks and explained to everybody that Mrs. Foley was not up to the strain of seeing so many people but sent her best wishes to all.

He was moving things around on the tool shelf. Soon he either found what he wanted or put back what he had intended to put back, and he switched off the light and left. He never knew that I was there.

I pulled up my bathing suit and got out of the water and went up the stairs. My body seemed such a weight to me that I was out of breath when I got to the top.

The sound of the cocktail party went on and on. I had to do something to hold my own against it, so I started to write a letter to Dawna, who was my best friend at that time. I described the cocktail party in lurid terms—people vomited over the deck railing and a woman passed out, falling down on the sofa in such a way that part of her dress slid off and exposed a purple-nippled old breast (I called it a bezoom). I spoke of Mr. Hammond as a letch, though I added that he was very good-looking. I said that he had fondled me in the kitchen while my hands were busy with the meatballs and that later he had followed me to the boathouse and grabbed me on the stairs. But I had kicked him where he wouldn't forget and he had retreated. *Scurried away* I said.

"So hold your breath for the next installment," I wrote. "Entitled, 'Sordid Adventures of a Kitchen Maid.' Or 'Ravaged on the Rocks of Georgian Bay.'"

When I saw that I had written "ravaged" instead of "ravished," I thought I could let it go, because Dawna would never know the difference. But I realized that the part about Mr. Hammond was overdone, even for that sort of letter, and then the whole thing filled me with shame and a sense of my own failure and loneliness. I crumpled it up. There had not been any point in writing this letter except to assure myself that I had some contact with the world and that exciting things—sexual things—happened to me. And I hadn't. They didn't.

"MRS. FOLEY ASKED ME where Jane was," I had said, when Mrs. Montjoy and I were doing the silver—or when she was keeping an eye on me doing the silver. "Was Jane one of the other girls who worked here in the summer?"

I thought for a moment that she might not answer, but she did.

"Jane was my other daughter," she said. "She was Mary Anne's sister. She died."

I said, "Oh. I didn't know." I said, "Oh. I'm sorry.

"Did she die of polio?" I said, because I did not have the sense, or you might say the decency, not to go on. And in those days children still died of polio, every summer.

"No," said Mrs. Montjoy. "She was killed when my husband moved the dresser in our bedroom. He was looking for something he thought he might have dropped behind it. He didn't realize she was in the way. One of the casters caught on the rug and the whole thing toppled over on her."

I knew every bit of this, of course. Mary Anne had already told me. She had told me even before Mrs. Foley asked me where Jane was and clawed at my breast.

"How awful," I said.

"Well. It was just one of those things."

My deception made me feel queasy. I dropped a fork on the floor.

Mrs. Montjoy picked it up.

"Remember to wash this again."

How strange that I did not question my right to pry, to barge in and bring this to the surface. Part of the reason must have been that in the society I came from, things like that were never buried for good, but ritualistically resurrected, and that such horrors were like a badge people wore—or, mostly, that women wore—throughout their lives.

Also it may have been because I would never quite give up when it came to demanding intimacy, or at least some kind of equality, even with a person I did not like.

Cruelty was a thing I could not recognize in myself. I thought I was blameless here, and in any dealings with this family. All because of being young, and poor, and knowing about Nausicaa.

I did not have the grace or fortitude to be a servant.

ON MY LAST SUNDAY I was alone in the boathouse, packing up my things in the suitcase I had brought—the same suitcase that had gone with my mother and father on their wedding trip and the only one we had in the house. When I pulled it out from under my cot and opened it up, it smelled of home—of the closet at the end of the upstairs hall where it usually sat, close to the mothballed winter coats and the rubber sheet once used on children's beds. But when you got it out at home it always smelled faintly of trains and coal fires and cities—of travel.

I heard steps on the path, a stumbling step into the boathouse, a rapping on the wall. It was Mr. Montjoy.

"Are you up there? Are you up there?"

His voice was boisterous, jovial, as I had heard it before when he had been drinking. As of course he had been drinking—for once again there were people visiting, celebrating the end of summer. I came to the top of the stairs. He had a hand against the wall to steady himself—a boat had gone by out in the channel and sent its waves into the boathouse.

"See here," said Mr. Montjoy, looking up at me with frowning concentration. "See here—I thought I might as well bring this down and give it to you while I thought of it.

"This book," he said.

He was holding *Seven Gothic Tales.*

"Because I saw you were looking in it that day," he said. "It seemed to me you were interested. So now I finished it and I thought I might as well pass it along to you. It occurred to me to pass it along to you. I thought, maybe you might enjoy it."

I said, "Thank you."

"I'm probably not going to read it again though I thought it was very interesting. Very unusual."

"Thank you very much."

"That's all right. I thought you might enjoy it."

"Yes," I said.

"Well then. I hope you will."

"Thank you."

"Well then," he said. "Good-bye."

I said, "Thank you. Good-bye."

Why were we saying good-bye when we were certain to see each other again before we left the island, and before I got on the train? It might have meant that this incident, of his giving me the book, was to be closed, and I was not to reveal or refer to it. Which I didn't. Or it might have been just that he was drunk and did not realize that he would see me later. Drunk or not, I see him now as pure of motive, leaning against the boathouse wall. A person who could think me worthy of this gift. Of this book.

At the moment, though, I didn't feel particularly pleased, or grateful, in spite of my repeated thank-yous. I was too startled, and in some way embarrassed. The thought of having a little corner of myself come to light, and be truly understood, stirred up alarm, just as much as being taken no notice of stirred up resentment. And Mr. Montjoy was probably the person who interested me least, whose regard meant the least to me, of all the people I had met that summer.

He left the boathouse and I heard him stumping along the path, back to his wife and his guests. I pushed the suitcase aside and sat down on the cot. I opened the book just anywhere, as I had done the first time, and began to read.

> The walls of the room had once been painted crimson, but with time the colour had faded into a richness of hues, like a glassful

of dying roses ... Some potpourri was being burned on the tall stove, on the sides of which Neptune, with a trident, steered his team of horses through high waves ...

I forgot Mr. Montjoy almost immediately. In hardly any time at all I came to believe that this gift had always belonged to me.

The New Family Robinson: A Chronicle of the End of the 20th Century

by

LUDMILA PETRUSHEVSKAYA

MY PARENTS DECIDED they would outsmart everyone. When it all began they piled me and a load of canned food into a truck and took us to the country, the far-off and forgotten country, somewhere beyond the Mur River. We'd bought a cabin there for cheap a few years before, and it just stood there and stood. We'd go at the end of June to pick wild strawberries, for my health, and then once more in August, in time for stray apples and plums and black cranberry in the abandoned orchards, and for raspberries and mushrooms in the woods. The cabin was falling apart when we bought it and we never fixed anything. Then one fine day late in the spring, after the mud had hardened a little, my father arranged things with a man with a truck and off we went with our groceries, just like the Swiss Family Robinson, with all kinds of yard tools and a rifle and a bloodhound called Red—who could, theoretically, hunt rabbits.

Now my father began his feverish activity. He plowed earth over in the garden, plowing the neighbours' earth in the process, so that he pulled out our fence posts and planted them over in the next yard. We dug up the vegetable patch, planted three sacks of potatoes, groomed the apple trees. My father went into the woods and brought back some turf for the winter. We suddenly had a two-wheeled wheelbarrow; in general my father was very active in the store-rooms of our neighbours' boarded-up houses, picking up whatever might come in handy: nails, old boards, shingles, pieces of tin, buckets, benches, door-handles, window panes, and all sorts of useful old things, like well buckets, yarn-spinners, grandfather clocks, and then not-so-useful old things, like old iron teakettles, iron oven parts, stove tops, and so on.

In the entire village there were just three old women: Baba Anisya; Marfutka, who had reverted to half-savagery; and the red-headed Tanya, the only one with a family: her kids would come around and bring things, take other things away, that is to say they'd bring canned food from the city, cheese, butter, and cookies, and take away pickled cucumbers, cabbage, potatoes. Tanya had a rich basement pantry, a good covered front yard, and one of her grandchildren, a permanently ailing boy named Valera, often stayed with her. His ears were always hurting, or else he was covered with eczema. Tanya herself was a nurse by training, which training she received in a labour camp in Kolyma, where she'd been sent at the age of seventeen for stealing a suckling pig at her collective farm. She was popular, she kept her stove warm, the shepherdess Vera came from the next village over and call out, I could hear her in the distance, "Tanya, put the tea on! Tanya, put the tea on!" Baba Anisya, the only human being in the village—Marfutka didn't count and Tanya was a criminal, not a human being—said that Tanya used to be the head of the health clinic here, practically the most important person around, she ran all sorts of schemes, she let half her house to the clinic and made some money that way, too. Anisya worked for her for five years, for doing which she lost her pension because it meant she didn't complete the full twenty-five years at the collective farm, and then five years sweeping up at the clinic don't count, especially with a boss like Tanya. My mom made a trip once with Anisya to the regional Party headquarters in Prizersk, but the headquarters had been boarded up long ago, everything was boarded up, and my mother walked the twenty-five kilometres home with a frightened Baba Anisya, who immediately began digging in her garden with renewed vigour, and chopping wood, and carrying firewood and twigs into her house—she was fending off a hungry death, which is what she'd face if she did nothing, like Marfutka, who was eighty-five and no longer lit her stove, and even the few potatoes she'd managed to drag into her house had frozen during the winter. They simply lay there in a wet, rotten pile. Marfutka had nibbled out of that pile all winter and now refused to part with these riches, her only ones, when one time my mother sent me over with a shovel to clean them out. Marfutka refused to open the door, looking out through the window that was draped in rags and seeing that I was carrying a garden spade. Either she ate the potatoes raw, despite her lack of teeth, or she made a fire for them when no one was looking—it was impossible to tell. She had no firewood. In the spring Marfutka, wrapped in layers of greasy shawls, rags, and blankets, showed up at Anisya's warm home and sat there like a mummy, not breathing a word. Anisya didn't even try to talk to her, Marfutka just sat there—I looked once at her face, that is to say what was visible of her face under the rags, and saw that it was small and dark, and that her eyes were like wet holes.

Marfutka survived another winter but no longer went into the yard—she'd decided, apparently, to die of hunger. Anisya said simply that, last year, Marfutka still had some life in her left, but this year she's done for, her feet don't look straight ahead but at each other, the wrong way. One day my mother took me along and we planted half a bucket of potatoes in Marfutka's yard, but Marfutka just looked at us and worried, it was clear, that we were taking over her plot, though she didn't have the gumption to make it over to us. My mother just went over to her and handed her some potatoes, but Marfutka, thinking that her plot was being bought from her for half a bucket of potatoes, grew very frightened, and refused.

That evening my father and mother and I went over to Anisya's for some goat milk. Marfutka was sitting there. Anisya said she'd seen us on Marfutka's plot. My mother answered we'd decided to help Baba Marfa. Anisya objected that Marfutka was going to the next world, she didn't need help, she'd find her way. It should be added that we weren't paying Anisya for the milk with money but with canned food and soup packets. This couldn't go on forever, since the goat made more milk every day, whereas the canned food was dwindling. We needed to establish a more stable equivalent, and so my mother said, directly after the discussion about Marfutka, that our canned foods were running out, we didn't have anything to eat ourselves, so we wouldn't be buying any more milk that day. Clever Anisya grasped the point at once and answered that she'd bring us a can of milk the next day and we could talk about it—if we still had potatoes, that is. Anisya was angry, apparently, that we were wasting our potatoes on Marfutka instead of paying her, Anisya—she didn't know how many potatoes we'd invested in Marfutka's plot during the hungry spring. Her imagination was working like a little engine. She must have been calculating that Marfutka didn't have long to go and that she'd gather her harvest in the fall, and was angry in advance that we were the rightful owners of those planted potatoes. Everything becomes complicated when it's a matter of surviving in times like these, especially for an old, not particularly strong person in the face of a strong young family—my parents were both forty-two then and I was eighteen.

That night we received a visit from Tanya, who wore a city coat and yellow rubber boots, with a new household bag in her hands. She brought us a little piglet smothered by its mother, wrapped in a clean rag. She wondered if we were officially registered to live in the Mur village. She pointed out that many of the houses there had owners, and that the owners might want to come out and see for themselves what was happening, if someone were to write them, and that all that we saw was not just riches lying by the roadside. In conclusion Tanya reminded us about the neighbour's plot that we'd encroached on, and also that Marfutka was still alive. As for the piglet, she offered to sell it to us for money, that is for paper rubles, and that night my father chopped and pickled the little baby pig, which in the rag looked like a little baby. He had lashes above his eyes and everything.

Later, after she left, Anisya came by with a can of goat's milk, and over tea we quickly negotiated a new price—one can of food for thee days of milk. With hatred in her voice Anisya asked why Tanya had come by, and she approved of our decision to help Marfutka, though she said of her with a laugh that she smelled bad.

The milk and the piglet were supposed to protect us from scurvy, and what's more Anisya was raising a little goat and we'd decided to buy it for ten cans of food—but only a little later, after it had grown some more, since Anisya knew better how to raise a goat. We never discussed this with Anisya, though, and one day she comes over, full of insane jealousy at her old boss Tanya, and proudly shows us that she's killed her little goat and wrapped it up for us. Two cans of fish were the answer she received, and my mom burst into tears. We tried to eat the meat, we broiled it, but it was inedible, for some reason, and my father ended up pickling it again.

We did end up buying a baby goat with my mom, we took a ten-kilometre walk to the village of Tarturino, but we did it as if we were tourists, as if it were old times. We wore backpacks, and sang, and when we got to the village we asked where we could drink some goat's milk, and when we bought a glass of milk from a peasant woman for a bread roll, we made a show of our affection for the little goats. I started whispering artfully to my mother, as if I wanted a goat for myself. The peasant woman became very excited, sensing a customer, but my mother whispered back to say no, at which point the woman began speaking very sweetly to me, saying she loved the little goats like her own children and because of this she'd give them both to me. To which I quickly replied, "No, I only need one!" We agreed on a price right away, the woman clearly didn't know the state of the ruble and took very little, and even threw in a handful of salt crystals for the road. She clearly thought she'd made a good deal, and, in fact, the little goat did begin to fade away pretty quickly after the tough long walk. It was Anisya again who got us out of it, she gave the baby goat to her own big goat, but first she covered it with some mud from her yard, and the goat took it as one of her own, didn't kill it. Anisya was beaming.

We had all the main things now, but my indomitable father, despite his slight limp, started going out into the forest, and every day he went further and further. He would take his axe, and some nails, and a saw, and a wheelbarrow—he'd leave with the sunrise and come back with the night. My mother and I paddled around the garden, somehow or other kept up my father's work of collecting window panes, doors and glass, and then of course we made the food, cleaned up, lugged the water for laundry, sewed and mended. We'd collect old, forgotten sheepskin coats in the abandoned houses and then sew something like fur ponchos for the winter, and also we made mittens and some fur mattresses for the beds. My father, when he noticed such a mattress one night on his bed, immediately rolled up all three and carted them away the next morning. It looked like he was preparing another refuge for us, except this one would be deep in the forest, and later on it came in very handy. But it also turned out later that no amount of labour and no amount of foresight can save you, no one and nothing can save you except luck.

In the meantime we lived through the hungriest month, June, which is when the supplies in a village usually run out. We shoved chopped dandelions into our mouths, made soup out of weeds, but for the most part we just gathered grass, pulled handfuls of it, and carried it, carried it, carried it home in sacks. We didn't know how to mow it, and anyway it hadn't really risen high enough for mowing yet. Finally Anisya gave us a scythe (in exchange for ten sackfuls of grass, which is not nothing), and Mom and I took turns mowing. I should repeat: We were living far away from the world, I missed my friends and girlfriends, but nothing reached us anymore. My father turned on the radio sometimes, but only rarely, because he wanted to save the batteries. The radio was full of lies and falsehoods, but we just mowed and mowed, and our little goat Raya was growing and we needed to find her a boy goat. We trod over to the next village again, but the peasant woman was unfriendly to us now, by this point everyone knew all about us, but they didn't know we had a goat, since Anisya was raising it—so the woman thought we'd lost Raya, and to hell with us. She wouldn't give us the other goat, and we didn't have any bread now, there wasn't any flour and there wasn't any bread, and anyway her little goat had grown, too, and she knew three kilos of fresh meat would mean a lot of money in this hungry time. We finally got her to agree to sell the goat for a kilo of salt and ten bars of soap. But for us this meant future milk, and we ran home to get our payment, telling the woman that we wanted the goat alive. "What," she answered, "I'm going to bloody my hands for you?" That evening we brought the little goat home and then began the tough summer days: mowing the grass, weeding the plot, grooming the potato plants, and all of this at the same pace as Anisya—we'd arranged with her that we'd take half the goats' manure, and somehow or other we fertilized the plot, but our vegetables still grew poorly and mostly produced weeds. Baba Anisya, freed from mowing grass, would tie up the goat and the little goatling kindergarten in a place where we could see them, and then gallop off into the woods for mushrooms and berries, after which she'd come by our plot and examine the fruits of our labour. We had to re-plant the dill, which we'd planted too deeply; we needed it for pickling cucumbers. The potatoes flourished mostly above ground level. My mother and I read "The Guide to Planting and Sowing," and my father finally finished his work in the forest, and we went to look at his new home. It turned out to be someone's hut, which my father had refurbished, put in window-frames, glass, doors, and covered the roof with tar. The house was empty. From then on at night we carried tables and benches and drawers and buckets and iron pots and pans and our remaining supplies, and hid everything, my father was digging a basement storage there, almost an underground home with a stove, our third. There were already some young vegetables peeking out of the earth in his garden.

My mother and I had become rough peasants over the summer, our fingers grew thick, with rough thick nails that the earth had eaten into, and the most interesting thing of all was that at the base of our nails we'd developed some sort of round calluses. I noticed that Anisya had the same thing on her fingers, as did Marfutka, who didn't do anything, and even Tanya, our most leisurely lady, a former nurse, had them too. Speaking of which, at this point Tanya's most constant visitor, Vera, the shepherdess, hung herself in the forest. She wasn't actually a shepherdess anymore, all the sheep had been eaten long ago, and at this time Anisya was very angry with Tanya and told us her secret, which was that Tanya didn't give Vera tea but instead some kind of medicine, which she couldn't live without, and that's why she hung herself, because she had no money anymore to pay for the medicine. Vera left behind her a little daughter, and without a father, to boot. Anisya, who had contact with Tarutino, the neighbouring village, told us further that the girl was living with her grandmother, but then it emerged that the grandmother was another Marfutka, only with a drinking problem, and so the little girl, already half insane, was brought home the next day by our mother in an old baby stroller.

My mother always needed more than the rest of us, and my father was angry, the girl wet her bed and never said a word, licked her own snot, didn't understand anything and cried at night for hours. Pretty soon none of us could live or sleep for these nighttime screams, and my father went off to live in the woods. There wasn't much for it but to go and give the girl back to her failed grandmother, but just then this same grandmother, Faina, appeared and, swaying on her feet, began demanding money for the girl and the stroller. In reply my mother went inside and brought out Lena, combed, showered, barefoot but in a clean dress. At this point Lena suddenly threw herself at my mother's feet, without a word, but like a grown-up, curling herself up in a ball and putting her arms around my mother's bare ankles. Her grandmother began crying and left without Lena and without the baby stroller—apparently, to die. She swayed on her feet as she walked and wiped her tears away with her fist—but she swayed not from drink but from hunger, as I later figured out. She didn't have any supplies, after all her daughter Vera hadn't earned anything for a long time. We ourselves mostly ate stewed grass in different forms, with plain mushroom soup being the most common dish.

Our little goats had been living for a while now with my father—it was safer there—and the trail to his house had almost disappeared, especially as my father never took the same path twice with his wheelbarrow, as a precaution, plotting for the future. Lena stayed with us. We would pour her off some milk, feed her berries and our mushroom soups. Everything became a lot more frightening when we thought of the coming winter. We had no flour and not a single grain of wheat; none of the farms in the area was operating, after all there hadn't been any gasoline or spare parts in ages, whereas the horses had been eaten even before that and there wasn't anything to work the fields on. My father walked around the abandoned fields, picked up some grain, but others had been by before him, he found just a little, a very small sack. He thought he'd figure out how to grow wheat under the snow on the little field near his house in the woods, he asked Anisya for when he should plant and sow, and she promised to tell him. She rejected the shovel, and there weren't any plugs to be found anywhere, so my father asked her to draw a plug and then began, just like Robinson Crusoe, to bang together some kind of contraption. Anisya herself didn't remember exactly how it worked, even though she's had to walk behind a cow with a plug a few times, in the old days, but my father was all aflame with his new engineering ideas and sat down to reinvent this particular bicycle. He was happy with his new fate and never pined for the life the city, where he'd left behind a great many enemies, including his parents, my grandmother and grandfather, whom I'd only seen when I was very little and who'd since been buried under the rubble of the arguments over my mom and my grandfather's apartment, may it rot, with its high ceilings and private bathroom and kitchen. We weren't fated ever to live there and now my grandparents were probably corpses. We didn't say anything to anyone when we left the city, though my father had been planning the escape a long time. That's how we managed to have so many sacks and boxes to take with us, because all of this stuff was cheap and, once upon a time, not subject to rationing, and my father, a farseeing man, collected it all over the course of several years. My father was a former athlete, a mountain climber and a geologist, he'd hurt his hip in an accident, and he'd long ago dreamed of escape, and here the circumstances came together with his still growing mania for running away, and so we did, we left, while the skies were still clear. "It's a clear day in all of Spain," my father would joke, literally every morning that it was sunny out.

The summer was a beautiful one, everything was blossoming, flowering, our Lena began to talk, she'd run after us into the forest, not to pick mushrooms but to run after my mother like she was tied to her, as if it were the main task of her young life. I taught her how to recognize edible mushrooms and berries, but it was useless, a little creature in that situation can't possibly tear herself away from grown-ups, she is saving her skin every minute of the day, and so she ran after my mother everywhere, on her short little legs, with her puffed-out stomach. She called my mother "Nanny." Where she picked up that word we had no idea, we'd never taught her it—and she called me that, too, which was very clever, actually.

One night we heard a noise outside our door like a cat meowing and went outside to find a newborn baby wrapped in an old, greasy coat. My father, who'd grown used to Lena and even came during the day sometimes to help around the house, now simply deflated. My mother didn't like it either, she immediately went over to Anisya to demand who could have done this—with the child, at night, accompanied by the quiet Lena, we marched over to Anisya's. She wasn't sleeping, she had also heard the child's cries and was very worried. She said that the first refugees had already arrived in Tarutino, and that soon they'd be coming to our village too, so we should expect more guests from here on out. The infant was squeaking shrilly and without interruption, he had a hard, puffed-out stomach. We invited Tanya over in the morning to have a look and without even touching him she said he wasn't going to survive—he had the infant's disease. The child suffered, yelled, and we didn't even have a pacifier, or any food for him. My mother dripped some water into his dried-out mouth and he nearly choked on it. He looked like he was about four months old. My mother ran at a good clip to Tarutino, traded a precious bit of salt for a pacifier, and returned full of energy, and the child drank a little bit of water from the bottle. My mother induced stool with some softening chamomile brew. We all, including my father, darted around as fast as we could, heating the water, giving the child a warm compress. It was clear to everyone that we needed to leave the house, the plot, our whole functioning household, or else we'd be destroyed. But leaving the plot meant starving to death. At the family conference my father announced that we'd be moving to the house in the woods and he'd be staying with a rifle and the dog in the shack next to the plot.

That night we set off with the first installment of things. The boy, whose name was now Nayden, rode atop the cart. To everyone's surprise, he'd recovered, then began sucking on the goat's milk, and now rode wrapped in a sheepskin. Lena walked alongside the cart holding on to the ropes.

At dawn we reached our new home, at which point my father immediately made a second run and then a third. He was like a cat carrying more and more of his litter in his teeth, that is to say all the many possessions he'd acquired, and now the little hut was smothered with things. That day, when all of us collapsed in exhaustion, my father set off for guard duty. At night he brought back some early vegetables from the garden on his wheelbarrow—potatoes, carrots, beets, and little onions. We laid this all out in the underground storage he'd created. The same night he set off again, but limped back almost immediately with an empty wheelbarrow. Gloomily he announced: That's it! Also he brought a can of milk for the boy. It turned out our house had been captured by some kind of squad, they'd already posted a guard at the plot, and Anisya's goat had already been taken to our former house. Anisya had lain in wait for my father on his escape path with that can of milk. My father was sad, but also he was pleased, he'd once again managed to escape, and escape with his whole family.

Now our only hope lay in my father's little plot and on mushrooms. Lena stayed in the house with the boy, we didn't take her with us to the forest now, we locked her in the house to keep her out of the way. Strangely enough she sat quietly with the boy, didn't beat her fists against the door. Nayden greedily drank the potato broth, while my mother and I scoured the woods with our bags and backpacks. We no longer pickled the mushrooms but just dried them, there was hardly any salt left now. My father began digging a well, as the nearest stream was very far.

On the fifth day of our immigration we were joined by Baba Anisya. She came to us with empty hands, with just a cat on her shoulder. Her eyes looked strange. Anisya sat for a while on the porch, holding the frightened cat on her lap, then gathered herself and went off into the woods. The cat hid under the porch. Soon Anisya came back with a whole apron's worth of mushrooms, though among them was a bright-red poisonous one. She remained sitting on the porch and didn't go into the house; we brought her out a portion of our poor mushroom soup in a can from the milk she used to give us. That evening my father took Anisya into the basement, where he'd built our third refuge, and she lay down and rested and the next day began actively scouring the forest for mushrooms. I'd go through the mushrooms she brought back, so she wouldn't poison herself. We'd dry some of them, and some we'd throw out. One time, coming home from the woods, we found all our refugees together on the porch. Anisya was rocking Nayden in her arms and just generally acting like a human being. She literally broke down and was telling Lena, choking on words: "They went through everything, took everything ... They didn't even look in on Marfutka, but they took everything of mine, they dragged the goat away by her rope." Anisya remained useful for a long time to come, took our goats out for walks, babysat Nayden and Lena until the frosts came. Then one day she lay down with the kids on the stove and left it only to use the outhouse.

The winter came and covered up all the paths that might have led to us. We had mushrooms, berries dried and boiled, potatoes from my father's plot, a whole attic filled with hay, pickled apples from abandoned gardens in the forest, even a few cans of pickled cucumbers and tomatoes. On the little field, under the snow, grew our winter crop of bread. We had our goats. We had a boy and a girl, for the continuation of the race, and a cat, who brought us mice from the forest, and a dog, Red, who didn't want to eat these mice, but with whom my father counted on hunting for rabbits soon. My father was afraid to hunt with his rifle, he was even afraid to chop wood because someone might hear us. He only chopped wood during the most vicious snow storms. We had a grandmother—the storehouse of the people's wisdom and their knowledge.

Cold desolate spaces spread out from us on all sides.

One time my father turned on the radio and tried for a while to hear what was out there. Everything was silent. Either the batteries had died or we really were the last ones left. My father's eyes shone: He'd escaped once again!

If in fact we're not alone, then they'll come for us. That much is clear. But, first of all, my father has a rifle, we have skis, and a smart dog. Second of all, they won't come for a while yet. We're living, and waiting, and out there, we know, someone is also living, and waiting, until our grain grows and our bread grows, and our potatoes, and our new little goats—and that's when they'll come. And take everything, including me. Until then they're being fed by our plot, and Anisya's plot, and Tanya's household. Tanya is long gone, but Marfutka is still there. When we're like Marfutka, they won't touch us, either.

But there's a long way to go until then. And in the meantime, of course, we're not just sitting here. My father and I have commenced work on our next refuge.

The View from the Balcony

by

WALLACE STEGNER

THE FRATERNITY HOUSE where they lived that summer was a good deal like a barracks, with its dormitory cut up into eight little plywood cells each with one dormer window, and its two shower rooms divided between the men and the women. They communized their cooking in the one big kitchen and ate together at a refectory table forty feet long. But the men were all young, all veterans, all serious students, and most of the wives worked part time in the university, so that their home life was a thing that constantly disintegrated and reformed, and they got along with a minimum of friction.

The lounge, as big as a basketball court, they hardly used. What they did use, daytime and nighttime, the thing that converted the austere barracks life into something sumptuous and country-clubbish, was the rooftop deck that stretched out from the lounge over the ten-car garage.

Directly under the bluff to which the house clung ran the transcontinental highway, but the deck was hidden and protected above it. At night the air was murmurous with insects, and sitting there, they would be bumped by blundering June bugs and feel the velvet kiss of moths. By standing up they could see the centerline of the highway palely emergent in the glow of the street lamp at the end of the drive. Beyond the highway, flowing with it in the same smooth curve, low-banked and smooth and dark and touched only with sparks and glimmers of light, was the Wawasee River.

More than a mile of the far shore was kept wild as a city park, and across those deep woods on insect-haunted nights, when traffic noise died for a moment and the night hung still around them, they could hear the lions roar.

The lions were in the zoo at the other side of the park. At first it was a shock to the students in the fraternity house to hear that heavy-chested, coughing, snarling roar, a more dangerous and ominous sound than should be heard in any American night, and for a moment any of them could have believed that the midland heat of the night was tropical heat and that real and wild lions of an ancient incorrigible ferocity roamed the black woods beyond the river. But after a week or two the nightly roaring had become as commonplace as the sound of traffic along the highway, and they rarely noticed it.

Altogether the fraternity house was a good place, in spite of the tasteless ostentation of the big echoing lounge and the Turkish-bath heat of the sleeping cubicles. They were lucky to be in it. They felt how lucky they were, and people who came out to drink beer on weekends kept telling them how lucky they were. So many less lucky ones were crammed into backstairs rooms or regimented into converted barracks. Out here there was a fine spaciousness, a view, a freedom. They were terribly lucky.

DEEP IN A SUN-STRUCK DAYDREAM, drowning in light and heat, the sun like a weight on her back and her body slippery with perspiration and her mouth pushed wetly out of shape against her wrist, Lucy Graham lay alone on the deck in the sultry paralysis of afternoon. Her eyes looked into an empty red darkness; in her mind the vague voluptuous uncoiling of memory and fantasy was slowed almost to a stop, stunned almost to sleep.

All around her the afternoon was thick, humid, stirring with the slow fecundities of Midwestern summer—locust-shrill and bird-cheep and fly-buzz, child-shout and the distant chime of four o'clock from the university's clock tower. Cars on the highway grew from hum to buzz-saw whine and slapped past and diminished, coning away to a point of sound, a humming speck. Deep inside the house a door banged, and she heard the scratch of her own eyelashes against her wrist as she blinked, thinking groggily that it was time to get up and shower. Everyone would be coming home soon; Tommy Probst would be through with his exams by four-thirty, and tonight there would be a celebration and a keg of beer.

For a while longer she lay thinking of Tommy, wishing Charley were as far along as that, with his thesis done and nothing but the formalities left. Then it struck her as odd, the life they all lived: this sheltered, protected present tipping ever so slightly toward the assured future. After what they had been, navigator and bombardier, Signal Corps major, artillery captain, Navy lieutenant and yeoman and signalman first class, herself a WAAF and two or three of the other wives WACS or WAVES—after being these things it was almost comic of them to be so seriously and deeply involved in becoming psychologists, professors, pharmacists, historians.

She sat up, her head swimming and the whole world a sheeted glare. Lifting the hair from her neck, she let the cooling air in and shook her head at the absurdity of lying in the sun until her brains were addled and her eyes almost fried from her head. But in England there had never been the time, rarely the place, seldom the sun. She was piggy about the sun as she had been at first about the food. From here England seemed very scrawny and very dear, but very far away. Looking at her arm, she could not believe the pagan colour of her own skin.

Quick steps came across the terrazzo floor of the lounge, and Phyllis Probst stepped out, hesitating in the door. "Have you seen anything of Tommy?"

"No," Lucy said. "Is he through his exams already?"

An extraordinarily complex look came over Phyllis' face. She looked hot, her hair was stringy, she seemed half out of breath. Her brows frowned and her mouth smiled a quick weak smile and her eyes jumped from Lucy out across the highway and back again.

Lucy stood up. "Is something wrong?"

"No," Phyllis said. "No, it's just ... You haven't seen him at all?"

"Nobody's been home. I did hear a door bang just a minute ago, though."

"That was me," Phyllis said. "I thought he might have come home and gone to bed."

"Phyllis, is he sick?" Lucy said, and took Phyllis' arm. She felt the arm tremble. Still with the terrified, anxious, distressed expression on her face, Phyllis began to cry.

"I've got to find him," she said, and tried to pull away.

"We'll find him," Lucy said. "What happened? Tell me."

"He ... I don't know. Helen Fast called me from the Graduate School office about two. I don't know whether he got sick, or whether the questions were too hard, or what. Helen said he came out once and asked for a typewriter, because he's left-handed and he smudges so when he writes, and she gave him a portable. But in a few minutes he came out again and put the portable on her desk and gave her a queer desperate look and walked out."

"Oh, what a shame," Lucy said, and with her arm around Phyllis sought for something else to say.

"But where is he?" Phyllis asked. "I called the police and the hospital and I went to every beer joint in town."

"Don't worry," Lucy said, and pushed her gently inside. "You come and take a cool shower and relax. We'll send the boys hunting when they come."

They came, half a household of them, before the two girls were halfway up the stairs; and they brought Tommy with them. He walked through the door like a prisoner among deputies, quietly, his dark smooth head bent a little as if in thought. Lucy saw his eyes lift and meet his wife's in an indescribable look. "Thanks for the lift," Tommy said to Charley Graham, and went up the stairs and took his wife's arm, and together they went down the corridor.

Lucy came back down to where her husband stood. "What on earth happened?"

He pursed up his lips, lifting his shoulders delicately, looked at the others, who were dispersing toward dormitory and shower room. "We cruised the park on a hunch and found him over there tossing sticks in the river," Charley said.

"Why didn't he take the exams?"

Her husband lifted his shoulders again.

"But it's so absurd!" she said. "He could have written the Lord's Prayer backward and they would have passed him. It was just a ritual, like an initiation. Everyone said so."

"Of course," he said. "It was a cinch." He put an arm across her shoulders, made a face as if disgusted by the coco-butter gooiness, and kissed her from a great distance. "Kind of dampens the party."

"We'd better not have it."

"Why not? I'm going to ask Richards and Latour to come over. They can straighten Tommy out."

"Will they give him another chance, do you think?"

"*Give* him?" Charley said. "They'll force it on him."

In the lounge after dinner the atmosphere was weighted and

awkward. Lucy had a feeling that somehow, without in any way agreeing on it, the whole lot of them had arrived at a policy of elaborately ignoring what had happened to Tommy. Faced with the uncomfortable alternatives of ignoring it or of slapping him on the back, encouraging him, they had chosen the passive way. It was still too hot on the deck for sitting; in the lounge they were too aware of each other. Some hunted up corners and dove into books. The others lounged and waited. Watching them, Lucy saw how the eyes strayed to Tommy when his back was turned, judging him. She saw that look even in Charley's face, the contempt that narrowed the eyes and fluttered the nostrils. As if geared up to play a part, Tommy stayed, looking self-consciously tragic. His wife was around him like an anxious hen.

Donna Earp stood up suddenly into a silence. "Lord, it's sultry," she said. "I wish it would rain."

She went out on the deck, and Lucy and Charley followed her. The sun was dazzling and immense behind the maple tree that overhung the corner. Shadows stretched almost across the quiet river. The roof was warm through Lucy's shoes, and the railing was hot to her hand.

"Has anyone talked to him at all?" she said.

Charley shook his head, shrugged in that Frenchy little way he had.

"Won't it look queer?"

"Richards and Latour are coming. They'll talk to him."

"What about getting the beer, then? It's like a funeral in there."

"Funeral!" Charley said, and snorted. "That's another thing that happened today. Quite a day." He looked at the sun, disintegrating behind the trees.

"Whose funeral?"

"Kay Cedarquist's."

"Who's she?"

"She's a girl," he said. "Maybe I'd better get the beer, I'll tell you later about the funeral. It's a howl."

"Sounds like a peculiar funeral."

"Peculiar is a small word for it," he said. In the doorway he met Art Morris, and haled him along to get the beer.

After the glare, the shade of the tree was wonderful. Lucy sat on the railing looking over the river, and a car pulled into the drive and parked with its nose against the bluff. Paul Latour, the psychology professor, and Clark Richards, head of the department of social science, got out and held assisting hands for Myra, Richards' young wife. For several seconds the three stood looking up, smiling. They seemed struck by something; none of them spoke until Professor Richards with his hand in his bosom took a stance and said:

O! she doth teach the torches to burn bright.
It seems she hangs upon the cheek of night
Like a rich jewel in an Ethiop's ear …

He was a rather chesty man, neat in a white suit; in the violet shadow of the court his close-clipped moustache smudged his mouth. Latour's grim and difficult smile was upturned beside him, Myra Richards' schoolgirl face swam below there like a lily on a pond. "Hi, lucky people," Myra said. "What repulsively romantic surroundings!"

"Come up," Lucy said. "It's cooler at this altitude."

They made her feel pretty, they took away the gloom that Tommy Probst's failure had dropped upon them all. When you were all working through the assured present to the assured future, it was more than a personal matter when someone failed. Ever since dinner they had been acting as if the foundations were shaken, and she knew why. She was glad Richards and Latour were here, outsiders, older, with better perspective.

As she sat waiting for them the lion roared, harsh and heavy across the twilight river. "Down, Bruno!" Henry Earp said automatically, and there was a laugh. The door banged open, and Charley and Art staggered the keg through, to set it up on a table. The talk lifted suddenly in tempo. The guests stepped out onto the deck in a chorus of greeting; the lounge emptied itself, lugubrious Probsts and all, into the open air. Gloom dissolved in the promise of festivity. Charley drew the first soapy glasses from the keg. Far across several wooded bends the university's clock tower, lacy and soaring, was pinned suddenly against the sky by the floodlights.

She saw them working on Tommy during the evening. Within the first half-hour, Clark Richards took him over in the corner, and Lucy saw them talking there, an attractive picture of *magister* and *studens,* Tommy with his dark head bent and his face smoothed perfectly expressionless, Richards solid and confident and reassuring. She saw him leave Tommy with a clap on the shoulder, and saw Tommy's smile that was like spoken thanks, and then Phyllis came slipping over to where Tommy stood, wanting to be told of the second chance. Some time later, when the whole party had been loosened by beer and a carful of other students had arrived, and the twilight was so far gone into dusk that the river was only a faint metallic shine along the foot of the woods, Paul Latour hooked his arm into Tommy's and unsmiling, looking glum as a detective, led him inside. By that time the party was loud.

Lucy stayed on the fringes of it, alert to her duties as hostess, knowing that the other girls forgot any such responsibilities as soon as they had a couple of drinks. She rescued glasses for people who set them down, kept edging through the crowd around the keg to get glasses filled, talked with new arrivals; circulated quietly, seeing that no bashful student got shoved off into a corner, making sure that Myra Richards didn't get stranded anywhere. But after a half-hour she quit worrying about Myra; Myra was drinking a good deal and having a fine gay time.

It did not cool off much with the dark. The deck was breathless and sticky, and they drank their beer fast because it warmed so rapidly in the glass. Inside, as she paused by the keg, Lucy saw Latour and Tommy still talking head to head in the lighted lounge. Cocking her head a little, she listened to the sound of the party, appraising it. She heard Myra's laugh and a series of groans and hoots from the boys, apparently at someone's joke.

She moved away from the brittle concentration of noise and out toward the rail, and as she passed through the crowd she heard Art Morris say, "... got the Westminster Choir and a full symphony orchestra to do singing commercials. That's what Hollywood is, one big assembled empty Technique. They hunt mosquitoes with .155's."

No one was constrained any more; everything was loose and bibulous. As she leaned on the rail a voice spoke at her shoulder, and she turned to see Professor Richards with a glass of beer in his hand and his coat off. But he still looked dignified because he had kept his tie on and his sleeves rolled down. Most of the boys were down to T-shirts, and a girl who had come with the carload of students was in a halter that was hardly more than a bra. She was out in an open space now, twirling, showing the full ballerina skirt she had made out of an India print bedspread.

"Find any breeze?" Richards said.

"No, just looking at the river."

"It's very peaceful," he said. "You're lucky to have this place."

"I know." She brushed an insect from her sticky cheek. It was pleasant to her to be near this man, with his confidence and his rich resonant voice, and a privilege that they could all know him on such informal terms. Until six months ago he had been something big and important in the American Military Government in Germany.

He was saying, "How do you like it by now? It's a good bit different from England."

"I'm liking it wonderfully," she said. "People have been lovely."

"Thoroughly acclimated?"

"Not quite to this heat."

"This just makes the corn grow," he said, and she heard in his voice, with forgiving amusement that it should be there in the voice of this so-distinguished man, the thing she had heard in so many American voices—the confidence they had that everything American was bigger and better and taller and colder and hotter and wider and deeper than anything else. "I've seen it a hundred degrees at two in the morning," Richards said. "Inside a house, of course."

"It must be frightful."

He shrugged, smiling with his smudged mouth in the semidarkness. "Myra and I slept three nights on the golf course last time we had that kind of weather."

"We've already slept out here a night or two," Lucy said. She looked across the shadowy, crowded, noisy deck. "Where is Myra? I haven't had a chance to talk to her at all."

"A while ago she was arguing Zionism with a bunch of the boys," Richards said. He chuckled with his full-chested laugh, indulgent and avuncular. "She knows nothing whatever about Zionism."

Lucy had a brief moment of wondering how a professor really looked upon his students. Could he feel completely at ease among men and women of so much less experience and learning, or did he always have a bit of the paternal in his attitude? And when he married a girl out of one of his classes, as Professor Richards had, did he ever—and did *she* ever—get over feeling that he was God omnipotent?

"I imagine you must feel a little as I did when I got back from Germany," he was saying. "After living under such a cloud of fear and shortages and loss, suddenly to come out into the sun."

"Yes," she said, "I've felt it. I take the sun like medicine."

"It's too bad we can't sweep that cloud away for the whole world," Richards said. He looked out over the river, and she thought his voice had a stern, austere ring. "England particularly. England looked straight in the face of disaster and recognized it for what it was and fought on. It's a pity the cloud is still there. They've earned something better."

"Yes," she said again, for some reason vaguely embarrassed. Talk about England's grit always bothered her. You didn't talk about it when you were in any of it. Why should it be talked about outside? To dispel the slight pompous silence she said, "I saw you talking to Tommy Probst."

Richards laughed. "Momentary funk," he said. "It's preposterous. He's one of the best students we've had in years. He'll come up and take it again tomorrow and pass it like a shot."

He touched her shoulder with a pat that was almost fatherly, almost courtly, and lifted his empty glass in explanation and drifted away.

IN THE CORNER BY THE BEER KEG, people were jammed in a tight group. A yell of laughter went up, hoots, wolf calls. As the lounge door let a brief beam of light across the deck Lucy saw Myra in the middle of the crowd. Her blond hair glinted silver white, her eyes had a sparkle, her mouth laughed. A vivid face. No wonder Professor Richards had picked her out of a whole class.

Charley broke out of the crowd, shaking his head and grinning, bony-shouldered in the T-shirt. He put a damp arm around her and held his glass for her to sip. "How's my Limey bride?"

"Steamed like a pudding," she said. "It sounds like a good party over here."

He gave her a sidelong down-mouthed look. "Doak was just telling the saga of the funeral."

Laughter broke out again, and Myra's voice said, "Doak, I think that's the most awful thing I've ever ..."

"Tell me," Lucy said, "what's so screamingly funny about a girl's funeral?"

"Didn't you ever hear about Kay Cedarquist?"

"No."

"She was an institution. Schoenkampf's lab assistant, over in Biology. She had cancer. That's what she died of, day before yesterday."

Lucy waited. "Is it just that I'm British?"

Wiping beer from his lips with his knuckles, Charley grinned at her in the shadow. "Nothing is so funny to Americans as a corpse," he said. "Unless it's a decaying corpse, or one that falls out of the coffin. Read Faulkner, read Caldwell. Kay sort of fell out of the coffin."

"Oh, my God," Lucy said, appalled.

"Oh, not really. See, she was Schoenkampf's mistress as well as his assistant. He's got a wife and four kids and they're all nudists, I'll tell you about them too some time. But Schoenkampf also had Kay, and he set her up in an apartment."

He drank again, raised a long admonishing finger. *"But,"* he said. "When Schoenkampf was home with Mrs. Schoenkampf and the four nudist children, Kay had a painter from Terre Haute. He spent a lot of time in our town and painted murals all over Kay's walls ... haven't I ever told you about those murals?"

"No."

"Gentle Wawasee River scenes," Charley said. "Happy farm children in woodlot and pasture, quiet creeks, steepled towns. Kay told Schoenkampf she had it done because art rested her nerves. She had this double feature going right up to the time she died, practically."

"You're making this all up," Lucy said.

He put his hands around her waist and lifted her to the rail. "Sit up here." Confidential and grinning, he leaned over her, letting her in on the inside. It was a pose she had loved in him when they walked all over Salisbury talking and talking and talking, when they were both in uniform.

"But if she had cancer," she said, "wasn't she ill, in bed?"

"Not till the last month." He knocked the bottom of his glass lightly against the stone and seemed to brood, half amused. "She was a good deal of a mess," he said. "Also, she had dozens of short subjects besides her double feature. Graduate students, married or single, she wasn't fussy. Nobody took her cancer very seriously. Then all of a sudden she up and died."

Lucy stirred almost angrily, moving her arm away from his sticky bare skin. "I don't think all that's funny, Charley."

"Maybe not. But Kay had no relatives at all, so Schoenkampf had to arrange the funeral. To keep himself out of it as much as possible, he got a bunch of students to act as pallbearers. Every one of them had passed his qualifying exams. That was what got the snickers."

"Graduate students?" Lucy said. "What have their qualifying exams to do... ?" Then she saw, and giggled involuntarily, and was angry at herself for giggling. Over the heads of the crowd she saw the group of students still clustered in the corner. They had linked arms in a circle and were singing "I Wanted Wings." Myra was still among them, between Doak and the girl in the bra and the India print bedspread.

"Who?" she said. "Doak and Jackson and that crowd?"

"They led the parade," Charley said, and snorted like a horse into his glass. "I guess there were three or four unfortunates who couldn't find an empty handle on the coffin."

Sitting quietly, the stone still faintly warm through her dress, she felt as if a greasy film had spread over her mind. It was such a nasty little sordid story from beginning to end, sneaking and betrayal and double betrayal and fear and that awful waiting, and finally death and heartless grins. "Well," Charley said, "I see you don't like my tale."

She turned toward him, vaguely and impulsively wanting reassurance. "Charley, was she pretty?"

"No," he said. "Not pretty at all, just easy."

What she wanted, the understanding, wasn't there. "I think it's wry," she said. "Just wry and awful."

"It ought to be," he said, "but somehow it isn't. Not if you knew Kay. You didn't."

With a kind of dismay she heard herself say, not knowing until she said it that there was that much distress and that much venom in her, the thing that leaped abruptly and unfairly to her mind, "Did *you*?"

He stared at her, frowned, looked amazed, and then grinned, and the moment he grinned it was all right again, she could laugh and they were together and not apart. But when he waved his glass and suggested that they go see how the beer was holding out she shook her head and stayed behind on the railing. As he worked his way tall through the jam of shadowy people she had an impulse to jump down and follow him so that not even twenty feet of separation could come desperately between, but the bray of talk and laughter from the deck was like a current that pinned her back against the faintly warm stone, threatening to push her off, and she looked behind her once into the dark pit of the court and tightened her hands on the railing.

SHE DISLIKED EVERYONE there for being strangers, aliens to her and to her ways of feeling, unable from the vast plateau of security to see or understand the desperation and fear down below. And even while she hated them for it, she felt a pang of black and bitter envy of that untroubled assurance they all had, that way of shrugging off trouble because no trouble that could not be cured had ever come within their experience. Even the war—a temporary unpleasantness. *Their* homes hadn't leaped into unquenchable flame or shaken down in rubble and dust. *They* had known no families in Coventry. Fighting the war, they could still feel not desperate but magnanimous, like good friends who reached out to help an acquaintance in a scuffle.

She hated them, and as she saw Paul Latour approaching her and knew she could not get away, she hated him worst of all. His face was like the face of a predatory bird, beaked, grim-lipped; because of some eye trouble he always wore dark glasses, and his prying, intent, hidden stare was an agony to encounter. His mouth was hooked back in a constant sardonic smile. He not merely undressed her with his eyes; he dissected her most intimate organs, and she knew he was a cruel man, no matter how consistently and amazingly kind he had been to Charley, almost like a father, all the way through school. Charley said he had a mind like a fine watch. But she wished he would not come over, and she trembled, unaccountably emotional, feeling trapped.

Then he was in front of her, big-shouldered for his height, not burly but somehow giving the impression of great strength, and his face like the cold face of a great bird thrust toward her and the hidden stare stabbed into her and the thin smile tightened. "Nobody to play with?" he asked. There was every unpleasant and cutting suggestion in the remark. A wallflower. Maybe halitosis. Perhaps B.O.

She came back quickly enough. "Too hot to play." To steer the talk away from her she said, "You've been conferring with Tommy."

"Yes," he said, and a spasm of what seemed almost contempt twisted across his mouth. "I've been conferring with Tommy."

"Is he all right now?"

"What do you mean, all right?"

"Is he over his … trouble?"

"He is if he can make up his mind to grow up."

Now it was her turn. "What do you mean?"

The dark circles of his glasses stared at her blankly, and then she realized that Latour was laughing. "I thought you were an intelligent woman."

"I'm not," she said half bitterly, "I'm stupid."

His laugh was still there, an almost soundless chuckle. Beyond him the circle of singers had widened to include almost everyone on the deck, and thirty people were bellowing, "We were sailing a-lo-o-o-ng, on Moonlight Bay …"

Latour came closer, to be heard, "You mean to tell me you haven't even yet got wise to Tommy?"

"I don't know what you mean. He's a very good student—"

"Oh, student!" Latour said. "Sure, he's a student. There's nothing wrong with his brains. He's just a child, that's all, he never grew up."

A counterattraction to the singing had started in the lounge. A few of the energetic had turned on the radio and were dancing on the smooth terrazzo floor. Lucy saw figures float by the lighted door: Donna and Henry Earp, the Kinseys, Doak and Myra Richards, Tommy and Phyllis. The radio cut quick and active across the dragging tempo of the singing.

"But he was in the air force three years," she said. "He's a grown man, he's been through a lot. I never saw anything childish in him."

He turned his head; his profile was cruel and iron against the light. "You're disgustingly obtuse," his mocking voice said. "What did *you* make of that show he put on today?"

"I don't know," she said, hesitating. "That he was afraid, I suppose."

"Afraid of what?"

"Of what? That he'd fail, that he wouldn't make it after all."

"Go to the foot of the class."

"Pardon?"

"Go to the foot of the class," Latour said. "Look at the record. Only child, doting mother. I knew him as an undergraduate, and he's been trying for five or six years to break loose. Or he thought he was. If it hadn't been for the war he'd have found out sooner that he wasn't. The war came just as he graduated, just right so he could hide in it. He could even make a show like a hero, like a flyboy. But not as a pilot, notice. He busted out in pilot training. Somebody else would have the real responsibility. After the war, back to school where he's still safe, with GI benefits and no real decisions to make. And then all of a sudden he wakes up and he's pretty near through. In about three hours he'll be out in the bright light all by himself with a Ph.D. in his hand and a career to make and no mother, no Army, no university, to cuddle him. He wasn't afraid of that exam, he was afraid of passing it."

Lucy was silent. She believed him completely, the pattern matched at every edge, but she rebelled at the triumph and contempt in his voice. Suppose he was completely right: Tommy Probst was still his student and presumably his friend, somebody to like and help, not someone to triumph over. Sticky with the slow ooze of perspiration, feeling the hot night dense and smothering around her, she moved restlessly on the rail. Latour reached into the pocket of his seersucker jacket and brought out a pint bottle.

"Drink? I've been avoiding the bellywash everyone else is drinking."

"No, thank you," Lucy said. "Couldn't I get you a glass and some ice?"

"I like it warm," he said. "Keeps me reminded that it's poison."

She saw then what she had not seen before, that he was quite drunk, but out of her vague rebelliousness she said, "Mr. Latour, all the boys are in Tommy's position almost exactly, aren't they? They're right at that edge where they have to be fully responsible adults. They all work much too hard. Any of them could crack just the way Tommy did. Charley could do it. It isn't a disgrace."

Latour's head went back, the bottle to his lips, and for a moment he was a bird drinking, his iron beak in the air, at once terrible and ridiculous. "You needn't worry about Charley," he said when he had brought the bottle down. "Charley's another breed of rat. He's the kind that wants to wear the old man's breeches even before they're off the old man's legs. Tommy's never got over calling me 'Sir,' Charley'd eat me tomorrow if he thought he could get away with it."

"Who'd do what?" Charley said. He had appeared behind Latour with two glasses in his hands. He passed one to Lucy with a quick lift of the eyebrows and she loved him again for having seen that she was trapped.

"You, you ungrateful whelp," Latour said. He dropped the bottle in his pocket; his blank stare and forward-thrusting face seemed to challenge Charley. "I'll tell you what you think. You think you're younger than I am. That's right. You think you're better-looking than I am. Maybe that's right too. You think you could put me down. That's a foolish mistake. You think you're as smart as I am, and that's even more foolish."

His thumb jerked up under Charley's wishbone like a disembowelling knife, and Charley grunted. "Given half a chance," Latour said, "you'd open your wolfish jaws and swallow me. You're like the cannibals who think it gives them virtue to eat their enemy's heart. You'd eat mine."

"He's distraught," Charley said to Lucy. "Maybe we should get him into a tepid bath."

"You and who else?" Latour said, like a belligerent kid. His sardonic fixed grin turned on Lucy. "You can see how it goes in his mind. I develop a lot of apparatus for testing perception, and I fight the whole damn university till I get a lab equipped with sound equipment and Phonelescopes and oscillographs and electronic microscopes, and then punks like this one come along and pick my brains and think they know as much as the old man. I give them the equipment and provide them with ideas and supervise their work and let them add their names to mine on scholarly articles, and they think they're all ready to put on the old man's breeches."

"Why, Paul," Charley said, "you've got an absolute anxiety neurosis. You should see a psychiatrist. You'll brood yourself into paranoia and begin to have persecution complexes. You've got one now. Here I've been holding you up all year, and you think I'm secretly plotting to eat you. You really should talk to a good psychologist."

"Like who?" Latour said, grinning. "Some punk like you whose soft spot hasn't hardened yet?"

"There are one or two others almost as good," Charley said, "but Graham is the best."

Latour took the bottle from his pocket and drank again and screwed on the cap and dropped the bottle back in the pocket. His stare never left Charley's face; his soundless chuckle broke out into a snort.

"A punk," he said. "A callow juvenile, a pubescent boy, a beardless youth. You're still in the spanking stage."

Winking at Lucy, Charley said, "Takes a good man."

"Oh, not so good," Latour said. "Any *man* could do it."

His hand shot out for Charley's wrist, and Charley jerked back, slopping his beer. It seemed to Lucy that something bright and alert had leaped up in both of them, and she wanted to tell them to drop it, but the noise of singing and the moan of dance music from the lounge made such a current of noise that she didn't trust her voice against it. But Latour's edged foolery bothered her; she didn't think he was entirely joking, and she didn't think Charley thought so either. She watched them scuffle and shove each other, assuming exaggeratedly the starting pose for a wrestling match. Latour reached in his pocket and handed her the almost empty whisky bottle; he removed his glasses and passed them to her, and she saw his eyes like dark holes with a glint of light at the bottom.

"For heaven's sake," she said, "you're not going to ..."

Latour exploded into violent movement, reached and leaned and jerked in a flash, and suddenly Charley's length was across his shoulder, held by crotch and neck, and Latour with braced legs was staggering forward. He was headed directly for the rail. Charley's legs kicked frantically, his arm whipped around Latour's neck in a headlock, but Latour was brutally strong. Face twisted under Charley's arm, he staggered ahead.

Lucy screamed, certain for a moment that Latour was going to throw Charley over. But her husband's legs kicked free, and he swung sideward to get his feet on the floor. Latour let go his neck hold, and his palms slapped against Charley's body as he shifted. Charley was clinging to his headlock, twisting the blockier Latour into a crouch. Then somehow Latour dove under him, and they crashed.

The whole crowd was around them, shutting off the light from the lounge so that the contestants grunted and struggled in almost total darkness. Lucy bent over them, screaming at Charley to quit it, let go. Someone moved in the crowd, and in a brief streak of light she saw Latour's hands, iron strong, tearing Charley's locked fingers apart, and the veins ridged on Charley's neck as he clung to his hold.

"Stop it!" she screamed at them. "You'll get all dirty, you'll get hurt, stop it, please, Charley!"

Latour broke free and spun Charley like a straw man, trying to get a hold for a slam. But as they went to the floor again Charley's legs caught him in a head scissors and bent him harshly back.

"Great God," Henry Earp said beside Lucy. "What is this, fun or fight?"

"I don't know," she said. "Fun. But make them stop." She grabbed the arm of Clark Richards. "Make them stop, please!"

Richards bent over the wrestlers, quiet now, Latour's head forced back and Charley lying still, just keeping the pressure on. "Come on," Richards said. He slapped them both on the back. "Bout's a draw. Let go, Charley."

"Okay with me," Charley said. "You satisfied with a draw, Paul?"

Latour said nothing. "All right," Richards said. "Let's call it off, Paul. Someone might get hurt."

As Charley unlocked his legs and rolled free, Latour was up and after him like a wolf, but Richards and Henry and several others held him back. He put a hand to his neck and stood panting. "That was a dirty hold, Graham."

"Not so dirty as getting dumped twenty feet into a courtyard," Charley said. His T-shirt was ripped half off him. He grinned fixedly at Latour. Sick and fluttery at what had happened, Lucy took his hand, knowing that it was over now, the support was gone, the rest of the way was against difficulties all the way. "You foolish people," she said. "You'll spoil a good party."

SOMEHOW, by the time she had got herself together after her scare, the party had disintegrated. The unmarried graduate students who had been noisily there all evening had vanished, several of the house couples had gone quietly to bed, The keg was empty, and a half-bottle of whisky stood unwanted on the table. A whole carful of people had gone out the Terre Haute road for sandwiches, taking Paul Latour with them. The court below the rail was empty except for Charley's jeep and Clark Richards' sedan, and the deck was almost deserted, when Richards stepped out of the lounge with his white coat on, ready to go home.

He came from light into darkness, so that for a moment he stood turning his head, peering. "Myra?" he said. "We should be getting on."

"She isn't out here," Lucy said, and jumped down from the railing where she had been sitting talking to Charley. "Isn't she in the lounge?"

"I just looked," Richards said. "Maybe she's gone up to the ladies' room."

He came out to lean against the rail near them, looking out across the darkness to the floodlighted clock tower floating in the sky. "It's a little like the spire of Salisbury Cathedral, isn't it?" he said. "Salisbury Cathedral across the Avon." He turned his face toward Lucy. "Isn't that where you're from, Salisbury?"

"Yes," she said, "it is rather like."

Then an odd thing happened. The southwest horizon leaped up suddenly, black and jagged, hill and tree and floating tower, with the green glow of heat lightning behind it, and when the lightning winked out, the tower went with it, leaving only the unbroken dark. "Wasn't that queer?" she said. "They must have turned off the floodlights just at that instant. It was almost as if the lightning wiped it out."

They were all tired, yawning, languid with the late hour and the beer and the unremitting, oozing heat. Richards looked at his watch, holding it so that light from the lounge fell on it. "Where can Myra be?" he said. "It's one o'clock."

Slowly Charley slid off the rail, groaning. "Could she be sick? Did she have too much, you think?"

"I don't know," Richards said. His voice was faintly snappish, irritated. "I don't think so, but she could have, I suppose."

"Let me just look up in the shower room," Lucy said, and slipped away from them, through the immense hot lounge. Art Morris was asleep on the big sofa, looking greasy with sweat under the bluish light. Down the long wide hall she felt like a tiny lost figure in a nightmare and thought what a really queer place this was to live in, after all. So big it forgot about you. She pushed the door, felt for the switch. Light leaped on the water-beaded tile, the silence opened to the lonely drip of a tap. No one was in the shower room, no shoes showed under the row of toilet doors.

When she got back to the deck, someone had turned on the powerful light above the door, and the party lay in wreckage there, a surly shambles of slopped beer and glasses and wadded napkins and trampled cigarette butts. In that light the Earps and Charley and Richards were looking at each other abashed.

"It's almost a cinch she went with the others out to the Casino," Charley was saying. "There was a whole swarm of them went together."

"You'd think she would have said something," Richards said. His voice was so harsh that Lucy looked at him in surprise and saw his mouth tight and thin, his face drawn with inordinate anxiety. "She wasn't upstairs?"

Lucy shook her head. For an instant Richards stood with his hands opening and closing at his sides. Abruptly he strode to the rail and looked over it, following it around to the corner and peering over into the tangle of weeds and rubbish at the side. He spun around as if he feared guns were pointed at his back. "Who saw her last? What was she doing? Who was she with?"

No one spoke for a moment, until Henry Earp said cautiously, "She was dancing a while ago, a whole bunch of us were. But that was a half-hour ago, at least."

"Who with?" Richards said, and then slapped at the air with his hand and said, "No, that wouldn't tell us anything. She must have gone for a sandwich."

"We can go see," Charley said. "Matter of fact, I'd like a sandwich myself. Why don't we run up the road and see if she's at the Casino? She probably didn't notice what time it was."

"No," Richards said grimly. Lucy found it hard to look at him, she was so troubled with sympathy and embarrassment. "Probably she didn't." He looked at Charley almost vaguely, and sweat was up on his forehead. "Would you mind?" he said. "Perhaps I ought to stay here, in case she ..."

"I'll stay here," Lucy said. The distraught vague eyes touched her.

"You'll want something to eat too. You go along."

"No," she said. "I'd rather stay. I would anyway." To Charley she said, "Why don't you and Henry and Donna go? You could look in at the Casino and the Tavern and all those places along there."

With his arm around her he walked her to the lounge door, and everything that had passed that evening was in their look just before he kissed her. When she turned around Richards was watching. In the bald light, swarming with insects that crawled and leaped and fluttered toward the globe above the doors, his eyes seemed to glare. Lucy clicked off the light and dropped them back into darkness.

"Should you like a drink?" she said into the black.

After a moment he answered, "No, thank you."

Gradually his white-suited figure emerged again as her eyes adjusted. He was on the rail looking out across the river and woods. Heat lightning flared fitfully again along the staring black horizon. The jeep started down below them; the lights jumped against the bluff, turned twisting the shadows, and were gone with the diminishing motor.

"Don't worry," Lucy said. "I'm sure she just forgot about the time and went for something to eat. We should have had something here, but somehow with so many to plan things, nothing ever gets planned."

"I don't like that river," Richards said. "It's so absolutely black down there ..." He swung around at her, "Have you got a flashlight?"

"I think so," she said, "but don't you suppose—"

"Could I borrow it, please?" he said. "I'm going down along the bank to look. If you'd stay here—if she should come back ..."

She slipped in and past the still-sleeping Art Morris and found a flashlight in the kitchen drawer, and now suddenly it was as if she were five years back in time, the cool tube in her hand, the intense blackout darkness around, the sense of oppression, the waiting, the search. That sense was even stronger a few minutes later as she sat on the rail and saw the thin slash of the light down along the riverbank, moving slowly, cutting on and off, eventually disappearing in the trees.

It was very still. Perched on the rail, she looked out from the deck they were so lucky to have, over the night-obliterated view that gave them such a sense of freedom and space, and in all the dark there was no sound louder than the brush of a moth's wings or the tick of an armoured bug against the driveway light. Then far up the highway a point of sound bored into the silence and grew and rounded, boring through layers of dark and soundless air, until it was a rush and a threat and a roar, and headlights burst violently around the corner of the bluff and reached across the shine of water and picked out, casual and instantaneous, a canoe with a couple in it.

It was there, starkly white, for only a split instant, and then the road swung, the curtain came down. She found it hard to believe that it had been there at all; she even felt a little knife-prick of terror that it could have been there—so silent, so secret, so swallowed in the black, as unseen and unfelt and unsuspected as a crocodile at a jungle ford.

The heat lightning flared again like the flare of distant explosions or the light of burning towns. Instinctively, out of a habit long outgrown, and even while her eyes remained fixed on the place where the canoe had been, she waited for the sound of the blast, but nothing came; she found herself waiting almost ridiculously, with held breath, and that was the time when the lion chose to roar again.

That challenge, coming immediately after the shock of seeing the silent and somehow stealthy canoe, brought a thought that stopped her pulse: "What if he should be loose?" She felt the adrenaline pump into her blood as she might have felt an electric shock. Her heart pounded and her breath came fast through her open mouth. What if he should be loose?

What if, in these Indiana woods by this quiet river where all of them lived and worked for a future full of casual expectation, far from the jungles and the velds where lions could be expected and where darkness was full of danger, what if here too fear prowled on quiet pads and made its snarling noise in the night? This fraternity house where they lived amicably was ringed with dark water and darker woods where the threat lay in wait. This elevated balcony which she could flood with light at the flip of a finger, this fellowship of youth and study and common experience and common hopes, this common belief in the future, were as friable as walls of cane, as vulnerable as grass huts, and she did not need the things that had happened that evening, or the sight of Clark Richards' tiny light flicking and darting back toward her along the riverbank, to know that what she had lived through for six years was not over and would perhaps never be over for any of them, that in their hearts they were alone, terrified, and at bay, each with his ears attuned to some roar across the woods, some ripple of the water, some whisper of a footstep in the dark.

Learning to Swim

by

GRAHAM SWIFT

MRS. SINGLETON had three times thought of leaving her husband. The first time was before they were married on a charter plane coming back from a holiday in Greece. They were students who had just graduated. They had rucksacks and faded jeans. In Greece they had stayed part of the time by a beach on an island. The island was dry and rocky with great grey and vermilion coloured rocks and when you lay on the beach it seemed that you too became a hot, basking rock. Behind the beach there were eucalyptus trees like dry, leafy bones, old men with mules and gold teeth, a fragrance of thyme, and a café with melon pips on the floor and a jukebox which played bouzouki music and songs by Cliff Richard. All this Mr. Singleton failed to appreciate. He'd only liked the milk-warm, clear-blue sea, in which he'd stayed most of the time as if afraid of foreign soil. On the plane she'd thought: he hadn't enjoyed the holiday, hadn't liked Greece at all. All that sunshine. Then she'd thought she ought not to marry him.

Though she had, a year later.

The second time was about a year after Mr. Singleton, who was a civil engineer, had begun his first big job. He became a junior partner in a firm with a growing reputation. She ought to have been pleased by this. It brought money and comfort; it enabled them to move to a house with a large garden, to live well, to think about raising a family. They spent weekends in country hotels. But Mr. Singleton seemed untouched by this. He became withdrawn and incommunicative. He went to his work austere-faced. She thought: he likes his bridges and tunnels better than me.

The third time, which was really a phase: not a single moment, was when she began to calculate how often Mr. Singleton made love to her. When she started this it was about once every fortnight on average. Then it became every three weeks. The interval had been widening for some time. This was not a predicament Mrs. Singleton viewed selfishly. Love-making had been a problem before, in their earliest days together, which, thanks to her patience and initiative, had been overcome. It was Mr. Singleton's unhappiness, not her own, that she saw in their present plight. He was distrustful of happiness as some people fear heights or open spaces. She would reassure him, encourage him again. But the averages seemed to defy her personal effort: once every three weeks, once every month ... She thought: things go back to as they were.

But then, by sheer chance, she became pregnant.

Now she lay on her back, eyes closed, on the coarse sand of the beach in Cornwall. It was hot and, if she opened her eyes, the sky was clear blue. This and the previous summer had been fine enough to make her husband's refusal to go abroad for holidays tolerable. If you kept your eyes closed it could be Greece or Italy or Ibiza. She wore a chocolate-brown bikini, sun-glasses, and her skin, which seldom suffered from sunburn, was already beginning to tan. She let her arms trail idly by her side, scooping up little handfuls of sand. If she turned her head to the right and looked towards the sea she could see Mr. Singleton and their son Paul standing in the shallow water. Mr. Singleton was teaching Paul to swim. "Kick!" he was saying. From here, against the gentle waves, they looked like no more than two rippling silhouettes.

"Kick!" said Mr. Singleton, "Kick!" He was like a punisher, administering lashes.

She turned her head away to face upwards. If you shut your eyes you could imagine you were the only one on the beach; if you held them shut you could be part of the beach. Mrs. Singleton imagined that in order to acquire a tan you had to let the sun make love to you.

She dug her heels in the sand and smiled involuntarily.

When she was a thin, flat-chested, studious girl in a grey school uniform Mrs. Singleton had assuaged her fear and desperation about sex with fantasies which took away from men the brute physicality she expected of them. All her lovers would be artists. Poets would write poems to her, composers would dedicate their works to her. She would even pose, naked and immaculate, for painters, who having committed her true, her eternal form to canvas, would make love to her in an impalpable, ethereal way, under the power of which her bodily and temporal self would melt away, perhaps forever. These fantasies (for she had never entirely renounced them) had crystallized for her in the image of a sculptor, who from a cold intractable piece of stone would fashion her very essence—which would be vibrant and full of sunlight, like the statues they had seen in Greece.

At university she had worked on the assumption that all men lusted uncontrollably and insatiably after women. She had not yet encountered a man who, whilst prone to the usual instincts, possessing moreover a magnificent body with which to fulfill them, yet had scruples about doing so, seemed ashamed of his own capacities. It did not matter that Mr. Singleton was reading engineering, was scarcely artistic at all, or that his powerful physique was unlike the nebulous treasures of her dreams. She found she loved this solid man-flesh: Mrs. Singleton had thought she was the shy, inexperienced, timid girl. Overnight she discovered that she wasn't this at all. He wore tough denim shirts, spoke and smiled very little and had a way of standing very straight and upright as if he didn't need any help from anyone. She had to educate him into moments of passion, of self-forgetfulness which made her glow with her own achievement. She was happy because she had not thought she was happy and she believed she could make someone else happy. At the university girls were starting to wear jeans, record-players played the Rolling Stones and in the hush of the Modern Languages Library she read Leopardi and Verlaine. She seemed to float with confidence in a swirling, buoyant element she had never suspected would be her own.

"Kick!" she heard again from the water.

Mr. Singleton had twice thought of leaving his wife. Once was after a symphony concert they had gone to in London when they had not known each other very long and she still tried to get him to read books, to listen to music, to take an interest in art. She would buy concert or theatre tickets, and he had to seem pleased. At this concert a visiting orchestra was playing some titanic, large-scale work by a late nineteenth-century composer. A note in the programme said it represented the triumph of life over death. He had sat on his plush seat amidst the swirling barrage of sound. He had no idea what he had to do with it or the triumph of life over death, he had thought the same thought about the rapt girl on his left, the future Mrs. Singleton, who now and then bobbed, swayed or rose in her seat as if the music physically lifted her. There were at least seventy musicians on the platform. As the piece worked to its final crescendo the conductor, whose arms were flailing frantically so that his white shirt back appeared under his flying tails, looked so absurd Mr. Singleton thought he would laugh. When the music stopped and was immediately supplanted by wild cheering and clapping he thought the world had gone mad. He had struck his own hands together so as to appear to be sharing the ecstasy. Then, as they filed out, he had almost wept because he felt like an insect. He even thought she had arranged the whole business so as to humiliate him.

He thought he would not marry her.

The second time was after they had been married some years. He was one of a team of engineers working on a suspension bridge over an estuary in Ireland. They took it in turns to stay on the site and to inspect the construction work personally. Once he had to go to the very top of one of the two piers of the bridge to examine work on the bearings and housing for the main overhead cables. A lift ran up between the twin towers of the pier amidst a network of scaffolding and power cables to where a working platform was positioned. The engineer, with the supervisor and the foreman, had only to stay on the platform from where all the main features of construction were visible. The men at work on the upper sections of the towers, specialists in their trade, earning up to two hundred pounds a week—who balanced on precarious catwalks and walked along exposed reinforcing girders—often jibed at the engineers who never left the platform. He thought he would show them. He walked out on to one of the catwalks on the outer face of the pier where they were fitting huge grip-bolts. This was quite safe if you held on to the rails but still took some nerve. He wore a check cheese-cloth shirt and his white safety helmet. It was a grey, humid August day. The catwalk hung over greyness. The water of the estuary was the colour of dead fish. A dredger was chugging near the base of the pier. He thought, I could swim the estuary; but there is a bridge. Below him the yellow helmets of workers moved over the girders for the roadway like beetles. He took his hands from the rail. He wasn't at all afraid. He had been away from his wife all week. He thought: she knows nothing of this. If he were to step out now into the grey air he would be quite by himself, no harm would come to him ...

Now Mr. Singleton stood in the water, teaching his son to swim. They were doing the water-wings exercise. The boy wore a pair of water-wings, red underneath, yellow on top, which ballooned up under his arms and chin. With this to support him, he would splutter and splash towards his father who stood facing him some feet away. After a while at this they would try the same procedure, his father moving a little nearer, but without the water-wings, and this the boy dreaded. "Kick!" said Mr. Singleton, "Use your legs!" He watched his son draw painfully towards him. The boy had not yet grasped that the body naturally floated and that if you added to this certain mechanical effects, you swam. He thought that in order to swim you had to make as much frantic movement as possible. As he struggled towards Mr. Singleton his head, which was too high out of the water, jerked messily from side to side, and his eyes which were half closed swivelled in every direction but straight ahead. "Towards me!" shouted Mr. Singleton. He held out his arms in front of him for Paul to grasp. As his son was on the point of clutching them he would step back a little, pulling his hands away, in the hope that the last desperate lunge to reach his father might really teach the boy the art of propelling himself in water. But he sometimes wondered if this were his only motive.

"Good boy. Now again."

At school Mr. Singleton had been an excellent swimmer. He had won various school titles, broken numerous records and competed successfully in ASA championships. There was a period between the age of about thirteen and seventeen which he remembered as the happiest in his life. It wasn't the medals and trophies that made him glad, but the knowledge that he didn't have to bother about anything else. Swimming vindicated him. He would get up every morning at six and train for two hours in the baths, and again before lunch; and when he fell asleep, exhausted, in French and English periods in the afternoon, he didn't have to bother about the indignation of the masters—lank, ill-conditioned creatures—for he had his excuse. He didn't have to bother about the physics teacher who complained to the headmaster that he would never get the exam results he needed if he didn't cut down his swimming, for the headmaster (who was an advocate of sport) came to his aid and told the physics teacher not to interfere with a boy who was a credit to the school. Nor did he have to bother about a host of other things which were supposed to be going on inside him, which made the question of what to do in the evening, at weekends, fraught and tantalizing, which drove other boys to moodiness and recklessness. For once in the cool water of the baths, his arms reaching, his eyes fixed on the blue marker line on the bottom, his ears full so that he could hear nothing around him, he would feel quite by himself, quite sufficient. At the end of races, when for one brief instant he clung panting alone like a survivor to the finishing rail which his rivals had yet to touch, he felt an infinite peace. He went to bed early, slept soundly, kept to his training regimen; and he enjoyed this Spartan purity which disdained pleasure and disorder. Some of his schoolmates mocked him—for not going to dances on Saturdays or to pubs, underage, or the Expresso after school. But he did not mind. He didn't need them. He knew they were weak. None of them could hold out, depend on themselves, spurn comfort if they had to. Some of them would go under in life. And none of them could cleave the water as he did or possessed a hard, streamlined, perfectly tuned body like he did.

Then, when he was nearly seventeen all this changed. His father, who was an engineer, though proud of his son's trophies, suddenly pressed him to different forms of success. The headmaster no longer shielded him from the physics master. He said: "You can't swim into your future." Out of spite perhaps or an odd consistency of self-denial, he dropped swimming altogether rather than cut it down. For a year and a half he worked at his maths and physics with the same single-mindedness with which he had perfected his sport. He knew about mechanics and engineering because he knew how to make his body move through water. His work was not merely competent but good. He got to university where he might have had the leisure, if he wished, to resume his swimming. But he did not. Two years are a long gap in a swimmer's training; two years when you are near your peak can mean you will never get back to your true form. Sometimes he went for a dip in the university pool and swam slowly up and down amongst practising members of the university team, whom perhaps he could still have beaten, as a kind of relief.

Often, Mr. Singleton dreamt about swimming. He would be moving through vast expanses of water, an ocean. As he moved it did not require any effort at all. Sometimes he would go for long distances under water, but he did not have to bother about breathing. The water would be silvery-grey. And always it seemed that as he swam he was really trying to get beyond the water, to put it behind him, as if it were a veil he were parting and he would emerge on the other side of it at last, on to some pristine shore, where he would step where no one else had stepped before.

When he made love to his wife, her body got in the way; he wanted to swim through her.

Mrs. Singleton raised herself, pushed her sun-glasses up over her dark hair and sat with her arms stretched straight behind her back. A trickle of sweat ran between her breasts They had developed to a good size since her schoolgirl days. Her skinniness in youth had stood her in good stead against the filling out of middle age, and her body was probably more mellow, more lithe and better proportioned than it had ever been. She looked at Paul and Mr. Singleton half immersed in the shallows. It seemed to her that her husband was the real boy, standing stubbornly upright with his hands before him, and that Paul was some toy being pulled and swung relentlessly around him and towards him as though on some string. They had seen her sit up. Her husband waved, holding the boy's hand, as though for the two of them. Paul did not wave; he seemed more concerned with the water in his eyes. Mrs. Singleton did not wave back. She would have done if her son had waved. When they had left for their holiday Mr. Singleton had said to Paul, "You'll learn to swim this time. In salt water, you know, it's easier." Mrs. Singleton hoped her son wouldn't swim; so that she could wrap him, still, in the big yellow towel when he came out, rub him dry and warm, and watch her husband stand apart, his hands empty.

She watched Mr. Singleton drop his arm back to his side. "If you wouldn't splash it wouldn't go in your eyes," she just caught him say.

The night before, in their hotel room, they had argued. They always argued about half way through their holidays. It was symbolic, perhaps, of that first trip to Greece, when he had somehow refused to enjoy himself. They had to incur injuries so that they could then appreciate their leisure, like convalescents. For the first four days or so of their holiday Mr. Singleton would tend to be moody, on edge. He would excuse this as "winding down," the not-to-be-hurried process of dispelling the pressures of work. Mrs. Singleton would be patient. On about the fifth day Mrs. Singleton would begin to suspect that the winding down would never end and indeed (which she had known all along) that it was not winding down at all—he was clinging, as to a defence, to his bridges and tunnels; and she would show her resentment. At this point, Mr. Singleton would retaliate by an attack upon her indolence.

Last night he had called her "flabby." He could not mean, of course, "flabby-bodied" (she could glance down, now, at her still flat belly), though such a sensual attack would have been simpler, almost heartening, from him. He meant "flabby of attitude." And what he meant by this, or what he wanted to mean, was that *he* was not flabby; that he worked, facing the real world, erecting great solid things on the face of the land, and that whilst he worked, he disdained work's rewards—money, pleasure, rich food, holidays abroad—that he hadn't "gone soft," as she had done since they graduated eleven years ago, with their credentials for the future and their plane tickets to Greece. She knew this toughness of her husband was only a cover for his own failure to relax and his need to keep his distance. She knew that he found no particular virtue in his bridges and tunnels (it was the last thing he wanted to do really—build); it didn't matter if they were right or wrong, they were there, he could point to them as if it vindicated him—just as when he made his infrequent, if seismic love to her it was not a case of enjoyment or satisfaction; he just did it.

It was hot in their hotel room. Mr. Singleton stood in his blue pyjama bottoms, feet apart, like a PT instructor.

"Flabby? What do you mean—'flabby!?'" she had said, looking daunted.

But Mrs. Singleton had the advantage whenever Mr. Singleton accused her in this way of complacency, of weakness. She knew he only did it to hurt her, and so to feel guilty, and so to feel the remorse which would release his own affection for her, his vulnerability, his own need to be loved. Mrs. Singleton was used to this process, to the tenderness that was the tenderness of successively opened and reopened wounds. And she was used to being the nurse who took care of the healing scars. For though Mr. Singleton inflicted the first blow he would always make himself more guilty than he made her suffer, and Mrs. Singleton, though in pain herself, could not resist wanting to clasp and cherish her husband, wanting to wrap him up safe when his own weakness and submissiveness showed and his body became liquid and soft against her; could not resist the old spur that her husband was unhappy and it was for her to make him happy. Mr. Singleton was extraordinarily lovable when he was guilty. She would even have yielded indefinitely, foregoing her own grievance, to this extreme of comforting him for the pain he caused her, had she not discovered, in time, that this only pushed the process a stage further. Her forgiveness of him became only another level of comfort, of softness he must reject. His flesh shrank from her restoring touch.

She thought: men go round in circles, women don't move.

She kept to her side of the hotel bed, he, with his face turned, to his. He lay like a person washed up on a beach. She reached out her hand and stroked the nape of his neck. She felt him tense. All this was a pattern.

"I'm sorry," he said. "I didn't mean—"

"It's all right, it doesn't matter."

"Doesn't it matter?" he said.

When they reached this point they were like miners racing each other for deeper and deeper seams of guilt and recrimination.

But Mrs. Singleton had given up delving to rock bottom. Perhaps it was five years ago when she had thought for the third time of leaving her husband, perhaps long before that. When they were students she'd made allowances for his constraints, his reluctances. An unhappy childhood perhaps, a strict upbringing. She thought his inhibition might be lifted by the sanction of marriage. She'd thought, after all, it would be a good thing if he married her. She had not thought what would be good for her. They stood outside Gatwick Airport, back from Greece, in the grey, wet August light. Their tanned skin had seemed to glow. Yet she'd known this mood of promise would pass. She watched him kick against contentment, against ease, against the long, glittering life-line she threw to him; and, after a while, she ceased to try to haul him in. She began to imagine again her phantom artists. She thought: people slip off the shores of the real world, back into dreams. She hadn't "gone soft," only gone back to herself. Hidden inside her like treasure there were lines of Leopardi, of Verlaine her husband would never appreciate.

She thought, he doesn't need me, things run off him, like water. She even thought that her husband's neglect in making love to her was not a problem he had but a deliberate scheme to deny her. When Mrs. Singleton desired her husband she could not help herself. She would stretch back on the bed with the sheets pulled off like a blissful nude in a Modigliani. She thought this ought to gladden a man. Mr. Singleton would stand at the foot of the bed and gaze down at her. He looked like some strong, chaste knight in the legend of the Grail. He would respond to her invitation, but before he did so there would be this expression, half stern, half innocent, in his eyes. It was the sort of expression that good men in books and films are supposed to make to prostitutes. It would ensure that their love-making was marred and that afterwards it would seem as if he had performed something out of duty that only she wanted. Her body would feel like stone. It was at such times, when she felt the cold, dead-weight feel of abused happiness, that Mrs. Singleton most thought she was through with Mr. Singleton. She would watch his strong, compact torso already lifting itself off the bed. She would think: he thinks he is tough, contained in himself, but he won't see what I offer him, he doesn't see how it is I who can help him.

Mrs. Singleton lay back on her striped towel on the sand. Once again she became part of the beach. The careless sounds of the seaside, of excited children's voices, of languid grownups', of wooden bats on balls, fluttered over her as she shut her eyes. She thought: it is the sort of day on which someone suddenly shouts, "Someone is drowning."

When Mrs. Singleton became pregnant she felt she had outmanoeuvred her husband. He did not really want a child (it was the last thing he wanted, Mrs. Singleton thought, a child), but he was jealous of her condition, as of some achievement he himself could not attain. He was excluded from the little circle of herself and her womb, and, as though to puncture it, he began for the first time to make love to her of a kind where he took the insistent initiative. Mrs. Singleton was not greatly pleased. She seemed buoyed up by her own bigness. She noticed that her husband began to do exercises in the morning, in his underpants, press-ups, squat-jumps, as if he were getting in training for something. He was like a boy. He even became, as the term of her pregnancy drew near its end, resilient and detached again, the virile father waiting to receive the son (Mr. Singleton knew it would be a son, so did Mrs. Singleton) that she, at the appointed time, would deliver him. When the moment arrived he insisted on being present so as to prove he wasn't squeamish and to make sure he wouldn't be tricked in the transaction. Mrs. Singleton was not daunted. When the pains became frequent she wasn't at all afraid. There were big, watery lights clawing down from the ceiling of the delivery room like the lights in dentists' surgeries. She could just see her husband looking down at her. His face was white and clammy. It was his fault for wanting to be there. She had to push, as though away from him. Then she knew it was happening. She stretched back. She was a great surface of warm, splitting rock and Paul was struggling bravely up into the sunlight. She had to coax him with her cries. She felt him emerge like a trapped survivor. The doctor groped with rubber gloves. "There we are," he said. She managed to look at Mr. Singleton. She wanted suddenly to put him back inside for good where Paul had come from. With a fleeting pity, she saw that this was what Mr. Singleton wanted too. His eyes were half closed. She kept hers on him. He seemed to wilt under her gaze. All his toughness and control were draining from him and she was glad. She lay back triumphant and glad. The doctor was holding Paul; but she looked, beyond, at Mr. Singleton. He was far away like an insect. She knew he couldn't hold out. He was going to faint. He was looking where her legs were spread. His eyes went out of focus. He was going to faint, keel over, right there on the spot.

Mrs. Singleton grew restless, though she lay unmoving on the beach. Wasps were buzzing close to her head, round their picnic bag.

She thought that Mr. Singleton and Paul had been too long at their swimming lesson. They should come out. It never struck her, hot as she was, to get up and join her husband and son in the sea. Whenever Mrs. Singleton wanted a swim she would wait until there was an opportunity to go in by herself; then she would wade out, dip her shoulders under suddenly and paddle about contentedly, keeping her hair dry, as though she were soaking herself in a large bath. They did not bathe as a family; nor did Mrs. Singleton swim with Mr. Singleton—who now and then, too, would get up by himself and enter the sea, swim at once about fifty yards out, then cruise for long stretches, with a powerful crawl or butterfly, back and forth across the bay. When this happened Mrs. Singleton would engage her son in talk so he would not watch his father. Mrs. Singleton did not swim with Paul either. He was too old, now, to cradle between her knees in the very shallow water, and she was somehow afraid that while Paul splashed and kicked around her he would suddenly learn how to swim. She had this feeling that Paul would only swim while she was in the sea, too. She did not want this to happen, but it reassured her and gave her sufficient confidence to let Mr. Singleton continue his swimming lessons with Paul. These lesson were obsessive, indefatigable. Every Sunday morning at seven, when they were at home, Mr. Singleton would take Paul to the baths for yet another attempt. Part of this, of course, was that Mr Singleton was determined that his son should swim; but it enabled him also to avoid the Sunday morning languor: extra hours in bed, leisurely love-making.

Once, in a room at college, Mr. Singleton had told Mrs. Singleton about his swimming, about his training sessions, races; about what it felt like when you could swim really well. She had run her fingers over his long, naked back.

Mrs. Singleton sat up and rubbed suntan lotion on her thighs. Down near the water's edge, Mr. Singleton was standing about waist deep, supporting Paul who, gripped by his father's hands, water-wings still on, was flailing, face down, at the surface. Mr. Singleton kept saying, "No, keep still." He was trying to get Paul to hold his body straight and relaxed so he would float. But each time as Paul nearly succeeded he would panic, fearing his father would let go, and thrash wildly. When he calmed down and Mr. Singleton held him, Mrs. Singleton could see the water running off his face like tears.

Mrs. Singleton did not alarm herself at this distress of her son. It was a guarantee against Mr. Singleton's influence, an assurance that Paul was not going to swim; nor was he to be imbued with any of his father's sullen hardiness. When Mrs. Singleton saw her son suffer, it pleased her and she felt loving towards him. She felt that an invisible thread ran between her and the boy which commanded him not to swim, and she felt that Mr. Singleton knew that it was because of her that his efforts with Paul were in vain. Even now, as Mr. Singleton prepared for another attempt, the boy was looking at her smoothing the suntan oil on to her legs.

"Come on, Paul," said Mr. Singleton. His wet shoulders shone like metal.

When Paul was born it seemed to Mrs. Singleton that her life with her husband was dissolved, as a mirage dissolves, and that she could return again to what she was before she knew him. She let her staved-off hunger for happiness and her old suppressed dreams revive. But then they were not dreams, because they had a physical object and she knew she needed them in order to live. She did not disguise from herself what she needed. She knew that she wanted the kind of close, even erotic relationship with her son that women who have rejected their husbands have been known to have. The kind of relationship in which the son must hurt the mother, the mother the son. But she willed it, as if there would be no pain. Mrs. Singleton waited for her son to grow. She trembled when she thought of him at eighteen or twenty. When he was grown he would be slim and light and slender, like a boy even though he was a man. He would not need a strong body because all his power would be inside. He would be all fire and life in essence. He would become an artist, a sculptor. She would pose for him naked (she would keep her body trim for this), and he would sculpt her. He would hold the chisel. His hands would guide the cold metal over the stone and its blows would strike sunlight.

Mrs. Singleton thought: all the best statues they had seen in Greece seemed to have been dredged up from the sea.

She finished rubbing the lotion on to her insteps and put the cap back on the tube. As she did so she heard something that made her truly alarmed. It was Mr. Singleton saying, "That's it, that's the way! At last! Now keep it going!" She looked up. Paul was in the same position as before but he had learned to make slower, regular motions with his limbs and his body no longer sagged in the middle. Though he still wore the water-wings he was moving, somewhat laboriously, forwards so that Mr. Singleton had to walk along with him; and at one point Mr. Singleton removed one of his hands from under the boy's ribs and simultaneously looked at his wife and smiled. His shoulders flashed. It was not a smile meant for her. She could see that. And it was not one of her husband's usual, infrequent, rather mechanical smiles. It was the smile a person makes about some joy inside, hidden and incommunicable.

"That's enough," thought Mrs. Singleton, getting to her feet, pretending not to have noticed, behind her sun-glasses, what had happened in the water. It *was* enough: they had been in the water for what seemed like an hour. He was only doing it because of their row last night, to make her feel he was not outmatched by using the reserve weapon of Paul. And, she added with relief to herself, Paul still had the water-wings and one hand to support him.

"That's enough now!" she shouted aloud, as if she were slightly, but not ill-humouredly, peeved at being neglected. "Come on in now!" She had picked up her purse as a quickly conceived ruse as she got up and as she walked towards the water's edge she waved it above her head. "Who wants an ice cream?"

Mr. Singleton ignored his wife. "Well done, Paul," he said. "Let's try that again."

Mrs. Singleton knew he would do this. She stood on the little ridge of sand just above where the beach, becoming fine shingle, shelved into the sea. She replaced a loose strap of her bikini over her shoulder and with a finger of each hand pulled the bottom half down over her buttocks. She stood feet apart, slightly on her toes, like a gymnast. She knew other eyes on the beach would be on her. It flattered her that she—and her husband, too—received admiring glances from those around. She thought, with relish for the irony: perhaps they think we are happy, beautiful people. For all her girlhood diffidence, Mrs. Singleton enjoyed displaying her attractions, and she liked to see other people's pleasure. When she lay sunbathing she imagined making love to all the moody, pubescent boys on holiday with their parents, with their slim waists and their quick heels.

"See if you can do it without me holding you," said Mr. Singleton. "I'll help you at first." He stooped over Paul. He looked like a mechanic making final adjustments to some prototype machine.

"Don't you want an ice cream then, Paul?" said Mrs. Singleton. "They've got those chocolate ones."

Paul looked up. His short wet hair stood up in spikes. He looked like a prisoner offered a chance of escape, but the plastic water-wings, like some absurd pillory, kept him fixed.

Mrs. Singleton thought: he crawled out of me; now I have to lure him back with ice cream.

"Can't you see he was getting the hang of it?" Mr. Singleton said. "If he comes out now he'll—"

"Hang of it! It was you. You were holding him all the time."

She thought: perhaps I am hurting my son.

Mr. Singleton glared at Mrs. Singleton. He gripped Paul's shoulder. "You don't want to get out now, do you Paul?" He looked suddenly as if he really might drown Paul rather than let him come out.

Mrs. Singleton's heart raced. She wasn't good at rescues, at resuscitations. She knew this because of her life with her husband.

"Come on, you can go back in later," she said.

Paul was a hostage. She was playing for time, not wanting to harm the innocent.

She stood on the sand like a marooned woman watching her ships. The sea, in the sheltered bay, was almost flat calm. A few, glassy waves idled in but were smoothed out before they could break. On the headlands there were outcrops of scaly rocks like basking lizards. The island in Greece had been where Theseus left Ariadne. Out over the blue water, beyond the heads of bobbing swimmers, seagulls flapped like scraps of paper.

Mr. Singleton looked at Mrs. Singleton. She was a fussy mother daubed with Ambre Solaire, trying to bribe her son with silly ice creams; though if you forgot this she was a beautiful, tanned girl, like the girls men imagine on desert islands. But then, in Mr. Singleton's dreams, there was no one else on the untouched shore he ceaselessly swam to.

He thought, if Paul could swim, then I could leave her.

Mrs. Singleton looked at her husband. She felt afraid. The water's edge was like a dividing line between them which marked off the territory in which each existed. Perhaps they could never cross over.

"Well, I'm getting the ice creams: you'd better get out."

She turned and paced up the sand. Behind the beach was an ice-cream van painted like a fairground.

Paul Singleton looked at his mother. He thought: she is deserting me—or I am deserting her. He wanted to get out to follow her. Her feet made puffs of sand which stuck to her ankles, and you could see all her body as she strode up the beach. But he was afraid of his father and his gripping hands. And he was afraid of his mother, too. How she would wrap him, if he came out, in the big yellow towel like egg yolk, how she would want him to get close to her smooth, sticky body, like a mouth that would swallow him. He thought: the yellow towel humiliated him, his father's hands humiliated him. The water-wings humiliated him: you put them on and became a puppet. So much of life is humiliation. It was how you won love. His father was taking off the water-wings like a man unlocking a chastity belt. He said: "Now try the same, coming towards me." His father stood some feet away from him. He was a huge, straight man, like the pier of a bridge. "Try." Paul Singleton was six. He was terrified of the water. Every time he entered it he had to fight down fear. His father never realized this. He thought it was simple; you said: "Only water, no need to be afraid." His father did not know what fear was; the same as he did not know what fun was. Paul Singleton hated water. He hated it in his mouth and in his eyes. He hated the chlorine smell of the swimming baths, the wet, slippery tiles, the echoing whoops and screams. He hated it when his father read to him from *The Water Babies*. It was the only story his father read, because, since he didn't know fear or fun, he was really sentimental. His mother read lots of stories. "Come on then. I'll catch you." Paul Singleton held out his arms and raised one leg. This was the worst moment. Perhaps having no help was most humiliating. If you did not swim you sank like a statue. They would drag him out, his skin streaming. His father would say: "I didn't mean ..." But if he swam his mother would be forsaken. She would stand on the beach with chocolate ice cream running down her arm. There was no way out; there were all these things to be afraid of and no weapons. But then, perhaps he was not afraid of his mother nor his father, nor of water, but of something else. He had felt it just now—when he'd struck out with rhythmic, reaching strokes and his feet had come off the bottom and his father's hand had slipped from under his chest: as if he had mistaken what his fear was; as if he had been unconsciously pretending, even to himself, so as to execute some plan. He lowered his chin into the water. "Come on!" said Mr. Singleton. He launched himself forward and felt the sand leave his feet and his legs wriggle like cut ropes. "There," said his father as he realized. "There!" His father stood like a man waiting to clasp a lover; there was a gleam on his face. "Towards me! Towards me!" said his father suddenly. But he kicked and struck, half in panic, half in pride, away from his father, away from the shore, away, in this strange new element that seemed all his own.

Flesh

by

ELIZABETH TAYLOR

PHYL WAS ALWAYS ONE of the first to come into the hotel bar in the evenings, for what she called her *aperitif*, and which, in reality, amounted to two hours' steady drinking. After that, she had little appetite for dinner, a meal to which she was not used.

On this evening, she had put on one of her beaded tops, of the kind she wore behind the bar on Saturday evenings in London, and patted back her tortoiseshell hair. She was massive and glittering and sunburnt—a wonderful sight, Stanley Archard thought, as she came across the bar towards him.

He had been sitting waiting for her. They had found their own level in one another on about the third day of the holiday. Both being heavy drinkers drew them together. Before that had happened, they had looked one another over warily as, in fact, they had all their fellow guests.

Travelling on their own, speculating, both had watched and wondered. Even at the airport, she had stood out from the others, he remembered, as she had paced up and down in her emerald green coat. Then their flight number had been called, and they had gathered with others at the same channel, with the same pink labels tied to their hand luggage, all going to the same place; a polite, but distant little band of people, no one knowing with whom friendships were to be made—as like would no doubt drift to like. In the days that followed, Stanley had wished he had taken more notice of Phyl from the beginning, so that at the end of the holiday he would have that much more to remember. Only the emerald green coat had stayed in his mind. She had not worn it since—it was too warm—and he dreaded the day when she would put it on again to make the return journey.

Arriving in the bar this evening, she hoisted herself up on a stool beside him. "Well, here we are," she said, glowing, taking one peanut; adding, as she nibbled, "Evening, George," to the barman. "How's tricks?"

"My God, you've caught it today," Stanley said, and he put his hands up near her plump red shoulders as if to warm them at a fire. "Don't overdo it," he warned her.

"Oh, I never peel," she said airily.

He always put in a word against the sunbathing when he could. It separated them. She stayed all day by the hotel swimming pool, basting herself with oil. He, bored with basking—which made him feel dizzy—had hired a car and spent his time driving about the island, and was full of alienating information about the locality, which the other guests—resenting the hired car, too—did their best to avoid. Only Phyl did not mind listening to him. For nearly every evening of her married life she had stood behind the bar and listened to other people's boring chat: she had a technique for dealing with it and a fund of vague phrases. "Go on!"she said now, listening—hardly listening—to Stanley, and taking another nut. He had gone off by himself and found a place for lunch: *hors d'oeuvre,* nice-sized slice of veal, two veg, *crème caramel,* half bottle of rosé, coffee—twenty-two shillings the lot.

"Well, I'm blowed," said Phyl, and she took a pound note from her handbag and waved it at the barman. When she snapped up the clasp of the bag it had a heavy, expensive sound.

One or two other guests came in and sat at the bar. At this stage of the holiday they were forming into little groups, and this was the jokey set who had come first after Stanley and Phyl. According to them all sorts of funny things had happened during the day, and little screams of laughter ran round the bar.

"Shows how wrong you can be," Phyl said in a low voice, "I thought they were ever so starchy on the plane. I was wrong about you, too. At the start, I thought you were … you know … one of *those.* Going about with that young boy all the time."

Stanley patted her knee. "On the contrary," he said, with a meaning glance at her. "No, I was just at a bit of a loose end, and he seemed to cotton on. Never been abroad before, he hadn't, and didn't know the routine. I liked it for the first day or two. It was like taking a nice kiddie out on a treat. Then it seemed to me he was sponging. I'm not mean, I don't think; but I don't like that—sponging. It was quite a relief when he suddenly took up with the Lisper."

By now, he and Phyl had nicknames for most of the other people in the hotel. They did not know that the same applied to them, and that to the jokey set he was known as Paws and she as the Shape. It would have put them out and perhaps ruined their holiday if they had known. He thought his little knee-pattings were of the utmost discretion, and she felt confidence from knowing her figure was expensively controlled under her beaded dresses when she became herself again in the evenings. During the day, while sunbathing, she considered that anything went—that, as her mind was a blank, her body became one also.

The funny man of the party—the awaited climax—came into the bar, crabwise, face covered shyly with his hand, as if ashamed of some earlier misdemeanour. "Oh, my God, don't look round. Here comes trouble!" someone said loudly, and George was called for from all sides. "What's the poison, Harry? No, my shout, old boy. George, if you *please*."

Phyl smiled indulgently. It was just like Saturday night with the regulars at home. She watched George with a professional eye, and nodded approvingly. He was good. They could have used him at The Nelson. A good quick boy.

"Heard from your old man?" Stanley asked her.

She cast him a tragic, calculating look. "You must be joking. He can't *write*. No, honest, I've never had a letter from him in the whole of my life. Well, we always saw each other every day until I had my hysterectomy."

Until now, in conversations with Stanley, she had always referred to "a little operation." But he had guessed what it was—well, it always was, wasn't it?—and knew that it was the reason for her being on holiday. Charlie, her husband, had sent her off to recuperate. She had sworn there was no need, that she had never felt so well in her life—was only a bit weepy sometimes late on a Saturday night. "I'm not really the crying sort," she had explained to Stanley. "So he got worried, and sent me packing." "You clear off to the sun," he had said, "and see what that will do."

What the sun had done for her was to burn her brick-red, and offer her this nice holiday friend. Stanley Archard, retired widower from Hove.

She enjoyed herself, as she usually did. The sun shone every day, and the drinks were so reasonable—they had many a long discussion about that. They also talked about his little flat in Hove; his strolls along the front; his few cronies at the club; his sad, orderly and lonely life.

This evening, he wished he had not brought up the subject of Charlie's writing to her, for it seemed to have fixed her thoughts on him and, as she went chatting on about him, Stanley felt an indefinable distaste, an aloofness.

She brought out from her note-case a much-creased cutting from *The Morning Advertiser.* "Phyl and Charlie Parsons welcome old friends and new at The Nelson, Southwood. In licensed hours only!" "That was when we changed Houses," she explained. There was a photograph of them both standing behind the bar. He was wearing a dark blazer with a large badge on the pocket. Sequins gave off a smudged sparkle from her breast, her hair was newly, elaborately done, and her large, ringed hand rested on an ornamental beer-handle. Charlie had *his* hands in the blazer pockets, as if he were there to do the welcoming, and his wife to do the work: and this, in fact, was how things were. Stanley guessed it, and felt a twist of annoyance in his chest. He did not like the look of Charlie, or anything he had heard about him—how, for instance, he had seemed like a fish out of water visiting his wife in hospital. "He used to sit on the edge of the chair and stare at the clock, like a boy in school," Phyl had said, laughing. Stanley could not bring himself to laugh, too. He had leaned forward and taken her knee in his hand and wobbled it sympathetically to and fro.

No, she wasn't the crying sort, he agreed. She had a wonderful buoyancy and gallantry, and she seemed to knock years off his age by just *being* with him, talking to him.

In spite of their growing friendship, they kept to their original, separate tables in the hotel restaurant. It seemed too suddenly decisive and public a move for him to join her now, and he was too shy to carry it off at this stage of the holiday, before such an alarming audience. But after dinner, they would go for a walk along the seafront, or out in the car for a drink at another hotel.

Always, for the first minute or two in a bar, he seemed to lose her. As if she had forgotten him, she would look about her critically, judging the set-up, sternly drawing attention to a sticky ring on the counter where she wanted to rest her elbow, keeping a professional eye on the prices.

When they were what she called "nicely grinned-up," they liked to drive out to a small headland and park the car, watching the swinging beam from a lighthouse. Then, after the usual knee-pattings and neck-strokings, they would heave and flop about in the confines of the Triumph Herald, trying to make love. Warmed by their drinks, and the still evening and the romantic sound of the sea idly turning over down below them, they became frustrated, both large, solid people, she much corseted and, anyhow, beginning to be painfully sunburnt across the shoulders, he with the confounded steering wheel to contend with.

He would grumble about the car and suggest getting out onto a patch of dry barley grass; but she imagined it full of insects; the chirping of the cicadas was almost deafening.

She also had a few scruples about Charlie, but they were not so insistent as the cicadas. After all, she thought, she had never had a holiday-romance—not even a honeymoon with Charlie—and she felt that life owed her just one.

AFTER A TIME, during the day, her sunburn forced her into the shade, or out in the car with Stanley. Across her shoulders she began to peel, and could not bear—though desiring his caress—him to touch her. Rather glumly, he waited for her flesh to heal, told her "I told you so"; after all, they had not forever on this island, had started their second, their last week already.

"I'd like to have a look at the other island," she said, watching the ferry leaving, as they sat drinking nearby.

"It's not worth just going there for the inside of a day," he said meaningfully, although it was only a short distance.

Wasn't this, both suddenly wondered, the answer to the too small car, and the watchful eyes back at the hotel. She had refused to allow him into her room there. "If anyone saw you going in or out. Why, they know where I live. What's to stop one of them coming into The Nelson any time, and chatting Charlie up?"

"Would you?" he now asked, watching the ferry starting off across the water. He hardly dared to hear her answer.

After a pause, she laughed. "Why not?" she said, and took his hand. "We wouldn't really be doing any harm to anyone." (Meaning Charlie.) "Because no one could find out, could they?"

"Not over there," he said, nodding towards the island. "We can start fresh over there. Different people."

"They'll notice we're both not at dinner at the hotel."

"That doesn't prove anything."

She imagined the unknown island, the warm and starlit night and, somewhere, under some roof or other, a large bed in which they could pursue their daring, more than middle-aged adventure, unconfined in every way.

"As soon as my sunburn's better," she promised. "We've got five more days yet, and I'll keep in the shade till then."

A CHAMBERMAID ADVISED yogourt, and she spread it over her back and shoulders as best she could, and felt its coolness absorbing the heat from her skin.

Damp and cheesy-smelling in the hot night, she lay awake, cross with herself. For the sake of a tan, she was wasting her holiday—just to be a five minutes' wonder in the bar on her return, the deepest brown any of them had had that year. The darker she was, the more *abroad* she would seem to have been, the more prestige she could command. All summer, pallid herself, she had had to admire others.

Childish, really, she decided, lying rigid under the sheet, afraid to move, burning and throbbing. The skin was taut behind her knees, so that she could not stretch her legs; her flesh was on fire.

Five more days, she kept thinking. Meanwhile, even this sheet upon her was unendurable.

ON THE NEXT EVENING, to establish the fact that they would not always be in to dinner at the hotel, they complained in the bar about the dullness of the menu, and went elsewhere.

It was a drab little restaurant, but they scarcely noticed their surroundings. They sat opposite one another at a corner table and ate shellfish briskly, busily—he, from his enjoyment of the food; she, with a wish to be rid of it. They rinsed their fingers, quickly dried them and leaned forward and twined them together—their large placid hands, with heavy rings, clasped on the tablecloth. Phyl, glancing aside for a moment, saw a young girl, at the next table with a boy, draw in her cheekbones to suppress laughter then, failing, turn her head to hide it.

"At *our* age," Phyl said gently, drawing away her hands from his. "In public, too."

She could not be defiant; but Stanley said jauntily, "I'm damned if I care."

At that moment, their chicken was placed before them, and he sat back, looking at it, waiting for vegetables.

AS WELL AS THE SUNBURN, the heat seemed to have affected Phyl's stomach. She felt queasy and nervy. It was now their last day but one before they went over to the other island. The yogourt—or time—had taken the pain from her back and shoulders, though leaving her with a dappled, flaky look, which would hardly bring forth cries of admiration or advance her prestige in the bar when she returned. But, no doubt, she thought, by then England would be too cold for her to go sleeveless. Perhaps the trees would have changed colour. She imagined—already—dark Sunday afternoons, their three o'clock lunch done with, and she and Charlie sitting by the electric log fire in a lovely hot room smelling of oranges and the so-called hearth littered with peel. Charlie—bless him—always dropped off amongst a confusion of newspapers, worn out with banter and light ale, switched off, too, as he always was with her, knowing that he could relax—be nothing, rather—until seven o'clock, because it was Sunday. Again, for Phyl, imagining home, a little pang, soon swept aside or, rather, swept aside *from.*

She was in a way relieved that they would have only one night on the little island. That would make it seem more like a chance escapade than an affair, something less serious and deliberate in her mind. Thinking about it during the daytime, she even felt a little apprehensive; but told herself sensibly that there was really nothing to worry about: knowing herself well, she could remind herself that an evening's drinking would blur all the nervous edges.

"I CAN'T GET OVER THAT less than a fortnight ago I never knew you existed," she said, as they drove to the afternoon ferry. "And after this week," she added, "I don't suppose I'll ever see you again."

"I wish you wouldn't talk like that—spoiling things," he said heavily, and he tried not to think of Hove, and the winter walks along the promenade, and going back to the flat, boiling himself a couple of eggs, perhaps; so desperately lost without Ethel.

He had told Phyl about his wife and their quiet happiness together for many years, and then her long, long illness, during which she seemed to be going away from him gradually; but it was dreadful all the same when she finally did.

"We could meet in London on your day off," he suggested.

"Well, maybe." She patted his hand, leaving that disappointment aside for him.

There were only a few people on the ferry. It was the end of summer, and the tourists were dwindling, as the English community was reassembling, after trips "back home."

The sea was intensely blue all the way across to the island. They stood by the rail looking down at it, marvelling, and feeling like two people in a film. They thought they saw a dolphin, which added to their delight.

"Ethel and I went to Jersey for our honeymoon," Stanley said. "It poured with rain nearly all the time, and Ethel had one of her migraines."

"I never had a honeymoon," Phyl said. "Just the one night at the Regent Palace. In our business, you can't both go away together. This is the first time I've ever been abroad."

"The places I could take you to," he said.

They drove the car off the ferry and began to cross the island. It was hot and dusty, hillsides terraced and tilled; green lemons hung on the trees.

"I wouldn't half like to actually *pick* a lemon," she said.

"You shall," he said, "somehow or other."

"And take it home with me," she added. She would save it for a while, showing people, then cut it up for gin and tonic in the bar one evening, saying casually, "I picked this lemon with my own fair hands."

Stanley had booked their hotel from a restaurant, on the recommendation of a barman. When they found it, he was openly disappointed; but she managed to be gallant and optimistic. It was not by the sea, with a balcony where they might look out at the moonlit waters or rediscover brightness in the morning; but down a dull side street, and opposite a garage.

"We don't *have* to," Stanley said doubtfully.

"Oh, come on! We might not get in anywhere else. It's only for sleeping in," she said.

"It *isn't* only for sleeping in," he reminded her.

An enormous man in white shirt and shorts came out to greet them. "My name is Radam. Welcome," he said, with confidence. "I have a lovely room for you, Mr. and Mrs. Archard. You will be happy here, I can assure you. My wife will carry up your cases. Do not protest, Mr. Archard. She is quite able to. Our staff has slackened off at the end of the season, and I have some trouble with the old ticker, as you say in England. I know England well. I am a Bachelor of Science of England University. Once had digs in Swindon."

A pregnant woman shot out of the hotel porch and seized their suitcases, and there was a tussle as Stanley wrenched them from her hands. Still serenely boasting, Mr. Radam led them upstairs, all of them panting but himself.

The bedroom was large and dusty and overlooked a garage.

"Oh, God, I'm sorry," Stanley said, when they were left alone. "It's still not too late, if you could stand a row."

"No. I think it's rather sweet," Phyl said, looking round the room. "And, after all, don't blame yourself. You couldn't know any more than me."

The furniture was extraordinarily fret-worked, as if to make more crevices for the dust to settle in; the bedside-lamp base was an old gin bottle filled with gravel to weight it down, and when Phyl pulled off the bed cover to feel the bed she collapsed with laughter, for the pillowcases were embroidered "Hers" and "Hers."

Her laughter eased him, as it always did. For a moment, he thought disloyally of the dead—of how Ethel would have started to be depressed by it all, and he would have hard work jollying her out of her dark mood. At the same time, Phyl was wryly imagining Charlie's wrath, how he would have carried on—for only the best was good enough for him, as he never tired of saying.

"He's quite right—that awful fat man," she said gaily. "We shall be very happy here. I dread to think who he keeps "His" and "His" for, don't you?"

"I don't suppose the maid understands English," he said, but warming only slightly. "You don't expect to have to read off pillowcases."

"I'm sure there *isn't* a maid."

"The bed is very small," he said.

"It'll be better than the car."

He thought, she is such a woman as I have never met. She's like a marvellous Tommy in the trenches——keeping everyone's pecker up. He hated Charlie for his luck.

I shan't ever be able to tell anybody about "Hers" and "Hers," Phyl thought regretfully—for she dearly loved to amuse their regulars back home. Given other circumstances, she might have worked up quite a story about it.

A tap on the door, and in came Mr. Radam with two cups of tea on a tray. "I know you English," he said, rolling his eyes roguishly. "You can't be happy without your tea."

As neither of them ever drank it, they emptied the cups down the hand basin when he had gone.

Phyl opened the window and the sour, damp smell of new cement came up to her. All round about, building was going on; there was also the whine of a saw-mill, and a lot of clanking from the garage opposite. She leaned farther out, and then came back smiling into the room, and shut the window on the dust and noise. "He was quite right—that barman. You *can* see the sea from here. It's down the bottom of the street. Let's go and have a look as soon as we've unpacked."

On their way out of the hotel, they came upon Mr Radam, who was sitting in a broken old wicker chair, fanning himself with a folded newspaper.

"I shall prepare your dinner myself," he called after them. "And shall go now to make soup. I am a specialist of soup."

THEY STROLLED IN the last of the sun by the glittering sea, looked at the painted boats, watched a man beating an octopus on a rock. Stanley bought her some lace-edged handkerchiefs, and even gave the lace-maker an extra five shillings, so that Phyl could pick a lemon off one of the trees in her garden. Each bought for the other a picture-postcard of the place, to keep.

"Well it's been just about the best holiday I ever had," he said. "And there I was in half a mind not to come at all." He had for many years dreaded the holiday season, and only went away because everyone he knew did so.

"I just can't remember when I last had one," she said. There was not—never would be, he knew—the sound of self-pity in her voice.

This was only a small fishing village; but on one of the headlands enclosing it and the harbour was a big new hotel, with balconies overlooking the sea, Phyl noted. They picked their way across a rubbly car park and went in. Here, too, was the damp smell of cement; but there was a brightly-lighted empty bar with a small dance floor, and music playing.

"We could easily have got in here," Stanley said. "I'd like to wring that bloody barman's neck."

"He's probably some relation, trying to do his best."

"I'll best him."

They seemed to have spent a great deal of their time together hoisting themselves up on bar stools.

"Make them nice ones," Stanley added, ordering their drinks. Perhaps he feels a bit shy and awkward, too, Phyl thought.

"Not very busy," he remarked to the barman.

"In one week we close."

"Looks as if you've hardly opened," Stanley said, glancing round.

It's not *his* business to get huffy, Phyl thought indignantly, when the young man, not replying, shrugged and turned aside to polish some glasses. Customer's always right. He should know that. Politics, religion, colour-bar—however they argue together, they're all of them always right, and if you know your job you can joke them out of it and on to something safer. The times she had done that, making a fool of herself, no doubt, anything for peace and quiet. By the time the elections were over, she was usually worn out.

Stanley had hated her buying him a drink back in the hotel; but she had insisted. "What all that crowd would think of me!" she had said; but here, although it went much against her nature, she put aside her principles, and let him pay; let him set the pace, too. They became elated, and she was sure it would be all right—even having to go back to the soup-specialist's dinner. They might have avoided that; but too late now.

The barman, perhaps with a contemptuous underlining of their age, shuffled through some records and now put on *Night and Day*. For them both, it filled the bar with nostalgia.

"Come *on*!" said Stanley. "I've never danced with you. This always makes me feel … I don't know."

"Oh, I'm a terrible dancer," she protested. The Licensed Victuallers' Association annual dance was the only one she ever went to, and even there stayed in the bar most of the time. Laughing, however, she let herself be helped down off her stool.

He had once fancied himself a good dancer; but, in later years, got no practice, with Ethel being ill, and then dead. Phyl was surprised how light he was on his feet; he bounced her round, holding her firmly against his stomach, his hand pressed to her back, but gently, because of the sunburn. He had perfect rhythm and expertise, side-stepping, reversing, taking masterly control of her.

"Well, I never!" she cried. "You're making me quite breathless."

He rested his cheek against her hair, and closed his eyes, in the old, old way, and seemed to waft her away into a different dimension. It was then that he felt the first twinge, in his left toe. It was doom to him. He kept up the pace, but fell silent. When the record ended, he hoped that she would not want to stay on longer. To return to the hotel and take his gout pills was all he could think about. Some intuition made her refuse another drink. "We've got to go back to the soup-specialist some time," she said. "He might even be a good cook."

"Surprise, surprise!" Stanley managed to say, walking with pain towards the door.

MR. RADAM was the most abominable cook. They had—in a large cold room with many tables—thin greasy chicken soup, and after that the chicken that had gone through the soup. Then peaches; he brought the tin and opened it before them, as if it were a precious wine, and no hanky-panky going on. He then stood over them, because he had much to say. "I was offered a post in Basingstoke. Two thousand pounds a year, and a car and a house thrown in. But what use is that to a man like me? Besides, Basingstoke has a most detestable climate."

Stanley sat, tight-lipped, trying not to lose his temper; but this man, and the pain, were driving him mad. He did not—dared not—drink any of the wine he had ordered.

"Yes, the Basingstoke employment I regarded as not *on,*" Mr Radam said slangily.

Phyl secretly put out a foot and touched one of Stan's—the wrong one—and then thought he was about to have a heart attack. He screwed up his eyes and tried to breathe steadily, a slice of peach slithering about in his spoon. It was then she realized what was wrong with him.

"Oh, sod the peaches," she said cheerfully, when Mr. Radam had gone off to make coffee, which would be the best they had ever tasted, he had promised. Phyl knew they would not complain about the horrible coffee that was coming. The more monstrous the egoist, she had observed from long practice, the more normal people hope to uphold the fabrication—either for ease, or from a terror of any kind of collapse. She did not know. She was sure, though, as she praised the stringy chicken, hoisting the unlovable man's self-infatuation a notch higher, that she did so, because she feared him falling to pieces. Perhaps it was only fair, she decided, that weakness should get preferential treatment. Whether it would continue to do so, with Stanley's present change of mood, she was uncertain.

She tried to explain her thoughts to him when, he leaving his coffee, she having gulped hers down, they went to their bedroom. He nodded. He sat on the side of the bed, and put his face into his hands.

"Don't let's go out again," she said. 'We can have a drink in here. I love a bedroom gin, and I brought a bottle in my case." She went busily to the wash basin, and held up a dusty tooth-glass to the light.

"You have one," he said.

He was determined to keep unruffled, but every step she took across the uneven floorboards broke momentarily the steady pain into burning splinters.

"I've got gout," he said sullenly. "Bloody hell, I've got my gout."

"I thought so," she said. She put down the glass very quietly and came to him. "Where?"

He pointed down.

"Can you manage to get into bed by yourself?"

He nodded.

"Well, then!" she smiled. "Once you're in, I know what to do."

He looked up apprehensively, but she went almost on tiptoe out of the door and closed it softly.

He undressed, put on his pyjamas, and hauled himself onto the bed. When she came back, she was carrying two pillows. "Don't laugh, but they're 'His' and 'His,'" she said. "Now, this is what I do for Charlie. I make a little pillow house for his foot, and it keeps the bedclothes off. Don't worry, I won't touch."

"On this one night," he said.

"You want to drink a lot of water." She put a glass beside him. "'My husband's got a touch of gout,' I told them down there. And I really felt quite married to you when I said it."

She turned her back to him as she undressed. Her body, set free at last, was creased with red marks, and across her shoulders the bright new skin from peeling had ragged, dirty edges of the old. She stretched her spine, put on a transparent nightgown and began to scratch her arms.

"Come here," he said, unmoving. "I'll do that."

So gently she pulled back the sheet and lay down beside him that he felt they had been happily married for years. The pang was that this was their only married night and his foot burned so that he thought that it would burst. And it will be a damn sight worse in the morning, he thought, knowing the pattern of his affliction. He began with one hand to stroke her itching arm.

Almost as soon as she had put the light off, an ominous sound zigzagged about the room. Switching on again, she said, "I'll get that devil, if it's the last thing I do. You lie still."

She got out of bed again and ran round the room, slapping at the walls with her *Reader's Digest,* until at last she caught the mosquito, and Stanley's (as was apparent in the morning) blood squirted out.

After that, once more in the dark, they lay quietly. He endured his pain, and she without disturbing him rubbed her flaking skin.

"So this is our wicked adventure," he said bitterly to the moonlit ceiling.

"Would you rather be on your own?"

"No, no!" He groped with his hand towards her.

"Well, then ..."

"How can you forgive me?"

"Let's worry about you, eh? Not me. That sort of thing doesn't matter much to me nowadays. I only really do it to be matey. I don't know ... by the time Charlie and I have locked up, washed up, done the till, had a bit of something to eat ..."

Once, she had been as insatiable as a flame. She lay and remembered the days of her youth; but with interest, not wistfully.

ONLY ONCE did she wake. It was the best night's sleep she'd had for a week. Moonlight now fell over the bed, and on one chalky white-washed wall. The sheet draped over them rose in a peak above his feet, so that he looked like a figure on a tomb. If Charlie could see me now, she suddenly thought. She tried not to have a fit of giggles for fear of shaking the bed. Stanley shifted, groaned in his sleep, then went on snoring, just as Charlie did.

HE WOKE OFTEN during that night. The sheets were as abrasive as sandpaper. I knew this damn bed was too small, he thought. He shifted warily onto his side to look at Phyl who, in her sleep, made funny little whimpering sounds like a puppy. One arm flung above her head looked, in the moonlight, quite black against the pillow. Like going to bed with a coloured woman, he thought. He dutifully took a sip or two of water and then settled back again to endure his wakefulness.

"WELL, *I* WAS HAPPY," she said, wearing her emerald green coat again, sitting next to him in the plane, fastening her safety-belt.

His face looked worn and grey.

"Don't mind me asking," she went on, "but did he charge for that tea we didn't order."

"Five shillings."

"I *knew* it. I wish you'd let me pay my share of everything. After all, it was me as well wanted to go."

He shook his head, smiling at her. In spite of his prediction, he felt better this departure afternoon, though tired and wary about himself.

"If only we were taking off on holiday now," he said, "not coming back. Why can't we meet up in Torquay or somewhere? Something for me to look forward to," he begged her, dabbing his mosquito-bitten forehead with his handkerchief.

"It was only my hysterectomy got me away this time," she said.

They ate, they drank, they held hands under a newspaper, and presently crossed the twilit coast of England, where farther along grey Hove was waiting for him. The trees had not changed colour much and only some—she noticed, as she looked down on them, coming in to land—were yellower.

She knew that it was worse for him. He had to return to his empty flat; she, to a full bar, and on a Saturday, too. She wished there was something she could do to send him off cheerful.

"To me," she said, having refastened her safety-belt, taking his hand again. "To me, it was lovely. To me it was just as good as if we had."

Lifeguard

by

JOHN UPDIKE

BEYOND DOUBT, I am a splendid fellow. In the autumn, winter, and spring, I execute the duties of a student of divinity; in the summer I disguise myself in my skin and become a lifeguard. My slightly narrow and gingerly hirsute but not necessarily unmanly chest becomes brown. My smooth back turns the colour of caramel, which, in conjunction with the whipped cream of my white pith helmet, gives me, some of my teenage satellites assure me, a delightfully edible appearance. My legs, which I myself can study, cocked as they are before me while I repose on my elevated wooden throne, are dyed a lustreless maple walnut that accentuates their articulate strength. Correspondingly, the hairs of my body are bleached blond, so that my legs have the pointed elegance of, within the flower, umber anthers dusted with pollen.

For nine months of the year, I pace my pale hands and burning eyes through immense pages of Biblical text barnacled with fudging commentary; through multivolumed apologetics couched in a falsely friendly Victorian voice and bound in subtly abrasive boards of finely ridged, prefaded red; through handbooks of liturgy and histories of dogma; through the bewildering duplicities of Tillich's divine politicking; through the suave table talk of Father D'Arcy, Etienne Gilson, Jacques Maritain, and other such moderns mistakenly put at their ease by the exquisite antique furniture and overstuffed larder of the hospitable St. Thomas; through the terrifying attempts of Kierkegaard, Berdyaev, and Barth to scourge God into being. I sway appalled on the ladder of minus signs by which theologians would surmount the void. I tiptoe like a burglar into the house of naturalism to steal the silver. An acrobat, I swing from wisp to wisp. Newman's iridescent cobwebs crush in my hands. Pascal's blackboard mathematics are erased by a passing shoulder. The cave drawings, astoundingly vital by candlelight, of those aboriginal magicians, Paul and Augustine, in daylight fade into mere anthropology. The diverting productions of literary flirts like Chesterton, Eliot, Auden, and Greene—whether they regard Christianity as a pastel forest designed for a fairyland romp or a deliciously miasmic pit from which chiaroscuro can be mined with mechanical buckets—in the end all infallibly strike, despite the comic variety of gongs and mallets, the note of the rich young man who on the coast of Judaea refused in dismay to sell all that he had.

Then, for the remaining quarter of the solar revolution, I rest my eyes on a sheet of brilliant sand printed with the runes of naked human bodies. That there is no discrepancy between my studies, that the texts of the flesh complement those of the mind, is the easy burden of my sermon.

On the back rest of my lifeguard's chair is painted a cross—true, a red cross, signifying bandages, splints, spirits of ammonia, and sunburn unguents. Nevertheless, it comforts me. Each morning, as I mount into my chair, my athletic and youthfully fuzzy toes expertly gripping the slats that make a ladder, it is as if I am climbing into an immense, rigid, loosely fitting vestment.

Again, in each of my roles I sit attentively perched on the edge of an immensity. That the sea, with its multiform and mysterious hosts, its savage and senseless rages, no longer comfortably serves as a divine metaphor indicates how severely humanism has corrupted the apples of our creed. We seek God now in flowers and good deeds, and the immensities of blue that surround the little scabs of land upon which we draw our lives to their unsatisfactory conclusions are suffused by science with vacuous horror. I myself can hardly bear the thought of stars, or begin to count the mortalities of coral. But from my chair the sea, slightly distended by my higher perspective, seems a misty old gentleman stretched at his ease in an immense armchair which has for arms the arms of this bay and for an antimacassar the freshly laundered sky. Sailboats float on his surface like idle and unrelated but benevolent thoughts. The soughing of the surf is the rhythmic lifting of his ripple-stitched vest as he breathes. Consider. We enter the sea with a shock; our skin and blood shout in protest. But, that instant, that leap, past, what do we find? Ecstasy and buoyancy. Swimming offers a parable. We struggle and thrash, and drown; we succumb, even in despair, and float, and are saved.

With what timidity, with what a sense of trespass, do I set forward even this obliquely a thought so official! Forgive me. I am not yet ordained; I am too disordered to deal with the main text. My competence is marginal, and I will confine myself to the gloss of flesh with which this particular margin, this one beach, is annotated each day.

Here the cinema of life is run backwards. The old are the first to arrive. They are idle, and have lost the gift of sleep. Each of our bodies is a clock that loses time. Young as I am, I can hear in myself the protein acids ticking; I wake at odd hours and in the shuddering darkness and silence feel my death rushing toward me like an express train. The older we get, and the fewer the mornings left to us, the more deeply dawn stabs us awake. The old ladies wear wide straw hats and, in their hats' shadows, smiles as wide, which they bestow upon each other, upon salty shells they discover in the morning-smooth sand, and even upon me, downy-eyed from my night of dissipation. The gentlemen are often incongruous; withered white legs support brazen barrel chests, absurdly potent, bustling with white froth. How these old roosters preen on their "condition"! With what fatuous expertness they swim in the icy water—always, however, prudently parallel to the shore, at a depth no greater than their height.

Then come the middle-aged, burdened with children and aluminum chairs. The men are scarred with the marks of their vocation—the red forearms of the gasoline-station attendant, the pale X on the back of the overall-wearing mason or carpenter, the clammer's nicked ankles. The hair on their bodies has as many patterns as matted grass. The women are wrinkled but fertile, like the Iraqi rivers that cradled the seeds of our civilization. Their children are odious. From their gaunt faces leer all the vices, the greeds, the grating urgencies of the adult, unsoftened by maturity's reticence and fatigue. Except that here and there, a girl, the eldest daughter, wearing a knit suit striped horizontally with green, purple, and brown, walks slowly, carefully, puzzled by the dawn enveloping her thick smooth body, her waist not yet nipped but her throat elongated.

Finally come the young. The young matrons bring fat and fussing infants who gobble the sand like sugar, who toddle blissfully into the surf and bring me bolt upright on my throne. My whistle tweets. The mothers rouse. Many of these women are pregnant again, and sluggishly lie in their loose suits like cows tranced in a meadow. They gossip politics, and smoke incessantly, and lift their troubled eyes in wonder as a trio of flat-stomached nymphs parades past. These maidens take all our eyes. The vivacious redhead, freckled and white-footed, pushing against her boy and begging to be ducked; the solemn brunette, transporting the vase of herself with held breath; the dimpled blonde in the bib and diapers of her Bikini, the lambent fuzz of her midriff shimmering like a cat's belly. Lust stuns me like the sun.

YOU ARE OFFENDED that a divinity student lusts? What prigs the unchurched are. Are not our assaults on the supernatural lascivious, a kind of indecency? If only you knew what de Sadian degradations, what frightful psychological spelunking, our gentle transcendentalist professors set us to, as preparation for our work, which is to shine in the darkness.

I feel that my lust makes me glow; I grow cold in my chair, like a torch of ice, as I study beauty. I have studied much of it, wearing all styles of bathing suit and facial expression, and have come to this conclusion: a woman's beauty lies, not in any exaggeration of the specialized zones, nor in any general harmony that could be worked out by means of the *sectio aurea* or a similar aesthetic superstition; but in the arabesque of the spine. The curve by which the back modulates into the buttocks. It is here that grace sits and rides a woman's body.

I watch from my white throne and pity women, deplore the demented judgment that drives them toward the braggart muscularity of the mesomorph and the prosperous complacence of the endomorph when it is we ectomorphs who pack in our scrawny sinews and exacerbated nerves the most intense gift, the most generous shelter, of love. To desire a woman is to desire to save her. Anyone who has endured intercourse that was neither predatory nor hurried knows how through it we descend, with a partner, into the grotesque and delicate shadows that until then have remained locked in the most guarded recess of our soul: into this harbour we bring her. A vague and twisted terrain becomes inhabited; each shadow, touched by the exploration, blooms into a flower of act. As if we are an island upon which a woman, tossed by her labouring vanity and blind self-seeking, is blown, and there finds security, until, an instant before the anticlimax, Nature with a smile thumps down her trump, and the island sinks beneath the sea.

There is great truth in those motion pictures which are slandered as true neither to the Bible nor to life. They are—written though they are by demons and drunks—true to both. We are all Solomons lusting for Sheba's salvation. The God-filled man is filled with a wilderness that cries to be populated. The stony chambers need jewels, furs, tints of cloth and flesh, even though, as in Samson's case, the temple comes tumbling. Women are an alien race of pagans set down among us. Every seduction is a conversion.

Who has loved and not experienced that sense of rescue? It is not true that our biological impulses are tricked out with ribands of chivalry; rather, our chivalric impulses go clanking in encumbering biological armour. Eunuchs love. Children love. I would love.

My chief exercise, as I sit above the crowds, is to lift the whole mass into immortality. It is not a light task; the throng is so huge, and its members so individually unworthy. No *memento mori* is so clinching as a photograph of a vanished crowd. Cheering Roosevelt, celebrating the Armistice, there it is, wearing its ten thousand straw hats and stiff collars, a fearless and wooden-faced bustle of life: it is gone. A crowd dies in the street like a derelict; it leaves no heir, no trace, no name. My own persistence beyond the last rim of time is easy to imagine; indeed, the effort of imagination lies the other way—to conceive of my ceasing. But when I study the vast tangle of humanity that blackens the beach as far as the sand stretches, absurdities crowd in on me. Is it as maiden, matron, or crone that the females will be eternalized? What will they do without children to watch and gossip to exchange? What of the thousand deaths of memory and bodily change we endure—can each be redeemed at a final Adjustments Counter? The sheer numbers involved make the mind scream. The race is no longer a tiny clan of simian aristocrats lording it over an ocean of grass; mankind is a plague racing like fire across the exhausted continents. This immense clot gathered on the beach, a fraction of a fraction—can we not say that this breeding swarm is its own immortality and end the suspense? The beehive in a sense survives; and is each of us not proved to be a hive, a galaxy of cells each of whom is doubtless praying, from its pew in our thumbnail or esophagus, for personal resurrection? Indeed, to the cells themselves cancer may seem a revival of faith. No, in relation to other people oblivion is sensible and sanitary.

This sea of others exasperates and fatigues me most on Sunday mornings. I don't know why people no longer go to church—whether they have lost the ability to sing or the willingness to listen. From eight-thirty onward they crowd in from the parking lots, ants each carrying its crumb of baggage, until by noon, when the remote churches are releasing their gallant and gaily dressed minority, the sea itself is jammed with hollow heads and thrashing arms like a great bobbing backwash of rubbish. A transistor radio somewhere in the sand releases in a thin, apologetic gust the closing peal of a transcribed service. And right here, here at the very height of torpor and confusion, I slump, my eyes slit, and the blurred forms of Protestantism's errant herd seem gathered by the water's edge in impassioned poses of devotion. I seem to be lying dreaming in the infinite rock of space before Creation, and the actual scene I see is a vision of impossibility: a Paradise. For had we existed before the gesture that split the firmament, could we have conceived of our most obvious possession, our most platitudinous blessing, the moment, the single ever-present moment that we perpetually bring to our lips brimful?

So: be joyful. Be Joyful in my commandment. It is the message I read in your jiggle. Stretch your skins like pegged hides curing in the miracle of the sun's moment. Exult in your legs' scissoring, your waist's swivel. Romp; eat the froth; be children. I am here above you; I have given my youth that you may do this. I wait. The tides of time have treacherous undercurrents. You are borne continually toward the horizon. I have prepared myself; my muscles are instilled with everything that must be done. Someday my alertness will bear fruit; from near the horizon there will arise, delicious, translucent, like a green bell above the water, the call for help, the call, a call, it saddens me to confess, that I have yet to hear.

Three Players of a Summer Game

by

TENNESSEE WILLIAMS

CROQUET IS A SUMMER GAME that seems, in a curious way, to be composed of images the way that a painter's abstraction of summer or one of its games would be built of them. The delicate wire wickets set in a lawn of smooth emerald that flickers fierily at some points and rests under violet shadow in others, the wooden poles gaudily painted as moments that stand out in a season that was a struggle for something of unspeakable importance to someone passing through it, the clean and hard wooden spheres of different colours and the strong rigid shape of the mallets that drive the balls through the wickets, the formal design of those wickets and poles upon the croquet lawn—all of these are like a painter's abstraction of a summer and a game played in it. And I cannot think of croquet without hearing a sound like the faraway boom of a cannon fired to announce a white ship coming into a harbour which had expected it anxiously for a long while. The faraway booming sound is that of a green-and-white striped awning coming down over a gallery of a white frame house. The house is of Victorian design carried to an extreme of improvisation, an almost grotesque pile of galleries and turrets and cupolas and eaves, all freshly painted white, so white and so fresh that it has the blue-white glitter of a block of ice in the sun. The house is like a new resolution not yet tainted by any defection from it. And I associate the summer game with players coming out of this house, out of the mysteries of a walled place, with the buoyant air of persons just released from a suffocating enclosure, as if they had spent the fierce day bound in a closet, were breathing freely at last in fresh atmosphere and able to move without hindrance. Their clothes are as light in weight and colour as the flattering clothes of dancers. There are three players—a woman, a man, and a child.

The voice of the woman player is not at all a loud one; yet it has a pleasantly resonant quality that carries it farther than most voices go and it is interspersed with peals of treble laughter, pitched much higher than the voice itself, which are cool-sounding as particles of ice in a tall shaken glass. This woman player, even more than her male opponent in the game, has the grateful quickness of motion of someone let out of a suffocating enclosure; her motion has the quickness of breath released just after a moment of terror, of fingers unclenched when panic is suddenly past or of a cry that subsides into laughter. She seems unable to speak or move about moderately; she moves in convulsive rushes, whipping her skirts with long strides that quicken to running. The whipped skirts are white ones. They make a faint crackling sound as her pumping thighs whip them open, the sound that comes to you, greatly diminished by distance, when fitful fair-weather gusts belly out and slacken the faraway sails of a yawl. That agreeably cool summer sound is accompanied by another which is even cooler, the ceaseless tiny chatter of beads hung in long loops from her throat. They are not pearls but they have a milky lustre, they are small faintly speckled white ovals, polished bird's eggs turned solid and strung upon glittery filaments of silver. This woman player is never still for a moment; sometimes she exhausts herself and collapses on the grass in the conscious attitudes of a dancer. She is a thin woman with long bones and skin of a silky lustre and her eyes are only a shade or two darker than the blue-tinted bird's-egg beads about her long throat. She is never still, not even when she has fallen in exhaustion on the grass. The neighbours think she's gone mad but they feel no pity for her, and that, of course, is because of her male opponent in the game.

This player is Brick Pollitt, a man so tall with such a fiery thatch of hair on top of him that I never see a flagpole on an expanse of green lawn or even a particularly brilliant cross or weather vane on a steeple without thinking suddenly of that long-ago summer and Brick Pollitt and begin to assort again the baffling bits and pieces that make his legend. These bits and pieces, these assorted images, they are like the paraphernalia for a game of croquet, gathered up from the lawn when the game is over and packed carefully into an oblong wooden box which they just exactly fit and fill. There they all are, the bits and pieces, the images, the apparently incongruous paraphernalia of a summer that was the last one of my childhood, and now I take them out of the oblong box and arrange them once more in the formal design on the lawn. It would be absurd to pretend that this is altogether the way it was, and yet it may be closer than a literal history could be to the hidden truth of it. Brick Pollitt is the male player of this summer game, and he is a drinker who has not yet completely fallen beneath the savage axe blows of his liquor. He is not so young any more but he has not yet lost the slim grace of his youth. He is a head taller than the tall woman player of the game. He is such a tall man that, even in those sections of the lawn dimmed under violet shadow, his head continues to catch fiery rays of the descending sun, the way that the heavenward pointing index finger of that huge gilded hand atop a Protestant steeple in Meridian goes on drawing the sun's flame for a good while after the lower surfaces of the town have sunk into lingering dusk.

The third player of the summer game is the daughter of the woman, a plump twelve-year-old child named Mary Louise. This little girl had made herself distinctly unpopular among the children of the neighbourhood by imitating too perfectly the elegant manners and cultivated eastern voice of her mother. She sat in the electric automobile on the sort of a fat silk pillow that expensive lapdogs sit on, uttering treble peals of ladylike laughter, tossing her curls, using grown-up expressions such as, "Oh, how delightful" and "Isn't that just lovely." She would sit in the electric automobile sometimes all afternoon by herself as if she were on display in a glass box, only now and then raising a plaintive voice to call her mother and ask if it was all right for her to come in now or if she could drive the electric around the block, which she was sometimes then permitted to do.

I was her only close friend and she was mine. Sometimes she called me over to play croquet with her but that was only when her mother and Brick Pollitt had disappeared into the house too early to play the game. Mary Louise had a passion for croquet; she played it for itself, without any more shadowy and important connotations.

What the game meant to Brick Pollitt calls for some further account of Brick's life before that summer. He was a young Delta planter who had been a celebrated athlete at Sewanee, who had married a New Orleans debutante who was a Mardi Gras queen and whose father owned a fleet of banana boats. It had seemed a brilliant marriage, with lots of wealth and prestige on both sides, but only two years later Brick had started falling in love with his liquor and Margaret, his wife, began to be praised for her patience and loyalty to him. Brick seemed to be throwing his life away as if it were something disgusting that he had suddenly found in his hands. This self-disgust came upon him with the abruptness and violence of a crash on a highway. But what had Brick crashed into? Nothing that anybody was able to surmise, for he seemed to have everything that young men like Brick might hope or desire to have. What else is there? There must have been something else that he wanted and lacked, or what reason was there for dropping his life and taking hold of a glass which he never let go of for more than one waking hour? His wife, Margaret, took hold of Brick's ten-thousand-acre plantation as firmly and surely as if she had always existed for that and no other purpose. She had Brick's power of attorney and she managed all of his business affairs with celebrated astuteness. "He'll come out of it," she said. "Brick is passing through something that he'll come out of." She always said the right thing; she took the conventionally right attitude and expressed it to the world that admired her for it. She had never committed any apostasy from the social faith she was born to and everybody admired her as a remarkably fine and brave little woman who had too much to put up with. Two sections of an hourglass could not drain and fill more evenly than Brick and Margaret changed places after he took to drink. It was as though she had her lips fastened to some invisible wound in his body through which drained out of him and flowed into her the assurance and vitality that he had owned before marriage. Margaret Pollitt lost her pale, feminine prettiness and assumed in its place something more impressive—a firm and rough-textured sort of handsomeness that came out of her indefinite chrysalis as mysteriously as one of those metamorphoses that occur in insect life. Once very pretty but indistinct, a graceful sketch that was done with a very light pencil, she became vivid as Brick disappeared behind the veil of his liquor. She came out of a mist. She rose into clarity as Brick descended. She abruptly stopped being quiet and dainty. She was now apt to have dirty fingernails which she covered with scarlet enamel. When the enamel chipped off, the grey showed underneath. Her hair was now cut short so that she didn't have to "mess with it." It was wind-blown and full of sparkle; she jerked a comb through it to make it crackle. She had white teeth that were a little too large for her thin lips, and when she threw her head back in laughter, strong cords of muscle stood out in her smooth brown throat. She had a booming laugh that she might have stolen from Brick while he was drunk or asleep beside her at night. She had a practice of releasing the clutch on a car and shooting off in high gear at the exact instant that her laughter boomed out, not calling goodbye but thrusting out one bare strong arm, straight out as a piston with fingers clenched into a fist, as the car whipped up and disappeared into a cloud of yellow dust. She didn't drive her own little runabout nowadays so much as she did Brick's Pierce-Arrow touring car, for Brick's driver's licence had been revoked. She frequently broke the speed limit on the highway. The patrolmen would stop her, but she had such an affability, such a disarming way with her, that they would have a good laugh together, she and the highway patrolman, and he would tear up the ticket.

Somebody in her family died in Memphis that spring, and she went there to attend the funeral and collect her inheritance, and while she was gone on that profitable journey, Brick Pollitt slipped out from under her thumb a bit. Another death occurred during her absence. That nice young doctor who took care of Brick when he had to be carried to the hospital, he suddenly took sick in a shocking way. An awful flower grew in his brain like a fierce geranium that shattered its pot. All of a sudden the wrong words came out of his mouth; he seemed to be speaking in an unknown tongue; he couldn't find things with his hands; he made troubled signs over his forehead. His wife led him about the house by one hand, yet he stumbled and fell flat; the breath was knocked out of him, and he had to be put to bed by his wife and the Negro yardman; and he lay there laughing weakly, incredulously, trying to find his wife's hand with both of his while she looked at him with eyes that she couldn't keep from blazing with terror. He stayed under drugs for a week, and it was during that time that Brick Pollitt came to see her. Brick came and sat with Isabel Grey by her dying husband's bed and she couldn't speak, she could only shake her head, incessantly as a metronome, with no lips visible in her white face, but two pressed narrow bands of a dimmer whiteness that shook as if some white liquid flowed beneath them with an incredible rapidity and violence which made them quiver ...

God was the only word she was able to say; but Brick Pollitt somehow understood what she meant by that word, as if it were in a language that she and he, alone of all people, could speak and understand; and when the dying man's eyes forcibly opened on something they couldn't bear to look at, it was Brick, his hands suddenly quite sure and steady, who filled the hypodermic needle for her and pumped its contents fiercely into her husband's hard young arm. And it was over. There was another bed at the back of the house and he and Isabel lay beside each other on that bed for a couple of hours before they let the town know that her husband's agony was completed, and the only movement between them was the intermittent, spasmodic digging of their fingernails into each other's clenched palm while their bodies lay stiffly separate, deliberately not touching at any other points as if they abhorred any other contact with each other, while this intolerable thing was ringing like an iron bell through them.

And so you see what the summer game on the violet-shadowed lawn was—it was a running together out of something unbearably hot and bright into something obscure and cool ...

THE YOUNG WIDOW was left with nothing in the way of material possessions except the house and an electric automobile, but by the time Brick's wife, Margaret, had returned from her profitable journey to Memphis, Brick had taken over the post-catastrophic details of the widow's life. For a week or two, people thought it was very kind of him, and then all at once public opinion changed and they decided that Brick's reason for kindness was by no means noble. It appeared to observers that the widow was now his mistress, and this was true. It was true in the limited way that most such opinions are true. It is only the outside of one person's world that is visible to others, and all opinions are false ones, especially public opinions of individual cases. She was his mistress, but that was not Brick's reason. His reason had something to do with that chaste interlocking of hands their first time together, after the hypodermic; it had to do with those hours, now receding and fading behind them as all such hours must, but neither of them could have said what it was aside from that. Neither of them was able to think very clearly about the matter. But Brick was able to pull himself together for a while and take command of those post-catastrophic details in the young widow's life and her daughter's.

The daughter, Mary Louise, was a plump child of twelve. She was my friend that summer. Mary Louise and I caught lightning bugs and put them in Mason jars to make flickering lanterns, and we played the game of croquet when her mother and Brick Pollitt were not inclined to play it. It was Mary Louise that summer who taught me how to deal with mosquito bites. She was plagued by mosquitoes and so was I. She warned me that scratching the bites would leave scars on my skin, which was as tender as hers. I said that I didn't care. "Someday you will," she told me. She carried with her constantly that summer a lump of ice in a handkerchief. Whenever a mosquito bit her, instead of scratching the bite she rubbed it gently with the handkerchief-wrapped lump of ice until the sting was frozen to numbness. Of course, in five minutes it would come back and have to be frozen again, but eventually it would disappear and leave no scar. Mary Louise's skin, where it was not temporarily mutilated by a mosquito bite or a slight rash that sometimes appeared after eating strawberry ice cream, was ravishingly smooth and tender. The association is not at all a proper one, but how can you recall a summer in childhood without some touches of impropriety? I can't remember Mary Louise's plump bare legs and arms, fragrant with sweet-pea powder, without also thinking of an afternoon drive we took in the electric automobile to the little art museum that had recently been established in the town. We went there just before the five o'clock closing time, and straight as a bee, Mary Louise led me into a room that was devoted to replicas of famous antique sculptures. There was a reclining male nude (the *Dying Gaul,* I believe) and it was straight to this statue that she led me. I began to blush before we arrived there. It was naked except for a fig leaf, which was of a different-coloured metal from the bronze of the prostrate figure, and to my astonished horror, that afternoon, Mary Louise, after a quick, sly look in all directions, picked the fig leaf up, removed it from what it covered, and then turned her totally unembarrassed and innocent eyes upon mine and inquired, smiling very brightly, "Is yours like that?"

My answer was idiotic; I said, "I don't know!" and I think I was blushing long after we left the museum ...

The Greys' house in the spring when the doctor died of brain cancer was very run down. But soon after Brick Pollitt started coming over to see the young widow, the house was painted; it was painted so white that it was almost a very pale blue; it had the blue-white glitter of a block of ice in the sun. Coolness of appearance seemed to be the most desired of all things that summer. In spite of his red hair, Brick Pollitt had a cool appearance because he was still young and thin, as thin as the widow, and he dressed as she did in clothes of light weight and colour. His white shirts looked faintly pink because of his skin underneath them. Once, I saw him through an upstairs window of the widow's house just a moment before he pulled the shade down. I was in an upstairs room of my house and I saw that Brick Pollitt was divided into two colours as distinct as two stripes of a flag, the upper part of him, which had been exposed to the sun, almost crimson and the lower part of him white as this piece of paper.

While the widow's house was being repainted (at Brick Pollitt's expense), she and her daughter lived at the Alcazar Hotel, also at Brick's expense. Brick supervised the renovation of the widow's house. He drove in from his plantation every morning to watch the house painters and gardeners at work. Brick's driving licence had been restored to him, and it was an important step forward in his personal renovation—being able to drive his own car again. He drove it with elaborate caution and formality, coming to a dead stop at every cross street in the town, sounding the silver trumpet at every corner, inviting pedestrians to precede him, with smiles and bows and great circular gestures of his hands. But observers did not approve of what Brick Pollitt was doing. They sympathized with his wife, Margaret, that brave little woman who had to put up with so much. As for Dr. Grey's widow, she had not been very long in the town; the doctor had married her while he was an intern at a big hospital in Baltimore. Nobody had formed a definite opinion of her before the doctor died, so it was no effort, now, to simply condemn her, without any qualification, as a strumpet, common in everything but her "affectations."

Brick Pollitt, when he talked to the house painters, shouted to them as if they were deaf, so that all the neighbours could hear what he had to say. He was explaining things to the world, especially the matter of his drinking.

"It's something," he shouted, "that you can't cut out completely right away. That's the big mistake that most drinkers make—they try to cut it out completely, and you can't do that. You can do it for maybe a month or two months, but all at once you go back on it worse than before you went off it, and then the discouragement is awful—you lose all faith in yourself and just give up. The thing to do, the way to handle the problem, is like a bullfighter handles a bull in a ring. Wear it down little by little, get control of it gradually. That's how I'm handling this thing! Yep. Now, let's say that you get up wanting a drink in the morning. Say it's ten o'clock, maybe. Well, you say to yourself, 'Just wait half an hour, old boy, and then you can have one.' Well, at half-past ten you still want that drink, and you want it a little bit worse than you did at ten, but you say to yourself, 'Boy, you could do without it half an hour ago so you can do without it now.' You see, that's how you got to argue about it with yourself, because a drinking man is not one person—a man that drinks is two people, one grabbing the bottle, the other one fighting him off it, not one but two people fighting each other to get control of a bottle. Well, sir, if you can talk yourself out of a drink at ten, you can still talk yourself out of a drink at *half-past* ten! But at *eleven* o'clock the need for the drink is greater. Now *here's* the important thing to remember about this struggle. You got to watch those scales, and when they tip too far against your power to resist, you got to give in a little. That's not weakness. *That's strategy!* Because don't forget what I told you. A drinking man is not one person but two, and it's a battle of wits going on between them. And so I say at eleven, 'Well, *have* your drink at that hour, *go on,* and *have* it! One drink at eleven won't hurt you!'

"What time is it, now? Yep! Eleven … All right, I'm going to have me that one drink. I could do without it, I don't crave it, but the important thing is …"

His voice would trail off as he entered the widow's house. He would stay in there longer than it took to have one drink, and when he came out, there was a change in his voice as definite as a change of weather or season, the strong and vigorous tone would be a bit filmed over.

Then he would usually talk about his wife. "I don't say my wife Margaret's not an intelligent woman. She is, and both of us know it, but she don't have a good head for property values. Now, you know Dr. Grey, who used to live here before that brain thing killed him. Well, he was my physician, he pulled me through some bad times when I had that liquor problem. I felt I owed him a lot. Now, that was a terrible thing the way he went, but it was terrible for his widow, too; she was left with this house and that electric automobile and that's all, and this house was put up for sale to pay off her debts, and—well, I bought it. I bought it, and now I'm giving it back to her. Now, my wife Margaret, she. And a lot of other folks, too. Don't understand about this …

"What time is it? Twelve? High noon! … This ice is melted …"

He'd drift back into the house and stay there half an hour, and when he came back out, it was rather shyly with a sad and uncertain creaking of the screen door pushed by the hand not holding the tall glass, but after resting a little while on the steps, he would resume his talk to the house painters.

"Yes," he would say, as if he had only paused a moment before, "it's the most precious thing that a woman can give to a man—his lost respect for himself—and the meanest thing one human being can do to another human being is take his respect for himself away from him. I. I had it took away from me …"

The glass would tilt slowly up and jerkily down, and he'd have to wipe his chin dry.

"I had it took away from me! I won't tell you how, but maybe, being men about my age, you're able to guess it. That was how. Some of them don't want it. They cut it off. They cut it right off a man, and half the time he don't even know when they cut it off him. Well, I knew it all right. I could feel it being cut off me. Do you know what I mean? … That's right …

"But once in a while there's one—and they don't come often—that wants for a man to keep it, and those are the women that God made and put on this earth. The other kind come out of hell, or out of … I don't know what. I'm talking too much. Sure. I know I'm talking too much about private matters. But that's all right. This property is mine. I'm talking on my own property and I don't give a s— who hears me! I'm not shouting about it, but I'm not sneaking around about it neither. Whatever I do, I do it without any shame, and I've got a right to do it. I've been through a hell of a lot that nobody knows. But I'm coming out of it now. Goddammit, yes, I am! I can't take all the credit. And yet I'm proud. I'm goddamn proud of myself, because I was in a pitiful condition with that liquor problem of mine, but now the worst is over. I've got it just about licked. That's my car out there and I drove it up here myself. It's no short drive, it's almost a hundred miles, and I drive it each morning and drive it back each night. I've got back my driver's licence, and I fired the man that was working for my wife, looking after our place. I fired that man and not only fired him but give him a kick in the britches that'll make him eat standing up for the next week or two. It wasn't because I thought he was fooling around. It wasn't that. But him and her both took about the same attitude toward me, and I didn't like the attitude they took. They would talk about me right in front of me, as if I wasn't there. 'Is it time for his medicine?' Yes, they were giving me dope! So one day I played possum. I was lying out there on the sofa and she said to him, 'I guess he's passed out now.' And he said, 'Jesus, dead drunk at half-past one in the afternoon!' Well. I got up slowly. I wasn't drunk at that hour, I wasn't even half drunk. I stood up straight and walked slowly toward him. I walked straight up to them both, and you should of seen the eyes of them both bug out! 'Yes, Jesus,' I said, 'at half-past one!' And I grabbed him by his collar and by the seat of his britches and turkey-trotted him right on out of the house and pitched him on his face in a big mud puddle at the foot of the steps to the front veranda. And as far as I know or care, maybe he's still laying there and she's still screaming, 'Stop, Brick!' But I believe I did hit her. Yes, I did. I did hit her. There's times when you got to hit them, and that was one of those times. I ain't been to the house since. I moved in the little place we lived in before the big one was built, on the other side of the bayou, and ain't crossed over there since …

"Well, sir, that's all over with now. I got back my power of attorney which I'd give to that woman and I got back my driver's licence and I bought this piece of property in town and signed my own cheque for it and I'm having it completely done over to make it as handsome a piece of residential property as you can find in this town, and I'm having that lawn out there prepared for the game of croquet."

Then he'd look at the glass in his hands as if he had just then noticed that he was holding it; he'd give it a look of slightly pained surprise, as if he had cut his hand and just now noticed that it was cut and bleeding. Then he would sigh like an old-time actor in a tragic role. He would put the tall glass down on the balustrade with great, great care, look back at it to make sure that it wasn't going to fall over, and walk very straight and steady to the porch steps and just as steady but with more concentration down them. When he arrived at the foot of the steps, he would laugh as if someone had made a comical remark; he would duck his head genially and shout to the house painters something like this: "Well, I'm not making any predictions because I'm no fortune-teller, but I've got a strong idea that I'm going to lick my liquor problem this summer, ha ha, I'm going to lick it this summer! I'm not going to take no cure and I'm not going to take no pledge, I'm just going to prove I'm a man with his balls back on him! I'm going to do it step by little step, the way that people play the game of croquet. You know how you play that game. You hit the ball through one wicket and then you drive it through the next one. You hit it through that wicket and then you drive on to another. You go from wicket to wicket, and it's a game of precision—it's a game that takes concentration and precision, and that's what makes it a wonderful game for a drinker. It takes a sober man to play a game of precision. It's better than shooting pool, because a pool hall is always next door to a gin mill, and you never see a pool player that don't have his liquor glass on the edge of the table or somewhere pretty near it, and croquet is also a better game than golf, because in golf you've always got that nineteenth hole waiting for you. Nope, for a man with a liquor problem, croquet is a summer game and it may seem a little bit sissy, but let me tell you, it's a game of precision. You go from wicket to wicket until you arrive at that big final pole, and then, bang, you've hit it, the game is finished, you're there! And then, and not until then, you can go up here to the porch and have you a cool gin drink, a buck or a Collins—Hey! Where did I leave that glass? Aw! Yeah, hand it down to me, will you? Ha ha—thanks."

He would take a birdlike sip, make a fiercely wry face, and shake his head violently as if somebody had drenched it with scalding water.

"This goddamn stuff!" He would look around to find a safe place to set the glass down again. He would select a bare spot of earth between the hydrangea bushes, deposit the glass there as carefully as if he were planting a memorial tree, and then he would straighten up with a great air of relief and expand his chest and flex his arms. "Ha, ha, yep, croquet is a summer game for widows and drinkers, ha ha!"

For a few moments, standing there in the sun, he would seem as sure and powerful as the sun itself; but then some little shadow of uncertainty would touch him again, get through the wall of his liquor, some tricky little shadow of a thought, as sly as a mouse, quick, dark, too sly to be caught, and without his moving enough for it to be noticed, his still fine body would fall as violently as a giant tree crashes down beneath a final axe stroke, taking with it all the wheeling seasons of sun and stars, whole centuries of them, crashing suddenly into oblivion and rot. He would make this enormous fall without a perceptible movement of his body. At the most, it would show in the faint flicker of something across his face, whose colour gave him the name people knew him by. Something flickered across his flame-coloured face. Possibly one knee sagged a little forward. Then slowly, slowly, the way a bull trots uncertainly back from its first wild, challenging plunge into the ring, he would fasten one hand over his belt and raise the other one hesitantly to his head, feeling the scalp and the hard round bowl of the skull underneath it, as if he dimly imagined that by feeling that dome he might be able to guess what was hidden inside it, the dark and wondering stuff beneath that dome of calcium, facing, now, the intricate wickets of the summer to come ...

II

For one reason or another, Mary Louise Grey was locked out of the house a great deal of the time that summer, and since she was a lonely child with little or no imagination, apparently unable to amuse herself with solitary games—except the endless one of copying her mother—the afternoons that she was excluded from the house "because Mother has a headache" were periods of great affliction. There were several galleries with outside stairs between them, and she patrolled the galleries and wandered forlornly about the lawn, and from time to time, she went down the front walk and sat in the glass box of the electric. She would vary her steps, sometimes walking sedately, sometimes skipping, sometimes hopping and humming, one plump hand always clutching the handkerchief that contained the lump of ice. This lump of ice to rub her mosquito bites had to be replaced at frequent intervals. "Oh, iceman," the widow would call sweetly from an upstairs window, "don't forget to leave some extra pieces for little Mary Louise to rub her mosquito bites with!"

Each time a new bite was suffered Mary Louise would utter a soft cry in a voice that had her mother's trick of carrying a great distance without being loud.

"Oh, Mother," she would moan, "I'm simply being devoured by mosquitoes!"

"Darling," her mother would answer, "that's dreadful, but you know that Mother can't help it; she didn't create the mosquitoes and she can't destroy them for you!"

"You could let me come in the house, Mama."

"No, I can't let you come in, precious. Not yet."

"Why not, Mother?"

"Because Mother has a sick headache."

"I will be quiet."

"You say that you will, but you won't. You must learn to amuse yourself, precious; you mustn't depend on Mother to amuse you. Nobody can depend on anyone else forever. I'll tell you what you can do till Mother's headache is better. You can drive the electric out of the garage. You can drive it around the block, but don't go into the business district with it, and then you can stop in the shady part of the drive and sit there perfectly comfortably till Mother feels better and can get dressed and come out. And then I think Mr. Pollitt may come over for a game of croquet. Won't that be lovely?"

"Do you think he will get here in time to play?"

"I hope so, precious. It does him so much good to play croquet."

"Oh, I think it does all of us good to play croquet," said Mary Louise in a voice that trembled just at the vision of it.

Before Brick Pollitt arrived—sometimes half an hour before his coming, as though she could hear his automobile on the highway thirty miles from the house—Mary Louise would bound plumply off the gallery and begin setting up the poles and wickets of the longed-for game. While she was doing this, her plump little buttocks and her beginning breasts and her shoulder-length copper curls would all bob up and down in perfect unison.

I would watch her from the steps of my house on the diagonally opposite corner of the street. She worked feverishly against time, for experience had taught her the sooner she completed the preparations for the game the greater would be the chance of getting her mother and Mr. Pollitt to play it. Frequently she was not fast enough, or they were too fast for her. By the time she had finished her perspiring job, the veranda was often deserted. Her wailing cries would begin, punctuating the dusk at intervals only a little less frequent than the passing of cars of people going out for evening drives to cool off.

"Mama! Mama! The croquet set is ready!"

Usually there would be a long, long wait for any response to come from the upstairs window toward which the calls were directed. But one time there wasn't. Almost immediately after the wailing voice was lifted, begging for the commencement of the game, Mary Louise's thin pretty mother showed herself at the window. She came to the window like a white bird flying into some unnoticed obstruction. That was the time when I saw, between the dividing gauze of the bedroom curtains, her naked breasts, small and beautiful, shaken like two angry fists by her violent motion. She leaned between the curtains to answer Mary Louise not in her usual tone of gentle remonstrance but in a shocking cry of rage: "Oh, be still, for God's sake, you fat little monster!"

Mary Louise was shocked into petrified silence that must have lasted for a quarter of an hour. It was probably the word "fat" that struck her so overwhelmingly, for Mary Louise had once told me, when we were circling the block in the electric, that her mother had told her that she was *not* fat, that she was only plump, and that these cushions of flesh were going to dissolve in two or three more years and then she would be just as thin and pretty as her mother.

Sometimes Mary Louise would call me over to play croquet with her, but she was not at all satisfied with my game. I had had so little practice and she so much, and besides, more importantly, it was the company of the grown-up people she wanted. She would call me over only when they had disappeared irretrievably into the lightless house or when the game had collapsed owing to Mr. Brick Pollitt's refusal to take it seriously. When he played seriously, he was even better at it than Mary Louise, who practised her strokes sometimes all afternoon in preparation for a game. But there were evenings when he would not leave his drink on the porch but would carry it down onto the lawn with him and would play with one hand, more and more capriciously, while in the other hand he carried the tall glass. Then the lawn would become a great stage on which he performed all the immemorial antics of the clown, to the exasperation of Mary Louise and her thin, pretty mother, both of whom would become very severe and dignified on these occasions. They would retire from the croquet lawn and stand off at a little distance, calling softly, "Brick, Brick" and "Mr. Pollitt," like a pair of complaining doves, both in the same ladylike tones of remonstrance. He was not a middle-aged–looking man—that is, he was not at all big around the middle—and he could leap and run like a boy. He could turn cartwheels and walk on his hands, and sometimes he would grunt and lunge like a wrestler or make long crouching runs like a football player, weaving in and out among the wickets and gaudily painted poles of the croquet lawn. The acrobatics and sports of his youth seemed to haunt him. He called out hoarsely to invisible teammates and adversaries—muffled shouts of defiance and anger and triumph, to which an incongruous counterpoint was continually provided by the faint, cooing voice of the widow, "Brick, Brick, stop now, please stop. The child is crying. People will think you've gone crazy." For Mary Louise's mother, despite the extreme ambiguity of her station in life, was a woman with a keener than ordinary sense of propriety. She knew why the lights had gone out on all the screened summer porches and why the automobiles drove past the house at the speed of a funeral procession while Mr. Brick Pollitt was making a circus ring of the croquet lawn.

Late one evening when he was making one of his crazy dashes across the lawn with an imaginary football hugged against his belly, he tripped over a wicket and sprawled on the lawn, and he pretended to be too gravely injured to get back on his feet. His loud groans brought Mary Louise and her mother running from behind the vine-screened end of the veranda and out upon the lawn to assist him. They took him by each hand and tried to haul him up, but with a sudden shout of laughter he pulled them both down on top of him and held them there till both of them were sobbing. He got up, finally, that evening, but it was only to replenish his glass of iced gin, and then returned to the lawn. That evening was a fearfully hot one, and Brick decided to cool and refresh himself with the sprinkler hose while he enjoyed his drink. He turned it on and pulled it out to the centre of the lawn. There he rolled about the grass under its leisurely revolving arch of water, and as he rolled about, he began to wriggle out of his clothes. He kicked off his white shoes and one of his pale-green socks, tore off his drenched white shirt and grass-stained linen pants, but he never succeeded in getting off his necktie. Finally, he was sprawled, like some grotesque fountain figure, in underwear and necktie and the one remaining pale-green sock, while the revolving arch of water moved with cool whispers about him. The arch of water had a faint crystalline iridescence, a mist of delicate colours, as it wheeled under the moon, for the moon had by that time begun to poke with an air of slow astonishment over the roof of the little building that housed the electric. And still the complaining doves of the widow and her daughter cooed at him from various windows of the house, and you could tell their voices apart only by the fact that the mother murmured "Brick, Brick" and Mary Louise still called him Mr. Pollitt. "Oh, Mr. Pollitt, Mother is so unhappy, Mother is crying!"

That night he talked to himself or to invisible figures on the lawn. One of them was his wife, Margaret. He kept saying, "I'm sorry, Margaret, I'm sorry, Margaret, I'm so sorry, so sorry, Margaret. I'm sorry I'm no good, I'm sorry, Margaret, I'm so sorry, so sorry I'm no good, sorry I'm drunk, sorry I'm no good, I'm so sorry it all had to turn out like this …"

Later on, much later, after the remarkably slow procession of touring cars stopped passing the house, a little black sedan that belonged to the police came rushing up to the front walk and sat there for a while. In it was the chief of police himself. He called

"Brick, Brick," almost as gently and softly as Mary Louise's mother had called him from the lightless windows. "Brick, Brick, old boy. Brick, fellow," till finally the inert fountain figure in underwear and green sock and unremovable necktie staggered out from under the rotating arch of water and stumbled down to the walk and stood there negligently and quietly conversing with the chief of police under the no longer at all astonished, now quite large and indifferent great yellow stare of the August moon. They began to laugh softly together, Mr. Brick Pollitt and the chief of police, and finally the door of the little black car opened and Mr. Brick Pollitt got in beside the chief of police while the common officer got out to collect the clothes, flabby as drenched towels, on the croquet lawn. Then they drove away, and the summer night's show was over ...

It was not quite over for me, for I had been watching it all that time with unabated interest. And about an hour after the little black car of the very polite officers had driven away, I saw the mother of Mary Louise come out into the lawn; she stood there with an air of desolation for quite a while. Then she went into the small building in back of the house and drove out the electric. The electric went sedately out into the summer night, with its buzzing no louder than a summer insect's, and perhaps an hour later, for this was a very long night, it came back again containing in its glass show box not only the young and thin and pretty widow but a quiet and chastened Mr. Pollitt. She curved an arm about his immensely tall figure as they went up the front walk, and I heard him say only one word distinctly. It was the name of his wife.

Early that autumn, which was different from summer in nothing except the quicker coming of dusk, the visits of Mr. Brick Pollitt began to have the spasmodic irregularity of a stricken heart muscle. That faraway boom of a cannon at five o'clock was now the announcement that two ladies in white dresses were waiting on a white gallery for someone who was each time a little more likely to disappoint them than the time before. But disappointment was not a thing that Mary Louise was inured to; it was a country that she was passing through not as an old inhabitant but as a bewildered explorer, and each afternoon she removed the oblong yellow wood box, lugged it out of the little building in which it lived with the electric, ceremoniously opened it upon the centre of the silken green lawn, and began to arrange the wickets in their formal pattern between the two gaudily painted poles that meant beginning, middle and end. And the widow, her mother, talked to her from the gallery, under the awning, as if there had been no important alteration in their lives or their prospects. Their almost duplicate voices as they talked back and forth between gallery and lawn rang out as clearly as if the enormous corner lot were enclosed at this hour by a still more enormous and perfectly translucent glass bell which picked up and carried through space whatever was uttered beneath it, and this was true not only when they were talking across the lawn but when they were seated side by side in the white wicker chairs on the gallery. Phrases from these conversations became catchwords, repeated and mocked by the neighbours, for whom the widow and her daughter and Mr. Brick Pollitt had been three players in a sensational drama which had shocked and angered them for two acts but which now, as it approached a conclusion, was declining into unintentional farce, which they could laugh at. It was not difficult to find something ludicrous in the talks between the two ladies or the high-pitched elegance of their voices.

Mary Louise would ask, "Will Mr. Pollitt get here in time for croquet?"

"I hope so, precious. It does him so much good."

"He'll have to come soon or it will be too dark to see the wickets."

"That's true, precious."

"Mother, why is it dark so early now?"

"Honey, you know why. The sun goes south."

"But why does it go south?"

"Precious, Mother cannot explain the movements of the heavenly bodies, you know that as well as Mother knows it. Those things are controlled by certain mysterious laws that people on earth don't know or understand."

"Mother, are we going east?"

"When, precious?"

"Before school starts."

"Honey, you know it's impossible for Mother to make any definite plans."

"I hope we do. I don't want to go to school here."

"Why not, precious? Are you afraid of the children?"

"No, Mother, but they don't like me, they make fun of me."

"How do they make fun of you?"

"They mimic the way I talk and they walk in front of me with their stomachs pushed out and giggle."

"That's because they're children and children are cruel."

"Will they stop being cruel when they grow up?"

"Why, I suppose some of them will and some of them won't."

"Well, I hope we go east before school opens."

"Mother can't make any plans or promises, honey."

"No, but Mr. Brick Pollitt—"

"Honey, lower your voice! Ladies talk softly."

"Oh, my goodness!"

"What is it, precious?"

"A mosquito just bit me!"

"That's too bad, but don't scratch it. Scratching can leave a permanent scar on the skin."

"I'm not scratching it. I'm just sucking it, Mother."

"Honey, Mother has told you time and again that the thing to do when you have a mosquito bite is to get a small piece of ice and wrap it up in a handkerchief and rub the bite gently with it until the sting is removed."

"That's what I do, but my lump of ice is melted!"

"Get you another piece, honey. You know where the icebox is!"

"There's not much left. You put so much in the ice bag for your headache."

"There must be some left, honey."

"There's just enough left for Mr. Pollitt's drinks."

"Never mind that ..."

"He needs it for his drinks, Mother."

"Yes, Mother knows what he wants the ice for, precious."

"There's only a little piece left. It's hardly enough to rub a mosquito bite with."

"Well, use it for that purpose, that purpose is better, and anyhow when Mr. Pollitt comes over as late as this, he doesn't deserve to have any ice saved for him."

"Mother?"

"Yes, precious?"

"I love ice and sugar!"

"What did you say, precious?"

"I said I loved ice and sugar!"

"Ice and sugar, precious?"

"Yes, I love the ice and sugar in the bottom of Mr. Pollitt's glass when he's through with it."

"Honey, you mustn't eat the ice in the bottom of Mr. Pollitt's glass!"

"Why not, Mother?"

"Because it's got liquor in it!"

"Oh, no, Mother, it's just ice and sugar when Mr. Pollitt's through with it."

"Honey, there's always a little liquor left in it."

"Oh, no, not a drop's left when Mr. Pollitt's through with it!"

"But you say there's sugar left in it, and, honey, you know that sugar is very absorbent."

"It's what, Mummy?"

"It absorbs some liquor and that's a good way to cultivate a taste for it, and, honey, you know what dreadful consequences a taste for liquor can have. It's bad enough for a man, but for a woman it's fatal. So when you want ice and sugar, let Mother know and she'll prepare some for you, but don't ever let me catch you eating what's left in Mr. Pollitt's glass!"

"Mama?"

"Yes, precious?"

"It's almost completely dark now. Everybody is turning on their lights or driving out on the river road to cool off. Can't we go out riding in the electric?"

"No, honey, we can't till we know Mr. Pollitt's not—"

"Do you still think he will come?"

"Precious, how can I say? Is Mother a fortune-teller?"

"Oh, here comes the Pierce, Mummy, here comes the Pierce!"

"Is it? Is it the Pierce?"

"Oh, no. No, it isn't. It's a Hudson Super Six. Mummy, I'm going to pull up the wickets, now, and water the lawn, because if Mr. Pollitt does come, he'll have people with him or won't be in a condition to play croquet. And when I've finished, I want to drive the electric around the block."

"Drive it around the block, honey, but don't go into the business district with it."

"Are you going with me, Mummy?"

"No, precious, I'm going to sit here."

"It's cooler in the electric."

"I don't think so. The electric goes too slowly to make much breeze."

If Mr. Pollitt did finally arrive those evenings, it was likely to be with a caravan of cars that came from Memphis, and then Mrs. Grey would have to receive a raffish assortment of strangers as if she herself had invited them to a party. The party would not confine itself to the downstairs rooms and galleries but would explode quickly and brilliantly as a rocket in all directions, overflowing both floors of the house, spilling out upon the lawn and sometimes even penetrating the little building that housed the electric automobile and the oblong box that held the packed-away croquet set. On those party nights, the fantastically balustraded and gabled and turreted white building would glitter all over, like one of those huge night-excursion boats that came downriver from Memphis, and it would be full of ragtime music and laughter. But at some point in the evening there would be, almost invariably, a startling disturbance. Some male guest would utter a savage roar, a woman would scream, you would hear a shattering of glass. Almost immediately afterward, the lights would go out in the house, as if it really were a boat that had collided fatally with a shoal underwater. From all the doors and galleries and stairs, people would come rushing forth, and the dispersion would be more rapid than the arrival had been. A little while later, the police car would pull up in front of the house. The thin, pretty widow would come out on the front gallery to receive the chief of police, and you could hear her light voice tinkling like glass chimes, "Why, it was nothing, it was nothing at all, just somebody who drank a little too much and lost his temper. You know how that Memphis crowd is, Mr. Duggan, there's always one gentleman in it who can't hold his liquor. I know it's late, but we have such a huge lawn—it occupies half the block—that I shouldn't think anybody who wasn't overcome with curiosity would have to know that a party had been going on!"

And then something must have happened that made no sound at all.

It wasn't an actual death, but it had nearly all the external evidence of one. When death occurs in a house, the house is unnaturally quiet for a day or two before the occurrence is finished. During that interval, the enormous, translucent glass bell that seems to enclose and separate one house from those that surround it does not transmit any noise to those who are watching but seems to have thickened invisibly so that very little can be heard through it. That was the way it had been five months ago, when the pleasant young doctor had died of that fierce flower grown in his skull. It had been unnaturally quiet for several days, and then a peculiar grey car with frosted windows had crashed through the bell of silence and the young doctor had emerged from the house in a very curious way, as if he were giving a public demonstration of how to go to sleep on a narrow bed in atmosphere blazing with light and while in motion.

That was five months ago, and it was now early October.

The summer had spelled out a word that had no meaning, and the word was now spelled out and, with or without any meaning, there it was, inscribed with as heavy a touch as the signature of a miser on a cheque or a boy with chalk on a fence.

One afternoon, a fat and pleasantly smiling man, whom I had seen times without number loitering around in front of the used-car lot which adjoined the Paramount movie, came up the front walk of the Greys' with the excessive nonchalance of a man who is about to commit a robbery. He pushed the bell, waited awhile, pushed it again for a longer moment, and then was admitted through an opening that seemed to be hardly wide enough for his fingers. He came back out almost immediately with something caught in his fist. It was the key to the little building that contained the croquet set and the electric automobile. He entered that building and drew its folding doors all the way open to disclose the ladylike electric sitting there with its usual manner of a lady putting on or taking off her gloves at the entrance to a reception. He stared at it a moment, as if its elegance were momentarily baffling. But then he got in it and he drove it out of the garage, holding the polished black pilot stick with a look on his round face that was like the look of an adult who is a little embarrassed to find himself being amused by a game that was meant for children. He drove it serenely out into the wide, shady street and at an upstairs window of the house there was some kind of quick movement, as if a figure looking out had been startled by something it watched and then had retreated in haste ...

Later, after the Greys had left town, I saw the elegant square vehicle, which appeared to be made out of glass and patent leather, standing with an air of haughty self-consciousness among a dozen or so other cars for sale in a lot called "Hi-Class Values" next door to the town's best movie, and as far as I know, it may be still sitting there, but many degrees less glittering by now.

The Greys were gone from Meridian all in one quick season: the young doctor whom everyone had liked in a hesitant, early way and had said would do well in the town with his understanding eyes and quiet voice; the thin, pretty woman, whom no one had really known except Brick Pollitt; and the plump little girl, who might someday be as pretty and slender as her mother. They had come and gone in one season, yes, like one of those tent shows that suddenly appear in a vacant lot in a southern town and cross the sky at night with mysteriously wheeling lights and unearthly music, and then are gone, and the summer goes on without them, as if they had never come there.

As for Mr. Brick Pollitt, I can remember seeing him only once after the Greys left town, for my time there was also of brief duration. This last time that I saw him was a brilliant fall morning. It was a Saturday morning in October. Brick's driver's licence had been revoked again for some misadventure on the highway due to insufficient control of the wheel, and it was his legal wife, Margaret, who sat in the driver's seat of the Pierce-Arrow touring car. Brick did not sit beside her. He was on the back seat of the car, pitching this way and that way with the car's jolting motion, like a loosely wrapped package being delivered somewhere. Margaret Pollitt handled the car with a wonderful male assurance, her bare arms brown and muscular as a Negro field hand's, and the car's canvas top had been lowered the better to expose on its back seat the sheepishly grinning and nodding figure of Brick

Pollitt. He was clothed and barbered with his usual immaculacy, so that he looked from some distance like the president of a good social fraternity in a gentleman's college of the South. The knot of his polka-dot tie was drawn as tight as strong and eager fingers could knot a tie for an important occasion. One of his large red hands protruded, clasping over the outside of the door to steady his motion, and on it glittered two bands of gold, a small one about a finger, a large one about the wrist. His cream-coloured coat was neatly folded on the seat beside him and he wore a shirt of thin white material that was tinted faintly pink by his skin beneath it. He was a man who had been, and even at that time still was, the handsomest you were likely to remember, physical beauty being of all human attributes the most incontinently used and wasted, as if whoever made it despised it, since it is made so often only to be disgraced by painful degrees and drawn through the streets in chains.

Margaret blew the car's silver trumpet at every intersection. She leaned this way and that way, elevating or thrusting out an arm as she shouted gay greetings to people on porches, merchants beside store entrances, people she barely knew along the walks, calling them all by their familiar names, as if she were running for office in the town, while Brick nodded and grinned with senseless amiability behind her. It was exactly the way that some ancient conqueror, such as Caesar or Alexander the Great or Hannibal, might have led in chains through a capital city the prince of a state newly conquered.

Early in the Summer of 1970

by

A.B. YEHOSHUA

I BELIEVE I ought to go over the moment when I learned of his death once more.

A summer morning, the sky wide, June, last days of the school year. I rise late, faintly stunned, straight into the depths of light; don't listen to the news, don't look at the paper. It is as though I had lost my sense of time.

I get to school late, search the dim green air in vain for a fading echo of the bell. Start pacing the empty playground, across squares of light and shadow cast by the row of windows, past droning sounds of classrooms at their work. And then, surprised, I discover that the Head is running after me, calling my name from afar.

Except that I have nearly arrived at my class, the Twelfth, their muffled clamour rising from the depth of the empty corridor. They have shut the door upon themselves not to betray my absence, but their excitement gives them away.

Again the Head calls my name from the other end of the corridor, but I ignore him, open the classroom door upon their yells and laughter which fade into a low murmur of disappointment. They had by now been certain I wouldn't show up today. I stand in the door waiting for them to sort themselves out, wild-haired, red-faced, in their blue school uniforms, scrambling back to their desks, kicking the small chairs, dropping Bibles, and gradually the desktops are covered with blank sheets of paper, ready for the exam.

One of them is at the blackboard rubbing out wild words—a distorted image of myself. They look me straight in the eye, impudent, smiling to themselves, but silent. For the present my grey hairs still subdue them.

And then, as I walk softly into the room, the exam paper in my hand, the Head arrives, breathless, pale. All eyes stare at him but he does not even look at the class, looks only at me, tries to touch me, hold me; he who has not spoken to me for the past three years is all gentleness now, whispers, pleads almost: Just a moment … never mind … leave them … you've got to come with me. There's some notice for you … come …

IT IS THREE YEARS NOW that no words have passed between us, that we look at each other as though we were stone. Three years that I have not set foot in the common room either, have not sat on a chair in it, not touched the teapot. I intrude into the school grounds early in the morning, and during break I wander up and down corridors or playground—in the summer in a large, broad-brimmed hat, in the winter in a greatcoat with the collar up—floating back and forth with the students. I pay my trips to the office long after school is out, leave my lists of marks, supply myself with chalk.

I hardly exchange a word with the other teachers.

Three years ago I had been due to retire, and had indeed resigned myself to the inevitable, had even considered venturing upon a little handbook of Bible instruction, but the war broke out suddenly and the air about me filled with the rumble of cannon and distant cries. I went to the Head to say I was not going to retire, I was staying on till the war would end. After all, now that the younger teachers were being called up one by one he would need me the more. He, however, did not see any connection between the war and myself. "The war is all but over," he told me with a curious smile, "and you deserve a rest."

No rest, however, but a fierce summer came, and flaming headlines. And two of our very young alumni killed one a day after the other. And again I went to him, deeply agitated, hands trembling, informed him in halting phrases that I did not see how I could leave them now, that is to say, now that we were sending them to their death.

But he saw no connection whatever between their death and myself.

The summer holidays started and I could find no rest, day after day in the empty school, hovering about the office, the Head's room, waiting for news, talking to parents, questioning them about their sons, watching pupils in army uniform come to ask about their exam results or return books to the library, and sniffing the fire-singed smell in the far distance. And again, another death, unexpected, an older alumnus, much liked in his time, from one of the first-year classes, killed by a mine on a dirt track, and I at the Head again, shocked, beaten, telling him: "You see," but he straightaway tried to brush me off: he has given instructions to prepare the pension forms, has planned a farewell party—which of course I declined.

A week before the new school year I offered to work for nothing if only he would give me back my classes, but he had already signed on a new teacher and I was no longer on the roster.

School starts. I arrive along with everyone in the morning, carrying briefcase and books and chalk, ready to teach. He spotted me near the common room and inquired anxiously what had happened, what was I doing here, but I, on the spur of the moment, did not reply, did not even look at him, as though he were a stone. He thought I had gone out of my mind, but in the turmoil of a new school year had no time to attend to me. And meanwhile my eyes had been searching out the new teacher, a thin, sallow young man, in order to follow him. He enters the classroom, and I linger a moment and enter on his heels. Excuse me, I say to him with a little smile, you must be mistaken, this isn't your class, and before he has time to recover I have mounted the platform, taken out my ragged Bible. He stammers an apology and leaves the room, and as for the dazed students who never expected to see me again, I give them no chance to say a word.

When after some moments the Head appears, I am deep in the lesson, the class listening absorbed. I do not budge.

I did not leave the room during the break, stayed planted in a crowd of students. The Head stood waiting for me outside but did not dare come near me. If he had I would have screamed, in front of the students I would have screamed and well he knew it; and there was nothing he feared as much as a scandal.

By sheer force I returned to teaching. I had no dealings with anyone but the students. For the first few weeks I scarcely left the school grounds, would haunt them even at night. And the Head in my wake, obsessed by me, dogs my steps, talks to me, appeals to me, holding, stroking, threatening, reproaching, speaking of common values, of good fellowship, of the many years of collaboration, coaxes me to write a book, is even prepared to finance its publication, sends messengers to me. But I would not reply—keeping my eyes on the ground, or on the sky, or on the ceiling; freezing to a white statue, on a street corner, in the corridor, in the empty classroom, by my own gate, or even in my armchair at home, during the evenings when he would come to talk to me. Till he gave up in despair.

He had meant to drag me into his office, but I did not wish to move out of the students' range. I walked a few paces out into the corridor and stopped, and before the attentive gaze of the students I wrung it all out of him.

Some five or six hours ago …

In the Jordan Valley …

Killed on the spot …

Could not have suffered …

Not broken it to his wife yet, nor to the university …

I am the first …

He had put my name on the forms and for some reason given the school for address.

Must be strong now …

And then the darkness. Of all things, darkness. Like a candle the sun going out in my eyes. The students sensed this eclipse but could not move, weren't set for the contingency of my needing help, whereas the Head talked on fluently as though he had been rehearsing this piece of news for the past three years. Till suddenly he gave a little exclamation.

But I had not fainted, only slumped to the floor and at once risen to my feet again, unaided, and the light was returning to me as well, still dim, in the empty classroom, seated on a student's chair, seeing people throng the room, teachers rushing in from nearby classrooms, curious students, office workers, the caretaker, people who had not spoken to me these three years. Here they were all coming back, some with tears in their eyes, surrounding me, a whole tribe, breaking my loneliness.

HE HAD RETURNED from the United States three months ago, after an absence of many years. Arrived with his family late in the night, on a circuitous flight by way of the Far East. For six hours I waited at the airport, thinking at last that they wouldn't arrive, that I would have to go back as I came. But at midnight, when I was by then dozing on some bench in a corner, they approached me, emerged from the obscurity of the runway, as though not coming off a plane but back from a hike; rumpled and unkempt, heavy rucksacks on their backs and in one of them a white-faced toddler who looked at me with gentle eyes.

I hardly recognized my son in him. Bearded, heavy, soft, my son's hair was already sprinkled with grey, and, in his movements, some new, slow tranquility. He, whom I had already given up for a lost bachelor, coming back a husband, a father, nearly a professor. I was dazzled by him. And he bringing his wife forward, in trousers, a slim girl, enveloped in hair, dressed in a worn-out tasselled coat, one of his students presumably; and then she is leaning towards me and smiling, her face clear. Very beautiful. At that moment anyway I found her so beautiful, touching me with cool, transparent fingers.

And I, my heart overflowing, rise at once to touch them, kiss them, kiss the child at least, but he is too high for me, hovering up there in the rucksack, and as soon as I touch him he starts chattering to me in English, and the thin student girl joins in as well, a shower of words, in two voices, pouring their incomprehensible English out over me. I turn to my son for illumination, and he listens with a smile as though he, too, could not take it in at first, then says they are amazed by the resemblance between us two.

And afterwards the customs inspection, a long, remorseless affair, as though they were suspected of something, myself looking on from afar, watching all their parcels being taken apart. And when at last we embark on the journey home, in a dark taxicab, through a gradually lightening spring night, the baby is already drooping with sleep, like a plucked flower, huddled in his rucksack between the two of them on the front seat; while I, behind them, among the luggage, among a guitar, typewriter, and rolled-up posters, watch the loosely tied parcels softly disintegrate.

My son fell asleep at once, enfolding his sleeping son, but my daughter-in-law was surprisingly wakeful. Not looking out at the road, not at this land she had never seen, not at the stars or the new sky, but her whole body turned towards me sitting in the back, her hair tumbling over my face, she was shooting questions at me, speaking of the war, that is, what do people here say, and what do they really want, as though accusing me of something, as though in some furtive manner I were enjoying this war, as though there existed some other possibility …

That or thereabouts, I mean, since I had much difficulty understanding her, I who was never taught English, and what I know is what I caught from the air, just so, from the air, from English lessons sounding out of adjacent classrooms when the hush of an examination is on mine, or when I pace the empty corridors waiting my turn to enter the class.

And I am straining to understand her, exhausted as I am from the long waiting hours in the night. And my sleeping son on the front seat, a heavy mass, his head wobbling, and I alone with her, observing the delicate features, the thin glasses she has suddenly put on, such a young intellectual, maybe this New Left thing, and for all that a trace of perfume, a faint scent of wilted flowers coming from her.

In the end I open my mouth to answer her. In an impossible English, a staggering concoction of my own make, laced with Hebrew words, lawless, and she momentarily taken aback, trying to understand, falling silent at last. Then, softly, she starts to sing.

And we arrive at my place, and though worn out they show the sudden efficiency of seasoned travellers, shed their sandals by the door and start walking about barefoot. Swiftly they unload their luggage and send the driver away. They pick up the sleepy child and quickly, both together, undress him, put him into some kind of sewn-up sheet like a little shroud and lay him on my bed. Then, as though suddenly discovering the immensity of their fatigue, they begin to undress themselves, right in front of me, move half-naked through the small flat, and dawn is breaking. They spread blankets over the rug, and I glimpse her bare breasts, very white, and she sends me a tired smile, and all at once I lose my own sleep, all desire for sleep. I shut the door upon them and start wandering through what little space is still left me, waiting for signs of the sun itself. They had sunk into a deep sleep, and before I left for school I went and covered up their bare feet. At noon I returned very tired and found them still sleeping, all three of them. I thought I'd burst, I who was aching to talk to them. I had lunch by myself, lay down beside the child who was wet by now and tried to get some sleep, but could not. I got up and began to search through their luggage, see what they had brought, a book perhaps, or a magazine, but after a few minutes my hands flagged.

Towards nightfall I could bear their silence no longer. Softly I opened the door and came upon them. They lay slumped each to himself, submerged, catching up on the time they had lost in their journey round the world. Once again I bent down to cover my daughter-in-law's feet, but I turned back the blanket under which my son lay.

Little by little he awoke, naked, hairy, heavy, his breath catching, opened his eyes at last and discovered me in the half-light standing over him, looking down. He gave a brief start as though for an instant not recognizing me. "What's with you?" he whispered from the floor.

"At school still, every morning, the Head keeping silent still," I whisper at him in one breath.

For a moment he is puzzled, even though I used to write to him about everything, devotedly, all the details. Perhaps he did not read my letters. The silence grows, no sound except the breathing of the young woman by his side who has thrown off her blanket again. Little by little he recovers his composure, slowly pulls the blanket over himself. His eyes lift in a smile.

"And you're still teaching Bible there …"

(Already he has nothing to say to me.)

"Yes, of course. Only Bible."

"In that case"—still smiling—"everything's as usual."

"Yes, as usual"—and another long silence—"except of course for my pupils getting killed," I spit out in a whisper straight into his face.

He shuts his eyes. Then he sits up, huddled in his blanket, his beard wild, picks up a pipe and sticks it into his mouth, begins to muse, like an ancient prophet, to explain that the war won't go on, haven't I noticed the signs, can't go on any longer. And now his wife wakes up as well, sits up beside him, likewise drapes the blanket about her, sends me a smile full of light, ready to make contact, join the conversation, explain her viewpoint, straightaway, without going for a wash, coffee, her eyes still heavy with sleep, in the shimmer of spring twilight, in the littered room filled with their warmth.

STRIDING THROUGH the corridors to the office, a little mourning procession, I in their midst, like a precious guest, like a captive. And classroom doors open a crack as though under the pressure of studies, and teachers' faces, blackboard faces, student faces, the entire school watching me as though discovering me anew.

… And we never knew he was back, you never told, your silence. I didn't think you'd remember him, though in fact he used to be a pupil here too. How old is he, was he? Thirty-one. God, when'll all this stop. So young. Not quite so young any more, took me aback when he got off the plane, aged some … And right away the army takes him? Give him no breathing space? How no breathing space, three months they gave him, everybody goes these days, and in the Six Day War he didn't take part, not before it either, and he's no better than everybody else, is he? But right away to the Jordan Valley? Yes, odd that, I never thought they'd still find a use for him, he himself was sure they'd send him to guard army stores in Jerusalem....

And we cut across the empty playground simmering in the sun.

... And how about his wife? American, doesn't even know Hebrew. And whom has she got here? No one. And the child, how old is the child? A toddler still. About three. Oh, God Almighty, enough to make you cry. Who's going to be with them now? I'll be with them ...

And another corridor, classrooms, doors, and a flushed student in light-blue uniform running after us.

... What's up? Teacher left his briefcase and book behind in class. Oh, never mind, leave them here, I'll take them for him. What are you doing in there now? Nothing ... I mean, waiting ... We're so sorry ... Maybe you could get on with that exam all the same? By ourselves? Yes, why not ...

And arriving at the office at last, heads bowed.

... Been years since I've set foot in your office. Yes, so pointless too, this breach between us, sit down a moment now, rest, a difficult time before you, I'm quite stunned myself, when they told me on the phone, I couldn't believe it. Would you like us to get in touch with the military now, maybe talk to them yourself. No, no need. Hadn't they better come here and pick you up, maybe let his wife know, the university. No, no need, I'll tell them all myself, I'll go to Jerusalem, I don't want anyone else to precede me. But that's impossible, you can't by yourself, must get in touch with the army, they'll pick you up, someone must go to the hospital too ... that is, to identify ... you know ... I'll identify him. Why are you getting up? What can we do for you? The entire school's at your service, say the word, what do you need? I need nothing, just to go, just want to go now. I'll take you, I'll come with you, it's madness for you to leave here by yourself, maybe somebody could drive you in their car. But why a car, I live so near, you're pressing me overmuch, I shall lose my breath again …

BUT HE INSISTS on coming along. Abandons the school, his humming empire, and takes my arm in the street, carries my briefcase, the jacket, the ragged Bible. There are tears in his eyes, as though not my son but his had fallen. At every street corner I try to detach myself, that's enough, I say, but he insists on tagging on after me as though afraid to leave me alone. By my gate, under a blue morning sky, we come to a halt at last, subside like two large, grey, moss-grown rocks, and as a vapour above us trail the words of condolence that he does not believe in and I do not hear.

Finally silence, his last word spent. I collect my things from him, the jacket, Bible, briefcase, urge him to go back to the students, but still he refuses to take his leave, as though he had detected signs of a new breakdown in me, in my silence. And I put out my hand and he takes it and does not let go, seizes me in a tight grip, as though I had suddenly mysteriously, gained a new hold over him, as though he would never be able to part from me again.

I leave him by the gate, go in and discover an unfamiliar kind of light in my flat, light of a weekday morning. I let down blinds (he is still standing by the gate), strip, and go to take a shower; knowing people will come close to me this day, touch me. Stand a long time naked under the streaming water, head throbbing, trying to tell his wife of his death in broken, water-swept English. Clean, cleanse myself, put on fresh linen, find a heavy black suit in the wardrobe and put it on. Peer through the blinds and see the Head still by my gate, rooted to the spot, sunk in thought, aloof as though he had really given up his school. And then I tidy up the flat, unplug the telephone, let down the last blinds and all of a sudden, as though someone had given me a hard push, I fall down sobbing on the rug where they lay that night. And when I get up it is as though the darkness had grown. My temples ache. Softly I call to the Head who is there no longer, who is gone and has left the street empty, accessible.

AND AFTERWARDS SUPPER, on the porch, on a spring evening filled with scents, under the branches of a tree in flower. And the three of them sit there, pink-cheeked, gorged with sleep, and I, very tired, knees trembling, bring them bread and water. They have brought out cans left from their travels and have spread a meal as though they were still on the road, a halt between inns. And the toddler still in his white shroud, sitting upright, clear-eyed, prattling endlessly, arguing with the crickets in the garden.

And my son is engrossed in his food, betrays a ravenous appetite, rummages among the cans, slices up bread, his eyes moist, and in vain I try to sound him out about his work, what exactly he is researching, what he intends to teach here, and has he perhaps brought some new gospel. He sits there and smiles, begins to talk, flounders, has difficulty explaining, doesn't think I'd understand him. Even if he should give me stuff to read he doubts I'd be able to follow, the more so as it is all in English. It is a matter of novel experiments, something in between history and statistics, the methods themselves such a revolution …

And he goes back to his food, his beard filling with crumbs, his head bent, chewing in silence, and I sink down before him, drawn to him, more than twenty-four hours without sleep, begin to speak to him softly, desperately, in a burning voice, about the endless war, about our isolation, about the morning papers, about the absent-mindedness of my pupils, about the bloodshed, about my long hours upon the platform, about history disintegrating, and all the time the child runs on, in non-stop English, babbling and singing, beating his knife on an empty can. And the night fills with stars, and my daughter-in-law, wide-eyed, restless, smiles at me, does not understand a word I say but nonetheless very tense, nodding her head eagerly. And only my son's attention wanders, the absent look in his eyes familiar, unhearing, already elsewhere, alien, adrift ...

And the night grows deeper and deeper, and every hour on the hour I turn on the radio to listen to the news, and the announcer's voice beats harsh and clear into the darkness. And my son swears at someone there who doesn't see things his way, then gets up and starts pacing the garden. And the child has fallen silent, sits bent over huge sheets of paper, painting the night, me, the crickets he has not seen yet. And my daughter-in-law at my side again, hasn't despaired of me and my English. She talks to me slowly, as if I were a backward pupil, her summery blouse open, her hair gathered at the back, a black ribbon encircling her forehead, all in all very much of a student still, of the kind that many years, eons ago, I might have fallen in love with, pursued in my heart, year after year.

And the night draws on, a kind of intoxication, dew begins to lap us. And she in a sudden burst of enthusiasm decides to sleep outside, fetches blankets from the house and covers up the child who has fallen asleep with his head on his papers, puts a blanket over me as well, and over her husband, and curls up in his lap, and he already puffing at his pipe, he who is thinking his own thoughts, whose heart there is no knowing, exchanges a few rapid sentences with her in English, kisses her with frightening intensity.

And I try to talk them into staying with me another day, but they cannot, must start getting organized, find a flat, a nursery school for the child, and I take leave of them, pick up the radio and go in, go to bed and fall asleep at once. And at daybreak, half in dream I see them load their bundles into a black cab, on their way to Jerusalem.

AND WITHOUT ANY PREPARATIONS, without longing, like a bird, you too find yourself on the way to Jerusalem. On a bright morning, a Friday, on a fast, half-empty bus, among newspaper-rustling passengers, and no longer toiling up the old, tortuous road but tearing with a dull hiss through the widened wadi, through trees that have receded, and there is no knowing any more whether one goes up to Jerusalem or down.

And suddenly you cry out, or think you do, and are amazed to see the people around you sink slowly into their tall seats, and for an instant the newspapers freeze in their hands. And you stand up, overcome, start crossing the aisle, and from the stealthy glances thrown at you you understand, they have made you out, you and your grief, but are powerless to help. And you want to vomit over the people, but they motion to the driver and he stops the bus, and you descend the iron steps into the roadside, near a painted yellow stripe, piles of earth and asphalt rubble and you want to vomit over the view, over the mountains, the pines, but it comes to nothing, a fresh breeze plays about you, you recover your breath, and far away in the opposite lane cars rush past on their way to the plain as on a different road. And you climb back into your bus, mumble apologies, and people look up kindly, say: That's all right …

And shortly afterwards on the Jerusalem hills, steeped in hard, hurting, almost impossible light, you make your way to the house of your dead son in an erstwhile border slum raised from the dust. Cobbled alleys have been paved over, ancient water holes connected to the drainage, ruins are turned into dwellings and in the closed courtyards new babies crawl. And you find the place at last, touch the ironwork door and it opens, and you lose your breath because the news has caught in your throat. And softly you enter into an apartment turned upside down for cleaning, bunched-up curtains, chairs lifted on to tables, flowerpots on the couch. Broom, dustpan, pail, rag, are strewn about the room. And the radio is singing Arabic in great lilting chorus and drums, heroic songs. And an Arab cleaning woman, very old, is wildly beating a red carpet. And his wife isn't there and nor is the child. And your strength is ebbing, you stumble over the large tiles worn smooth by generations. And from great depths, through the loud singing, you try to dredge up forgotten Arabic words. "*Ya isma'i* … *el wallad* … *ibni* … *maath* …"

(Listen … the child … my son … dead …)

AMAZING THAT MY CRY does not frighten her, that she understands at once that I belong here, that I have rights, and perhaps she perceives traces of others in my features. Slowly she approaches me, the carpet-beater in her hand, an old crone (where did they dig her up?), her face crumpled, deaf apparently, for the radio is still going full blast.

Again I shout something, point at the radio, and she goes over to it at once, stoops by an elaborate device with multiple microphones, turns the knobs till the singing fades and only drums still rumble from some hidden microphone. Then she comes back to me, withered monkey, bent, swathed in skirts, her head covered with a large kerchief, waiting.

"*Ibni* …" I try again and fall silent, tears choke me, begin moving through the apartment, between upturned chairs, dripping flowerpots, between packing cases (still not unpacked), transformers, records, exploring amid this American clutter the apartment I never knew, and she in my wake, with the thudding drums, barefoot, still holding the carpet-beater, picking up things from under my feet, shifting chairs, letting down curtains, and increasing the confusion beyond repair.

And I reach the bedroom and find the bedclothes tumbled, long dresses strewn about, the imprint of her body on the sheet, the pillow; and in a corner still the inevitable packing cases, one on top of the other.

The place will have to be arranged for mourning …

I sit on the bed, study the vaulting lines, begin to perceive the structure of the building, and the old woman by my side, imagines I ought not to be left alone, wishes to help me, serve me, expects me to lie down perhaps so as to cover me, and once more I try to explain very softly.

"Ibni maath … walladi …"

And finally she understands.

"El zreir?" (The little one?) she asks, as though I had many sons.

And I stand up, hopeless, try to send her away, but she has already grown attached to me, such faithfulness, my being such an old man perhaps, she awaits orders, apparently used to the fact that she will never understand what is said to her in this house, but totally overcome when she sees me begin to tidy up the room. Folding the bedclothes (discover a telephone between the twisted blankets and unplug it), spreading a rug over the bed, returning clothes to cases and discover nappies in one of them, new, whole stacks of them in transparent wrappings, as though they planned to beget an entire tribe.

And in the next room still the beating drums …

And the old woman restless, fidgeting about me, wishing to help and not knowing how, begins to speak suddenly, or to sob, or scream, repeats the same phrase over and over, tirelessly, till I understand. She thought I had meant the child.

"La, la, la zreir," (No, no, not little one). I lean towards her, breathing the scorched smell of dead bonfires in her clothes. *"Abuhu …"* (His father …)

But at that she seems ten times worse stricken:

"Eish abuhu …?" (How, his father …?)—stunned, unbelieving, taking a pace backward.

But I am seized with a sudden anxiety for the child, begin to look for him, want to fetch him home, and she grasps my intention at once, pulls me to the door, and on the doorstep, facing the little alleys, gesturing and yelling, she shows me the way to the nursery school.

AND IN A ROOM drenched in sun, smelling of bananas—the story hour; in a circle, upon tiny chairs, arms folded, all in blue pinafores, I haven't identified him yet, all of them very still, listening tensely to the slow, confident, melodious voice of a little teacher. It is years since I have known so deep a silence among children, had not imagined them capable of it.

And dropping into this, me, in black, flushed, stepping over piles of huge blocks, still trying to spot him, and something cracks in me, here of all places, and I wish to sink down beside the little towels hung up in a row, under the paintings scattered on the wall. And the brief shout of the teacher.

A bereavement in our family …

Before dawn …

But she, pale, misses the name, thinks I am rambling, thinks I belong at another nursery school perhaps, but then he stands up, rises like a slender stalk from his place, arms still folded, very grave, silently admits to the connection between us, listens to the teacher who has suddenly understood, has gone over to put her arms about him, addresses him in English, picks him up, lifts him out of the circle.

And at once the little lunch box is hung around his neck, a blue cap placed on his head, and he asks for something in his language and is immediately given a painting he has made that morning, and through the mist that veils my eyes I see—the page is filled with a red sun sparking splinters all around. And his little hand in mine, and my fingers closing over it. They have given him to me, even though I haven't told everything yet, could have been any old man entering a nursery school wishing to take away a child.

BACK IN THEIR APARTMENT. Soundless, barefoot, the Arab woman pads about in the kitchen. The child is with her, eating an early lunch. Now and then a few soft phrases reach me, she talking to him in Arabic, he answering her in English. A distant rustle from the open windows. We are waiting only for her. Everything will be turned upside down here in a day or two, people will fill the rooms. In a month or two nothing will remain. She will stow the child in a rucksack and go back where she came from. I find his study, go in and shut the door upon myself. Dim and cool in here. Stacks of books on the floor, the desk littered with papers. Left everything as it was and went to the army. Confusion of generations. I circle his desk, lightly touch his papers. Who could make order in this chaos. Fifteen years since I have inspected his exercise books. Vainly I try to let in some light. The blind has stuck, won't open. I come back to the desk. What had he been working on, what planned, and how can I link up with this? I touch the first layer and at once telephone bills, electricity bills, university circulars, come fluttering down. He is something of a teacher himself. I peel off a second layer—accounts, thick magazines in English, unfamiliar, pictures of men posing for advertisements, some half-naked, all of them long-haired, fat and lean revolutionaries displaying novel ties or striped trousers, small electric instruments of doubtful purpose. And suddenly I also find a pipe of his, and a smell of unknown tobacco. Tokens of my son's mystery. Son, child of mine. Another spell of dizziness. My eyes grow dim. I return to the window and strain all my powers to wrench the blind loose. Specks of light, a thin current of air; through the slats I discover a novel angle of a teeming wadi, and beyond it new buildings of the university. I return to my rummaging about the desk. Transcripts sent him by colleagues. Diagrams of statistical data. Will have to try and read these as well. Notes in his handwriting, book titles. Promises of new ideologies. I stuff some in my pocket. And now something genuinely his, a sheaf of papers in his handwriting, half in English, half in Hebrew, entitled "Prophecy and Politics." A new book perhaps, or an article. I pull drawers, perhaps there will be a personal diary as well, but they turn out to be almost empty. More pipes, a broken camera, old medicine bags, and snapshots of his girl-wife—by some trees, by a hill, a car, a river. And beyond the pictures, in a far corner of the drawer, I find a small knife, sharp, ornamented, inscribed with the word PEACE.

And the front door opens, and the house fills with the sound of light steps and with her laughter. The child's singsong, then the hectic whispering of the Arab woman. And now light streaming at me from the opening door. And she—in a light dress, still hot and sweaty from walking, her bag on her shoulder, sunglasses on her eyes, such a tourist. Stands there surprised at the depth of my intrusion, tries a smile for me at once, but I am buried in the chair, behind the desk, black-suited, heavy, the knife between my fingers.

She takes a few quick, airy steps towards me but suddenly she halts, has sensed something, dread seizes her, as though she had perceived the marks of death upon me.

"Something wrong ..." her voice trembles, as though it were I on the point of death, concealing a mortal wound beneath my garments.

And I straighten up, drop the knife, a burst of hot light hits me, begin to move, past her. Mumble the morning's tidings in an ancient, biblical Hebrew, and know she will not understand, the words dart back at me. And I am filled with pity for them, stroke the child's hair, incline my head before the old Arab woman, and am drawn onwards to the hot light in the rooms, through the still open front door, towards the looming wadi, to the university. Will have to enlist their help.

AND IN A STRAIGHT LINE, almost as the crow flies, I cross the wadi towards the university, and in a tangle of thicket, in the depth of a teeming ditch, for a moment I lose the sky. Suddenly I think of you and you alone, ardently, hungrily. My killed, mine only son. Out of the depths I cry, noon is passing, the Sabbath near, and in Jerusalem they still know nothing of your death. Your wife has not grasped the tidings. I was wrong, I should have let the authorities perform their duty.

And here rocks, and a very steep slope, and bushes growing out of an invisible earth tangling underfoot, and who would have imagined that near the university there could be such a wilderness still.

At last I have seen your papers. Vainly you feared that I would not understand, I understood at once, and I am inspired, burnt and despairing of you. You came back to preach your gospel, I am with you, my son, I have filled my pockets with your notes, shall learn English properly, shall go up into the mountains and wait for the wind.

And I crash through the barbed-wire fence surrounding the university, behind one of the marble buildings, a gnarled branch in my hand, a long time since I have been here, am confounded anew by the sequence of the buildings. Start looking for your faculty, wander along corridors, between oxygen bottles, dim laboratories, small libraries, hothouses, humming computers, and the campus emptying before my eyes, students receding.

And in the compound of the main library, defeated, I detain a last, book-laden, hurrying professor, but he has never heard your name and, embarrassed, he shows me the way to the offices. And a flock of clerks, just leaving, listen to me attentively, advise me that the telephones are disconnected already, that moreover they are not authorized to handle such tidings, perhaps I had better go to the police. And I realize suddenly: they take me for mad, or for some eternal student, a crank wishing to draw attention to himself. In a black suit slightly earth-caked, and hands holding a branch. It is the branch that makes me so suspect.

And I throw it away at once, in the middle of the square, and hasten back to the faculty building, into a lighted, balcony-tiered lobby. And on the top landing a stout porter moves about, letting down blinds. I, from my depth down below, in a shout, ask him about you, and he *has* heard your name, knows you by sight at least. "That professor with the wild beard"—he says, and comes down to me, jangling his keys, and takes me up to your office at the end of a corridor. And on the door I find a long list of students who want to consult you, and near it a typed announcement of your absence due to reserve duty, and on one side a list of books that you are asking your students to read pending your return. And I turn all these papers over, combine them and write a first death notice, my dearly beloved. And the porter reads it over my shoulder and believes it straightaway, brings me more thumbtacks to pin the paper to the door.

And we descend the stairs, and I tell him all about you, and our steps echo in the empty building. And the dusky light is pleasant, gentle to the eyes, I hang back, my steps waver, I would fain linger here awhile, but the porter is suddenly impatient, resolutely turns me out, back into the sun.

AND IT BLAZES with such passion, softening the world for a final conflagration. And I had said in my haste: early summer, and here it is high summer already. And back to drifting, in sweltering clothes, between the white buildings, the locked laboratories of the spirit, tramping across limp Jerusalem grass, drawing, drawn, towards a lone remnant of American students sprawled on one of the lawns, abandoning themselves to the sun, barefoot, bearded, half-naked some of them, nodding over copybooks and English Bibles, playing pop songs to themselves on small tape recorders. Calling me from afar—"You guy"—as though inviting me to accost them. And I do, I butt in, start walking among them, over them, step on their flabby, diaspora limbs, strike at them lightly with the branch that has reappeared in my hand. I could have been appointed professor here myself if I had really been determined, couldn't I?

And far away, somewhere on the horizon—the Hills of Moab.

They laugh, so passive are they, maybe even slightly drugged, "You old man," they say to me, taking me for who knows what, for some waster, someone come to peddle drugs perhaps. They are pleased with me, "You're great," they say, twisting on the ground, wallowing in the sparse grass, no word of Hebrew do they speak, it is only two days since they were set down at the airport. And I bend over them, am even prepared to examine them there and then, test their Bible knowledge, and I start talking to them in my broken, impossible English, which has all at once become intelligible to them.

"Hear me, children. My son killed at night. In Jordan. I mean, near the river," and I point at the horizon which is fading in a blue haze. And they laughing still, "Wonderful," they say, delighted, slap my back, eager to draw me in, make me join their crowd, assimilate me in the swelling beat of their song.

". . . I AM GRATEFUL TO YOU, my dear friend and Principal, for letting me address our students on this solemn occasion of their graduating from our school. I know, it wasn't easy for you to cede me this privilege for once. You, after all, haven't given a single lesson for years, not stained your hands with chalk, not touched a red pencil to correct a paper. You no longer stand for hours in front of a class, for you are busy with the administrative part of education, which you much prefer to any education proper. Nevertheless, and precisely therefore, you would always look forward impatiently to this moment when, before our anxious parents, you could hold forth as a guiding spirit to these youngsters; and all the more so in these troubled times.

"And who is not eager to address the young these days? We are all seized with a veritable passion for speaking to you, dear students, long-haired, inarticulate, slightly obtuse students, vague graduates without ideals, with your family cars, your discotheques and pettings at night in doorways. And with all that—with the strength and readiness to die. To burrow in bunkers for months on end, under constant fire, to charge at unseen wire fences in the night, so young, and in fact so disciplined, amazing us over and over with your obedience. Isn't that so, dear parents?

"Ladies and gentlemen, I am not speaking to you as senior teacher, but as one who was a father and is so no more. I came here the way I am and you see me with my beard of mourning, my dark clothes. I have no message, but I want to encourage you. See, I too have lost a son, though he was not quite so young any more. We thought he would go to guard army stores in Jerusalem, but they sent him to the Jordan Valley. Thirty-one years old. An only, beloved son. Dear parents, students, I do not want to burden you with my grief, but I ask you to look at me and guard yourself against surprise, because I was prepared for his death in a manner, and that was my strength in that fearful moment.

"And even on that very Friday I was informed of his death, before going to identify him, very lonely, wandering across lawns, between university buildings, under a fierce sun, even then I began to think of you, of the things I should say to you, how out of my private sorrow a common truth would illumine us all ..."

FROM A GREAT DISTANCE, beyond the summer clouds, as from a bird's-eye view, I look down upon myself. A tiny speck, abandoning the pale cubes and rolling slowly through a great splash of asphalt. An intersection. And all about—the heart of the dominion, a pile of government offices, reddish Parliament, sheer white museum, pine trees like soft moss, nibbled hills, blasted rocks, ribbons of road one atop the other—a plain attempt to transform the scenery. And a black dot comes spewing smoke from the east, stops beside the speck and swallows it.

It is an old taxi, some charred relic, and I drop on to torn and sweaty upholstery and wave the driver on.

Southwards. Through the stifling air—the stubbornness. Cemetery Hill, twisted lines of graves as a wild scrawl, and on all sides still more buildings, big housing projects, scaffolding, cranes—like rocket pits. Houses copulating with houses. The Kingdom of Heaven by force of stone.

And the driver—an unshaven ruffian, ageless, cracking sunflower seeds, hums under his breath, peers at me constantly through his mirror, ready for contact.

But I shut my eyes.

The taxi worms its way down the slope to a wadi, leaving a thick trail behind it. The hospital comes into view. A red rock dropped there once and turned into a windowed dam, hushed in the midday air, a small helicopter hovering above like a bird of prey.

My clothes are shedding wisps of grass. I doze, dream. The car rattles, its doors shake, windows subside. The hum of the springs sends the driver's spirits soaring and, having given me up, he starts singing aloud, with abandon, vigorously banging his steering wheel.

But I am transcending the heights, dominating the view. Long wadis drawing from Jerusalem to Mount Hebron, pouring, delving into bare eternal hills. Olive groves, stone walls, flocks of sheep, the beauty of it, ancient kingdom changeless for thousands of years, and in the same glance, higher up, the sea appears and the mouth of the desert. Heavily does this fearful land seize me by the neck.

I touch the back of the driver's neck lightly, his singing is cut short at once. I begin to talk. He does not understand at first, thinks I have gone out of my mind. But over the short distance remaining to the hospital I manage to convey the essential.

Yes, at thirty-one …

Only son …

Before dawn …

THEY WERE EXPECTING ME, as indeed they had said this morning, in the heart of the tiled compound, in the heart of the mountains, an army chaplain, heavy-limbed, his beard red and savage, a khaki-clad prophet, stands with the sun in his eyes, waiting. And when I arrive in my taxi he spots me at once, as though bereavement had marked me already, hurries to catch me before I should vanish through one of the glass doors gaping on all sides.

"You the father?"

"I am the father."

"Alone?"

"Alone."

He is astounded. His eyes burn. How on earth? How could they have let you come alone? For it isn't merely a matter of identification but a last leave-taking as well.

I know, but have no answer. Only cling to him with speechless fervour. At last a real rabbi, a man of God at my disposal. And silently I attach myself to his sweat-stained clothes, lightly touch his officer's insignia, and he, surprised at my clutching hands, surprised too at my weakness stirring at him through my hot clothes, puts his arm about me in embarrassment, his shoulders sag, tears in his eyes, and slowly, in the same embrace, he turns me towards the sun's radiance pouring out of the west, and softly pulls me inside.

Into an enormous and empty lift, and at once we sink slowly to the depths, no longer touching each other now, he beside the panel of buttons, I in a far corner, an empty stretcher between us.

He listens, his head tilted, his face blank, eyes extinguished; I am apparently talking again, not listening to myself, mechanically, probing the pain, the words happening far away, on some vague horizon, words already spoken several times today: thirty-one years old, nearly professor. Only son. Though saw little of him these past few years. A matter of months since he came back from the United States, grown a beard, hardly recognized him. Beloved son. Now he is leaving a wife, American, young, obscure. Leaving me a child. Leaving manuscripts, unfinished researches, packing cases scattered through his house, leaving wires and transformers. Enough to drive one mad. Our children getting killed and we left with things …

I am still speaking of him as though he were far away from me, lying in some desert somewhere, as though he weren't a couple of yards away, as though I weren't moving towards him in a slow but certain falling, which is arrested at last with a soft jolt that kindles the chaplain's eyes anew. Automatically the doors tear open before us …

He takes hold of me. I must have shown signs of wanting to escape. Leads me through lighted corridors of a basement filled with the breathing of engines. At the crossings between corridors, sudden gusts of wind blow at us. In a little room people rise to meet us, doctors, officials, bend their heads when they see me enter, close their eyes for an instant. Some retreat at once, begin to slip away, some are, on the contrary, drawn towards me, want to touch me. The chaplain whispers: "This is the father who's come alone," and I, terrified, start mumbling again, the familiar formula. And someone at once steps nearer to listen, and a hush all around.

There is a wonderful gentleness in their attitude towards me, in the way they place me in a chair, put a skullcap on my head, in the swiftness with which they extract the identity card from my clothes, write something down, open a side door; and when they help me up I seem weightless, drawn floating by their hands into a vault, a bare concrete floor, screens everywhere, beating of white wings.

I shiver.

There is an unmistakable sound of flowing water in the room, as though springs were bubbling up in it.

The shed blood.

The child. This curse fallen upon me.

Someone is already standing beside one of the screens, draws a curtain aside, turns the blanket back, and I still afar, swept by a dreadful curiosity, my breathing faint, fading, heart almost still, slip out of the hands holding me, glide softly, irresistibly over there, to look at the pale face of a dead young man, naked under the blanket, at thin lines of blood circling blank half-open eyes. I shrink back slightly, the skullcap slips off my head.

A deep hush. Everyone is watching me. The chaplain stands motionless, his hand in his waistcoat, any moment now he will come out with a ram's horn, blow us a feeble blast.

"It isn't him ..." I whisper at last with infinite astonishment, with growing despair, with the murmur of the water flowing in this damned room.

SOMEONE SWITCHES on more lights, as though it were a question of light. The silence lasts. I realize: no one wants to understand.

"It isn't him," I say again, say without voice, without breath, gasping for air, "you must have made a mistake ..."

Amazement comes to them at last. The chaplain attacks a scrap of paper tied to the stretcher, reads the name aloud.

"Only the name is right ..." myself still in a whisper, and I retreat, and in the deep silence, the murmur of water flowing unseen, the sweet smell of decay, return to the little cabinet which has already grown to be my oasis.

Behind my back the chaplain begins to swear at someone and the little group collapses.

Friday afternoon, and though I see neither sun nor mountains, I know—we are on the outskirts of town, deep in the vaults of a hospital that leans heavily into a wild plunging wadi. The people around me want to go home, the nearer the Sabbath the further the town draws away from them. They had been waiting for me in patience, knowing how brief the ceremony, a few seconds—enter, look, weep, part; sign a paper too perhaps, because somewhere the evidence must be left. I am not the first to come here after all, nor the last.

Now I am keeping them back. How distressing therefore to see the people enter the room with eyes lowered as in guilt. And when they see me sitting in a corner words fail them. Such a terrible mistake.

And behind the walls I hear the whirring of bells, frantic telephones. They are trying to sort out the confusion before I should start fanning false hopes.

But I am not fanning a thing. Only straighten up suddenly and stand on my feet, watching the others in silence. It is only a truce, I tell myself, a little cease-fire. But they are dismayed at my rising, believe I am going violent on them, are already resigning themselves to it, except that I am nothing of the kind, only start moving slowly and dazedly about the room, from wall to wall, and, like a dog, find a plate in some corner with a few stale biscuits on it, take one and start munching. I have eaten nothing since this morning.

But it sticks in my throat at once, as though I were chewing dust or ashes, dust mingled with ashes.

I vomit.

At last …

They had been waiting for this, had been prepared. Used to it apparently. They sit me in a chair at once, clean up, offer me some smelling salts.

"It wasn't my son …" I mumble at them with a face drained of blood.

Again the chaplain appears, looking very sombre, his eyes glowing, desperate, his beard unkempt, cap awry, the badges on his shoulder shining, invites me in a low voice to return to the room of the murmuring water.

Now I am faced with three screens. The light is glaring, they have turned it full on, thinking again that it is a question of light, that it is with light they'll convince me. Never has such a thing happened to them, and they suspect some fearful muddle may be at the bottom of it. And again I stagger, the shed blood. My son. This curse. And again my breathing grows faint, fades, heart still. Glide softly from stretcher to stretcher, lost faces, young men, like faces in my class, only the eyes closed, slightly rolled upward.

Not him …

They take me back to the first stretcher again, as though they were really resolved to drive me out of my mind.

"I'm sorry …" I falter and collapse against the chaplain, against the open water channels running along the walls that my eyes detect at last.

I BELIEVE I MUST GO over the moment when I learned of his death again.

Summer morning, the sky torn wide from end to end, June, last days of the school year. I rise late, languid, faintly stunned, unaware of time, straight into the glare of light.

Climb the school steps after the bell has faded. An echo still lingers among the treetops, in the dim green air. Start pacing through the emptying corridors, among last stragglers hurrying towards classrooms, make my way slowly for my class, from afar already sense their nervousness, their restive murmur.

Those huddling in the doorway spy me from afar and curse, hurry inside to warn the others. A last squeal of the girls. I by the door, and they tense and upright by their chairs, the white sheets of paper spread on their desks like flags of surrender, Bibles shelved deep inside.

The tyranny I enforce by means of the Bible.

Each examination takes on a fearful importance.

I greet them, they sit down. I call one of the girls and she comes over, long-haired, delicate, wordlessly receives the test papers, passes softly between the rows distributing them. The silence deepens, heads bend. The frozen hush and excitement of the first rapid survey.

I know: it is a hard test. Never before have I composed such a cruel text.

Slowly they raise their eyes. Their faces start to burn, a dumb amazement seizes them. They exchange despairing glances. Some of them raise their fingers at me, standing over them high on my platform, but I mow them down with a gesture of my hand. They are stunned, fail to see my purpose. They cannot utter a word before I silence them. Each of them forlorn in his seat. And suddenly, as though it were light they lacked, someone gets up and pulls the curtains, but to no avail. The new light trickling in at them only exasperates them the more. They try writing something, nibble their pens, but give up, a few already tearing up the papers. Someone rises and leaves the room with flaming face. Another follows, and a third, suddenly it seems as though they were up in revolt. At last.

And at that moment the quick steps of the Head sound, as though the rumour had reached him. He opens the door and enters, very pale, out of breath, does not look at the class but makes straight for me, mounts the platform, takes hold of me, three years that we haven't spoken and suddenly he clasps me to him hard, before the astonished eyes of the pupils. Whispers at me: Just a moment … leave them … never mind … come with me …

ONE POSSIBILITY—not to insist. To release these people, give them time; not to struggle against the waning sun, let the Sabbath descend upon Jerusalem in peace, let the rabbi reach home in time. And for the time being sever contact, depart, come down from the mountains, arrive in the evening, steal softly through our shadowy street. Enter the house through the back door, undress, not think, not tell, wait, the telephone disconnected, the door locked. To make the bed, try to sleep; and wait for a new, more authoritative call.

A second possibility—to insist, shout, tear clothes. To assail the chaplain, the others, demand immediate proof. To rout out additional people, organize a search party. A procession through the streets of Jerusalem on the Sabbath eve, wandering from one hospital to the next, to comb the cellars, descend into hell, find him.

Another possibility—not to stir. Do nothing. Go on lying on this stretcher, covered with a blanket, in this hospital, in the little cabinet.

There, someone is already holding a glass of water to my lips.

I open my eyes. It is the chaplain, wild and woebegone prophet, surrounded by doctors, who gives me a drink with his own hands and with infinite tenderness.

He feels they owe me some explanation …

But he has none.

Groping in the dark.

Has no words even.

Nothing like it ever happened to him.

The people here are baffled as well.

Something very deep has gone awry …

Telephone calls will solve nothing, he knows. What ought to be done is to go back to sources: to the brigade, the battalion, maybe to the company itself.

My suffering is great, but who knows, perhaps out of it a new rising may come.

He had not wanted to use that expression, it is too big.

He is very much afraid of false hopes.

There is a wonderful *midrash,* full of wisdom, only loath to trouble me now.

Such violent times, appalling.

Runs from one funeral to the next.

At night sits at home amending funeral orations.

And he bends over me: to stay here, on this stretcher, rolled up in a blanket, serves no purpose. We ought to go to Jerusalem.

If possible before the onset of the Sabbath …

Suggests therefore that I collect myself, that is, if I still have some strength left. That I remove the blanket, get off the stretcher. They won't leave me to wander about by myself any more.

Incidentally, my status is dubious from the point of religious law as well—should my garment be rent or not. However, to be on the safe side, to ward off illusions, and again, before Sabbath sets in—

And he takes a small penknife out of his pocket, removes my blanket, and as I lie there, everyone watching, he makes a long tear in my coat.

AND WE START the ascent, out of the depths, in the same lift and at the same slow speed, stumble out into the same compound and find a different light, different air, signs of a new hush. And climbing up out of the wadi, out of the heart of the mountains, and with us the sun, caught on the roof of the chaplain's small military car. He is driving zealously, sounding his horn to high heaven, his beard blowing, the steering wheel digging into his stomach, hurtles between near-empty buses, trying to overtake the Sabbath, which is descending upon him from the hazy eastern sky.

There is something desolate about the summery streets of Jerusalem vanquished by the Sabbath's might. I think of my house, of our street at this hour, decked in greenery, with a heavy perfume of blossoming, a swish of cars being washed, and the water murmuring along the curb.

And a taste of autumn suddenly, clouds caught in pines and cypresses. And we burst at a gallop into a large, empty military camp scattered through a grove on a hill, and just at that moment the Sabbath siren rises from the town like a wail. The chaplain stops the car at once, kills the engine, drops his hands off the wheel, listens to the sound as though he were hearing some new gospel, then goes to find someone from brigade staff.

But there is no one, only barracks with boarded-up windows, stretches of cracked and barren concrete, and small yellow signs with military postbox numbers. The army has migrated to the firing lines and left only whitewashed skeletons behind, and legends on blank walls: COMPANY A., MESS, Q.M., SYNAGOGUE.

And torn, sagging wire fences, and weeds rustling underfoot, and I still trailing behind the chaplain who circles the barracks, knocks on imaginary doors, recedes from view, is lost and reappears, his beard shining through the trees.

And I, who never served in the army, and in the War of Independence only stood beside road barriers, double up at last upon a rock in the centre of a crumbling parade ground, the torn flap dangling on my breast, and the smell of ancient hosts about me.

Such despair—

Since morning I have been rolling down an abyss.

This sad hush around me.

And then, as though sprung from the soil, people collect round me, hairy half-naked soldiers, their shoelaces untied, carrying towels and tiny transistors purring Sabbath songs, weary drivers emerging from one of the barracks on their way to the shower. They surround me silently in the middle of the parade ground, and once again I, grey and tired, with the same story: Thirty-one. Informed of his death this morning. Lecturer at the university. Left a wife and child. They know nothing yet. Myself come to Jerusalem to identify him, and then find—it's not him... .

Their amazement—

The towels crumple in their hands—

How not him?

Not him. Not his body. Someone else.

Who?

How should I know?

And what about him?

That's what I'm asking. Maybe you know someone who could help.

They tremble. Something in the story has shaken them, hairy men with towels and soap dishes, they silence the transistors at once, forget about their shower, take my arms and pull me up, supporting me, cursing the army. Never in their life heard of such a thing happening. It looks as though they would like to beat somebody up, some officer perhaps. And one of them recalls having seen the jeep of the Brigade Intelligence Officer under a tree somewhere, and at once they take me there. And in a coppice, beneath foliage, beside a locked barrack-turned-storehouse, the jeep stands, loaded with machine-guns and ammunition, its front wheels grazing one of the doors. They try to break down the door but fail, break through a window and peer into a dim room filled with ammunition boxes. And in the corner a camp bed. Someone vaults into the room and wakes up a boy in khaki, a lean officer, curled up like a fetus, in his clothes, shoes, revolver on his thigh, fallen asleep amid the explosives.

He wakes up at once, opens his eyes and waits. They tell him breathlessly, shouting, pointing their fingers at me rooted outside, by the window, like a frozen picture. But he does not look at me. Sits bent over on the bed in his crumpled clothes, indifferent to the general excitement. And only when the confusion of voices dies down, and the wind whispering in the pines is suddenly heard, does he begin to talk to me from afar in a slow, quiet voice.

What's your name?

I give it.

What's his?

I give it.

And it's not him.

Not him.

Who brought you here?

The chaplain.

His eyes darken, a lengthy silence, and at last very softly:

And what do you want?

To find him …

He makes no response, as though fallen asleep again. Then he gets up, tired, dream-wrapped, but suddenly assuming the airs of a general, folds up the blanket, opens the door which he had barred upon himself from within, goes out and vanishes among the pines, into their soft whisperings. The drivers follow, find him by a rusty tap half buried under a drift of dead pine-needles, holding his head under it and letting the cool water splash over him. Then he steps aside, not looking, letting the drops trickle. Now the drivers are really ready to hit him. But with the water drying, his eyes quickening, his head bent, he has made up his mind already, and in a quiet voice starts giving out commands to the drivers. He sends one of them to find the wandering chaplain, orders another to bring the jeep around and fill it up, and the rest have already seized me, lifted me, as though I were paralyzed. They clear a place for me in the jeep and wedge me in between a greasy machine-gun, cartridge cases, and smoke shells, place a helmet on my grey hairs, and firmly secure the strap around my chin.

And someone switches on the field radio by my side and it stirs into life with a thin shriek. And as though of its own accord, so slow as to be imperceptible, the jeep begins to move, surrounded by drivers half pushing it, half tagging in its wake. And from somewhere, at the last minute, they have fetched back the chaplain as well, sweat-drenched, lost, burnt out, dreaming of his Sabbath, and he too joins the slow procession, lagging a little behind. Notices me driven off, sitting pinioned between machine-guns, and is unamazed. They are taking me away from him and he yields me up, is even ready to give his blessing to the journey. What's to be done? He has found no one at staff quarters, tried to get in touch with front staff and failed. But has left instructions behind, written out the full story.

And still he trudges behind the slow jeep, through the trees, the humming of the field radio. What else? What else is bothering him? It appears that something has turned up after all, the dead man's personal file, lying on some table. And a sudden thought strikes him—maybe it's all a mistake, maybe only the name is identical but it's not my son. And maybe it would be well if, at the last moment, before going down into the desert, I took a glance at the picture at least. And he pushes a brief khaki folder into my hands, and the men crowd around to look at it with me And I open it to the first page and find the picture of a thin boy, just out of high school, fifteen years back, my son, in khaki shirt, cropped hair, looking at me with obstinate eyes.

THE TIME IS HALF-PAST FIVE in the afternoon. A tall aerial scratches the last of the sun. A hesitant jeep is crossing Jerusalem as though in search of a missing person, someone to obviate the purpose of its journey, and meanwhile a Jerusalemite orange-red Sabbath is trampled under dusty wheels.

Passers-by stop to gaze at the elderly civilian, dressed in black, helmeted, his eyes red with weeping. There is something in the way I grip the machine-gun that poses a menace for the Jerusalemites—the Jews in its western half first, then the Arabs; as though I intended to mow them down, I who do not even know where the trigger is.

I ask the little officer.

He shows me—

I finger it—

(So tiny.)

And then the final collapse of the Sabbath beyond East Jerusalem, the last signs of green dissolving, and the stark white of bare stone houses, of pale, powdery soil at the roadside, bluish smoke from invisible fires in courtyards, and near them Arabs, glancing up and away from us.

And then another collapse, of the road itself towards a grey, sunless desert appearing beyond a bend in a setting of smoky clouds.

At last, my solemn and fully armed entry into the Jordan Valley, where I have never yet set foot.

And to look at once for signs of a dead, distant, biblical deity among the arid hills flanking the road, in the sun-cracked face of an elderly soldier lifting the barrier.

And from here, I have been waiting for this, I knew, I knew, a great burst of speed, a resurgence. The jeep spins forward, and the officer, as though wrestling with someone, his lips set tight, eyes narrowed, starts driving wildly, greedily. And I cling to the gun in the face of a great sweeping wind, thrust my hand into my clothes and start weeding out papers—bus tickets, old receipts, lists of students, notes from my son's desk, the draft of a speech, text of the morning's examination.

AND THEN, at last, the army proper, and in the falling light. The sad, pellucid desert light dying over a camp of tents, barracks, tanks and half-tracks and immense towering aerials, and smoke spiralling from a chimney as though a different kind of Sabbath reigned here. And old, scorched soldiers in outsize overalls opening still another barrier before us, as though the desert were carved up by barriers.

People crowd around us—

They have been expecting us—

They even run after the jeep.

"The old father's arrived," someone shouts, as though I were a sacred figure.

And before long they have unloaded me, detached me carefully from the machine-gun, loosened the cartridge belt that has coiled itself about me, dislodged a bullet which I have inserted into the barrel by mistake, and lower me, dusty and old, the helmet askew, lead me in the gathering darkness to their commanding officer.

And suddenly, deep in the distance, beyond the hills, shots resound.

My heart freezes—

Such warmth in the touch of their hands on my body, their gladness that a really old man has come among them, in a helmet, a civilian dimension in their desert night, that they dare blurt in an initiatory whisper as if it were a sinful thought: "He's not been killed," "It isn't him," "You've been misled ..."

But the commander's voice asserts itself, carries firmly through the new darkness, and without seeing his face, listening to a voice heard before sometime, an old pupil doubtless, I nearly identify the voice, impossible that I should not ...

The encounter happened at night and the body was transferred to hospital before dawn. The men hardly know each other. Some of them haven't been with the unit for years. The clerk was only given an identity tag to go by, and from that set the chain of documents moving. He never looked at the dead man's face. They had taken everything to be in order, and then they received a phone call from headquarters in Jerusalem a short while back, someone giving them the whole story, saying we were on the way. And at once they had put their entire radio network into action. The men are scattered over a huge area. They inquired about the name right away, was there anyone answering to this name, and then, just a while back, someone was found. A man of thirty-one, from Jerusalem. And his military number too, corresponding to that of the body's. That is, the tags must have got shuffled somehow. And they'll still have to get to the bottom of that. Anyhow, they asked no more questions, did not want to alarm him, tell him his family had already been informed. But they are certain it is my son. Bound to be. And so long as I'm here, maybe I'd better see him with my own eyes after all. That way everybody's mind will be at ease. And better before the night is through. Look, he's with the patrol, they'll be here soon, and they've already arranged for them to be waiting at a little distance from here, so if I've come as far as this ... the forward position ... maybe I'd go on just a bit farther ... that is, if I have the strength ... Here, get up on this armoured car ... The word had got down from command about my pluck, considering ...

And suddenly it strikes me. He is afraid of me. This silence of mine, the endless patience, the way I stand there facing him, limp, demanding nothing; the passivity with which I still wear the crushing helmet on my head. Something has gone wrong within his sphere of command and he is alarmed by the tyranny of my silence.

And again, from the distance—long volleys, strung out, echoes splintering.

This time it is a heavy half-track they take me to. They open an iron door, install me, seal the armoured slits. Two or three soldiers clamber up and position themselves beside the machine-guns, someone bends over the field radio and starts muttering.

With infinite slowness, with extinguished lights, tracks churning, cooped in an iron hutch dark except for the glimmer of a tiny red bulb—I understand. We are returning to the Jordan, they want to send me over to the other side, take me out unto the source. All that has happened has been but a prelude.

AND SUDDENLY WE STOP. The engine falls silent. Someone lowers himself and opens the iron door from without, releases me. A junction of dirt tracks, desert and yet not-desert, reeds and shrubs in a narrow ditch beside the road. And silence, no shooting, and a light breeze, and a star-studded sky. We wait. Crouched low upon stones beside the track, in the thicket. And once again I find myself delivered into new hands. Someone not young and not old. An intelligent, sympathetic face, watching me intently, smiling. Something about me seems to amuse him, the helmet perhaps, I attempt to pry it loose. The smile persists. It turns out to be my age that bothers him.

"Seventy years old."

Sabbath eve. Matches flicker on the half-track, cigarettes are lit. The soldiers are talking in low voices, cursing softly, calculating the number of Sabbaths still left them here. The field radio splutters feebly, someone distant signalling, "Can you hear me? Hear me?" but no one takes the trouble to reply.

What do I do?

I tell him.

He smiles. He had thought as much.

"It's my Hebrew," I say quietly.

What about it?

"Some rhetoric still left perhaps."

No, he smiles, not at all, but the eyes, the expression in them. He used to have a history teacher with just the same look.

"What history?"

"Jewish history."

"And he looked like me?"

"Yes."

"Despite the difference."

"What difference?"

"Between history and Bible."

"Why difference?"

And I rise, the torn flap drops from my heart, and I begin to explain with quiet fervour.

"... I AM COMING to the main point of my speech. All this has been nothing but a prelude. Mr. Principal, colleagues, ladies and gentlemen, dear students, forgive me but I feel the need to say a few words to those among us who may disappear.

"On the face of it, your disappearance is nothing, is meaningless, futile. Because historically speaking, however stubborn you are, your death will again be but a weary repetition in a slightly different setting. Another tinge of hills, new contours of desert, a new species of shrub, astounding types of weapon. But the blood the same, and the pain so familiar.

"Yet another, other, glance reverses it all, as it were. Your disappearance fills with meaning, becomes a fiery brand, a source of wonderful, lasting inspiration.

"For to say it plainly and clearly—there is no history. Only a few scraps of text, some potsherds. All further research is futile. To glue oneself to the radio again and again, or seek salvation in the newspapers—utter madness.

"Everything fills with mystery again. Your notebooks, your chewed pencils, each object left behind you fills with longing. And we who move in a circle behind you and unwittingly trample your light footsteps, we must be vigilant, as in a brief nightly halt in the desert, between arid hills, upon barren, unmurmuring soil ..."

AND THEN out of the vastness a murmur rises, and from the east or west or north—I for one have lost my bearings—the patrol arrives, shining in a cloud of dust, two or three armoured vehicles, with growing clatter, in the dark, now and then sending a strong beam of light at the embankment, then brandishing it about the arid hills, at the sky.

And there, in that booming clatter, my son must be too. A thirty-one-year-old private whose desk is littered with drafts for researches is now stuck in a half-track, beside a machine-gun or mortar, flashing a beacon upon me and aiming his barrel at me.

Their beam hits us—

Someone fires a shot in our direction.

They have forgotten who we are, take us for infiltrators—

Only everyone shouts at once with all their might.

They would have killed us—

They pull up at some distance, two half-tracks and a tank, engines roaring, and the wadi stirs into life. Vague nightly shapes, faces indiscernible. The officer beside me goes to look for the man in charge. And I, in my darkness, planted on my spot, scan the dim silhouettes and suddenly give up, convinced it is all for nothing, tremble in every limb, am ready to admit to the first identification.

A few soldiers jump off to urinate on the chains, and all of a sudden I discover him too, heavy, long-haired, sleep-walking, lonely, he too urinating.

Myself unseen I make no move, watch him from afar; know, his linen must be foul. As a boy he would come home like that from any hike of a day or two, as filthy as if he had crossed a desert.

Meanwhile they have located him. The commander calls his name. He turns, does up his buttons, comes over, a lumbering shape. Strange, he is not surprised to find me, his old father, late in the evening, in a helmet, a few paces from the river Jordan.

Two officers take hold of him. The half-track engines fall silent. And suddenly a deep hush.

"This him?"

"Yes." I touch him lightly.

He smiles at us, his beard ragged, understanding nothing, very tired, stands before me hung about with grenades, the rifle dangling from his shoulder like a broomstick.

"What's happened?"

How to explain it to him.

"Anything wrong at home?"

How tell him that I had already given him up, intruded into his room, ruffled his papers, that I had planned to collect them for a book.

"You were reported killed …"

Not I, someone else said that.

He does not understand, how could he, stooping a little under his kit, his helmet pushed back, his face inscrutable, his eyes holding me, like his son's eyes, like mine gazing at him. This is how he would look at me when he was small, when I would beat him.

He is asked to show the tags—

Gradually a crowd of soldiers is piling up about us.

He starts hunting through his pockets with surprising meekness, takes out bits of paper, shoelaces, rifle bullets, white four-by-two flannel, more flannel, sheds flannel like notes, but the tags fail to turn up. Lost them. Thought they were tied to his first-aid dressing.

"Where's the dressing?"

Gave it to the medic after the encounter. It follows that he gave the tags as well. I begin to suspect that he, too, had considered disappearing, here beside the Jordan, or perhaps he just wanted to signal to me.

The medical orderly is summoned—

Out of the darkness they fish up a scraggy little fellow, middle-aged, embittered, smoking hungrily, who does not remember a thing. Yes, some people gave him their dressings, but he doesn't know about tags. Found tags on the dead man and put them around his neck. Was useless dressing him anyway. Halfway through had realized the man was dead. Finished the job anyway. No, didn't identify him. Doesn't know who it was. Knows hardly anyone here. Himself belongs to a different brigade altogether anyhow, attached here by mistake. Wants to get back to his own unit. Why've they stuck him here in the first place? He misses his pals, and besides, they're getting their discharge soon, and then where will he be? …

They remove him—

Little by little, in the massing darkness, understanding comes to my son. His face unfolds, his eyes clear, his figure straightens. He adjusts the rifle and comes to life. And I who feel my collapse imminent want to climb on to him.

"This morning, at school, the Head informs me," I speak to him at last, "it's been a mad day …"

The ring around us tightens, the men cleave to us. The story of his death and resurrection thrills them. They press jokes upon the two of us, want to hear all the particulars. We both stand trembling, smiling weakly.

The officers start breaking it up, sending the men back to the half-tracks. The night deepens, the patrol ought to be on its way, there is still a war on.

And we are suddenly alone, both of us in helmets but myself unarmed, with only the torn flap on my heart.

"What's with you?" I whisper at him rapidly, with the last of my strength.

And only now he looks at me, stunned, that I have closed with him, come as far as this and by the very border hemmed him in.

"You can see for yourself ..." he whispers with something of despair, with bitterness, as though it were I who issued call-up orders, "such a loss of time ... so pointless ..."

And how to give him some point, some meaning, but quickly, hurriedly, in the shadow of the vehicles which are starting up their engines again, before he disappears to the vague nightly lines of the desert, and before I myself should fall before him into a deep slumber.

NOT DREAMING YET, but asleep. I mean: my heart asleep. Nod on my feet, with weakness, with hunger, and diminish under a star-tossed sky and a moon rising in the east. Clouds start to move, the setting changes and consciousness fades. Little by little the senses are quenched as well. I do not hear the shots flaring up again in the distance, do not smell these rushes, the desert mallow; and what I hold in my hand drops soundlessly; it is from a blurring figure that I take leave, flutter my hand like a defeated actor to the beam of light cast at me from one of the half-tracks, and yield my body to someone willing to take it (someone different again, very young) and get me back on to some tank, shut the steel plate upon me. And once again beside a red bulb, without headlights, in the dark, I begin the journey back.

And it was then that I noticed for the first time that I had lost the text. Entire chapters. I would not have passed a single test, not the easiest of tests. The last verses were slipping and being ground by the creaking chains.

After this opened Job his mouth and cursed his day—

A prayer of Habakkuk the prophet upon Shigionoth—

A Psalm of David when in the wilderness of Judah—

In the year that King Uzziah died—
To the Musician upon Shoshanim—
The song of songs—
Hallelujah—

NOT ALLOWED TO dream yet. By the light of a clouded moon, at the forward position, I discover a civilian car, headlights burning, engine humming softly, no one inside. Next they are taking, almost pushing me, towards one of their huge tents, and there, by the light of one pale bulb, between field radios, twisted telephone cables, and nude photographs stirring against the tent-flaps my daughter-in-law, standing between the beds, surrounded by signallers who are gazing enchanted at the young, wind-blown woman who has turned up at nightfall in their tent.

"He not killed," I tell her at once in my broken English, grimy, on the verge of dreams.

But she knows already, and all she wants now is to fall upon me, wild with excitement, having been certain all along it was nothing but a private delusion of mine.

But I forestall her, and insensibly, drowsily, through a thousand veils, I take two steps, getting entangled in cables, rubbing against the pinups, fall upon her, kiss her brow, stroke her hair, and a delicate smell of perfume steals into my first dream, the cool touch of her skin, smooth, lacking warmth.

This New Left—
Surreptitiously perfumed—
Seeking warmth—

And then she breaks down. The signallers are stunned. About to cry, but first she says something in rapid English, repeating it more slowly, unexpectedly casting about for Hebrew words as well, and at last crying, silently, making no sound.

And only now I become aware of an old signaller in a corner of the tent, bent over a field telephone, trying to find out, unhopefully, with someone very distant, the dead man's true identity.

And again someone comes to fetch me, leads me and her to a tent at the far end of the camp and offers us the rumpled beds of soldiers out on ambush, to sleep in till morning. Then they bring food in mess-tins, a bottle with some leftover wine in honour of the Sabbath eve, light a candle on the floor, and leave us to ourselves, my daughter-in-law and me, in the translucent darkness of one quivering candle, in the close air of the Jordan Valley.

And I, crazed and exhausted with hunger, am stupefied by the smell of the food. And thus, seated on the bed, the dishes on the floor at my feet, without looking at her, without strength left to speak English, I stoop and eat like a savage, crouching over the food, with a misshapen fork and without a knife, sleepily devouring the army food that tastes wonderful to me, mingled with the smells and flavours of gunpowder, saltpetre, desert, dust, sweat; I set the bottle to my lips and gulp down cheap wine, sweet and tepid and reeking of rifle grease and tank fuel, and right away getting drunk, as though someone were striking me with dull inward remote blows that are growing sharper and sharper.

Shots. Human beings shooting at each other again. I wake up, find myself lying on the bed, the helmet that I had grown used to as to a skullcap taken off my head, my shoes removed. The moon is gone, the candle extinguished and the darkness grown deep. A new wind has set up, gently beating against the tent flaps, bringing in a current of cool desert air. Without lifting myself up, very heavy, my face sticky with food remnants like a baby's, I make out her profile; sitting up on the other bed, her long hair in wild confusion about her, a soldier's battle dress over her shoulders, her face open, feet bare, sitting and sucking upon a cigarette. Half the night gone and she still awake. Hasn't touched the food. Her head turned towards me, gazing at me in fascination, in wonder, and the dread that drove her through several barriers last night in order to reach this place deepens, as though by my power I had killed him, as though by my power brought him hack to life, as though I had not wished but to indicate one possibility ...

The firing does not stop. Single shots, and it is as if they had changed direction. But I feel I am growing more and more used to them. She is not frightened either, does not stir, even though now he might really get killed, somewhere out there, on his half-track slowly grinding down a trail.

I MUST STILL GO over the moment when I learned of his death.

Summer morning, the sky a deep clear blue, June, last days, I rise late, stunned, as after an illness, straight into the sun.

The bells are ringing and I am swept slowly up the stairs upon the turmoil of students who suck me upwards in their tide, into the corridors. Move along the open classroom doors, past weary teachers' faces, arrive at my class and find them quiet, aloof, long-haired, Bibles dropping to the floor. One of them is by the blackboard filling it with flowers, dozens of white crumbling bowers.

I mount the platform and they raise their eyes at me. The room is dim, curtains drawn. And I realize: I am not important to them any more, have lost my power over them, they have done with me, I already belong to the past.

How well I know that look; yet I never feared it, for I knew—they would come back in the end. In a few years I would find them about, with their wives or husbands, running after their babies with a faint stoop, and when I would meet them—self-conscious, holding shopping baskets—in the street, I would regain my power over them. If only for an instant, for a split second.

But these last years the parting becomes difficult. They are off to the deserts, far away; I mean, this supple flesh, the erect heads, the young eyes. And there are those who do not come back. Several class-years already. Some disappear. And some balance is upset with me. I remain troubled. This pain of theirs, the advantage of an experience in which I have no share. And even those who do come back, though they walk with their children and their shopping baskets, there is something veiled in their eyes, they stare at me blankly, almost ignore me, as though I had deceived them somewhere. I mean, as though with the material itself I had deceived them. As though everything we taught them—the laws, the proverbs, the prophecies—as though it had all collapsed for them out there, in the dust, the scorching fire, the lonely nights, had all failed the test of some other reality. But what other reality? Lord of Hosts, Lord God—*what* other reality for heaven's sake? Does anything really change? I mean, these imaginary signs of revolution.

And I am seized with a feeling of unease, start handing out the test papers, pass between the rows myself and lay them on their desks. And the silence around me deepens. They read, give a little sigh, then pull out clean sheets of paper and start drafting their straightforward, efficient, unimaginative answers in the bald, arid style that may suddenly, unaccountably, take a lyrical turn, only to dry up again and expire in the desert.

They'll be the death of me—

And there is my son, returned from the United States, clumsy, hair grown, such a gentle professor, no longer so young. Has brought along a campus girl, a slender student, cloaked in a worn and tasselled garment, and on her shoulders, strapped into a sort of rucksack, a small, pale child who speaks only English. And they alight from the plane and look at me as though they had brought some new gospel, tidings of a revolution, of some other reality, wonderful and unknown....

And I suddenly feel tears spring to my eyes. Still wandering between the desks, past Bibles on the floor, stoop and pick one up here and there. The students follow me with their eyes, already longing to crib, or at least pass on a whisper that they believe might help them, might add another fraction to their marks, even though they are abandoning it all soon, leaving empty classrooms behind them, a pile of chairs in a corner, a clean blackboard, traces of their names scored on desks as on tombstones.

And all of a sudden I long for a different parting, one that will be scored on their memories. In a whirl of emotion I cross to the windows and jerk the curtains aside, bespatter them with heavy splashes of sunlight as drops of blood. Go to the door and open it wide, stand on the threshold, half my face to the corridor and half to the class. And I know the suspense they are in. Am I setting them a trap? Am I here or am I not?

And then I see the Head from afar, striding sadly and pensively along the empty corridor. Approaches slowly, heavily, like an obsolete tank. Something deep has aged in him these past few years. In a year or so he too will have to retire. He lifts his head and sees me standing on the threshold, lowers it again as though I were a stone or spirit. He still assumes I do not want to talk to him. As though three years had not sufficed us. And in the room the whispering swells, and the swish of papers. Passing on the answers to each other. But I make no move. My face is turned to the corridor window, its display of summer bright and full. The Hills of Judaea in the distance, the Hills of Moab, and all the rest. And the image of the students behind me is reflected in the window as well, fused upon the scenery, on a patch of blue, on the treetops, faraway aerials, the hum of aircraft.

And the Head stops beside me. For the first time in three years. Very pale. And must break the silence at once.

Five or six hours ago …

In the Jordan Valley …

Killed on the spot …

The Authors

Margaret Atwood (Canada, 1939–) Poet, novelist, and essayist. Her first collection of poetry, *The Circle Game,* appeared in 1966. Among her many novels are *Surfacing* (1972), *The Handmaid's Tale* (1985), *The Robber Bride* (1993), *Alias Grace* (1996), and *Oryx and Crake* (2003). *The Blind Assassin* won The Booker Prize for 2000.

Ray Bradbury (U.S.A., 1920–) One of the masters of modern science fiction, Bradbury began publishing in pulp magazines at a very early age. He became famous with a short-story collection, *The Martian Chronicles* (1950), followed by *The Illustrated Man* (1951). His masterpiece is *Fahrenheit 451* (1953). He wrote the film script for John Huston's *Moby Dick* (1954).

Italo Calvino (Italy, 1923–1985) Though born in Cuba, Calvino was brought to Italy at the age of two. His many books include *The Baron in* *the Trees* (1957), *Invisible Cities* (1972), *If on a Winter's Night a Traveller* (1979), and *Mr. Palomar* (1983). Calvino was a member of the experimental literature group OULIPO.

Albert Camus (France, 1913–1960) Born in French Algeria, Camus wrote novels, essays, and plays. Among the former, his best known is *The Outsider* (1942); among the latter, *The Plague* (1947). He is also the author of an essay on suicide, *The Myth of Sisyphus* (1942). Camus won the Nobel Prize for Literature in 1957.

Mohamed Choukri (Morocco, 1935–) Choukri did not learn to read or write until he was twenty-one. Ten years later, he published his first short story, "Violence on the Beach." Choukri has since published several novels and autobiographical books, among them *For Bread Alone* (1981) and *Streetwise* (1992). He has also written essays on Tennessee Williams, Jean Genet, and Paul Bowles.

Julio Cortázar (Argentina, 1914–1984) Born in Brussels, he soon moved back to Argentina with his family. He is the author of *Hopscotch* (1965), an important experimental novel, and of many collections of short stories: *End of Game* (1964), *The Secret Weapons* (1964), *Bestiary* (1951), *All Fires the Fire* (1966), and *Cronopios and Famas* (1962).

Anita Desai (India, 1937–) Her books include children's novels, collections of short stories, and novels, among them *Clear Light of Day* (1980) and *In Custody* (1984)—both shortlisted for The Booker Prize—*Journey to Ithaka* (1995), *Diamond Dust* (2000), and *The Zigzag Way* (2004).

Helen Garner (Australia, 1942–) Novelist, film scriptwriter, and essayist, she published her first novel, *Monkey Grip,* in 1977. Her books include *Honor & Other People's Children* (1980), *The Children's Bach* (1984), *Postcards from Surfers* (1985), *Cosmo Cosmolino* (1992), and two books of non-fiction, *The First Stone* (1995) and *True Stories* (1996).

Isabel Huggan (Canada, 1943–) Best known as a short-story writer, Huggan has published two collections: *The Elizabeth Stories* (1984) and *You Never Know* (1993). She is also the author of a book of non-fiction, *Belonging* (2003).

Shimaki Kensaku (Japan, 1903–1945) He lived in extreme poverty for the first part of his life and became a member of the Japanese Communist Party. His first novel, *Rai* [Leprosy], was published in 1934, based on his prison experience. Among his many books are *Momoku* [Blindness] (1936), *Goku* [Prison] (1937), and *Seikatsu no Tankyu* [The Quest for Life] (1939).

Bernard MacLaverty (Ireland, 1945–) Novelist and short-story writer, he began his writing career with *Secrets and Other Stories* (1977). His other books include *Lamb* (1980), *A Time to Dance and Other Stories* (1982), *Cal* (1983), *Grace Notes* (1997), and *The Anatomy School* (2001).

Daphne du Maurier (England, 1907–1989) The granddaughter of the Victorian novelist George du Maurier, she is the author of many best-selling novels, including *Jamaica Inn* (1936), *Rebecca* (1938), and *My Cousin Rachel* (1951). She also published several volumes of short stories and of memoirs.

Gabriel García Márquez (Colombia, 1928–) The author of the now-classic *One Hundred Years of Solitude* (1967) has published several other novels and collections of short stories, including *In Evil Hour* (1966), *The Autumn of the Patriarch* (1975), and *Love in the Time of Cholera* (1985). He was awarded the Nobel Prize for Literature in 1982.

Alice Munro (Canada, 1931–) Munro has published twelve books, as well as *Selected Stories*. She has won three Governor General's Awards, two Giller Prizes, and the Trillium Book Award in Canada, and numerous international prizes, including the W.H. Smith Award in the U.K. and the National Book Critics Circle Award in the United States. Like many of her stories, "Hired Girl" first appeared in *The New Yorker*.

Ludmila Petrushevskaya (Russia, 1938–) Best known for her controversial plays, she published her first book of collected stories after the end of glasnost: *Immortal Love* (1989). Among her plays, her most successful one is *Songs of the Twentieth Century* (1989).

Wallace Stegner (U.S.A., 1909–1993). Among his many novels are *Remembering Laughter* (1937), *The Big Rock Candy Mountain* (1943), *Joe*

Hill (1950), *All the Little Live Things* (1967), *Angle of Repose* (1971), and *Crossing to Safety* (1987). *The Spectator Bird* won the American National Book Award in 1977. His non-fiction includes *Wolf Willow* (1963) and *The Sound of Mountain Water* (1969). His *Collected Stories* were published in 1990.

Graham Swift (England, 1949–) Novelist and short-story writer. His books include *The Sweet-Shop Owner* (1980), *Shuttlecock* (1981), *Waterland* (1983), *Out of This World* (1988), *Ever After* (1992), and *The Light of Day* (2003). His novel *Last Orders* won The Booker Prize in 1996.

Elizabeth Taylor (England, 1912–1975) Her first book, *At Mrs. Lippincote's* (1946), began her series of novels dealing with English bourgeois life. It was followed by *Palladian* (1947), *A Wreath of Roses* (1950), *The Soul of Kindness* (1963), *Mrs. Palfrey at the Claremont* (1972), and *Blaming* (posth. 1976). Her collections of short stories include *Hester Lilly* (1954) and *The Devastating Boys* (1962).

John Updike (U.S.A., 1932–) Mainly known as a novelist and short-story writer, he has also written essays, poems, and a play: *Buchanan Dying* (1974). His best-known books are *The Poorhouse Fair* (1959), *Rabbit Run* (1960), *The Centaur* (1963), *Couples* (1968), *Marry Me* (1976), *The Coup* (1978), *The Witches of Eastwick* (1984), *Roger's Version* (1986), and *Villages* (2004). In 1989 he published a volume of memoirs, *Self-Consciousness.*

Tennessee Williams (U.S.A., 1914–1983) (pseudonym of Thomas Lanier Williams) His first success came with *The Glass Menagerie* (1945), followed by *A Streetcar Named Desire* (1947), *Summer and Smoke* (1948), *The Rose Tattoo* (1951), *Cat on a Hot Tin Roof* (1955), *Orpheus Descending* (1957), and *Sweet Bird of Youth* (1959). His collections of short stories include *Hard Candy* (1954) and *Three Players of a Summer Game* (1960).

A.B. Yehoshua (Israel, 1936–) He is the author of eight novels, including *The Lover* (1977), *Five Seasons* (1987), *Mr. Mani* (1989), *A Journey to the End of the Millennium* (1998), *A Woman in Jerusalem* (2006), and a collection of short stories, *The Continuing Silence of the Poet* (1976). He lives in Haifa.

GRATEFUL ACKNOWLEDGMENT IS MADE FOR PERMISSION
TO REPRINT THE FOLLOWING COPYRIGHTED WORKS

"Death by Landscape" from *Wilderness Tips* by Margaret Atwood © 1991, published by McClelland & Stewart. Used with permission of the publisher.

Dandelion Wine by Ray Bradbury. Reprinted by permission of Don Congdon Associates, Inc. Copyright © 1957, renewed 1985 by Ray Bradbury.

Under the Jaguar Sun by Italo Calvino. Copyright © 1988 The Estate of Italo Calvino. Translated by William Weaver. Reprinted with the permission of the Wylie Agency Inc.

"The Adulterous Woman" from *Exile and the Kingdom* by Albert Camus, translated by Justin O'Brien, copyright © 1957, 1958 by Alfred A. Knopf, a division of Random House, Inc. Used by permission of Alfred A. Knopf, a division of Random House, Inc.

"Le Chevalier" from *Streetwise* by Mohamed Choukri. Copyright © the estate of Mohamed Choukri, 1996 and 2007. Translation copyright © Ed Emery, 1996 and 2007. By kind permission of Telegram Books.

"Deshoras" by Julio Cortázar. Copyright © 2004 by Julio Cortázar. Translated and reprinted as "Summer" from *Unreasonable Hours,* translated by Alberto Manguel. Used by permission of Carmen Balcells.

"Games at Twilight" from *Games at Twilight and Other Stories* by Anita Desai. Copyright © 1978 Anita Desai. Reproduced by permission of the author c/o Rogers, Coleridge & White Ltd., 20 Powis Mews, London W11 1JN.

"Postcards from Surfers" from *Postcards from Surfers* by Helen Garner. Copyright © 1981 by Helen Garner. Used by permission of Penguin Group (Australia).

"On Fire" extracted from *You Never Know* by Isabel Huggan. Copyright © 1993 by Isabel Huggan. Reprinted by permission of Knopf Canada.

"The Wasps" from *A Late Chrysanthemum* by Shimaki Kensaku. Copyright © Shimaki Kensaku, 1970. Originally published by Chikuma Shobo. Translation copyright © Lane Dunlop, 1986. Used by permission of Lane Dunlop.

"A Pornographer Woos" from *Secrets* by Bernard MacLaverty. Copyright © 1977 Bernard MacLaverty. Reproduced by permission of the author c/o Rogers, Coleridge & White Ltd., 20 Powis Mews, London W11 1JN.

"The Pool" from *The Breaking Point* by Daphne du Maurier. Reproduced with permission of Curtis Brown Group Ltd, London on behalf of the Estate of Daphne du Maurier. Copyright © Daphne du Maurier 1959.

"El Verano Feliz de la Señora Forbes" from *Doce cuentos peregrinos* by Gabriel García Márquez. Copyright © 1994 by Gabriel García Márquez. Translated and reprinted as "Miss Forbes's Summer of Happiness" from *Strange Pilgrims,* translated by Edith Grossman. Used by permission of Carmen Balcells.

"Hired Girl" from *The View from Castle Rock* by Alice Munro copyright © 2006. Published by McClelland & Stewart Ltd. Used with permission of the publisher.

"The New Family Robinson" copyright © 1985 by Ludmila Petrushevskaya, translated by Keith Gessen and Anya Gessen. Translation copyright © 2006 by Keith Gessen and Anya Gessen. Reprinted with permission of The Wylie Agency Inc.

"The View from the Balcony," from the *The Collected Stories of Wallace Stegner* by Wallace Stegner, copyright © 1990 by Wallace Stegner. Used by permission of Random House, Inc.

"Learning to Swim" by Graham Swift from *Learning to Swim and Other Stories* (London Magazine Editions, 1982). Used by permission of Enitharmon Press.

"Flesh" from *The Devastating Boys* by Elizabeth Taylor. Copyright © Elizabeth Taylor, 1972. Used by permission of AM Heath.

"Lifeguard," from *Pigeon Feathers and Other Stories* by John Updike, copyright © 1962 and renewed © 1990 by John Updike. Used by permission of Alfred A. Knopf, a division of Random House, Inc.

"Three Players of a Summer Game" by Tennessee Williams, from *The Collected Stories of Tennessee Williams,* copyright © 1948 by The University of the South. Reprinted by permission of New Directions Publishing Corp.

"Early in the Summer of 1970" from *The Continuing Silence of the Poet* by A.B. Yehoshua. Copyright © 1988 by A.B. Yehoshua. Translated by Miriam Arad and Pauline Shrier. Used by permission of The Liepman Agency.